Evernight Publishing

www.evernightpublishing.com

SIN'S FLOWER

DEDICATION

For my mom who gave me life, love and music.

ACKNOWLEDGMENT

Sometimes a lifelong obsession really pays off. Thank you to my favorite band of all time, Depeche Mode, for three decades of inspiration! My eternal gratitude goes to the Evernight family. A hug to my Aunt Terry who helped with all my sewing questions. And to my boys, I love you.

SIN'S FLOWER

SIN'S FLOWER

A Sin Pointe Novel, 2

Carlene Love Flores

Copyright © 2013

Prologue

Tail end of July; Bugscuffle, Tennessee; the curb next to Tris's house...

Lily Elstone could either pee herself in her car or make like a big girl and march right up to her older sister's front door. It looked inviting enough if she squinted to see that far, with a family of sculpted, wooden bear cub statues stationed on either side. Were they smiling huge smiles or baring their sharp teeth? An empty porch swing tottered forward and back like a weak little ghost child was standing behind, giving tiny pushes but making very little progress through the thick, hot air.

Lily shivered under her warm clothes, petting the soft cotton of her long sleeves over her arms.

Ghosts and childhood loomed right up there with stilettos and potato chips on her list of things to avoid. Great, now her nervous tummy was hungry too. She rubbed at it as if she were carrying twins. Unfortunately, there was no turning back from this house. Not today.

No point really. She wouldn't go back to Oklahoma. As a freshly divorced woman from a small town, she was better off here, in this even smaller but secluded town, awkward as she felt. A shiver that had no place pimpling her skin in late, humid July sprang all the way up to her shoulders as she realized there was no way she was gonna be able to avoid those first two topics. She'd already driven the 739 miles and terrified or not, she was getting out of her tired old Jetta. She was walking up the driveway, knocking on that door and having a proper reunion with the sister she hadn't truly spent time with since they were little girls.

Lily bailing on Tris three weeks ago when they'd miraculously bumped into each other in line for the women's restroom at a Sin Pointe concert, didn't count.

Quickly, she recited aloud a rehearsed opening line with her hands curled like a strangler over the steering wheel. "Knock, knock. Okay, then Tris opens the door. Then I say surprise or maybe just hello and she probably frowns at me and makes to slam the door but I jam my foot in there first and tell her how sorry I am for not meeting up with her after the concert." She needed to remember to stop and take a breath there. "Look Tris, I know it was crappy the way I chickened out about finding you after the show but it's just that I hadn't seen you in over twenty years…I wanted to go to you more than anything, I was just dealing with my own junk and…"

A long, tall man with long, wavy dark blond hair nearly gave her a heart attack when he leaned in, interrupting her, and tapped on her window, motioning to roll it down. She did so once she realized Tennessee appeared just as country as Oklahoma. He could probably shoot her just for being parked so suspiciously on his curb. Oh man, his curb. Was this the husband Tris had been so over the moon for her to meet?

"Lily?" he asked while she remembered to close her mouth.

"H-How did you know?" She stared up at him, noticing how his soft smile touched his blue eyes. Her rigid hands eased up on the victim. The steering wheel, she meant the steering wheel.

"Well, turns out I'm a pretty good lip reader and caught mostly everything after 'Look Tris, I know it was crappy.' Why don't you pull all the way in to the drive and come on inside? Trista...well, let's just say she's been waiting for this day for a few weeks now." He just crooked an eyebrow and stood there, like they'd known each other forever and she should understand exactly what he meant.

Funny thing was, she sorta did. It was then that she let herself start to consider coming here hadn't been a mistake. Maybe her sister didn't hate her for the things Lily suspected her father had done when they were but nine and twelve—and as had just been pointed out to her, for bailing on this reunion three weeks ago.

Oh but God please let me be more than just an ugly reminder of our past. She fisted her fingers around her tote and climbed out of her car.

The husband smiled and then reached behind her, opening her rear door and grabbing the large bag containing everything material she had left in the world. He easily slung it over his shoulder and closed her door.

She started to protest, not planning on staying past her welcome today but instead finding a nearby motel for the night. "Oh, you don't have to do that."

He gave her an assessing look like she'd imagine a big, bossy brother doing. "I'm Lucky, by the way." He stuck out his hand to shake. She obliged. "Don't worry about your bag. I'll go ahead and put it in the room your sister made up for you. Come on, let's go inside."

Lily's arms hung at her sides like string cheese— sorta stiff, sorta limp. Never had she thought a past as horrible as theirs could have allowed for anything remotely resembling promising.

She didn't realize she'd been standing there stuck in place like a log in cement mud.

"Well, are you comin'?"

Well, was she? Did this glowing, helpful man mean Tris had managed to successfully leave her monsters in the past where they belonged? Lily's ex-husband's cruel face flashed through her mind right before a vision of her dead father careened in behind it. Well, there was no going back to Oklahoma.

"You're sure she's gonna be okay with having me here? I can only imagine the pain my coming around would bring to her. Lucky, you can tell it to me straight if you think this is a bad idea," Lily assured her sister's husband. He seemed to genuinely care.

"I did mention the part about the room she's made up for you, right?" He took a few steps back to stand at her side and with the hand not supporting her bag, patted her shoulder. "Listen Lily, we all come from somewhere and we all end up somewhere. Sometimes bad stuff brings you to a good place. I love your sister more than life itself and whatever brought you here today, well, I'm thankful." He blinked and she watched the patch of whiskers flex under his bottom lip. "She needs her sister. And the baby...he or she is gonna need an auntie."

"Really?" She'd give anything to trust someone at their words, face value.

Everything so far here in this quiet, out of the way town had fallen over her like a safe, new beginning. Maybe she didn't have to think about deceitful men. In fact, she didn't have to think about men period. What was the use if they all kept their true colors hidden so you never really knew them anyway? This was to be her time with her sister. *We might just be able to make this work,*

she thought with a fierce sense of hope. If not, she was a
screwed, divorced, thirty-one year old woman with
nowhere to go but back out on the road.

Out of habit, she glanced quickly over her
shoulder before walking Lucky's way. "Lucky, I think I
just need a second to go over what I'm gonna say again."

But as soon as the last word left her lips, an
embodiment of feminine warmth outlined herself against
the other side of the screen door. It eased open in the
next second and then Lily was being held.

"I'm so sorry, Tris," she managed to get out in a
shaky hush.

"I'm not." Her beautiful, earthy big sister pulled
back only after what felt like assuring they'd made a real
connection this time. "Promise me you'll stay," Tris
tittered then let out a weepy sniffle. "Don't leave until
we've worked through this together. Even if it takes
forever. We need that, baby sis."

Adrenaline born from fear brought fire to her
joints and she rubbed at her elbows to try calming down.
In a world where she'd only ever acted courageously
when forced to it, Lily wished away her fear so that she
could make her sister a promise. "Until we're good as
new."

No doubt. That just might take forever. And a
whole lot of heartbreak in between.

*Please don't let me find out my father really was a
monster.* But in her heart, she knew. She hugged her
half-sister tighter, letting Tris's messy hair blot away her
tears. *Until we're good as new...*

SIN'S FLOWER

Chapter One

Not forever but five months later; Beginning of December; Bugscuffle, Tennessee; Lily's new hometown...

"Tris, stop beating yourself up. You're on doctors' orders to avoid long bumpy rides in your hubby's beloved old truck. Going the sixty miles to the airport would have been a bad idea. Don't worry, I'm sure Lucky will call soon to say Maryella has arrived safe and sound."

Lily reached into the full laundry basket she had set on the dining room table and handed her sister a few dish towels to fold. It was the only thing she'd been able to think up in order to keep Tris seated rather than pacing the house.

"I know, I just can't help it. I wanted to be there to greet her. It's been so long since I saw Maryella. I can't believe she's already seven," Tris said as her exuberance faded quickly and her head dipped to the side.

"Hey, what's the matter? You were so excited just a second ago."

Tris let out a sigh. "I was just trying to remember the last time I spent quality time with her and I couldn't picture anything past her first birthday party."

"Oh wow." Lily wasn't great at first responses, especially when they came with such sudden instances of sadness. She fished around the basket and handed Tris a clump of Lucky's long white socks, then tried again. "She sounds really special to you. So tell me about that birthday party." Tris had indicated it had been a happy time so maybe that would bring back her sister's smile.

"Oh, she is special. When she was born, she brought this spark of happiness and light into our otherwise dark world out there in California. You should have seen how pink we decorated the house for that first birthday party. All the Sin Pointe guys were there too, thankfully showered and dressed. Maryella and I, we twirled, a little too much, because she puked all over me. But it was the best. I can still smell the sweet top of her head tickling my nose. It was the first and the last time I got to hold her in my arms for more than a few seconds. Her mother showed up late and that was that."

"Oh geez. I'm sorry to hear that."

"It's okay. It's in the past, where it belongs." Tris abandoned the large white undershirt she was folding to reach out and plant her hand on top of Lily's. "You're really easy to talk to, you know that little sis? And I'm sorry I've been so up and down lately. I've just got a lot on my mind. But I can't tell you how much it means that you agreed to stay here with us."

Only a cold hearted son of a gun would have been able to say no to the silent pleading Tris had done with her that first night she'd shown up. Within seconds, Tris's arms had wrapped around Lily and dragged her inside. And that room she'd indeed prepared. Lavender, Lily's favorite color, had greeted her in the pillows, blankets, curtains and even the vase with fresh cut asters. Everything about her sister was honest and therefore calming. Which was why hearing her speak about this troubled relationship had Lily's ears perking up and heating.

"Well, I'm only easy to talk to because I feel like nothing's off limits with you. That right there is priceless." Lily paused to check that Tris's hands were folding more socks without the jitters. They appeared calm so she continued. "So hey, why did things go so badly after that first party? What's happened since then to make it so that Maryella is getting to spend Christmas with you now? Unless you'd rather not talk about it. Which, by the way, is totally fine." Sometimes Lily felt like Tris might only be so open with her because she felt obligated. Which she wasn't. If anything, it was the other way around. Unfortunately, Lily worried she'd never be able to make up for the ways her father, Tris's stepdad, had indeed hurt her sister when they were kids.

"Well, it's no big secret. Maryella's mother, Vangie, and I never got along because she was convinced I was after Jaxon. Which, hello, is just gross. He couldn't be more like a big brother to me."

Yeah, Lily was still trying to wrap it around her head that Tris was basically an adopted member of the Sin Pointe family from her days as their personal assistant. And they were talking about the band's leader like he was Joe Schmoe.

"Wow. Why did this Vangie woman think that?" Lily asked, trying not to be overwhelmed with curiosity. It was surreal on steroids to think that the rock star's daughter was on her way to visit them for the holidays which was why Lily did her best to banish that star struck train of thought.

"You know, looking back, Jaxon and I did spend a lot of time together but that was only because we had been roommates at one point and the work was non-stop. When the band was on tour, we were basically all living on top of each other for months at a time. So I could see where it would be hard for her, for any woman really. Maybe if Vangie hadn't been such a witch, we could have had a legitimate conversation about things and settled it early on. But it didn't go that way which made sticking it out in Jaxon's world so ridiculously hard."

"What do you mean?"

"When things were bad, they were really bad. Vangie had these horrible ways of using Maryella to

15

control Jaxon. I nearly left so many times that last year I lived in Cali because it was just so painful to watch and even worse to be a part of. You know?" She tugged at the wadded up toe of a sock. "I mean, yeah, Jaxon had his crap load of problems, but he was a good dad and no matter what Vangie thought, he was devoted to her."

"It sounds like you miss him too and that this Vangie woman is no longer in the picture."

Lily watched her sister swallow, shrink and then blink. "Well, when Maryella turned five, we had another blowout birthday party. I shouldn't have shown up. It got ugly fast. By that time, I was beyond turning my cheek to look the other way when Vangie started making her accusations and threats. Jaxon actually stood up for me that day and boy did it cost him. Initially Vangie took off with Maryella and stayed gone for a while which was strange because whenever she'd stormed out on Jaxon before, she'd come back the next day dangling his parental rights until he caved to her demands. But from what I've heard, it's been two years now and she's disappeared. It's so sad. I mean to the point that I actually pray for her."

Now that's saying something, Lily thought. "Man, it sounds like she needs it. What a horrible situation." Lily tried for one minute to see herself praying for her ex to become a better man. The pressure built in her temples immediately. Tom had been so cruel to her the four years they'd been married. So deceitful. Lily couldn't do it. Apparently her sister was a saint. Feeling sorry for herself was off the table so she channeled it to someone who sounded like they deserved it. "At least Maryella has your friend, Jaxon."

Tris wiped at her runny nose and Lily handed her one of the clean, folded hand towels to help. "Yeah, that's true. I'm sure things have got to be better now than when I left. But he hasn't had such a good life either, Lily." The telltale signs of pending tears took up in Tris's shiny eyes as she pinched the bridge of her nose to try and stop them.

"Oh hey, it's okay. I didn't mean to get you crying. Remember we're supposed to be happy that Lucky will be here soon with Maryella? Shush, I'm sorry, Tris." Lily abandoned her folding and hugged Tris tightly in her chair.

It was hard to understand all the words through Tris's breathing that kept hitching. "It, it's just that I left you behind and then I left Jaxon behind and now I'm here living this dream life while the people I care about are still hurting."

"Hey, hey, no, that's not true." Lily patted her sister's head under the pile of hair as best she could. "You didn't leave me when we were kids, you were taken away. And now that I know why, I'm thankful for that."

Nothing could be truer. Lily had always wondered why she'd found Tris at the creek by their old house, soaking wet and stained red from the sopping Oklahoma clay. But she'd never gotten any answers because Tris's grandma, Grace, had rolled into town the next day to visit and taken her big sister away for good. It wasn't until five months ago when Tris sat Lily down and answered her questions in an all-night conversation that she'd insisted they get through together. The red covering her skin, dress and tights had been a mixture of the Oklahoma clay and Tris's blood. And Lily's father had been sexually abusing Tris for the two years since their mother had died. Tris had gone to the creek to escape. She'd slit her wrists on a sharp rock. But Lily had found her.

"You know, your friend, Jaxon, is a grown man. It's up to him to leave or stay where he is. Trust me, that's something I know all about. Adults have to make hard choices sometimes, just like you did to come here with Lucky."

"You did it too, sweetie. I'm very proud of you for leaving that jerk all on your own," Tris said, giving her face a few wipes with the mascara streaked small towel.

"Thanks." Lily paused to focus the conversation back to someone else. "Hey sis, out of curiosity, why didn't you ask Jaxon to come along with Maryella? I keep thinking of him as your distant friend but he's blood relation, right? Lucky's cousin because he's Bear's son? It sounds like his being here might ease your worry and I bet it would mean the world to his father."

There had been a family dinner over at Lucky's father and uncle's house a few nights ago and when Tris had mentioned Maryella was confirmed to arrive this week, both Luke and Bear Mason had become mirror images of jolly, but tall, old men. Then Bear had inquired about Jaxon and Lucky had said something about not being sure of his plans yet. You could have heard a pea split at the table for the next few minutes.

Tris grabbed for the towel again. Oh no, Lily had said the exact wrong thing apparently.

"I did. He refused."

"But you wish he was coming…I can hear it in your voice."

Unfortunately, that was when her sister closed up on the topic. "Lily, I'm tired and I should lie down until Lucky and Maryella arrive."

Lily noted it was the first time she'd felt her sister pull away from one of their conversations.

Tris spent the next half hour watching TV then zonked out. Lily covered her with a homemade quilt, admiring the rounded hump of Tris's belly and what a wonderful mom she was going to be. She then gave her thoughts too much leave and they instantly jumped to a vision of two pregnant sisters shopping for baby clothes and spending hours crocheting blankets together. A fog of depression fumigated her heart because something that perfect wasn't in her deck of cards. Tris's baby had a doting daddy awaiting its arrival while Lily still had days of looking over her shoulder to be sure her lousy choice in husband material hadn't found her.

She shook off the impossible fantasy and then made her way to the baby-to-be's nursery to ensure it was all set for Maryella. Lily dressed the air mattress on the floor with the soft pink pillows and comforter Tris had set out earlier on a yellow changing table.

She smoothed everything until it was perfect for the little girl she felt like she already knew in a big way. What a huge trip for such a young child to make alone.

But the only trip Lily could truly picture was the crazy one forming in her overwhelmed mind.

The one that would take her to California to fetch Jaxon James.

She owed her sister so much.

Not many people would be able to take in a daily reminder of the abuse they'd suffered as a child. Tris had done it with open arms. Now it was Lily's turn to return the favor. There was no question this had to be done.

* * * *

Los Angeles Airport, aka the last place Jaxon James wanted to be…

Shit, he knew this was going to be tough but Maryellie might not be making this flight after all. Not if he couldn't let go and hand her over to the awaiting airline agent. Good thing the woman hadn't started tapping her navy blue pointy shoed toes. He'd have twisted that into an excuse of not letting his baby girl go with someone so impatient and unreliable. But nope, the honey-colored-hair lady just stood there looking pleasant as ever, not a twitch of her skirted hips nor a glance to her watch to say he needed to get the show on the road broke her unquestionable professionalism. *Fuck.*

"Mr. James, I promise we'll take excellent care of your daughter. We actually have two other unaccompanied minors on this flight so Maryella will have a great time sitting up front with them. The receiving agent in Nashville will contact you once the plane has landed and then again when…let's see here…" She checked her small clipboard and read from what he guessed was Maryellie's itinerary. "Here it is, when Mr. and Mrs. Lucky Mason's identification cards are verified on site and Maryella is formally released to them."

Not having risen from his knees yet, he nodded at the long legged agent. Then he leaned into his baby girl's face and nuzzled her nose for an Eskimo kiss, knocking his Dodgers baseball hat back on his head.

"Daddy, I want to see you for Christmas. Do you promise to come on another airplane after you finish your work with Uncle Stefan and Uncle Benny?"

God, he was going to start blubbering right there in the damned airport. He wished it were that easy.

"Sweetums, Daddy is going to do his very very best to be with you okay? But for now I want you to go have lots of fun with Auntie Trissy and Uncle Lucky. And, you get to see—"

"I know! I get to meet Grampa Bear," she said his father's name with an adorable growl, apparently stoked that she had a grandpa and that he had such a cool name.

Man, Jaxon was an ass for keeping her away for so long. The guilt hit him hard as her tiny button nose slid to his cheek and then her long eyelashes kissed him like a butterfly. "I have to get on the airplane now, Daddy. Be good and be nice to Uncle Benny." She kissed her palm and then smeared it into his. "That is Uncle Benny's kiss. Since he couldn't come up here with you to say goodbye. You can give it to him when you go back down the escalagator."

Her way with words made his eyes all wet.

"Okay sweetums. I love you. I'll talk to you as soon as you land. Be sure you stay with the nice airline lady, okay?"

She nodded and her uneven, blonde braided piggy tails that he and Benny had tag-teamed that afternoon bounced up and down.

They waved and he stood watching as she disappeared hand in hand with the airline agent down the tunnel to the plane. Not caring for any undue attention, he made sure to tug his hat back down to shade enough of his face. Hopefully that and the lighter colored clothes he was wearing had made him look less like Jaxon James of Sin Pointe and more like a daddy who was about to have a major moment there in the gate area.

"Sir, if you sit over here, you can see her plane until it takes off," the agent who had escorted Maryellie said, respecting his space. Hopefully she wasn't secretly texting his whereabouts. He was not in the mood.

Jaxon blew out a gust of breath which dried out his mouth even more. He rubbed hard at his eyebrows, feeling the spread of his skin as it tightened under his fingertips. "Yeah, all right. Thanks." He dipped his head to her and forced himself away from the gate where he'd just handed his baby girl over to strangers.

Was he fucking living on planet earth? All this just because he couldn't find his balls and show up at the Mason family Christmas? He shook his head and caught sight of the leggy agent looking over at him from his right side. She smiled a small, closed mouth smile. "Hey, thank you for doing such a good job with my baby girl. I appreciate it."

"Oh, you're welcome, Mr. James. On behalf of the airline, it was my pleasure to assist you and your daughter."

"So formal, good on you," he'd just said except for then he caught her chewing at her bottom lip. "Um, was there anything else you needed from me?" He never assumed people knew who he was. Once he'd offered to take a picture with a cab driver who it turned out had never heard of Sin Pointe. The guy was instead looking to report Jaxon and Stefan for dressing obscenely while riding in his car. But this girl looked like when out of her proper bun and skirt, she'd fit right in with the rest of the tank top wearing females at his concerts.

She twisted her mouth like she wanted to ask but couldn't. Ah hell, here he went. This would backfire, he knew it. He quickly thought of something clever. "Hey um, so I do some scrapbooking with my daughter and with this being her first plane ride, I bet she'd like a photo of the nice young lady who helped her onto the plane. Would you mind taking one with me?" This one was a good girl with manners. She'd never have gotten around to asking him for the pic.

"Oh my God, are you sure? Really?"

"Yep. Quick, go get your phone." She turned to grab it from the gate check-in desk and then returned. No one seemed to have noticed her rapid movements. He pulled her in closely to his side and hooked his arm over her shoulder. He snapped the photo since his arms were longer and they were doing this self-portrait style. "Say cheese, darl'."

A shudder went through her upper body that he felt too. "Wow, thank you very much Mr. James. That wasn't for your daughter, was it?"

"No darl'. That's for you. Thanks for being a fan of the music." He leaned in to whisper his own favor. "Be a sweetie though and wait until tomorrow morning if you plan to share that. Deal?"

She nodded and he wanted to believe her.

"Oh look, your daughter's plane is taxiing away now. Should be in the air within minutes."

He smiled then left her to go stand right up against the ceiling to floor glass window and watch his heart fly off into the fucking big ass sky without him.

He couldn't miss Christmas with her. Who the fuck did that shit? Not him. But the thought of standing toe to toe with his father after deserting him twenty-seven years ago nearly caused Jaxon to choke. And Trissy. Shit, they had unresolved demons to address too. Shit, something had to give if he was gonna face a house full of people he'd fucked over in his practicing days as an idiot. He tugged off his hat to rip a hand through his hair before remembering who and where he was.

* * * *

Later that night, a creak sounded in the hallway by Lily's open bedroom door, startling her awake. She recognized Lucky's deep voice humming a child's lullaby in the nursery next door. She tip toed over to get a peek at their new pint-sized houseguest. *Oh my goodness, what a doll.* And already asleep. Both Tris and Lucky came out of the room after they'd seen Lily in the doorway.

"Hey, so that's her. What a cutie," she whispered to her sister.

Her answer was a big old face full of Tris's wild hair and a belly bump as she came in for a hug. "Get back to sleep; I'll introduce you in the morning." Tris yawned at the end and slid her feet along the wooden floor until she disappeared into hers and Lucky's room. Once it was just her and Lucky milling about in the kitchen, cleaning up the few stray dishes from some surprisingly tasty, midnight pudding sandwiches Tris had made, Lily asked him the favor she hadn't wanted to in front of her sister.

"Hey Lucky, I actually could use your help in the morning."

"Sure Lily, anything. Whatcha need?" He passed her a hand towel.

"Thanks." She stalled for a moment realizing how crazy this would sound. "I need a ride to the bus stop."

"The bus stop?" Lucky asked, his blue eyes scrutinizing her as if she'd just declared her own insanity. "Any chance you're willing to share the why, when and where with me?" He gulped down a glass of water.

"That might not be a good idea." She was afraid if she told Lucky he'd end up telling Tris and her sister didn't need any more stress right now. Not with the early contractions that Lily would bet had been caused by the whole "Jaxon's not coming" situation.

"Lily, you know your sister would kill me if you left here, something happened, and I not only didn't tell her but then had no idea where you'd gone. She just got you back, kiddo. You understand, right?" His country boy features were handsome—Tris had great taste—but his tone was entirely too scolding.

Lily nodded. "I do. But I'm also thirty-one years old, not a kiddo. And this is very important. It's not like I'm not coming back. I just have to go away for the weekend." She had no idea how long it would actually take but there were only a couple weeks left before Christmas.

"I don't know, Lily. I mean, the bus? Can't we at least get you a round trip flight somewhere if you're being serious? I'm happy to take care of that for you if it's a money issue."

Truth be told, yes, it was a money issue, but the whole point of this mission was to do something for Tris, get out of that indebtedness she felt to her sister and brother-in-law. Not bury herself any deeper, personally handing Lucky the shovel. Besides, it wasn't like she was hitch-hiking. She clicked her tongue against her teeth and then made Lucky an offer.

"I'll tell you where I'm going and how long I plan to be there as long as you promise not to tell Tris."

"You know I can't lie to her. Why the need for secrecy?"

She passed over most of what he'd just said. "I don't want you lying either, and I didn't say I was giving you the specifics. Just enough so that in case of an emergency, you know where to start looking."

"That's not funny, Lily."

"You're right; I'm sorry. Lucky, are you gonna help me or not? I could just take a taxi." Man, if only Tris's Gramma Grace was still there. But she'd taken off last week for a spur of the moment RV trip with the gals to go visit a dear friend with pneumonia. Lily knew she'd have taken her as far west as she could. Grace didn't interject much around here, mostly keeping to the garage they'd transformed to her cozy little apartment, but the few things she'd said about this Jaxon had all been kind. Lucky, on the other hand, seemed wishy-washy. Like he wished his cousin the best but would be happy to wash his hands of him.

"No, I'll at least get you to the bus stop safely."
He gnawed at his lip. "All right, give me the non-
specifics. Just in case."

"Thanks, you're the best." She nearly cheered her
surprise. "I'm planning on being in Southern California
for the weekend. I've got an old friend to look up." It
was the truth. This guy was an old friend, just not hers.
"See, no big deal. And if Tris asks, that's what you can
tell her."

The dark blond scruff growing under his bottom
lip must have gotten itchy because he started scratching
at it like crazy. "Mm-hmm. Sweetie, you know he's not
gonna come. If Jaxon had planned on being here, he'd
have flown in with his daughter tonight. Just be happy he
sent Maryella to us for the holidays."

Caught red-handed, Lily let down all her
pretenses. "I don't understand. Why won't he just
come?"

"It's complicated. He's probably just not ready,"
Lucky said, raising one brow like it was something that
made all the sense in the world.
The look in Lucky's eyes socked her in the heart. There
were obviously things she, as a newcomer, wasn't privy
to. Maybe her brother-in-law was jealous that his wife's
best friend was a guy, and not just any guy. Nah, that
didn't suit Lucky at all. But she'd blundered the judging
of men's character worse in the past. A jar of green
olives with the red pimientos setting on the counter
reminded her of Tom's deceitful eyes. She longed to
squish her fingers into a few of the sour, green and red
garnishes until they turned to mush.

"Look, Jaxon is family. He's not a bad guy but
the last time I saw him, he had a lot on his plate," he said,
emphasizing *a lot.* "And my guess is that he needs to stay

away to deal with it. Which is probably best for now. Maybe he'll come around next year."

She was glad for the level-headedness shining through Lucky's southern voice. How many times had she told herself the past was the past? Bugscuffle and this good home were the last places she wanted Tom's cruel likeness pushing its way in. "Gosh, I feel kind of bad for him. I didn't realize." It sounded like Jaxon was facing a lot alone.

"He'll be all right. And we'll help out by making sure Maryella has a wonderful Christmas. I really don't think there's any point in you going to California, if that's who you were after."

Lucky was a logical guy but maybe he couldn't see what she saw in Tris's eyes. That pain of separation others would miss but Lily and her sister knew oh so well. A stray thought of their estranged younger brother, Jack—who had managed to stay deployed since 9-11, marched back and forth in her heart, making her even more determined not to fail. Every time Tris had mentioned Jaxon's name tonight, she'd gotten all weepy eyed. And every time Lily saw that happen, she pictured the day when Jack was seven, she was nine, and Tris was twelve and a bloodied Tris had been driven away.

It was just silly that Jaxon wasn't here. This was his family too. Heck, she wasn't just doing Tris a favor; she would be coming back with a chum cousin for Lucky, a sorely missed daddy for Maryella, and Bear's one and only son. Then Grace would hopefully pull back into town just in time and everyone would be happy. Heck, it might even snow. She pulled the lower layers of her disobedient hair and tucked them behind her ears then pressed her palms firmly to the cool counter. She gave the olives trapped in the glass jar a fixed last glance.

"You're still going, aren't you?" He popped his knuckles until they refused to make any more noise. "Well, you make sure and take your cell phone with you, and the charger. And if you need anything, I mean anything, you call me. Deal?"

She stuck out her hand to shake on it like the two southerners they were, glad for the overprotective brother in him. "Deal," she said.

Lucky gave her a goodnight nod and walked off toward his and Tris's room. Lily sat there at the breakfast bar on her stool and traced the black and white swirls of the countertop.

This was important. She'd be back way before Christmas. It was all gonna work out just fine.

Elusive rock stars were just normal people on the inside.

God, she'd almost forgotten that detail about Jaxon James. At least it wasn't Stefan Calderon, Sin Pointe's lead singer, she had to go after. That man made her hum, all over, with his black hair, golden brown eyes and deep chocolate honey voice. A zoomy feeling raced around her pulse points. If only it had truly stemmed from Stefan lust. But no. She was scared she'd fail. That Jaxon James would take one look at Lily and see her as nothing special. She might not even get as far as explaining whose little sister she was. With her hands glued to the sides of her head and the bones of her elbows digging against the hard counter, she practiced the Lamaze breathing she'd learned with her sister.

Lily's life had been a trapeze act for too long and now, thanks to Tris, it was better. But still, a girl needed her best friend. If there was even the slightest possibility she could bring her sister's back, she was gonna do whatever she had to do to make that happen. *I won't leave 'til he at least hears me out…Until we're good as new*. Maybe this was the missing piece to making good on that promise.

"Now to go pack," she whispered to the pine scented candle and then blew out its woodsy flame. Before making her way back to her room, she chucked the jar of olives into the wooden kitchen trash bin where they landed with a heavy thud but no sound of shattering glass. Good, she didn't want to disturb anyone here; she just wanted that crap gone.

SIN'S FLOWER

Chapter Two

The next day; San Luna, California, Sin Pointe's personal studio...

"Where in the hell is yesterday's mail?" Or better than that, where in the hell was Benny? "Benny!"

Hell's piss! Paper had come to litter and then die on his webmaster's desk. He scanned the postal mess for this month's ballet bill. A snide personal letter from the dance teacher reminding him it was in bad taste for Maryellie to be missing December's lessons had already surfaced. "Benny, where the hells are you, mate?" *Fuck. Me.*

A toilet flushed.

Benny.

"Sorry, Jaxon. Were you calling me? I was just..."

"Yeah, I got it. We all have to shit around here."

Benny sighed and then his slumping, abnormally large shoulders sagged even more.

Great, he'd gone and scared the sweetest dude he knew. Benny was like a gifted genie on the computer. The band wouldn't have such well-informed, fervent fans, stalking their every move, had it not been for him. But the kid sucked just as badly as Jaxon did at keeping the studio organized.

"Since she's been gone, this place has turned to shit," Jaxon sang under his breath to the tune of the poppy Kelly Clarkson hit, changing the words as he saw fit. Benny cranked up a brow so Jaxon answered. "What? I'm well-versed. And don't look like that, mate. I'm not really that pissed." He'd have thought Benny would have figured this out by now that they spent so

much time together, both at home and the studio. *Maybe he has but I'm just a scary fucking shit head.*

That was more like it.

Jaxon rubbed at his sore triceps as he reminded himself he'd decided not to be that ass anymore. *More good deeds, less dickhead moves.*

"Hey, um, so what did you need, boss?" Benny asked, hands tucked into the pockets of a vest that did ridiculously embarrassing things to Jaxon's psyche. The girl who'd made that vest for Benny was the missing mortar to the walls of this studio. Without Trissy, well, the place just wasn't the same.

It's good she's not here anymore. She made it out, now shut up and get on with your life.

Jaxon tried focusing on Benny's question again, although tenderness took up beside the pain because he knew his Maryellie was now safe in Tennessee, enjoying a wholesome holiday with Trissy and her family.

"Yeah man, have a listen. I've got to call the ballet studio and make nice with the teacher. Find last week's mail, will you? I need the numbers—account, phone." Who was the wanker who said time healed all wounds? He launched into a few neck stretches until a goody cracked its way out. God, that felt amazing.

"Sure, it's all right here." His horrible temporary assistant pointed to a stash of envelopes tucked to the side of his monitor and a dripping can of Dr. Pepper. "Woops. It's kinda wet," said Benny.

"Hand it here." Jaxon poked through, still not finding the invoice he needed.

Oh fuck it, I'll just send in a check covering this year's tuition and next.

He tossed the sticky pile of crap back onto the cluttered desk. "Benny, do me a favor and just find the

studio's address. And if you can, a dry envelope."
Benny nodded while Jaxon tugged on his pocket chain.

A postcard hidden between soggy guitar mags caught his eye. He rescued it and flipped it over to see the distinct handwriting of his horribly missed assistant and best friend. On the other side was a photo of his cousin, Lucky, and Trissy, sitting posed with her growing, preggy belly. "Did you know Trissy had sent this, mate?" He held up the Christmas photo card.

"Sorry, it must have gotten lost in the..."

"In the sopping mess you call your desk nowadays?"

Benny's eyes showed a kid about to be, no, way past being fed up with his boss as they popped open wide and stopped just in time from rolling around in their sockets.

"Shit." Jaxon tapped the edge of the card on the desk.

"What is it, boss?"

"Don't call me that."

"Fine."

Jaxon rocked back on his heels and blinked, hoping to get some moisture to his eyes. "I've got work to do down the hall. Clean this up. And by the end of this week, I want at least three choices in my office for a new assistant. No blondes and no brunettes." Benny gave him a snide salute that Jaxon knew he'd earned. "Hey, ignore most of what I say. Except for the part about the new assistant. We suck dick at this, mate. Truly, like a big giant dick."

He left the front desk, then, and headed to his private studio room, tugging at his hair and stretching his arms over his head as he went. The tight, wanking muscles in his neck and shoulders ached for him to shut everything down. For five minutes, he needed a break from worrying about Maryellie, the inadequacy of a Trissy-less studio, avoiding his father…hell, his lack of a woman's touch in nearly two years. His ex, Vangie.

He needed to write a song. Or get laid. Where had the days gone when he'd have enjoyed those two things all at once? How long had it now been since he'd done either? He knew better than to be longing for those selfish days. But under a constant cloud of guilt battling his former desires, Jaxon's current desires roared back to life.

Warmth. Goodness. Light.

He'd driven and sent them all away and whether he'd invited it or not, the dark cold he secretly hated surrounded him now, smiling.

Fuck a new assistant, he and Benny needed the hell out of here.

Too bad that was impossible.

Chapter Three

Jaxon would never get this song to come out right. He dropped out of his chair and sat legs stretched out on the cushiony floor. Every time he came at it, the thing became more gnarled and twisted. And without it, he had no way to tell the girl how sorry he was. How scared he'd been that night with her. Shit, enough time had gone by since he and Trissy had been brutalized by that group of psychos after the show. But, his knees still locked up on him whenever he slipped and forgot to keep the visions of that horror locked up.

Trissy was safe in Tennessee with his cousin now, thank God. Maryellie, he reminded himself again how it was the right decision to send her there too. And for him to stay far away. Was he the only one who understood his showing up would ruin the holidays?

He glanced back down at his blank page and rubbed at his eyes. He could see the words fighting the page. They were dirty and full of his failure. Damn good apology gift, right? Yeah. So it's not bad enough that he had been forced to nearly rape Trissy that night. And now he was going to write her a song about that messed up shit?

Rolling onto his back, he blew out hard with frustration.

"Merry fucking Christmas." He tossed his pen up at the ceiling and caught it, lucky it hadn't speared his eye on the way back down. He did it again, trying to get past all the crap blocking the words.

This time it landed square on his forehead, close enough to his eyes, which gave him a scare if he was being honest. Jaxon ground out a cough but then lit up at a quick vision of pip squeak-sized sparkle boots and bouncy braids marching down the airplane tunnel like a big girl. The thought managed to warm his stiff hands as he sat up and grabbed for his guitar. He strummed, finding the most familiar chord, the darkest one as always.

But, his fingers pulled back from the strings as his worries again drowned out the song. Was he really willing to let his baby girl down? Hells no. Her mother had that covered. Along with proving to him he had regrettably horrible taste in women.

Where the hell was Vangie? When she'd called last Christmas, and tried to pull another "give me money or I'll yank Maryellie away from you", he'd lied and told her he'd already tasked his lawyer to have Maryellie's birth certificate amended to include Jaxon's name. So Vangie could go screw herself. And then he'd promptly given a call to his trusted manager and made good on the threat. Unfortunately, a change like that required Vangie's signature since she was the only parent listed. They'd put one of those ads in the paper and if Vangie didn't respond in another two weeks, the birth certificate would be amended.

Jaxon scattered a stack of publicity photos he'd left after his last floor session in here reminding him of yet more responsibilities he couldn't drop. The shots were for upcoming CD art he and the guys had done a few weeks ago and they'd actually come out all right. He grinned at Stefan's bad boy pout, Marion's perfectly sculpted sideburns and Will's hand stretched across his heart holding a lone drumstick to his bare chest.

Yeah, they needed him too. Poor bastards.

But it was Trissy's god-damned, wrecked face and tangled hair that wouldn't leave him alone.

"*I only need her because she's gone,*" he sang to the empty studio room.

He scribbled that down on the blank page, feeling an energy start to flow through his veins. With songwriting, he could be anyone.

He could be a different friend. A different boss. He could deserve the praise he got from strangers who wanted to love him but had no idea what that required in the real world. Right now, with this pen, he could be better.

Something inside sparked and he knew it meant he wouldn't be leaving this room for a very long time. He reached over his knees and squeezed the pen in his fingers. Blood swelled to his temples.

But tapping against the sound booth glass continued until he acknowledged it, forcing him to leave behind the hero he'd imagined being for the hour. Jaxon looked up and watched Benny's lips moving in silence.

Jaxon should have paid Benny more respect but he didn't want to lose this lyric. After a pause, he strung some words together, etching out the beginnings of the song. *"I have no idea where she is and I couldn't care less. You were always my chosen mess,"* he sang.

Yeah, I might get out of this booth yet.

Jaxon had looked away but turned his face back to Benny just in time to see his middle finger daftly trying to blend back in with the rest of his fist.

Jaxon grinned, and flipped Benny off in return.

But his mate didn't smile.

"I'm not the only one who needs you; wish I could say the same for myself. I'll never get another chance and I won't ask for help." The song would sound better when it was sung by Stefan but Jaxon always liked hearing his own throaty voice before their team turned it into a production.

That was it for now. It was awfully short but better than anything he'd come up with in a long time.

He peeled off his headphones and spied Benny walking away so he tossed a flip-flop at the window. It plinked softly back to the ground. *Useless rubber.* Story of his life.

He tossed the other one with the same effect. Benny was almost down the hallway, out of sight, so Jaxon went to the window to bang at it with his hands. But when he got there, he saw that Benny was already back at the front desk. His lips were moving so Jaxon gathered he was talking with someone out of his view. Good for Benny and whoever it was. Probably their fruit guy who brought bananas which Stefan somehow blended into flipping delicious smoothies.

Benny knew better than to lead anyone back here down the hall.

He didn't want to be bothered with anyone else's shit. Not while he was figuring out how to become a hero. He slid his butt down to the floor, back against the padded wall and half sang the words he'd hand over to Stefan to sing from his heart someday soon.

"I only need her because she's gone. I have no idea where she is and I couldn't care less. You were always my chosen mess. I'm not the only one who needs you; wish I could say the same for myself. I'll never get another chance if I won't ask for help. Just change me, then someone can save me. I'm the mess. I'm the mess."

Jaxon's toes wiggled in response to the gritty melody.

I can never expect this kind of insane attention from another woman again.

Man, he needed out of this room before he went bananas. From the ground, he pushed himself up and went to retrieve his flip-flops. His empty tummy urged him to wander out and snag some fruit before Benny ruined it in their blender.

As he made his way down the hall, Jaxon saw that there was a girl standing at the front desk. This time he thanked God for the rubber sole that stopped his skidding step.

That was no fruit man.

He was about to disregard their visitor when the tantalizing back view of pale blonde hair tumbling into a teasing vee whacked his ability to do so. He should curse Benny for not adhering to the "No Blondes" policy. Jaxon took a long breath and backed out of view. But he stayed propped in the dark hallway and watched.

What was it about this girl? Sure, her curves put her at knockout level and made him fond of her jeans. Tight jeans that hugged her so intimately in all the right places. His fingers would have to dig deep to get between her skin and the tight fitting material. Without thinking, he rubbed his fingertips into the palms of his hands like they were eight tiny fires he had to put out. Hell, it had been a solid decade since a girl's figure had held him in place for this long. That couldn't be it. Just then he heard her voice raise and those fingers he'd imagined touching her with fell motionless at his sides. It was crazy and strange, but she sounded like home. Like if every song he'd ever written had been sung by his feminine side, that's exactly how it would sound. *Holy shit.*

Shaken, he tugged his hand through his hair and inched further back, knowing he needed to do an about face and go pick that pen back up and pretend to be someone's hero. That thought finally won out and he turned, not needing a final glance at what he was leaving up front. He added her memory to those who would haunt him for some time to come.

He'd never felt like more of a coward than he did just then. He rubbed his eyes until it hurt.

But staying away was the only way to keep women safe. He went back to knock out more of his song, apologizing to Stefan for the even darker-than-normal shit he was gonna have to sing. But like that voice he'd just heard trickle out from a faceless angel, it was right and it was what his heart ached to say. The thing his body burned for sat pouting in the corner of his mind. It was pissed he was denying them that angel, knowing damn well he could have had her with one look.

Chapter Four

Lily sat waiting in the car because Benny had asked her nicely to do so. That and it was obvious either someone in the studio didn't want to see her, or didn't want to be seen. That was okay for now because she still had a few days to convince Jaxon James he needed to come visit Tris and his daughter. She would not be intimidated by this elusive man who hadn't bothered to come out and shake her hand just now.

Benny stuck a key in the front door to the mission-styled, stucco studio behind him and fished another set of keys from the front of a very familiar, two-pocketed style vest she'd bet anything her sister had made. Its colorful stripes reminded Lily of bad wall paper from the old church daycare she used to attend but Benny's loping stride left her with a much happier memory of that place. Musical chairs had been her favorite game as a little kid, running around on bare feet in the dry Oklahoma winter air, usually chasing after Tris. It still hurt to think that those good old days hadn't necessarily been so good.

But for sure, there hadn't been a trace of ocean anywhere. Here, it smelled like a sandy, salty, mermaid heaven touched by the faint fragrance of honeysuckle. And it had saturated every expanding strand of her ridiculously wavy hair. Good thing she'd opted to stuff her small Stefan Calderon pillow in her bag and not a useless flat iron. Wherever she slept tonight, the pillow would be tucked between her knees and under her blanket as always. Her shoulders pulled in at the secret thought.

She rubbed her fingers up her other arm and smoothed the sheer mist of dew into her skin. This was the life, wasn't it? How was she ever gonna get a rock star to leave this gig? Benny hadn't even turned the key in the ignition and she already felt miles away from the impossible task.

He bent down into the driver seat and with a lips-pulled-in grin, they were off.

"So, where are we headed first?" she asked.

"Have you eaten today?"

To Lily's dismay, Greyhound buses didn't provide snacks. Neither did cab drivers following iffy directions she'd fished out of Lucky. "No, not yet."

"Then In'n'Out it is," he said, backing up his answer with a grin and maybe a slurp or two.

"Oh God, what's In'n'Out?" She was excited to be in "Rock Star" California and all, but a meal at a strip club was not on her menu right now. God, that's all the confidence sucker she needed, to have to eat around a bunch of sexy, bendy women.

He thought about it for a second. "Like Sonic, only better."

She burst out laughing which seemed to diminish his fast food superiority grin quickly. "Oh, so burgers, huh? Well, we'll see about that," she challenged, feeling relieved.

Gosh, he was so cute and friendly, not at all aware of his status and nothing like what she'd expected from anyone working for the bad boy rock gods of Sin Pointe. It didn't mean Jaxon James would follow suit, but a girl could be hopeful...and then highly disappointed.

That thought reminded her again of the husband she'd fled.

Hopefully the final judgment papers of her divorce would be waiting at Tris's when she got home. She knew it was silly to place so much importance on a sheet of paper but she'd never wanted to offer something to a burning fire and watch it go up in flames more. To say her marriage had been disappointing would be like calling the guys of her favorite band *just all right* in the deep, hot and sexy department. Her years wasted with Tom had been debilitating and Sin Pointe, namely Stefan Calderon, were...*oh no, what if she met him this weekend?* She blew out a charged breath and hoped Benny didn't smell the lust. Man, who knew the more western state lines you crossed, the bolder you felt.

Twenty short minutes later, because wherever you needed to get, there was a freeway waiting, Lily was stuffing a tiny piece of mustardy ketchup-covered pickle she'd somehow missed into her mouth while Benny watched. She was sure he'd eaten his burger in three bites about ten minutes ago. *Show off.* But she loved him already. Enough so that she felt she could ask him a question that had been eating at her ever since he'd whisked her out into the recording studio parking lot.

"So Benny, what's Jaxon James like?"

His eyes popped, reminding her of that cartoon movie where the little girl was kidnapped by jewel thieves and they sewed this gigantic diamond into the girl's teddy bear. Those huge, glass stones were Benny's eyes, except his were green. He refused to stop sucking pop through his fat straw and she heard slurping sounds that said he'd emptied it.

"Never mind. I'll find out soon enough for myself."

"Oh no, no, no," he said in a blur.

Great. Had Lucky called and gotten to him already? Oh boy, or better yet had Lucky spilled the beans to her sister? That was way more likely. "What, did Tris give you orders, too? Am I to stay away from the big bad wolf, Grams?"

"Hey, don't call me that. I'm not your granny."

Benny was way too cute to stay mad at. Lily tugged on his beanie and he showed her how much he didn't like it with a twisted mouth. But she did it again. "How old are you, Benny?"

"Twenty-nine."

"Well good then. That makes me your elder and someone you're supposed to respect and…"

"Nuh-uh. Nice try. I don't believe you. No way are you in your thirties."

"Oh yes I am. Thirty-one, as a matter of fact. Better get those eyes checked." But she'd just found another reason to love him. "Are you up for adoption? You are so cute." Maybe if she found a way to take this one home with her, Jaxon James would have a good reason to follow.

"You will not distract me," he chanted twice.

Oh my. He had a serious fear of something or someone. Lily would lay odds it was her sister. When big sis meant business, she meant business. If Benny had been told not to spill the beans, those puppies were staying put in the old pot with the lid tightly secured. Maybe she could throw him off with a jolt of pure, straightforward honesty.

"How old is Jaxon James?"

"Sixty-three," he shot out quickly.

She slapped his arm and a thick shock of black, rubber bangles shifted around his wrist. "No he's not. Why are you being so silly? I bet he's in his early forties, max."

The next words out of Benny's mouth were so profound she almost choked on her last salty fry. "Let's hope you're as good a judge of character."

After a quick recovery, she couldn't help but stutter out the first thing that came to her. "Guess we'll see if I've gotten any better at that."

He shook his head, sending locks of long, russet bangs into his eyes which he tucked back into his wool hat. But then he went silent again.

Lily tried a different approach. "So, how well do you know my sister? I assume we're allowed to talk about her."

At that, Benny didn't hesitate. "I'd do anything for Trista, including following her wishes when it comes to you."

Ugh! She popped an imaginary bubble in the air with the tip of her pointer finger.

So flipping things on Benny wasn't gonna work. He was way too smart. Laid back, grungy skater look was a total put-on. The guy could drive on the freeway at insane speeds and still remain stoic and evasive. Her attempt would have to be much more clever. "Why do you think I'm out here, Benny? Huh?" She didn't let him answer because she already had one prepared. "Jaxon James is needed in Tennessee, and not just by his daughter, hello," she said smartly, "but by my sister, that girl you care about. That's why I'm here to convince her best friend to go see her. That's all I'm interested in."

He looked at her with a tight lip. She guessed he had nothing to say. They sped up the coast, giving her a few moments to regroup and strategize. It was Christmas time, dammit. There would be cheer and joy in her sister's house if she had to tie it up, stuff it in a trunk, and drive it to Tennessee herself.

"Oh my God, is that the ocean?"

Benny, who seemed more like a race car driver than genius, bangle-wearing Sin Pointe webmaster, continued to tear them up the coastal highway. Lily could barely catch her breath. Palm trees really did line the hills and the tanned cliffs were magnificent. She could be stuck in traffic all day long with this view. A sea gull swooped down to the right of them just then, and she was close enough to see it dive bomb into the not so distant sea. She wiggled out of her tennies, her feet itching to be bare and running through all that sand.

"Benny? Is there any chance I could convince you to pull off at the next exit and let me get my feet wet? I've never been, you know."

He grinned and even though his eyes were hidden behind a pair of charcoal gray Ray-Bans, she knew he was peacocking under the shades. She would be, too, if this was what she called home. He didn't bother answering but hit his blinker and jammed toward the exit.

So he's a quiet one, Lucky told me that. And he's pretty sweet. He told me that too.

In fact, Benny was the only one she'd been permitted to ride alone in a car with, according to big, protective Lucky, when he'd waited with her at the bus stop. Speaking of her sizable brother-in-law, she'd never seen Jaxon James close up and wondered how much like Lucky he would be.

Tall and naturally muscled? At the handful of Sin Pointe concerts she'd attended, the stage had been too far away for her to see their leader all that well. But he had a super muscly build that was evident even under the solid black he wore.

Gosh, how embarrassing, but she realized then that with all the magazine photos she'd hoarded and the concert t-shirts she cherished, her focus had always been on Stefan. The most accurate description she could give of Jaxon James was that he had dark blond hair that was very short on the sides with long bangs on top that reminded her of Elvis' pompadour. Oh, and some infamous neck tattoo he blew off when asked about in interviews. That was it. That was all she had on the man. Well, that and he wrote some disturbingly good songs.

But since it was Stefan's voice who sang them, that's who she had always been most attracted to. There was that humming sensation again making her dizzy and unexpectedly hot.

She clicked through the list of forbidden boys. Absolutely no solo rides with Stefan Calderon. As if Lily would be able to breathe in a car with him. He was all about the "P" word according to Lucky. The other no-no for absolute alone time was Mr. James. They were just gonna have to fudge on that one a wee bit. She had time to deal with that anyhow, since sweet Benny appeared to be detouring her through the dusty green hills, down a winding road to the ocean. The houses here were amazing. Everyone must be beautiful. Lily could see how Trishad fit in when she'd lived here.

She could just make out small tips of waves peaking and then tumbling back in with the rest of the salty smelling water when they pulled into a private driveway.

Benny stepped out, walked around to her side and opened the door like a true gentleman.

"Benny, can we be parked here? Do you know whose...mansion...this is?"

Magenta pink bougainvillea draped itself over everything. She was sure some Spanish king and queen were missing their retirement home, and then she prayed they didn't come walking out of the gorgeous villa archways anytime soon.

"My place," he said.

"Your place?" she squeaked. "Benny, is there something you need to tell me?" she stuttered.

Like your title and given royal name?

"Well, mine and Jaxon's. I figured why drive you all the way down when I could just park and we could walk. Plus, I have to pee super bad."

If he said this beach was private, as in only for the owner of this…palace, she was going to asphyxiate herself with a face dive into the bougainvillea. "Are you serious? This is where you guys live and this is your own piece of beach?"

He nodded.

"Benny, I'm going to cry. This is too much. Way too much."

He seemed touched or maybe that was the pee pee dance. Lily's heart sank even through her awe. How in the world did she convince a sand flea, let alone Jaxon James—the rock star who owned the ocean—to leave and come to Bugscuffle, Tennessee? Not a one idea bothered to come to mind. Her gut warned that she didn't figure this problem out by turning to jelly every time she saw the life-altering view of the water. She pulled herself together and made an offering for all the drooling she'd done since she'd rolled bus wheels into the state of California.

"Benny, if you could just show me inside the house, you know, where to stow my bag… I'd like to get started on a thank you meal for you and your roommate. Southern style. And if you say no, I'll be all kinds of offended."

"But, but what about the beach?"

It sure was tempting, but now the tightness of her schedule flared to mind. Oh, and the miracle she had to perform.

Benny let out one giant, genius groan and then stuffed his hands into his pockets, only to pull the left one back out and lock a stare on his watch face. That's when his toe started tapping. She wasn't sure if it was from his full bladder or his pending knowledge of when a certain off-limits roommate might be coming home, but he wasn't the only one not taking no for an answer. "Come on, we have a few minutes. You came all the way out here, and if nothing else, you should at least see the ocean." He shrugged and looked up at her like he hoped his offer was sufficient.

At least. She'd have to do better than that. Lily tugged down on the hem of her blouse and took a moment to really think about where she was and what she was doing. Maybe it was the calling of the crashing waves and the way they changed the ripples in the sand each time they came in. She was here for Tris, but Lily needed to believe in herself again if she wanted to accomplish her mission. Otherwise, Benny was right. The ocean might be the only awe-inspiring thing she saw. And that wouldn't do Tris any good.

SIN'S FLOWER

Chapter Five

If she'd had the idea of walking in the front door, setting her bag down and getting straight to business, it was gone now. Her toes threatened to cramp from all the curling she'd just done in the cool, silky sand. Benny passed her by several times, bumping her arm, as he bouncily moved here and there. Straightening?

He finally noticed she was frozen in place and gently took hold of her at the elbow. "Hey, let me show you where to put your stuff." The sweat from his hands moistened her skin. She guessed he had no idea what else to do with her than bring her here to stay and the place was so big, she could see how people could live here and never bump into each other. She'd bet that was his hope for her and Jaxon James.

"Okay." She wanted to follow after him but she was dying to get her tennies off again and feel the soft fur of the rug spread out on the hard wood floor. In a second, the loose shoes were in her hand while her toes unfurled into the fabric she'd only ever imagined on a fine coat. Quickly, she stepped from it, feeling like her feet had no business mashing around on such luxury. She had a meal to make. And hopefully more than one to cook for. She wondered where Jaxon James was and then let her mind try and place the man she knew from Sin Pointe, clothed in black and zippers, walking down that elegant, dark wooden staircase.

Following long, lanky Benny up the regal stairs, she asked, "So what time do you guys normally eat supper around here?" He turned around and faced her with a smirk. Well, that was deliberate. "What, you don't eat at home?"

"Oh, we eat. Just not together. I'm a day walker and Jaxon, well, he's a night owl."

Really? Was this what boys said when they were offered a free, homemade meal? No. It couldn't be true. She'd never had to convince a person to accept her food. "Okay, well, I'm gonna be hungry in a couple hours and if either of you are around, there will be plenty to share."

She blinked so exaggeratedly that she felt her lashes tickle the skin beneath her eyes. She was trying to pull off vague and unoffended. But Benny must have seen that look before. "Lily, I'm sorry. Look, I didn't meant to be rude, but we might as well get something out in the open now about you showing up here and…well, me bringing you back to this house."

She waited for him to continue but he just quieted all the more and continued onto a room where he gestured for her to enter first. She set her bag down, and then took a seat on the edge of the heavily blanketed bed. It was plush and promised a regal night's sleep. The creamy colors reminded her of vanilla ice cream and hot buttered toast. Her tummy groaned. "I'm listening."

Benny stood tall and lanky in the doorway; Lily had no idea where his burgers went. He leaned against the frame, filling it to the top and brushed his long chocolate bangs away from his eyes in the adorable way he had of doing. "I get it that you came here to convince Jaxon he should pay Trista a visit in Tennessee."

She interrupted him. "Not just Tris, but his family. You know his father and uncle, and Lucky. And yes, little Maryella. They all will want to see him."

He nodded in acceptance but continued, effectively ignoring her point. "I get it. And Trista is your sister and Jaxon's her best friend. Trust me, I understand. It's why he agreed to fly Maryella back there for Christmas, to spend time with her family."

Lily couldn't help throwing out her two cents. "So, what's his problem?"

Two large hands shot up into midair. "Whoa, that's not fair, Lily."

"Maybe not. It just feels like he's got something against them. I mean, what's the deal? They're good enough for his daughter; they should be good enough for him, too."

"That has nothing to do with it. Don't be like that."

She really was sorry and hadn't meant to have gone off on a man she'd never even officially met yet. Huffing, she silently admitted to not knowing whether Jaxon James thought he was better than the rest of them or not. The things she'd heard from Tris and Lucky didn't really lead her to believe that.

As if reading Lily's thoughts, Benny started again. "Think about it, Lily. Jaxon has to have a good reason for keeping his distance, right?"

She guessed he had a point. She knew all about keeping her distance. And her reasons for it. Suddenly, she was aware of how awkward it was going to be when Jaxon James came home and found her there.

"And do you know what that reason is?" she asked Benny. The man lived in a mansion overlooking the Pacific Ocean. Maybe if you were used to getting and having whatever you wanted, it could be a pretty big blow to suddenly not get it. The word selfish popped into mind.

Benny just stood there, eyeballing her. "I do," he said in a near whisper.

But he apparently wasn't gonna tell her. "Listen, let's forget all my judging and prying. It's really not what I intended to do. I would like to spend the next couple days getting to know the both of you better and I'm sorry, but with me, that means over a meal."

He seemed to accept that she'd be cooking and he'd be eating. She'd convince Benny to help her wheel in Jaxon James once he tasted her peanut butter, bacon and sausage sandwich. He should be easy pickings after that.

They glided down the grand staircase and traveled an apartment length to a brilliant wine, olive and cream colored kitchen. There wasn't a drop of grease to be seen.

She had one thought.

The kitchen was the heart of any home, and it had been sorely neglected here. Suddenly, Lily didn't see Jaxon James as the untouchable rock star who was too good to pay his family a visit. She sensed he might be just a little more human than that, something she could relate to. Now if he'd just show up and prove it.

* * * *

If he didn't know better, Jaxon would have sworn Benny had ordered Denny's take out again. The guy had a strange all-day love thing for breakfast, particularly bacon. The house currently smelled like he'd greased the walls with it.

Jaxon just wanted a hot shower and then an unforgiving set of laps in the pool. And then a word with Benny. He was never allowed to leave the studio again. Jaxon had spent too many minutes on the phone convincing a spirited young lady who claimed to work for the local radio station that he was not Jaxon James and didn't know anything about a new Sin Pointe record or a new tour. At least some of it had been true. Purposefully losing his Aussie accent had helped in the end. Then on a much scarier note, he imagined hearing the captivating voice of their curvy blonde visitor from earlier. That voice could have strung him along over miles of hot burning coals with a mere whisper of his name. It was a good thing she'd come and gone and he'd stayed hidden. He would not ask Benny about her.

Jaxon took the stairs two at a time, stripping on the way, eager to feel the high-powered water jets pounding his back and neck. As he stood under the streaming hot water, a lonely hand made its way down his chest and to his dick. He wasn't sad Vangie was out of the picture, but he did miss a woman's touch. Even though hers had been hurtful, it had been something. He stroked himself roughly, spitting water a few times when he forgot to close his mouth, thinking instead of the mystery woman, her faceless shapely legs and her stranger's feminine, curvy hips. After a couple minutes, he turned away from the showerhead so he could open his eyes and watch his body release when he came. He didn't know why he liked that. Shit, he didn't know why he got off on most of the stuff he did. With that over, he grabbed a towel and made his way to his bedroom.

Strange…Jaxon heard Benny talking, hopefully to another person and not himself, poor guy. Jaxon went to close his door, assuming they had a visitor and that Benny hadn't lost it. For all he knew, Benny had been duped by another cute face who had convinced him she had no idea who Sin Pointe was but it was so cool that Benny worked for them like had happened last week. Unable to worry about anything else these days, Jaxon fell backwards onto his mattress, moisture still clinging to the backs of his knees, shoulders and ass which he wiggled to get dry. He swiped a hand through his hair, sending sprinkles all over the satin sheets.

When he reached for the remote and clicked on his sound system, dirty deep notes oozed from the ceiling-mounted speakers.

Shit, he must finally be growing up. The song didn't turn him on like it had in his twenties and thirties. A worse thought sank his mood. What if he didn't want women anymore? Vangie had been the last bitch on heels to get him hard. Then that shit that had gone down with Trissy had really fucked with his head which was why his reaction to the backside of that blonde today at the studio had been such a shock. He stroked his chest casually, not particularly caring whether he got off again or not. It was the sensation of his skin being touched that kept his hand slowly rubbing and warming with its circles. He could talk that "no women" crap all he wanted but the truth was he loved sex. Loved a woman's body. Her curves, her hips, her lips, her hands. Loved tucking her into him, if she'd let him. Vangie hadn't cared for that so he'd stopped bothering to try.

He could pick a thorn out of a bushel of roses every time.

Hell, that was probably no angel who'd happened into the studio today. Not with his luck. The outline of Vangie's sharp red lips cursed his brain while a completely foreign afterthought slammed him from beyond. His mother. He'd loved her dearly and still mourned her which made understanding how she'd lied to him his whole life inconceivable.

Frustrated with his mind, Jaxon stopped torturing his body and sat up. "This is my fucking house," he muttered and then stood up to go downstairs, leaving his clothes in a heap on the floor. Benny's friend was about to get an eyeful and Jaxon didn't care. Thirty laps around his pool should be a good start at getting the blood pumping back up to his brain and thinking about the important stuff. His daughter, his life, what was left of it. What kind of substance-free mind trip he'd have to take to make the trip out to Trissy's. Being a better person, a better dad. And if those laps in the heated pool were too kind to him, there was always the freezing cold ocean not too far from the house.

After considering for only a moment the familiar tone to the female's voice, he ignored her chattering coming from his kitchen, not bothering to look in that direction. As he made his way toward the back patio door, he knew Benny's guest might be getting a pretty good view of his ass.

Good for her. Souvenir.

He flung the back door open and let it slam shut. He was done with people for the night. Benny knew better than to let anyone through that back door. Jaxon jumped into his saltwater pool, thankful the door hadn't opened up behind him. *Good on you, Benny.* Thank God for his friend who put up with all his bull. *Let me not piss that away too.* He dove under the water, holding his breath all the way to the other end.

* * * *

"Lily, don't go out there. Please."

She'd cared about Benny the moment she'd met him, so she stayed put on her stool at the kitchen's center island.

"Will he be back?"

"Eventually."

SIN'S FLOWER

Chapter Six

She hadn't been properly introduced yet, but already, she was heartbroken for that man who had just made his way so carelessly out the back door.

Lily got up from her stool, Benny's watchful, uneasy eye on her the whole time. Holding up her hand and settling her new buddy back onto his stool, she waved for him to calm down. Walking up the stairs, she saw the only other opened doorway besides her own and assumed it must be Jaxon James'. There was a pile of black clothes on the floor so she picked it up and quickly bundled it in her arms and made her way back down to the first floor.

Benny had one of those perplexed thinker looks plastered to his face so she helped him out. "He's going to be cold when he comes back in." She handed Benny the pile of clothes. "Please put these where he'll find them. I'll go upstairs." Not that she wasn't curious about the front view since the back view had been surprisingly nice. And yes, she realized she was giving up a prime chance to have him cornered. But just then, it hit her how much that man had going on and no way did he need her or anyone else ogling his man parts. "Let me know when it's safe to come out," she yawned around her words, leaving Benny's jaw hanging low.

Benny stuttered at first, as if in total disbelief she wasn't camping out for the return show. "I will. Thanks, Lily. You're all right."

"That's what they say, anyway." She winked and crawled her lazy, tired bones up the stairs to her comfort-food-colored guest room. Which she felt lost in, again, the moment she stepped inside.

The truth? Dipping her toes into that fantasy pool she'd glimpsed out back had her seriously considering stumbling back down. It was like everything cool about the beach had been scooped up and transplanted to this back yard. Things only accomplished with loads of money too. A sculpted stone wall that dipped in a few places to show the actual ocean in the distance provided the privacy she guessed was necessary for a man so comfortable with his naked body.

Her stomach tightened at the thought before the rest of her body tensed as well.

She'd probably throw up before skinny dipping unless the pool was indoors, with no windows. And no lights. And no one else around. The waterfall in the corner was man made but could have rivaled Mother Nature's handy work. Actual mist crept up from the pool water and out onto her favorite part—the small slide made to look like a glittering lavender seashell and the initial M carved in deep jewel green. Lily could live a thousand fantasies on that deck alone.

She'd never be surrounded by such luxury again. The impossible scene in her head seemed harmless enough as she brought a pillow from the bed to the floor and lay out on her belly, stretching. With her face buried in a mix of her crossed forearms and the pillow, Lily pictured the silky black hair and intense golden brown eyes of the man she'd drifted off to many a nights during her harsh marriage.

She loved the way his tan skin took on the softness of velvet in her dreams but kept its edge with scattered tattoos. This version stepped out of the pool water, drenched and combing his hands through that touchable hair and met her at the edge with a present. It was his gentle hand cupped at her cheek. This was where he always leaned into her ear and whispered *"It will be okay. Don't cry,"* while stroking his fingers through her dry hair. It had been blown crazy from her running so feverishly down her street to get to this safe spot with him.

His voice, dripping sweet with deep, raspy honey, touched a different part of her just now. Her fantasy self, usually the confident junior college graduate she'd been before marrying, and especially tonight with a pool and possible bathing suit involved, released her grip on the loose hand of his she'd been holding. She took a step back, her clothes from the front wet from touching against his solid, sleek chest. This wasn't her Stefan Calderon. This man's dark blond hair had looked darker when he emerged from the pool because it was saturated with water, fooling her at first, and this chest was dusted with short hairs. She should have known when the voice had sounded wrong, rougher but with holes in it where it should have been Stefan's steady baritone.

She made a few odd movements with her shoulders, trying to inch back but he wouldn't let her hand go, now just as slick as his from the water. At first she kept trying but after a glance at his face, was drawn to his beaten down eyes, rimmed with deep shadows. He stared at her, letting her see the pain that had caused those bruises and was trying to drown out his nearly teal-colored eyes. But for one small glimmer of light that somehow shone through and let her know he was hurting, but he would be okay. As long as she stayed there with him. She hadn't been asked a question, but Lily nodded at Jaxon, feeling him pull her less padded, twenty-year-old's hips until they met his muscled upper thighs.

His swim trunks had either magically disappeared from when she'd thought he was Stefan or he was as bare as when he'd first climbed out of the pool. And she just hadn't noticed. She was noticing now. And about to break out into fantasy hives. That never happened before in her dreamy escapes. A few deep breaths later and she gave the real Lily's nerves the boot, recalling her younger, pre-Tom self. That felt better. Everywhere. Truly, it felt like Jaxon was everywhere on her skin. Not because he was kissing her or running his hands over her superb, body, but because he had just laid her down on an extra-large towel and had draped himself over her. She chanced a peak down to admire the teeny bikini she imagined herself wearing to find it missing. Prepared to freak out, she waited. But she had a tight hold on this fantasy and was handling her nakedness like a swimsuit model.

And admiring Jaxon's. The warmth she'd felt all over everywhere turned to a tingling sensation. That combined with the dead cocktail mix of teal and purple in his eyes killed her ability to think of anyone else.

"Stay with me, Lily."

"For how long? You won't even say hello to me. *"*

"Shh. I'm here now."

She supposed fantasy Jaxon was right and she wasn't used to talking back whenever Stefan had whispered she was safe with him. It made her wonder.

"Am I safe with you, Jaxon?"

His battered eyes closed and then reopened. *"Stay."*

So she wasn't getting the pretend answer she wanted, even though this was her imagination running loose. But she couldn't leave. And when he slid his hands beneath her bum and cuddled her to his chest, she didn't want to. In a swift move only an experienced, sensual man could pull off, he made his way up onto his knees and then to standing and walked her down the pools steps into the water.

The most amazing part of this fantasy happened next. She felt his body react to hers. The muscles of his chest and shoulders and thighs that she'd been able to press into earlier had now hardened under her hold on him. Even in the water as they were now immersed to the shoulders, she could feel his new, stimulated flesh. Holy cow, she'd done that to him.

Curious, she wiggled her hips, looking for his while they floated together near one of the waterfalls, mostly hidden under the night time sky. He seemed to notice her not so clever move and took each of her legs in his well-sized hands and wrapped them around his waist, hugging her against him. His hard body said he wanted to make love to her. This was a brand new sensation, a brand new fantasy and she nearly died at how far she knew she'd go with him. Except for when he brought his face back from her hair and stared at her again, she saw that a tear had fallen down his cheek.

"Stay, Lily." His voice had those same holes. He was afraid of something. She knew it.

"Shh, it's okay. I've got you, Jaxon."

He gently hiked her up his body and laid his cheek between her breasts while she made sure to cradle his head with care.

Lily shook herself back to reality, giving up on the moment that had been touching in a whole different way than what she'd planned.

But who in the world lived like this? A princess, a queen? Hokie Okie Lily Elstone? Surely not. Then she remembered that Tris had, for a very long time. So why had her sister left it all behind? Lily put that thought together with the one of the broken man who had drifted outside, naked for the world to see but just as closed off and then nicked her Stefan fantasy.

Maybe Benny was right. Jaxon might have a very good reason for keeping his distance. While she had no intentions of prying, she would be lying if she said she didn't feel the immediate need to help the guy out. But, it was late. She was tired. So she rolled over on the room's furry rug and scratched softly at her scalp to ease her nerves. Bundling her knees to her chest in an effort to feel snug, she imagined holding that distant, naked man tightly in her arms.

Then the door opened and Benny stepped in.

"Hey, you're still up," he said and then stooped down to pick up her Stefan throw pillow and walked it over to her spot. "This must belong to you."

"Don't laugh," she said taking it and tucking it under her knees, face down.

"So you like Stefan, eh?"

Shyness flipped on her quiet, retreat-inside-herself switch. "Yep, you caught me."

"That actually makes me feel a lot better. Strangely. So you seem pretty tired."

She was sure he meant *instead of Jaxon*.

"Yeah, it usually takes me at least a few minutes to fall asleep. And that's when I'm somewhere familiar." *And not dreaming of swimming naked with your roommate.*

"Man, and we've been doing our best to make you feel at home, haven't we?"

She snickered at his joke. "Yeah, you guys really know how to make a girl feel welcome," she teased back. "So, what's up Benny?" she asked, wondering why he'd come to see her when she'd just barely left him.

"Well, I had an idea that might up your chances of meeting with Jaxon and have it sting him a little less."

She didn't need a mirror to know her face was all scrunched up. Plus Benny was basically pulling the same faces she felt herself making. Mostly confused and frowny ones.

"What idea is that?"

"Well, he's got this hang up about certain hair colors and yours is one of them."

Not in my fantasy he doesn't. Seriously, she had to stop adlibbing to every comment made. The truth was the conversation she was having right now. Jaxon wasn't asking her to stay in real life. He wasn't even saying hello.

"You're telling me Jaxon won't see me because I'm blonde? Benny, that's really weird."

His long spindly fingers splayed wide in the space between them. "It was just an idea and if you're not up for it then I totally understand. Totally."

"Okay valley boy, what's your big idea? I mean, if it'll get me some face time with Mr. James, I suppose I should hear you out."

"Coolio. Follow me blondie no more."

She only understood half the things he said and had no idea what was up but at this point, Benny had tugged her by the wrist and she'd better start taking some pretty big steps to keep up. They skipped down the hall to his room and landed in his private bathroom.

"You color your hair, Benny? So that's the secret to your auburn tones. Pretty."

"This one's for me," he said showing her a russet color, and then reached down and brought up another box. "And this one's for you. Before you freak, it's only a temporary dye. Washes out in six shampoos. But it'll do the trick for while you're here."

Something had flipped to bring him over to her side. He seemed to want this now just as badly as she did.

"Okee dokee." Lily picked up her box and read the color that looked beautiful on the model. "Dead Set Red Head." Wow, this was for real, even if it wasn't permanent. She looked over to Benny who had already donned his colorist gloves and was mixing his concoction and flashed him a big smile. "So you really think this will help?"

He paused while pulling his long bangs back from his forehead. "It gives my hair deep red tones. On yours, it should come out nice and vibrant. And to answer your real question, the boss never said anything about red heads being forbidden." That was as hopeful a look as she'd ever seen. Benny snickered. "And, it's Stefan's favorite shade."

Secretly, she didn't care so much about what Stefan was into right now. Which sucked because she knew what that meant. Something inside her had shifted. And as much as she needed this, she was in no way ready for it in the real world. Fantasy Lily could hold Fantasy Jaxon to her bare chest. The real Lily needed lots more air than she was currently getting and a cauldron of magic potion that both shrank her curves and boosted her confidence.

God I hope this turns out. Taking Benny's lead, she stared into the mirror and parted her very light blonde hair into sections. This was one gigantic way of trusting in someone else. She prayed her new buddy's great idea paid off.

* * * *

Jaxon walked inside the main house, his muscles spent from the exhaustive swim. Oddly, he found his clothes folded neatly and sitting on a chair. He had wrapped his towel around his waist but with the living room being empty and the house quiet, assumed Benny's friend had left. Good for her. He gave the towel a tug and enjoyed the feeling of free flowing air on his skin. The list of benefits of being alone wasn't a long one, but walking around butt naked topped it. He didn't count Benny, who he knew didn't care. He'd seen it all and was over it.

Too bad his brain was still cycling through the problem he'd failed to solve or he'd have enjoyed his nakedness more. It was really tearing him up—whether to have Trissy put Maryellie back on a plane home or suck it up and get himself out there to Tennessee to see the family. His muscles flinched while the two-year-old scar bisecting his eyebrow heated with a fresh sting. It was where he'd been beaten with a metal pole and made it impossible to forget that night he and Trissy had been attacked while hanging out in Stefan's borrowed car. He owed Lucky and Stefan his soul for showing up just in time and finding them.

Shit, was he finally up for a real face to face meeting with Trissy?

How could they be in the same room and not talk about it? But how the fuck did he bring it up two years after the fact? At Christmas no less?

He cursed the sadistic pricks who'd attacked them with a long, painful life followed by a death that matched.

Jaxon also knew he couldn't keep avoiding his family. Not now that Trissy, his adopted little sister for all intents and purposes, had gone and married his cousin. And Maryellie, devoid of her mum's love, deserved more than he could give alone. The family he'd kept separate had grown together without asking him if he was ready and now he knew he had to decide if he could handle the closeness.

With his towel draped over his shoulder, he grabbed a quick drink of water from the kitchen and then made his way up the stairs.

Benny was still up as light filtered through the bottom of the door. Something didn't feel right about the extra guest room. They never closed that door because Maryellie played in it so often. Shit, had Benny put his friend up in there for the night? They were going to have to have a talk. If his roomy wanted to have girls over this week with his daughter gone, that was fine; at least one of them should be enjoying themselves. But the stud needed to bed them down in his own room. Jaxon walked to the door to check out Benny's catch for the night.

He couldn't see very well from the doorway but she looked pretty cute, definitely Benny's type with the crazy red hair. *Good on you, Benny Ben.* Maybe he'd finally realized he didn't have a chance in hell with the spunky singer Erby. He closed the guest room and left the red head sprawled out across all four corners of the bed. *Man, what a waste.*

Back in his own bed, admiring the guts it took to sleep that comfortably in a stranger's house, Jaxon remembered something about Benny's friend. The temperature liked to drop at night with them being beachside and he hadn't seen a blanket. Not wanting the girl to catch a chill, he moved out of his grand bed, scratching at his bare ass, and made his way back to the guest room. He'd be quick.

A faint aroma of fruit laced with hair dye bugged his nose as he leaned in to her. With her sprawled out over the covers, he went to the closet to pull down the extra blanket which pricked his overly sensitive side. It was a quilt Trissy had made for him the year he didn't even see her at Christmas because Vangie had been such a bitch.

It would fit just perfectly over Benny's friend. He held it under his nose for a few steps to soak up the earthy smell of the fibers. Leaning closer, his arms spread wide to fan the quilt over her body. The craziest thoughts began multiplying in his head. Her hair, even in the dark, was a visible mess of bright red waves, but something about her seemed familiar. Shit, he rubbed his ass again, assuming that's where cupid would have shot him. What else explained his sudden connection to the girls popping up in his path today? His bare ass felt fine. Smooth as always. Her skin was what he found so remarkable. He studied its suppleness, glowing but pale like it hadn't seen much sun, showing strong, filled out arm and leg muscles below. He made his way to the other side of the bed so he could see her turned face as she laid there flat on her stomach.

Fuck, was it crazy that he was contemplating sitting there until she woke up so he could hear her speak? All he needed was one word to convince him whether he'd truly lost his mind. This couldn't be the girl from earlier today. The hair was all wrong, but the curves were all right. The jeans were perfectly tight. He hardened at the thought.

No. Absolutely not, mate. Get your naked, starved for love, perverted ass up and out of this room and leave Benny's catch alone.

After another few beats of watching her sleep, fighting his hand not to pat the back of that mussed up, fragrant hair, he lifted up off the floor and left the room.

Jaxon's back sank into his bed while he petted the black silk sheets with his calloused fingertips. There had been a point when such luxuries had impressed him but he'd forgotten over time. Now, tonight, he felt and remembered each exquisite thread like he was that hungry seventeen year old kid again. Decent and hardworking but fucking naïve as shit. He let out a hard sigh.

The wild red hair was just a cover up.

Whoever that was in his guest room, she was a good girl. Even in sleep, people like him kept traces of their grit displayed on their face. Not this one. She was decent and her sleeping face was calm and unspoiled. He made the wickedly hard decision not to come out the next day until Benny verified with him she was gone.

His eyes closed before he was ready, he was that damn tired. But if he'd have known the image paying him a visit, he'd have clamped them shut the second he'd laid down. Rubbing at his chest and dragging it slowly up and down his torso, a burst of wavy red hair made its way to him from across his room. Her walk was half lamb half tiger which brought him a bit of amusement, making it obvious she was trying hard for him. He let her. She was fucking sexy, short on her bare feet and stacked with soft curves. He could tumble with her all over his bed, if she'd just make her way to him and stop torturing him with this slow, adorable strut.

By the time his inexperienced temptress was close enough for him to grab, her hair had changed to angelic light blonde. He noticed that although not a single expression moved a muscle in her face, tears were silently dripping from her eyes while she stood there trying to cover her nakedness from him.

Even in that state, she reached out and took his hand from his chest and tugged him up. In the next second she was leading him outside through some unfamiliar dark place, his heart thumping at her spontaneity and the chance to follow such a sexy yet innocent creature.

"I'm looking for someone." It was the voice that had touched and haunted him as he'd hid in the hallway at the studio today. And he was sure he'd heard those same words. *"Can you help me find him?"*

No, he didn't want her looking for anyone but him. She had to stay at his side, holding his hand because he could feel the monsters pretending to be men making their way closer to this dark location. Quickly, he thought to at least strip his clothes and give them to her so she could cover up but of course he had none. Distorted faces surrounded them but as he looked closer, the faces all belonged to him. He did the only thing he could, he told her to run and when he did so, he was back in his bed, alone.

His eyes shot open while he lay there staring up at the ceiling's sky light and he caught a handful of silk sheet.

There was no way he could go back to Bugscuffle this out of control. Maryellie would have to be flown home in time for Christmas so they could spend it together. As long as he was an embarrassing, emotional mess, Jaxon was not making that trip to Tennessee.

SIN'S FLOWER

Chapter Seven

Mission Day Two...

Lily couldn't keep cooking for ghosts.

Not a one of these boys had come down this morning for the sad little eggs and bacon she'd fried up. Jaxon, the man she had to convince to come back to Tennessee with her who she'd yet to officially meet...while staying in his house...directly across the hall from him at night. It was some really odd stuff Lily assumed only mega-reclusive-millionaires were able to get away with. Try pulling that number back home and you'd be lucky not to have the whole town intervening on your butt. And after last night's pool fantasy, he'd been haunting her like crazy.

Lunch was just as pathetic and lonely. Lily had wiped her sandwich's bread bits into her hand and then tossed them to a pair of wild birds chirping about on the patio, happy to have fed somebody.

"Guess I'll plan dinner for my ghosts," she muttered to herself and went back inside.

A few hours later and it was dinner time but still not a single hide nor hair of the boys. Maybe Lucky had caved and confessed to Tris who had called and warned both Benny and Jaxon they were to steer clear of Lily. Each thought like that knocked a few of her hard earned adulthood pegs from the board. While being worried over had its perks, she also longed for the respect a thirty-one-year old, life-experienced and divorced woman should have earned.

The bachelor stash of food in the refrigerator was close to being gone. Lily decided to pop a bag of Orville Redenbacher she'd seen in the cupboard but she had to scale the counter to grab it. She'd bet this was Benny's since he was the only long-limbed person in the house. She began sizing up her elusive hosts as she hefted herself up and planted her knees on the hard granite counter. Her head banged into a cupboard that should have caused her to get her wits back but she kept on. Benny probably had an inch or two on Lucky who was a good six feet. Jaxon wasn't quite as tall as either of them; he hadn't had to duck when he'd walked out onto the patio last night.

The patio.

His beautiful back...patio.

She'd bet he was five-ten, maybe five-eleven. Not too tall and not at all short. Built like no guy she'd ever seen before. She liked that Jaxon's strength was evident in his thickset build, not like undefined Tom who had surprised her so many times. Damn him for her bruised wrists. *Oh boy*, she sighed, trying to cover up yet again for her past. She re-focused on Jaxon. Tris would flip out if she knew Lily had seen him walking around butt naked.

"Thank God I didn't see his stuff from the front. That would be bad," she whispered softly as she found delicious Mr. Orville. "But, it would have made my fantasy a whole lot better." Shocked at her lusty mind, she knew that would make the very serious conversation she needed to have with him by tomorrow night all the more awkward.

While the salty, buttery good stuff popped in the shiny microwave, she remembered Tris. The pain Lily had witnessed cloud her sister's face every time she mentioned this man's name was why she had to get him to come back with her.

She began a mental bullet list of Bugscuffle's top draws. Privacy had to be important for a guy like Jaxon and there was plenty of that in the tiny river front town.

While thinking of more plusses, she became distracted and started to wonder if Jaxon had somehow snuck out of the villa. But after shaking the bag of popped corn, footsteps made their way noisily in her direction.

She expected Benny.

She got Benny.

"Hey you, where've you been all day? I've basically killed your snack stash all on my own. Sorry." She held up the hot, fragrant bag.

Looking sheepish, he grinned. "Hey Red."

Her hair felt silkier as she ran her fingers from her top part down to the ends, eyeballing them. Holy spitfire! She'd nearly forgotten about her midnight transformation. It appeared her flaming do hadn't faded any during the night. She'd envisioned Lucille Ball but appeared to have gotten The Fifth Element's Leeloo. Well, what was done was done. Today she'd find out if it had been worth it. Maybe Jaxon was a sci-fi fan. Too bad Benny didn't have a magical bottle that would give her Leeloo's body too. A hurtful memory of Tom calling her a short Charlize Theron, which had made her happy for one moment, before he told her it was from the movie where they'd harshened the beautiful actress up for the role, burned her. *Jerk.* Even if he was right.

She coughed to clear the tears traveling up her throat. "So hey, if I'm gonna stick it out here one more day, I think I'll need a ride to a grocery store."

"We could go now." He had a bright and hopeful look on his face.

She hated to shoot him down, but this was the second day and she'd yet to speak the word hello to

Jaxon. "Actually, Benny, can you please get your roommate to come out and say hi first? Then we could go."

He shook his head like that still wasn't going to happen. Even though she'd gone all Little Mermaid for the man.

But then, just past Benny's shoulder, she saw him. The rest of Jaxon James.

Wow.

He was clothed now, stalking down the stairs dressed in a black shirt and black pants with a few conveniently placed zippers. Boys didn't wear that many zippers back home. Lily couldn't help but try following the path of the one that started below his belly button and continued way past where most flies stopped. She snapped her attention back to his eyes. The man was built for women but everything she needed to see was in his face.

A tight, ticking jaw.

Sparking teal eyes muddled by dark shadows.

Muscled arms folded across his chest, gave wrinkles to his soft black shirt and her quickening pulse. The man's penetrating stance made her feel sexy. Despite what she knew to be the truth—that she just wasn't.

Hip dark blond hair, disheveled and longer on top, shaved close at the sides knocked years from his chronological age.

He had a scar cutting right through his one eyebrow. The tattoo she hadn't seen clearly last night as he'd strutted out of the house in his birthday suit peeked from his shirt collar and climbed up his thick neck on the left side. And it wasn't alone. More tattoos colored the fronts of his arms. Lily forced herself to take a few steps closer to offer him her hand. She'd never been around someone with such a daring aura.

"Lily." It's all she managed to say now that she was a few feet away from him at the base of his stairs. She reminded herself to smile but the truth was, it was the last thing her face wanted to do. Melting would have been more appropriate. The man radiated raw power, sexy power.

"Lily?" he asked in his faded Australian accent. Did he not realize who she was? What? Benny really hadn't said anything? At all? Good lord, didn't these boys talk?

"Yes. Tris's sister. Younger." She wanted to add *but not baby* except for he'd just swallowed and Lily couldn't help but watch his throat and neck. And the tattoo she could make out better of teeth markings, not like a vampire bite but more like a shark's. "You must be Jaxon. Nice to meet you." Thank God she didn't say *finally* or *see you.* That would've been a nice reminder that she'd already seen some of him. Which she didn't want to think about just then. Great, his perfectly manly, tight buns were now strutting their way around in her head.

"Lily, Trissy's baby sister, Lily? From Oklahoma?" He frowned.

"Yes, but I've been staying with her in Tennessee since this summer."

She could see the beginnings of a 'w' forming in his puckered lips. Finally he spoke again. "Why are you here, exactly?" he asked looking more concerned than pleased.

Why did he have to sound so rude? He cut a side glance to Benny, showing her what Jaxon looked like when he was pissed. A second later, Jaxon's face focused back on her and she tried for a soft smile. *Ease into it,* she told herself.

"I needed to talk to you." *Please don't make some snide, backward remark about Tennessee not having phones.* "In person."

He squeezed his hands inside his armpits which made his noticeable arm muscles bulge even more and then let them fall to his sides.

"Are you hungry, Lily?" he asked to her complete shock.

Normally, yes. Lily lived in a constant state of hunger. She hated that fact because it sucked that no matter how much she ate, it never seemed to be enough. Her tummy rumbled, even though she'd doubled up on breakfast and lunch so the boys' portions hadn't gone to waste. She shouldn't be hungry, but felt ravenous, and nodded yes.

"I'll go grab us dinner. We'll talk when I get back. Benny, you're coming with me."

Oh hell. If that look didn't say it all. She and Benny were in big trouble as the baseball cap Jaxon donned and pulled down low over his forehead didn't quite hide his mood.

Benny followed Jaxon through the villa door to his garage. A couple minutes later, she watched them drive away in a silver Range Rover. Lily wondered what it would be like to ride shotgun with Jaxon James all the way back to Tennessee in that…a lifestyles of the rich and famous luxury mobile.

A sense of extreme pride shot from her cherry red toe nails to her traffic cone hair strands that she'd somehow kept her cool and a meal was about to take place with these real, live men. Benny was an absolute genius. And probably getting an earful right about now.

* * * *

"What the fuck is going on, mate?" Jaxon let out, as he drove them to his favorite taco shop. "How the bloody hell is Trissy's little sister bunking at my fucking house?"

The word fuck hadn't been said nearly enough to get his point across right now. Hell, Jaxon hadn't realized how hot his temper had boiled over until it all welled up and he fast-balled it at Benny without care of how hard it hit. "Fuck, you know as well as I do why she shouldn't be here."

"Can I talk for a second?" Benny didn't dare look at him right now but stared out the tinted side window. "Look I'm sorry. But she just showed up and it's not like I was gonna turn Trista's little sister away after I found out that's who she was."

The thought did worry him, he supposed, and blew out a breath. Although having this girl at his house had gifted him instant heartburn. "After all that shit getting Trissy…out of this hell hole, Benny. Come on, man. Really? Our house?" He shook his head, worsening the pounding at his temples, thinking of a safe hotel he could have Benny drive her to after giving her some food.

"I get it, okay. I remember those days too. But will it really kill you to hear Lily out?"

Ah shit. Benny knew more than what he was letting on and he'd clearly already made friends with the unwelcome guest, the way he said her name. "And what the fuck would that be about, exactly?" He couldn't wait to hear this as much as he detested it.

Benny cleared his throat and adjusted his wool hat. "Okay. So, like I said, she showed up out of the blue, looking like she was gonna cry if I didn't give her the time of day…"

"Get to the point." Jaxon rubbed his face as he drove the memorized route to El Ranchito's.

"Trista isn't doing so hot, Jaxon. Lily's worried about her."

He hated to admit that changed things, but it did. Fuck. "What exactly do you mean?"

"I guess all the stress is hurting her pregnancy."

"What? What stress?" Trissy was supposed to be living her life out in the country with Lucky and all that was simple and good.

Benny looked like he'd rather not say, with his lips clamped shut from the inside.

"Fucking spill it now, mate."

"Lily's convinced that Trista's really upset you didn't show up with Maryella. And..."

"There's more? Shit, how much time have you spent with this girl?"

"Not much, actually. She kind of poured most of this out to me the other morning at my desk. I've been totally trying to avoid getting involved because I knew how thrilled you'd be."

The girl must have been desperate, showing up like this. That didn't matter. Fuck, yes it did. He knew it. Questions flooded his aching head at everything from how Trissy had reconnected with a little sister he knew little about and now this.

"Shit, Benny. I stay away for two damn years and it's all for nothing."

For the first time since they'd sped away, Benny looked over at him. Oh hell, that look.

"Maybe it's as easy as having a conversation with this girl who cares about Trista as much as we both do. Maybe there's something you can do to help."

They pulled up to the drive-thru just in time, keeping Jaxon from exploding with a huge blur of profanities. The cashier's voice warbled through the speaker while he and Benny sat there silent.

"Three fish tacos and an horchata," Benny said to him.

Realizing he had to order, Jaxon leaned out his window. "Fish taco platter and three horchatas."

They pulled forward in a fit of extremely uncomfortable funk and waited for their food until he couldn't stand ignoring their breathing sounds anymore.

"What exactly does she want?" Jaxon had forced himself to forget how drawn he'd been to her voice, oh hell…the thoughts he'd had about her body and holding her naked, tumbling around on his bed with Trissy's baby sister.

Benny huffed, sending loose wisps of bangs skyward. "For you to go back to Bugscuffle with her so Trista will stop stressing. And, hopefully stop her from having early contractions. I guess the baby's way too young to be born yet."

"Fuck, this isn't good. What the hell do I do?"

"You got me, boss."

He pulled them into the drive, not bothering to use the garage. This was going to be quick and to the point.

Inside, she had set the table with plates and cloth napkins he was surprised she'd found.

"I hope you like fish tacos. And uh, be ready to go first thing tomorrow."

Benny was to find the three of them a flight out to Tennessee. Jaxon's mind was gone. He took his tacos out to the patio, uncomfortable with the grateful look lifting her face. Had she missed his sharp tone and short words? Did she have any idea of the demons she was forcing him to face? Why did she have to smell so damn good?

Chapter Eight

For what she'd envisioned of mild winters in Southern California, it was downright cold. The sea outside the guest room's window pounded loudly, obviously as restless as Lily. She flipped over with a huff and tried her right side. But that ear had been giving her problems ever since she'd gotten carried away and let the powerful showerhead pound her face. Knowing that getting to sleep would quicken tomorrow's arrival, Lily closed her eyes. As soon as she did, he was there, inviting her back into that pool. But could she trust him? Was he really interested in her? She didn't think so, but a girl could hope.

A few hours later, she woke with the need to know she was somewhere safe. Lily wrung her clammy hands together as if she'd just squeezed out way too much lotion and no one wanted to share any. It took another couple minutes before she'd woken enough to be able to move any other part of her body. And yet a few more to realize she was doing something very unnatural. As her mind finished waking, the reality of what she'd done left her humiliated.

Oh my God, the bed was soaking wet and the unmistakable odor of urine coated the air.

She sprang up from the soiled mattress in disbelief. In her dream, she'd been squatting in the creek behind her house in Oklahoma. She'd gone to the creek looking for Tris when the warmth from her pee felt so good against that icy cold creek water.

Panicked, she scrambled around the guest room, flipped on the light switch and stripped the sheets from the bed. What would she do if she were at home? She needed to get a grip. This was worse than accidentally bleeding through on a girlfriend's bed when you had your period. And hello? She wasn't some awkward pre-teen anymore at the rare sleepover she'd attended as a kid with a harrowing history of bladder infections. She was a grown woman and no way in heck did thirty-one-year olds wet the bed. Oh, and not just any bed, of course. But one of Jaxon James'. She realized there wasn't much else she could do. Standing there in the middle of the floor on a nice and dry, warm rug, petrified, she remembered the last piece of her dream, when the door came slightly open from the other side.

"Lily? Are you okay?"

She expected Benny.

She got Jaxon.

* * * *

From the doorframe, he could see her arms trembling.

"Lily." He walked into the room and made sure she wasn't standing up asleep. Jaxon didn't want to scare her. He'd done that once to Trissy and she'd nearly scratched him blind. "Lily," he said softly, remembering the way he spoke to his baby girl when she'd had a bad dream and needed daddy to tuck her back in. "Let's get you back to bed."

Her head was shaking no before it dipped altogether, bringing her hands up to hide the rest of her face framed by that bright hair. "I'm sorry," she said.

"No need to be sorry. Come on." He knew he was supposed to be keeping his distance but reached his hand out and grasped her lightly by the elbow which pulled her one hand from her face. She looked like she was holding on to tears. Jaxon had no idea what was going on and he'd started to feel highly out of his element. Not to mention worried. Obviously Lily was awake. Maybe getting her to talk would help. She was eyeing the bed like it had the plague, so he offered her a seat on the small sofa in the room.

"Hey, are you okay?" *You shouldn't be coddling her like this.* "I know I haven't given you a reason to trust me, but you can talk to me, Lily." *Fuck what was he saying?* Then he realized she probably had no idea what to expect if she agreed to talk with him now.

"I promise, I'll just listen. I'm actually not a bad listener when I try," he said. Why was he trying so hard? Probably because she looked about as inadequate as he felt right now.

She watched his face and then blinked. Then it was eyes back down to her lap, hands back up so her face was shielded from his view. Maybe she wasn't capable of a conversation and her aversion to the bed had him wondering what was wrong with it. He was so completely unsure of what to do for her in that moment that he got up from the sofa and walked over to the bed. He didn't make it two feet.

"Jaxon, I...I ruined your bed. I'm sorry." Her voice shook.

He took a good long look at it now and for the first time noticed the blankets and sheets had all been stripped and lay in a large pile on the floor. He ran a hand over the bare mattress and stopped at the ring mark of moisture. "Oh shit," he muttered to himself. Apparently Lily had been sleeping in a bed that had been wet during one of Maryellie's sleepovers. Lily was probably one of those girls with a sensitive nose, just like Trissy, and hadn't wanted to say anything about the odor. But then his fingers caught the edge of the mark. Strangely, it was wet to his touch.

"I'm so so sorry," she said again to his back. When he turned around, she was looking up at him. The realization must have dawned heavily across his face because her body started to shake. Was she afraid he was angry? What in the hell had happened to this poor girl to make her think he'd be angry with her? But worse than that, what kind of traumatic shit was she dealing with that had her wetting the bed as a grown woman?

His worst fears snapped into place. Trissy had been taken from home because she'd been abused by her step-father. And Lily…Lily had been left behind.

Jaxon walked back to the sofa and took a seat by her side. "Lily, don't worry about the bed," he assured her.

She was still holding in her tears. He could tell by the deep frown in her brow, the odd way her mouth was clamped shut and the sniff she allowed through her nose every few seconds. But she nodded, apparently trusting that he could give a shit about a ruined mattress. The important thing, he realized in that instant, was that he wanted her to know he cared about her situation. No matter the way he'd completely ignored her until today. He hated that. A sudden realization scared the crap out of him. It was way too deep, the way all he wanted to do just then was hold her in his arms and keep her safe.

Jaxon found Lily's two hands in her lap and cupped them inside his. Her eyes looked so tired, whatever sleep she'd managed tonight hadn't been restful. It was highly unlikely she was up for talking so his priority was to get her somewhere comfortable so she could sleep. He was usually up all hours of the night; he didn't need his bed.

"Lily, come with me please."

Surprisingly, she followed, still rattled, but not disagreeing.

He led her by the hand to his room and offered her his bed by letting go of her to turn down the covers he hadn't yet used that night.

"There you go. It's pretty comfy and it's all yours." He was doing his best to be tender but stop himself from caring too much. Who knew if it was working? She looked hesitant standing there at the edge of the bed. "Don't worry, I'll be downstairs. I've got a sleeper sofa in my studio."

He must have read her pretty well because finally, Lily sat down where he'd pulled back the covers.

She deflated right there in front of him. "I'm afraid it might happen again. I...I don't want to ruin your..."

In a second, he was at her side, oddly wanting to hold her hand as she sat. He didn't touch her though. "Shhh, don't worry. It's okay, even if it does. I don't care about the fucking beds."

She ran her left hand through her hair at the top of her head, looking very nervous. "I don't know. I..."

"Hey, are you worried about getting back to sleep?"

She nodded her head. "Yeah."

"Would you like me to sit with you for a bit?" Jaxon fought against how badly his body called for him to soothe her. He clamped down on his bottom lip in an effort to feel something other than desire to be closer.

She shrugged. Her covered shoulders were still soft in the moonlight filtering from the bathroom window into his room. "I don't want to keep you up."

"It's all right. I don't sleep at night anyway."

She laid her head back against the pillow but stayed propped up in a sitting position. Knowing his proximity was dangerous, Jaxon took a few steps back toward the chair in the corner where he usually tossed his clothes and filled it with his mixed up ass instead. Even though it was only a good six feet, it was too far away. He'd picked up on a need in her, even though she'd been holding most everything in. Her arms didn't seem to be holding her tight enough and her shaking hadn't gone away yet.

Finally, the tears began to flow. He was up and out of his chair and sitting on the bed with her within a second. Jaxon hesitated, knowing he shouldn't, but then held her while she cried.

"Hey, Lily, it's going to be okay. Whatever it is, it'll be okay."

"Thank you."

Those two words tore him in more ways than he realized. He'd treated her like a leper but all he heard was the gratitude in her tattered voice. How could he leave her right now? Why did he care this much already? Fuck with the questions. Holding her reminded him he was human. For better or worse, he did have a heart. No, he couldn't stay too long. Only until she fell back to sleep, with him counting the hours until they packed and he returned Lily to her big sister.

Her lips puffed out from a deep breath and a faint sigh. She must like the way he was rubbing her scalp.

"You could have asked me to leave today. You didn't," she murmured softly.

God, she had to stop talking to him like that.

"A couple years ago, I would have." And then he thought what an idiot he was for toying with her like this, alluding to a transformation he still struggled with daily.

She sniffed and rubbed her sleeve against her nose and then an awkward giggle escaped her sweet lips. "Two years ago, I needed permission to so much as leave my house."

"Seriously?" Stunned wasn't a strong enough word.

She nodded. "Yeah," she said and closed her eyes. A tear fell down her cheek. "I was an idiot. Now

I'm just embarrassed." The joking end of her remark was obviously for his benefit. She held it together for exactly seven more seconds before her breath hitched again.

That was it. After hearing that last bit, his macho side cranked into protective mode. Which in turn ignited his true nature. It was going to be a long night of ignoring his body's reaction to this vulnerable young woman. Desperate for a distraction to his sudden and unexpected arousal, he began humming a lullaby. Fuck if it wasn't the first time he'd ever done that with such a voluptuous woman in his bed. *Forbidden Jaxon, forbidden.*

SIN'S FLOWER

Chapter Nine

Someone had done his best to sing her to sleep. It just hadn't worked.

"Jaxon, there's something I should tell you. I would have said it sooner but…" she started to say as they began their walk.

"But I was a dick and haven't been around. It's not your fault."

"Okay, so we agree on that." She smiled and tried to hold on to the easy feeling that came from it. "Thanks for taking this walk with me." Thick sand and a few broken sea shell fragments masked her toes all the way to the middle bridge of her foot. "I can't remember the last time I was out this late and never somewhere so stunning."

Lily could see why Tris had held on so tightly to Jaxon's friendship, staying through all that mess with Vangie.

"Sure. I used to come down here a lot more. It's nice seeing someone appreciate it. Reminds me I ought to do the same." He rubbed the back of his neck, thumbing his tattoo several times.

She hadn't asked him about it yet. They stood a safe distance from the shoreline, a foot or so separating them from each other. "That's an interesting tattoo on your neck. It must have hurt."

He must have heard that line a million times before because he smirked and then looked to be chewing the inside of his cheek. She guessed she'd blown that attempt and didn't expect an answer. But he surprised her.

"It hurt a little. Not so much the inking but having to hold my neck at that angle for so long." He may have become self-conscious of it from their conversation because Jaxon dropped his hand to his side, leaving red marks from where his fingers had dragged at it. "What about you?"

"What about me what?"

He snickered and then spoke more slowly. "Do you have any tattoos?"

"Nope. None." Wonderful, this was off to a great start but he didn't let go of it.

"What, are you afraid of the pain?"

Was he taunting her? Poking fun that she wasn't as tough as him? Unfortunately, she'd had her strength proven a time too many. But that's not what he meant. Was she afraid of the pain? No, that wasn't it. "I'm not afraid. But I'd have to love something for a really long time before I made that type of commitment."

"You and me both," he said, pulling at his shirt collar, making it snugger around his thick neck.

And that was it. He didn't say another word for a full five minutes. The moon dangled above them making the ocean shiny and black and even more immense than it was in the daytime. Thoughts of Jaxon's tattoos faded away along with everything else in that moment. She didn't realize how intently he'd been watching her until he pushed his foot into the sand, touching his toes to hers.

She coughed to clear her tightening and anxious throat. Now that the moment had passed, she couldn't seem to swallow enough times to get her voice and wits back.

"So I have an idea. You obviously enjoy the water, how about I run back up to the house, grab some chairs, and we sit here for a bit. Hmm?"

Really? Was this all real? She had to remind herself to say something. If it wasn't enough she'd fallen under the spell of the enormity of the ocean, it was clearly evident Jaxon had his own special hold over her.

Oh all right, maybe that had more to do with her fiery red hair and the passionate woman inside challenging her to act and feel instinctive. Her priorities had been shuffled like a deck of trick cards. She could keep telling herself she was only here for Tris. But the truth was, ever since Jaxon had strutted past her, not caring about his nakedness, she'd been absorbed in figuring him out. And in a very odd way, she felt both safe and sexy with him. If only she could trust that. "Sounds good," she finally answered.

"All right, are you okay on your own for a few minnys?"

She nodded, smiling at his unique speech. He took off in the direction of his house. His house, for goodness sake, which she could easily see being it was right there. What she wouldn't do to help him see the beauty in his life. Maybe the only place she'd find that answer was in Tennessee. At least she'd have her chance. Smiling, she drew a silly heart in the sand with her toe but quickly erased it for fear of him seeing.

* * * *

Lily sat with her back to him, hair blowing in the breeze. It was the sexiest look he'd seen on a woman. Half of her neck bared to him. The other half hidden by loose cinnamon curls. She was a beautiful woman. How she'd found her way to him was just bananas. Kind of like Stefan who had just kept him on the phone way too long. Band business could wait. Hopefully his mate wouldn't actually show up tonight. Jaxon didn't care to explain or introduce his guest. Especially since Stefan was the horniest man he knew and had a thing for red heads.

Jaxon watched Lily's hands sinking down into the sand from behind as hesitancy chopped up his steps. Years of ending up in dire situations had made him a decisive man when he needed to be. He was making one of those executive decisions right now. It didn't matter why she'd come. And he was close to dismissing his reluctance over whose baby sister she was. Not when she wore that swishing angelic lavender top that covered her from neck to shoulder to fingertip, driving him insane with curiosity. God, and that flaming hair which had gone from neon just yesterday to a flattering shade of cinnamon temptation tonight. His grip tightened around the folding chairs he'd gone to fetch. Purposefully, he slowed down.

Then stopped.

Wanting her was one thing, but hurting this young woman was not okay.

Standing back, he took another couple minutes to contemplate what could happen tonight. What he could control and make happen.

He knew they should talk. He just hoped she didn't mind how close he intended on being to her while that happened. His grip loosened and one of the folding lounge chairs fell to the sand. There would be plenty of room for the both of them on the one. He walked until he made it back to her side and unfolded the chair to its full length.

"Uh, hi," she said shyly, her brow furrowing in concentration.

"Hey." He sat down and held his arms out to assist her. "Sit with me?" He hadn't given her much of a choice and caught her eye scanning the sandy trail where he'd come from. "Yeah, I figured we didn't need that one."

"Oh, okay. Wait, just so we're clear here. You want me to sit, where exactly?"

God, she would kill him tonight. That amount of cute couldn't be faked. "Here, with me." Her eyes widened in disbelief so he scooted until he was flush with the back of the nylon chair and then opened his legs, letting one straddle each side. "There's room."

"You're crazy," she said shaking her head.

He let out a faked huff. His quick decision had been too fast for her and she wouldn't believe this was his way of comforting her. "I'll go fetch the other chair."

She gouged her hand into her hip. "Wait. It's just…I really don't think I'm gonna fit."

A hurricane couldn't have swayed her decision to stay put. But she eventually bent her knees, bracing herself with strong hands, and lowered herself until her squeezable bottom met the chair. Because he wanted her closer, he took the liberty of placing his hands at each side of her waist and scooted her back until she was flush with his chest and his lap.

On second thought, that was way too close.

Someone would kill him for the throbbing going on so close to their little sister. He wiggled an inch of space between Lily and his now obvious and straining erection. The last thing he wanted to do was leave her thinking he was incapable of a conversation without sex ending up front and center. He had amazing amounts of control in that department. It came along with all the years he'd practiced on the road. Tonight, plainly put, he just wanted to be close to someone, to Lily. And this was the way he knew how to do that.

"So what did you want to talk about?" he asked.

"I, I don't know." It sounded like nerves had her.

They didn't have to start with words. Fuck him for his appetite but he could say more by doing this anyway.

Hey you, horny fucker. This is the part where you pat her on the head, say you're sorry, and send her back to her big sister. This is not the time for indulging. Pack it up, Jaxon.

Yeah, no questions about it. That's what he should do.

He leaned in to her back until his nose brushed up against her sweet neck, nuzzling little circles in her fine baby hairs. Tiny goose bumps rose across her skin so he breathed his warm breath in an effort to chase away the chill. She squirmed, sending his muscles into tight spasms. God, this was so wrong but he needed it so bad. *Fucking bananas karma.*

"Oh, I, uh, so you met Tris when she was sixteen. How old were you?"

"I was twenty-six," he said, dropping into her neck a fraction more with each word.

"And you never wanted to kiss her?"

He should pull back from her, at least an inch or two, to answer but he was so close to finding the exact right spot. "No, I can honestly say I didn't." He waited to plant his lips in the sweet spot since tickling her with his nose seemed to be so pleasing. He should not be doing this. The craziest part was that he knew it. But just like during the talk they'd had in his room, he couldn't seal himself off from her right now and she wasn't saying no.

"Well knowing my sister, I bet there were times when she wanted to kiss you."

"There may have been a couple times but she quickly got over it." Even he could hear the haste in which he'd delivered that one. To keep the slow rhythm he refused to lose with her, he slowed to a pause and then answered. Hell, maybe he was just trying to scare her straight. *This is the real me, I will take you and you will regret it. Here's a little taste.*

"You know I never wanted to kiss your sister, but you on the other hand. I'm not gonna lie, I could definitely kiss you. I won't, of course."

"You won't?"

He paused again to consider the green light she'd just given him with that hopeful lilt tagging the end of her response.

"You have a great accent," he said. As much as he'd love to keep her talking just so he could hear her southern quirky drawl, it was time to start winding down.

"So do you," she said.

"I really like your voice, Lily." He was about to say *But I can't lick and talk at the same time so let's shush now and we'll get to that talk later,* when she made a tiny movement that pressed her neck into his lips. Their little word play was helping her relax so he held off on asking for her silence.

"I like yours too."

"I like your mouth," he said.

"I like your...lips."

"Lily, I changed my mind. I am going to kiss you."

"Jaxon, what are we doing?"

"Talking." He blew another breath into his favorite little place on earth right now.

* * * *

There was no way she could possibly talk and make any sense if he kept doing that blowing thing on her neck. How had they ended up here again? As hard as it was to pull away, she did it. And then pivoted so that she was still seated in his lap just in a sideways kind of way. So this was why Lucky and Tris wanted her to stay away from Jaxon. The man couldn't help himself when it came to women. She wasn't surprised given his occupation. At least he wasn't trying to hide the fact.

Lily needed to see his face if they were going to talk. At least that's what she thought at first. Now she wasn't so sure. Under the moonlight, with the waves sounding off behind them, and wrapped in a blanket on the same chair, she could see Jaxon's appeal to the masses. He was handsome. No, scratch that. He was striking mixed with the rawest, natural sexuality she'd ever dared to imagine existed.

In all the years she'd been a fan of Sin Pointe, this was the first time she'd ever noticed Jaxon over Stefan. All the anxiety of coming here washed away for the moment. Her lips found their way to the very outer edges of his. Her eyes closed. She waited. They could talk later.

* * * *

"Open your eyes, Lily. Please."

"Wh-what?"

Tracing her lip with his fingertip was his way of telling her he wanted the kiss she offered. He outlined it softly until she opened her eyes back up for him.

"Thank you," he said.

"I don't understand. I thought—I just thought you wanted…"

"Shh. I do." He did. Strangely, more than anything he'd wanted in a long time. But in the second she'd taken control of the situation by offering him her kiss, he realized there wasn't a right way to do this. He'd find a way to fuck it up. Sadly, he knew that wouldn't stop him.

She looked doubting as her chin started to fall. He caught it with his hand. And then gave her a quick peck on the nose. "I want more of these from you. Believe me. But not yet. And we need to talk first." Mmm, the countdown was on and he fought not to slide her under him and make her his. God, what was he thinking? "Lily, please, talk."

"Okay. Um, well, I guess I need to be completely honest with you." Her voice started off shaky but the more words that spilled from her perfect pink lips, the more confidence she regained. *Good girl.*

"So you obviously know the reason I came here is to ask you to come back to Tennessee with me." Yes, Benny had done that bidding for her. She took in a big mouthful of cool air and let it back out, which smelled incredibly good gusting over his face. "Tris has been all over the place lately, happy one day, sad and in tears the next. Lucky's tried, I've tried, Luke, Bear. We've all tried but it doesn't last long. I know she's pregnant and has all those hormones to deal with, but there's just something else I see in her eyes." She stopped and stared directly into his, like she was trying to find out whether or not he had an answer that would explain her sister's behavior.

Unfortunately, he did. And he had no idea how to talk about it with Lily.

He gathered his thoughts before going any further. "Lily, I want you to know something. Okay? If there was anything I could do to help your sister, I would. My showing up there isn't gonna make anything better for her. You've gotta trust me on that one."

"But you're her best friend. You know her better than any of us." Lily's eyes saddened to a shade closer to Trissy's ocean blue.

"I was." He couldn't bring himself to say he'd hurt Trissy so badly that he couldn't think of himself that way anymore.

"She hasn't forgotten about you. And before you say it, yes, she has Lucky now."

"And you," he pointed out.

"And me. But something's still missing. The way her eyes lit up when Lucky came back from the airport and then got all sad again, it dawned on me. It's you. You're what's missing. She was hoping you'd flown in with Maryella."

God, was there any turning back from that? "You see a lot," he finally said.

"I see what's laid out in front of me."

She made him want to share the safer parts of it with her. Those eyes of hers. Fine, let it be a lesson. Let her hear his truth and let any decision she made tonight be based on what he was about to share.

"Lily, you have to understand something. When your sister moved out here and took the job with the band, she was only sixteen. I was too young and stupid to realize it then, but she had no business touring around with us. We didn't know what to do with her, so we treated her like one of the guys. I didn't find out until a couple years later that she'd...well, she'd come to us from a really fucked up situation. We all loved her by that point, but the best thing that could have happened would have been for her to leave then and there. Instead she stuck around, became our family. Sixteen years later, we'd...I—I had ruined her. If Lucky hadn't come around..."

"What do you mean, you ruined her? Why do you feel that way?"

"You won't understand this because you're obviously a good person." He paused and shrugged, debating whether or not to take her hand into his. He decided not to. "She was my best friend. Always there for me, always ready to help me when I got in trouble. I started expecting that constant attention from her. But never gave her anything in return."

"That's not what she says. That's not how she talks about you."

"No. Lily, listen to me. I was a dick to her. Okay? Yeah, things were great for a long time. Then I started doing my own stupid shit and then Maryellie's mum came into the picture. So I had less and less time for Trissy, but I never let her off the hook. You know? I never let her go to find her own happiness. That's just what I do to friends."

"I don't believe that."

"Don't be that girl, Lily. Please. Be smarter than that."

"I'm not going to say that you couldn't have been a better friend and made better decisions. It sounds like you could have. We all could stand to do that. Okay, but you have to know that you weren't the monster who hurt her."

He watched Lily swallow around a giant spasm that nearly shook her whole body. Her evident pain invaded his heart, leaving him at a loss. Words were his specialty and he knew the times when they'd be useless. This was one of them. "I don't know what to say to that."

"It's okay. It's not exactly the easiest thing to talk about for me either. But I'd rather be up front and honest than running away from demons my whole life," she said.

Shit. Trissy had some badass demons. He hated thinking Lily shared them. "Like your sister."

She nodded yes. So she did know what had happened to Trissy when she was a little girl. He wouldn't push any further on that topic. He didn't want to hurt Lily and had no idea what to say. But she continued.

"I showed up at Tris's door this summer, with my basket full of questions. Why I'd found her bleeding by the creek by our house the way I had when we were kids. Why she'd left me when she did. What she remembered of our momma and our brother. Soon enough, she sat me down and I had all my answers. It was the absolute worst I've ever felt in my entire life." He could see that in her face as she took a second to compose herself. "But, I know there's no way we could have become close again if we hadn't gotten it out. There were things I had to hear, no matter how horrible they were."

"You're an easy person to open up to, Lily."

"Really? Am I?" She tried tucking a few stray pieces of long cinnamon bangs behind her ears but they wouldn't stay against the will of the ocean's night breeze to keep them freed.

Jaxon helped secure the longer pieces on the left. "Obviously or we wouldn't be sitting here together," he said to her as he caught her hand in his once they'd both given up on her hair.

He felt the sting of his words as they left his tongue. She curled back from him. He remembered how he couldn't get a word out of her earlier when he'd found her with the wet bed.

"Do you trust me, Lily?"

"Obviously or we wouldn't be sitting here together." She rolled her eyes. "Sorry."

Shit. That mocking comment told him she needed to get something off her chest. "It's all right. Hey, so those answers you got from Trissy, did they include, um, those times she was abused as a kid?"

"By my father, yes. It's not a secret."

"Ah baby, I wish that wasn't the case." Where did he touch her now? Every place seemed inappropriate but he longed to give this girl some comfort.

"Me too."

"Are you okay? I mean, if you need to talk...."

"Jaxon, one of these days, I think I might need a friend to talk to."

"But not tonight?"

"No, not tonight."

Had her bastard father fucked her up too? Too bad that asshole was dead. He took a breath to calm down and be there for her now. "It's all right." He pulled her face into his chest and held her like one of Maryellie's precious baby dolls. Time for another quick decision. He wouldn't make her beg for that favor she'd traveled forty-eight hours on a bus to ask him. "Baby." Yes, she'd become baby to him. He whispered into her hair. "We should try and get some rest. It's gonna be a long trip to your sister's place."

A shuddered breath tumbled out onto his chest as he gently rubbed circles into her back.

SIN'S FLOWER

Chapter Ten

She still couldn't believe he'd agreed. Like it hadn't taken her a secret trip out west and then nearly two full days to even get a hello from him.

"We should probably go inside," he said while rubbing her back and arm.

"Well first I think I should say thank you."

He just nodded and parted his pompadour styled bangs with his fingers.

They'd walked halfway back up the beach toward his house before he answered. "Don't thank me."

"Okay."

His tone had changed. She was sure of it. Like she was getting her wish but losing the connection they'd made in exchange. They walked quietly back to his house and went inside through the back patio doors. Waiting for them, sprawled out on the couch, was the man she'd dreamed of marrying since she'd turned sixteen.

Holy cow, Stefan Calderon was six feet from her. In the flesh. She should be hyperventilating right now but someone's hand in the small of her back seemed to have control of her breathing. And it was unusually calm.

"Stefan, what the fuck are you doing here, mate?"

"Well hello to you too, sweetie," Stefan cooed to Jaxon in rhythm with his waggling brows. Lily tried to step out of the way so they could talk but Jaxon kept her situated just off to his side. She nearly laughed when Jaxon flipped Stefan off. "I told you I was coming by. B-a-n-d business to discuss. Remember?"

"Yeah, yeah. Well, you suck at follow through," Jaxon threw back.

Stefan coughed while Jaxon's chest made full contact with Lily's back and he scooted them closer to the lead singer of Sin Pointe.

"Hi there, Red. I'm Stefan, nice to meet you."

"Hi," she grunted out.

Not that she could have come up with another syllable, let alone word, but she didn't have the chance because Jaxon pressed his hand to her back again and guided her right past Stefan and to the stairs then took a couple steps back. He plunged his hands deep into his zippered jeans. "Remember we've got an early start tomorrow. Get some good sleepies."

And with that she was evidently dismissed. Lily made her way in shock up the stairs to Jaxon's room. She hoped that's what he'd meant but he'd all but yellow police-taped off the room with the peed-on mattress which she had to somehow replace for him.

Her feet gave out and she fell onto his giant bed with the absolute absurdity of the last few hours and the insane curiosity of whether Stefan ever slept over scattering her thoughts. She sighed and hoped the next few hours would pass by at lightning speed. And that she'd wake up still feeling like Lily in Wonderland.

* * * *

Jaxon was busy thinking about how Stefan had just saved his butt again with the miraculous perfect timing of his showing up when Stefan managed to bring him back to the real world where nothing they ever did involving a girl could be considered good. "She's cute. Spicy red heads are my specialty though."

"She's a no-no."

"A no-no for me or for you?"

"Next," Jaxon said with a knife sharp tone.

Stefan made a smacking sound. "Fine. So hey, I, uh. I wanted to make a suggestion."

Stefan's suggestions were always worth a listen especially when Jaxon needed a laugh. But his band mate and dear friend was all clenched up looking. Ah shit, he better not be here to get all "let me help you past that fucking night" again.

"What?" Jaxon asked through a squinted eye.

"Shit. I don't want to say this, but the songs you're bringing to rehearsals, man, they're…"

"They're bad."

"Yeah dude, they're pretty bad. That's why the guys and I think you should take a break. Get out and see some different stuff. Find a new muse. Or…"

"Or?"

"Well, the rest of us agreed to step up to the plate. Will scribbled out a few workable lyrics the other night. I think he's still pretty haunted by Honey but it could make for a good song or two. I mean shit, I could even give it a try. Girls like songs about sex." Stefan's gaze drifted off to someplace else.

"Yeah, well usually only if you're clever about it."

Jaxon wasn't sold on the idea but apparently the guys weren't buying his crap lyrics anymore. He didn't blame them. But whether they realized it or not, Sin Pointe was bigger than the four of them now. It was a distinct sound. His sound. Stefan might see this as selfish, but Jaxon really was trying to think of the band and what their fans expected. "No, that's not gonna work. The songs, not saying they wouldn't be good songs, but they wouldn't be Sin Pointe."

Stefan walked into the kitchen and helped himself to a beer. "Near beer man, you want one?" Jaxon knew Stefan must have stopped and bought the stuff on the way over. His mate would never drink that piss otherwise. Nope, that was just for his recovering alcoholic benefit.

"Fuck no."

Stefan plopped back down on to the couch and gagged after taking a long swig. "Ack."

"Told you."

"Yeah, so hey. Since when do you ever get an early start to anything? Who's that curvy babe we'll call your motivation upstairs?"

"Nice try. You gonna hang for a bitty?" He wasn't sharing; soon Stefan would realize that.

"Fuck. I guess so."

"What, no *motivation* to get home to tonight? That fruit sample girl at the smoothie shop is into you."

"She's too sweet."

"Maybe that's why she makes such good smoothies."

"Fuck you. Feel like getting your ass kicked in *Fall for Duty?*"

He knew he should be forcing himself to sleep since he'd promised Lily they'd take off in the morning. Well, looks like he was gonna have to smooth-talk his driver who hadn't gotten around to booking them any flights. He'd make sure and tell Benny to pack a bag before he turned in. Stefan grabbed his joystick and started up where they'd last saved their game.

Two hours later, his rubber necking had become obnoxious. He cut out on his game with Stefan. "Hey man, stay as long as you want but I gotta get some sleepies."

"That's right. Your secret big day. Night, sweetie."

"Night, asshole," Jaxon said and then made his way up to his room.

Lily apparently didn't like choosing sides as she was curled up smack in the middle of his bed. He undressed and then lay with as many good manners as he could at her left side.

* * * *

Lily was having the hardest time waking up from her dream. She was snuggled between Stefan Calderon and Jaxon James. The room was mostly dark but the space on either side of her was filled with hunky, manly shoulders. Jaxon's extremely buff and muscled, Stefan's tanned and kissable. Even though her mind was trying to force her to question it, there was no doubt, she was lying in the middle of two sexy, musical gods.

Stefan's snores were the loudest sound in the room and she wondered if it was because he was drunk. A funky smelling beer cloud hovered near his otherwise kissable lips. It was funny that with all Stefan's kissable parts, Lily kept inching closer to Jaxon. Her feet rubbed up against the soft hairs of Jaxon's shin. Her hands were in nervous fists but the silk sheets balled up inside them felt like pure luxury. Her face was cool. Trepidation filled her silly heart. She sensed nearly every detail of this dream and the last thing to hit her was the taste of morning breath coating her tongue. Trying to work up enough saliva to wash some of it away, she realized this was no dream. She feared them coming to when she realized she was the only one awake. Quickly, she closed her eyes tight and swore not to be the first to reopen them. The things her red hair had gotten her into. Magnificent, once in a lifetime things.

* * * *

What the fuck was Stefan doing in bed with them?

A sudden drowning feeling began to fill Jaxon's lungs.

As much as he had already begun to like having Lily there with him, this scared the shit out of him. The fun was over because no matter how hard he tried, his expertise was in blurring lines. He had to get her out of here as soon as possible. And even though he'd just promised to go with her, he knew that was a bad idea.

He was skirting some pretty serious danger. Lily had a raging crush on his lead singer. He could tell the minute they'd walked in the room and she practically drooled. Stefan had that affect. Trissy would kill Jaxon if she knew he'd made a Stefan-Jaxon sandwich out of her baby sis.

And here he'd thought he could spend one night with Lily and not hurt her.

But wasn't that the damned funniest thing?

Here was a girl who thought Stefan Calderon was the ultimate sexy rock god yet her temptress toes were rubbing up against Jaxon's very sensitive shins.

Shit motherfucker. He was fully aroused now.

He had to get her out of there. He had absolutely no idea if he should let her at least finish sleeping or snatch her up and stick her in his car and send her and Benny on their way. No way did he belong with her on the road.

No fucking way. That was just bananas.

He stayed alert, making sure Stefan's wandering hands didn't get anywhere near her tempting curves. And then he tried to think with his head and not his dick and prayed Stefan would roll off the bed onto the floor. Jaxon prayed her sweet eyes wouldn't flicker open and realize what he'd let happen.

What a beautiful woman she was. He'd never felt the things he did during their moment on the beach last night. If he could keep her and hang out, he'd do it in a heartbeat. Too bad that wasn't possible. When would he ever learn?

SIN'S FLOWER

Chapter Eleven

The next day; the town of Jaxon-less Bugscuffle, Tennessee...
Lily was busy cursing Stefan Calderon for crawling into Jaxon's bed with them and ruining everything, when a man she didn't know waved his hands in front of her face. "Weight loss group meets on the third floor, young lady, up the stairs, all the way at the end of the hall."

"Gee, thanks," she muttered absentmindedly. *Do I look that bad? Great, are my underwear grooves showing tonight?*

Her fire engine red Leeloo hair on day three had washed halfway out, just as Benny had said it would, leaving her a dark strawberry golden blonde hue. With the loss of vibrancy she'd also bid goodbye to the little boost of sexy confidence she'd felt in California at Jaxon's villa. Her feelings about how that had gone were just too messy to figure out right now. And to top it all off, here she was at the community center to pick up some new Lamaze flyers, alone, being mistaken for an overeater. Guess the joke was on her. That overstepping stranger had gotten Lily exactly right. She hadn't been able to stop snacking since she'd been given the black leather steel-toed boot from Jaxon's.

Lily just stood there in the community center hallway, hoping her observant, gentlemanly helper would keep on his way. She didn't know what his business was up the flight of stairs he took—he was a slim fellow—but she knew where she was headed. And it wasn't where he'd assumed. Yeah, that made her feel all kinds of wonderful inside. *Ah, what's the use? I've got nothing to complain about and I know it.* Reconsidering that thought, she pushed open the Lamaze Center's door with a nice big breath. She wished like hell Tris was at her side but understood why she couldn't be, and tried to forget the man who had stopped short of calling her fat.

She pretended to adjust her top but really checked for hip flab. Yep, it was there, that inch, inch and a half that seemed to really love being a part of her body, no matter how much she told it she hated it. She tugged on the shirt hem poking out under her sweater.

She let a giant, pregnant woman exit the Lamaze room door and then made her way inside to collect Tris's brochures. Anything they could suggest to help alleviate stress was welcome Tris' doctor-ordered bed rest had been extended to her due date.

Yep, that was Lily's fault. She'd been so close to bringing home the cure for her sister's blues and then it had all slipped away. Damn that Stefan Calderon. Now Lily was back to scrambling for ways to be everything else Tris might need in a sister since there was no best friend coming to her aid.

Lily thumbed through the spiritual section of the brochure rack. She still struggled with the fact that she and her big sister were the girls who had grown up across the street from a church in a podunk Oklahoma town. These thoughts sometimes trickled in, unwelcome. It might take the rest of her life to understand how she'd lived with the same man, under the same roof, yet knew nothing except his good, fatherly concern. And still, she knew enough about the way Tris had always been so sad and preoccupied that she had no doubts her sister had told her the truth. He was dead now, her father, Tris's step-father.

I honestly don't know what I'm doing here.
Her head popped up at a female voice.

"Where's your sister tonight, Lily?" asked Tris's Lamaze coach.

"Oh, she's home, having some of those early contractions."

Lily wanted to add that Tris was happily married to a man named, of all things, Lucky, and that she and her sister had opened and were running their very own dress shop. Painting a happy picture had saved her from many pitiful days back in Oklahoma.

"Oh, I'm sorry to hear that. She's how far along?"

"Six months." They both nodded at how serious the situation was. "She's on doctor-ordered bed rest but I thought I might find some breathing tricks to help too."

"Well," the coach pulled out two pamphlets and pressed them into Lily's hands. "I'll keep her in my prayers, hun. How good of you to be here thinking of her. She's lucky she has you."

Lily wanted to feel like the good sister, but didn't. One thing for sure was Lily didn't have any answers tonight. What she did have was a dress shop to run in her sister's absence, a backlog of Christmas orders to produce, and a fear of their screwy, ancient sewing machine which would mean a long night of painstaking hand-stitching. There were also the images of Jaxon James and how stupidly close she'd gotten to him. She left the building and hopped up into her Jetta.

At seven o'clock on the dot, her cell phone rang.

"Hey Lily, everything all right? You on your way home?" his voice crackled with bad reception.

God, her sister was lucky. "Hey Lucky. Yep, everything's fine. But I'm stopping by the shop so don't worry if I'm not there for a while. How's Tris?"

"Aww, she's, you know, a little…tired."

"You mean cranky."

"Naw, she's perfect," he chuckled. "Don't be out too late. We worry, you know."

"I do and I'll try to finish up as soon as I can." The road was already dark, the air cold and her Jetta's heater sucked.

"All right. Hey Lily?"

"Yeah?"

"Thanks, darlin'. Really, for everything. You don't know how much it means to your sister the things you've tried to do for her. She hates being condemned to bed."

Tried, and failed. Was it really best she'd gone out and embarrassed herself to get Jaxon James back? Not if this pain inside didn't go away soon. She would have responded sooner but tears were gonna make her voice quiver like a Billy goat and she didn't want Lucky worrying about anyone but his pregnant wife.

"Me too. See you guys soon," she said keeping it simple and then made her way through the tree-lined darkness to the dress shop.

"Hello, Trista and Lily's Pad—ow, may I help you?"

Ouch. Dang it. She rubbed her foot, cursing its bareness. It hurt so bad she forgot about there being someone on the phone. She licked her finger and rubbed at the tiny blood-pricked spot on her heel and vowed to vacuum the shop once she got the orders catalogued and in the ledger.

"Hello? Anybody there? Hello?" a sexy, prickly male voice called to her insides but they must have had a bad connection because she could barely hear him. *Bugscuffle, land where cellphone calls go to die.*

"Sorry, sorry, sorry. I'm here," she remembered to respond. She sighed, missing Jaxon sorely. "Sorry again," she stuttered after the line became overly quiet. "Hello?"

Scratchy air whooshed over the cell waves. "Are you okay?" came the rough voice again.

"Yeah," she said, surprised the stranger on the other end hadn't chosen to cuss her out. "Just stabbed myself," she blurted, figuring he wouldn't hear anyway.

"Whoa, and you're sure you're okay?" asked the stranger.

"Oh yeah, I guess stabbed is a bit dramatic. Just a prick." Why was she telling him all this and why hadn't he hung up on her yet? She tested her heel against the cool wood of the shop floor. "All better. Now that I'm done wasting your time, what can I do for you?" She eyeballed the stack of dress orders yet to be logged and cursed Lucky for getting Tris pregnant. "Yeah, uh, I'm not even sure I have the right number. I'm trying to get a hold of Triss…um, Trista Hart, uh Mason. Trista Mason. Is this her business number?"

He sounded familiar but that was probably because she'd compared every male voice she'd heard that day to Jaxon's and now, apparently, her ears were worn out. Lily wondered what this guy would sound like without the white noise of their bad connection. More importantly, why was he stuttering over her sister's name? "Well, you've got the right number. She's just not here today." *Or this month. Or next.* "Can I take a message?"

She was pretty sure he let out a loud breath. "Well, yeah, you see, it's kind of personal. Can you just tell her Jaxon called and I really need her to call me back because if she doesn't…."

"Jaxon? As in Jaxon, Jaxon?"

"Yeah. Sure. I'm sorry, I can barely hear you." He was in and out.

He must be dealing with the same impersonation of hurricane force winds on his end because admitting he hadn't recognized her voice hurt worse than being mistaken for the wrong self-help group. She blew out three short puffy exhales like she'd seen Tris and Lucky practicing the past two months. Instead of calming her anxiety at having him on the phone, it left her light headed. She grabbed the counter.

"Well, yes. Sort of." *We slept together the morning I left. In your bed. With Stefan. No, no, no. Don't say that. It sounds horrible and lame and actually...kind of exciting.* But that wasn't exactly what had happened. *And then you sent me packing.* "Um, it's me? Lily, the little sister?" she eeked out.

Silence greeted her. What? Had Jaxon forgotten the scene he'd made that morning the three of them had woken up together? She'd just barely squirmed off the bed in time before Jaxon, half dressed, pummeled Stefan, completely naked, to the floor. It had taken exactly one second for Stefan to accidentally uncover himself with the sheet in a yawning stretch before the two guys became a blur of tanned flesh and burly muscles before her woozy eyes.

"Hello? Jaxon?"

"Sorry, Lily. Of course I remember you. Guess I'm, you know, still not used to Trissy having a baby sister and her answering the phone."

She told herself he sounded distant but not like he was being a jerk. Jerks had that certain venom to every slimy word that fell out of their spoiled mouths. While it was rare for Tris to talk badly about Jaxon, she did occasionally throw out the word selfish. Lily breathed in a fresh gulp of good attitude and tried to forget the butterflies kicking her belly like she was carrying five thousand of them. She remembered he'd sounded urgent.

"It's okay. That's what I get for making it a habit of showing up on peoples' doorsteps, unannounced." Okay, so that was the oddest thing she could have said out of a thousand other awkward choices. Jaxon hadn't responded, again. "Jaxon, I'll try and get whatever message you have to Tris as soon as I can. I'm actually planning on seeing her at some point tonight if she's up for it."

Lily wondered if he was okay. It was too quiet for a second.

"Is she okay?" he asked her in a rush.

"Sort of," she sputtered out in an effort to make the heart attack in his voice go away.

"Sort of? Oh my God, is she okay?"

Well, it had taken her long enough to realize the reason for Jaxon's call. He was worried about Tris. She twisted her lips, wondering what that felt like.

"Hello? Lily?"

She smiled at finally hearing her name by way of his soft Aussie voice. "I'm sorry, Jaxon. Tris's now officially on doctor-ordered bed rest for the rest of her pregnancy."

Maybe she should have nipped this convo in the bud and told him to call Benny, who was at Tris and Lucky's as they spoke. It was why she wasn't hating on Jaxon right now. He'd cared enough to send her packing with a proper escort and the Range Rover had been a wonderful ride. She just wished it had been Jaxon driving. She eyed the stack of dress orders threatening to topple over and knew she wouldn't make it home anytime soon.

"Well I hope she's really all right. Listen baby, the reason I'm calling is because we…"

Jaxon called me baby, just like he did on our one special night. But she knew who she really wished had called her that. *Sweet, one-chaired, beach-night Jaxon.* Not this version who was just worried about Tris and trying to be nice to Lily. He had changed his mind where Lily was concerned and as much as it had hurt, she could see the reason behind his actions, as much as she hated it and wished people would let her be the deciding factor. She cracked her knuckles and found a new pile of fabric samples to busy her silly brain.

Jaxon's soft, deeply sexy voice trailed off, well not so much his voice as her mind. She was still clamping back the bitter sweetness at being called baby when the shop doors jingled open, signaling a new customer.

"Well Jaxon, it was nice talking to you again but I'm sorry, I have to go."

"Don't go yet." He paused for a long time, long enough for Lily to look up, see the back of a customer's head browsing some handmade gift items toward the front entrance, and then spin two times on her short stool. "Lily, how is Maryellie doing?" he asked.

That was the sound of a daddy missing his little girl. There was no mistaking the desperation in his now hearty voice.

"She's doing great. Between everyone here, she's in good hands. Probably getting just a wee bit spoiled. But you had to expect that. She's my assistant chef and doing a great job."

He humphed. "That's a goody to hear. So, uh, Lily, are you being straight with me? Is Trissy gonna be okay? With the baby and all?"

She really felt for him. "I mean yeah, she's going to live. She's not too thrilled having to be on her back for the foreseeable future. I'm sure you remember how stubborn she can be." Okay to be honest, this was starting to hurt. In a weird way she didn't understand. His concern belonged exactly where he'd placed it.

With her big sis. With Maryella. Not with Lily. So what they'd spent one really great night together? Oh, she was such a fool. She shook her head, realizing Jaxon hadn't even tried to sleep with her. Not really. What did that say, given who he was?

So why did she suddenly feel like chucking the phone and burying her face in her favorite quilt? He owed her nada. Zip. Zilch. She should have never gone to Tennessee. Seeking out Jaxon James was beginning to hurt in an all too humiliating and familiar way. Thank goodness he hadn't ended up coming back here with her. It was bad enough playing third fiddle on the phone. In person, she imagined it would be downright painful. She had no idea what else to say to the man.

* * * *

Jaxon had no idea if there was really anything left to say. He'd found out exactly what he'd needed to know. Maryellie was soaking up all the lovey dovey family stuff he'd selfishly been denying her. Trissy was in a bad way with the baby. All because of stress, Lily had said. And Lily, sweet, lovely Lily. Even planted as far away from him as she was, he couldn't quash the tenderness she blanketed him with.

"Jaxon, I'm really gonna need to let you go now. I have a customer in the store."

"Okay. Well, I guess I'd better get. Can you tell the girls I said hi?"

"Sure." She sounded flat. "Okay, bye." And short. And irritated.

God, he wasn't even trying and he was still coming off like a dick. *New and improved me.* He blew out away from the phone's mouthpiece.

"Lily, actually, please tell my Maryellie that Daddy wishes he could be there for Christmas."

"Oh, okay. Sure. You, Maryella, Christmas."

"Hey, are you sure you're okay?" he asked, worried about the young woman he'd fallen for so quickly.

* * * *

No. "Yes. Thanks. I'll pass along your message."

She held the phone in her hand, barely. She'd thought he was on the verge of saying he was coming. Disappointment at how wrong she was must have left her hallucinating. She blinked but could swear her ex-sister-in-law was standing near an empty dress stand Lily was using to catch up on their orders. Lily's breath hitched from shock and the uncanny resemblance in this woman's dark hair and tall slender build to Steph and her twin brother, Tom.

Lily did her best to act like she wasn't completely on the verge of throwing up, biting her lip in anticipation of the woman turning enough so she could see her face and be sure it wasn't Steph. *Lay off the Kool Aid, Lily. Get a grip.*

She suddenly realized how much effort Stephanie or more importantly, Tom, would have had to put into finding Lily in Bugscuffle. She glanced outside the shop's windows, looking for Steph's purple Dodge Neon parked in one of their three spaces. It wasn't there. *Of course it's not there, silly. She would have had to have driven eleven hours.*

The woman finally spun to check out another table of crochet work but Lily still couldn't get a good look at her face. She'd never seen Steph in that exact style of sweater but the boot cut jeans and ballet flats were right on the mark. Really, what would Stephanie have stalked Lily here to do? Plead Tom's case? They'd already gone those rounds back in Oklahoma and Lily had been clear. For the one and only time in her life, she'd been strong enough to stand up for herself. It had taken years of extreme humiliation to arrive at that point but she'd done it. And she didn't appreciate being reminded of how she'd barely been able to handle that struggle.

If that was the reason for her visit, it was bound to get real uncomfortable, real fast. Maybe Lily could pretend she was still on the phone. She fished around her apron pocket for her cell and shook her head. Then to make it look real, she falsely punched in the digits of the last number on her call log. She was about to pretend-talk when the phone actually rang. *Dang it, I hit talk. Crap.* She was about to hang up when he answered. At the same time, the woman became distracted by Tris's handmade pet clothing, leaving Lily hanging on by the cash register.

"Hey-yo? Anybody there? I know you're there, I can hear you breathing. If this is a fan, I truly appreciate your support but I can't be getting these kinds of calls at this number."

Geez, did he have to be so smart-allicky? Whoever this was? Definitely not Jaxon because she'd know his voice now, bad connection or not.

Well, before the...the non-Australian sounding man on Jaxon's phone hung up, apparently thinking she was a stalker, she'd better say something. And then figure out what to do, if anything, about Stephanie's doppelganger. God, this was so weird.

"I'm sorry. I uh, I think I dialed the wrong number, sir."

He stalled but didn't hang up like she'd expected. "You sound cute. What's your name, sweetheart?"

Oh no. How dense could she be? The non-Australian. Who also has fans. Drops in on Jaxon whenever he feels like it. Sexy. Ornery. Stefan Calderon. Her brain was boinking around at how ludicrous it was to now be having her second conversation with a hot rock god while at the same time, scouting out this poor woman who probably just wanted to find a gift and could have used Lily's help with the selection. It was called customer service and Lily knew she ought to be giving it a lot more effort.

"Mate, who is it? Is it about Trissy?" Jaxon's voice sounded dark with worry in the background.

"Nah man." And then an annoyed sounding rash of words came her way. "Like I said, who is this?"

"Lily." She said her name, shy all of a sudden, keeping an eye on her customer. Only a table away now, the woman scanned the crocheted pet dress she'd picked up. Lily could see enough that the nose was different, pointier than Steph's more button-like features. She relaxed a drop.

"Lily…that's a nice name. Did you know how sexy you sound, sweetheart?"

Are you kidding me right now? He doesn't remember me?

"Lily," she said quietly, as if testing Stefan's theory. She sounded nothing like sexy; of course he didn't remember her. Lily's hands squeezed the tomato-shaped pin cushion she'd thought was empty until one bit into her palm.

She then heard Stefan muffle a few words, "It's a chick named Lily. You know her?" And just like that, she'd been branded as forgettable. Oh well, what did she expect?

A few curse words were exchanged by the men on the other end of the phone while she started what must look like the peepee dance in front of the customer who wasn't Stephanie.

Whether Stefan was listening or not, she started jabbering away to cover up for her staring problem. "Yes. She's my sister. You and I, we met last week, at Jaxon's. I should probably let you go." She really needed to get off the phone, help her customer, and then leave the shop for the rest of the night. Things had just gotten too psychic-network weird in there. But there were all these orders to produce and it was even more important now that she show Tris she was serious about their new relationship and the life she wanted as part of her family. This was a shared dream of running a dress shop in Momma's honor. Being distracted by those who couldn't even remember her name was a waste of time.

"Hello? Did you hear me? I need to go," she said.

He chuckled. Which was entirely too sexy and surreal. "If you insist. "

"Yep. I do," she said unceremoniously. "Listen, I hate to be rude, but I'm having the most crapalicious day so far so can you please tell me why you called?"

"Sweetheart, you called me."

Oh yeah, he was right. Point taken.

Jaxon's accent thickened as he ordered Stefan to give him the phone in the background.

Then finally, Non-Stephanie's gaze trapped Lily. The woman appeared ready to finish up her browsing.

"Yes well, I'll have to get back to you about that," Lily pretend-talked into the phone. Lord knows where that had come from.

The last thing she heard was a confused "What?" on the other end and then she hung up.

"Hi, did you need any help finding anything?" she tried to ask in her most polite voice.

The woman eyed her for the longest time, playing with the charcoal gray and lime green stitching on the dog sweater. "Nope, I think I found the perfect thing for my husband's Chihuahua."

Lily just smiled and had a healthy back and forth with the woman while going the extra mile and gift wrapping the sweater for her as they spoke. Turned out her name was Vanessa, hubby was Charlie, Chihuahua was Rusty. They lived in nearby Wartrace and had heard from a friend who had heard from a friend about the dress shop. If Lily ever needed her tires rotated or her brakes checked, she could stop in at Charlie's mechanic shop which wasn't far at all.

Harmless, safe, and perfectly representative of her new hometown.

The fears that her ugly past had followed her here had been pure paranoia. No matter how lonely she'd felt since returning from Jaxon's, there was no reason to ever go leaving here again. He'd made that abundantly clear and she didn't need to be told twice.

The cuckoo clock on the wall sounded and Mr. Blue Jay chirped eight times. She'd better call it a night. Ducking under the counter to gather her things, she found the stack of mail that had gone missing from last week. She quickly flipped through the envelopes, hoping for the final judgment papers from the state of Oklahoma when she saw one with very familiar hand-writing. The return address was Stephanie's.

Chapter Twelve

"Really, world? You have to be this loopy on me all in one night? Well, looks like I'm not going anywhere just yet." She dropped her bags and plunked down on the floor to read the letter.

"Hey, long time no see, or hear. Jenn says hi. She told me you'd moved out to some tiny little town that's beyond small. Even smaller than Shawnee. She says you're pretty secluded out there. Something about a raging river. I guess that's why you haven't kept in touch."

Lily just shrugged, dumbfounded at the conclusions Stephanie had come to about her distance and silence. She would have to make time and shoot Jenn an email and ask her to keep her lips shut from now on. Lily continued reading, glad to see the letter was short.

"Well, Lily, you should know my brother hasn't left the house since you dumped him."

Good, was all she could think. The best thing for the both of them would be for Lily to ask Steph not to write anymore. Or call or share her likeness with unsuspecting dress shop customers. The coincidence of Vanessa's looks and now this letter had her freaked out. Oh boy, she saw the next line of the letter was written in all caps.

"DON'T YOU HAVE ANYTHING TO SAY FOR YOURSELF?"

Well, Steph's anger was definitely saying something to Lily right now. Lily reminded herself that Steph had no idea why after four years, she'd seemingly suddenly left Tom. Even he would have kept the reason a secret. Being so cruel you had to bully your wife to be with you wasn't brag-worthy. *Jerk.*

"It's personal, Stephanie," she muttered to the lined stationary as she read the last few lines.

"I expected more from you. I thought we were friends. I know you and Tom had your problems, but doesn't every married couple go through that? You owe it to my brother, your husband, to give Tom another chance. He's miserable. At least call him, for me? Please?"

She'd signed it *Your sister, Steph.*

They weren't *that* close and Lily had a real sister who loved her and would never have written such things to put her in such an awful spot. Adding to that, Lily knew that if Tris had ever told Lucky he'd done something to make her feel uncomfortable, he'd have spent his every breath making up for it. Lily had to stop thinking about this damn letter and catch a good full breath. Not to mention all the excitement of the last hour had left her stressed and therefore hungry. Her stomach rumbled.

She peered up from the floor and had a look around the shop. Just a little straightening and she'd feel okay about calling it quits for the night. Lily took care to fold the afghans on the back shelves.

She shook her head, but it did nothing to erase Stephanie's maddening letter. What in the world could she say to that? There was no way she'd ever go back to Tom. Period. Did she really have to write this girl a letter explaining things once again? Hello? That's what the divorce and the move to a secluded place protected by a raging river was supposed to say for her. Done, finito. Your brother is a living memorial to manipulative pricks everywhere and I'm done visiting. Obviously, Stephanie didn't know how Tom had treated her. The perfect gentleman when everyone was around, the uncomfortable control freak with a nasty budding desire to record them in bed even though she hated it and had often told him so.

"I don't owe him or his family anything," she said, until she'd made every shelf in the shop stand out with the lovely handmade wares that she and her real sister had created.

Standing at the shop's entrance with her bags once again strapped over her shoulders and the rest of the mail tucked to her chest, Lily flipped the "We're Open" sign over and headed out. With much needed Christmas spirit, the door's bells jingled closed behind her.

The darkness of nighttime here had never scared her. She prayed it would always be this way. But wow, what a day.

So completely surreal. That turned her thoughts back to her call from one half of the world's greatest band. Namely...Jaxon. If only he'd been calling to check on her tonight. What a feeling that would have been. The cold sounding rain plinked steadily against the shop's walls, but she was starving. She shuffled her toes snugly into her thin pair of flats and hurried out into the storm, scanning the lot as she went.

* * * *

If Stefan wasn't the absolute only person in the world he trusted to sing his songs, he'd be sporting a sore jaw right now. His mate just stood there with that "I told you so" scowl on his face, taunting Jaxon like usual.

"I just don't understand why you bothered calling in the first place if you're too chicken shit to get your ass on a plane and see her for yourself."

Jaxon rubbed at his jaw. "I was worried. And Maryellie is there. It's not like I have no reason to be calling."

"Thank you for making my point. Your daughter is out there, Jaxon. Your best friend. Let's see who else? Oh yeah, your father, your uncle, your cousin."

"You forgot Benny." There was one more name but he didn't want to share anything about Lily with Stefan, ever again.

"Shit, that's right. Even poor Benny is out at *your* family's holiday celebration but here you are. What gives, man?"

"I know. It's bananas. I get it, okay? But, maybe it's just best if they're all there, and I'm here. Besides, I can't just leave you all alone, can I?"

"Fuck that. You're chicken shit, Jax. I'm calling you on it. And don't give me that lame bullshit that they're better off away from you." Stefan paused. "What happened in that field wasn't your fault. Yeah, I'm going there right now. You need to get right with that. Dude, I can't believe you'd miss Christmas with your daughter because of one fucked up night two years ago. Your girls need you, bro."

Jaxon considered everything Stefan said. Even though he wanted to pummel him to the ground, he was right. Heartburn steamed and bubbled through his innies. Maybe it was time to put this new and improved version of himself to the test. He slapped his thighs. "Come with?"

"Nah, maybe next time. Ma's having some problems back home. I fly out tomorrow to see her."

"Sorry to hear that, mate. Anything I can do?"

"Yeah, get your sorry ass to Buttscuffle." Stefan grinned at his mispronunciation.

"Drive me to the airport in the morning?"

"At your service, boss."

Jaxon punched Stefan in the chest before his good friend snuck in a hug and then whispered, "Go to

Tennessee. Clear your head. Then get your ass back here with some *good* songs for me to sing."

So Stefan was fed up with the old material. That made two of them. Maybe some new experiences, new places, would help.

"You know what you need?" Stefan said before heading to Jaxon's couch.

"What, mate?" But he knew what was about to come out of Stefan's mouth...pussy.

"A new girl. Maybe someone nice for a change," he said and then disappeared to the living room.

"A new girl," Jaxon mumbled to himself while a vision of Lily snuggled up to his side, rubbing her foot up and down his shin drove him upstairs to pack. Fuck, the thought of her had him rock hard.

* * * *

Stone cold with indecision, Lily went inside, sat down and looked for something scorching hot from the menu. Her toes tingled and ached as the blood must be thawing back out. She reached a hand under her table to rub the stabbing feeling away. The waitress came by and took her order, ignoring the fact she'd let her shoes fall to the floor.

"Coffee please."

"Sure thing, sweetie. And what can I getcha to eat?"

Her stomach was a ball of haywire nerves that were shouting "no" but she'd already dreamed of how flaky the top crust would taste and how ooey gooey the bottom crust would feel smooshing through her teeth. "Mmm, chicken pot pie please."

"Good choice. You okay?" the waitress asked.

Lily shook her head side to side at first but then feared the questions a small town diner confession on her part would bring. "I'm fine. Just a long day at work."

"You work at the dress shop with your sister, Trista, right?"

See, she thought to herself and then nodded yes.

"I'll bring you out something special, hun." The waitress walked back to the counter.

Lily watched the sidewalk outside through the diner's window. Why was she still nervous? If only she'd had the guts to plead a little harder for Jaxon to come back with her, not just for her sister's sake, but for hers. Then she wouldn't be sitting here paranoid and alone. She slid a wayward set of salt and pepper shakers back to the center of her table and then fidgeted with color-coding the artificial sweeteners. If her pot pie didn't get here soon, mentally, there'd be nothing left of Jaxon James. Because thoughts of him devouring her were the only thing keeping Lily from losing it right now.

Chapter Thirteen

Jaxon looked at the return address from Trissy's Christmas card. This was the place. He parked his car and then shoved at Benny who had shown up at the airport so dead tired, Jaxon didn't trust him not to fall asleep on the ride home. Needless to say, it was a fucking miracle they'd made it back to this dinky little town. Benny sat motionless in the passenger seat while Jaxon cracked each knuckle and then went through doing it again. The first Christmas with his family in over twenty-five years. Maryellie's first ever.

"Hey man, we're here. Come on, mate." That last shove at Benny had probably been unnecessary but he was on edge. In any case, it hadn't done any good. Benny let out a choppy snore.

Jaxon eyeballed the place. The basics hadn't changed. Still out in the middle of nowhere. Trissy's house and yard were dark except for the yellow porch light shining. It was cold. He felt his skin chill under the thin black shirt he'd put on that morning in sunny California. Leaving Benny to apparently sleep in the car for now, he made his way up the porch steps.

"Hello," he called without getting an answer back.

He double checked the address again and then walked inside since the door was open. A familiar fluff of gray fur sat curled on the coffee table. "Hey Figjam, old buddy." The cat hissed at him, not caring that he'd been the one to rescue his adorable kitty ass from the parking lot all those years ago.

Jaxon made his way through the interior of the house and nearly tripped over his own feet when he found Trissy doubled over, head plastered to the dining room table. She looked dead asleep. No wonder she and

Benny had always worked so well together. They both mistakenly thought nighttime was meant for sleeping. He smiled—happy for one second, but full of regret in the next.

It would have been wrong to everyone else in the world, but for Jaxon, wanting a hug from his best friend was the undeniable feeling bouncing around in him at that moment.

He was glad for it because it shoved the thoughts of running into his father on the back burner. Maryellie had been so excited to meet her grandpa for the first time when Jaxon put her on the plane. It broke his heart. He forced that particular thought from his head and made his way quietly to stand behind Trissy's seat. He leaned over and smelled her messy cherry almond scented hair, as usual, forced into some kind of bun at the nape of her neck. She made a small movement and he hovered over her without touching. When she relaxed back onto her folded arms, he knelt down on one knee, gently laid an arm across her shoulders, still rigid even in sleep, and whispered into her ear. "It's so good to see you, Trissy."

At that, her head shot up, leaving his lip numb where the hard bone of her skull clipped his mouth.

"Jaxon?" she asked.

"Lily?" he choked out.

"Ouch," they said in unison.

Mmm, she sounded so good though.

* * * *

An immediate sense of belonging in the arm that had been draped across her back soothed Lily's startled heartbeat. The warmth he'd given off in those few seconds should be counted in the droplets of sweat beading up and dampening her bra. But the second he choked on her name, she snapped out of that balmy lullaby and back to reality. Jaxon had thought she was Tris.

She rubbed at her breastbone, nearly flipping out at how many mini-coronaries she'd had the last twenty-four hours. But as she watched him rub at his lip, it reminded her she had a pretty hard head, so she took a turn at trying to sooth him at the same time he reached to her. Their hands crashed in midair.

"Hi, Jaxon."

"Hi, Lily. Looks like you're just as surprised to see me as I am to see you."

"You have no idea. It was that kind of day." What time was it? Past midnight?

"So is your foot okay?"

"My foot?"

"Yeah, you hurt it during our last phone call. And then things got all weird. I guess that's partly the reason I'm here."

"Because you were worried about my foot?" *Oh dear God, please let him stop talking so he doesn't ruin this moment and say no.*

"Well, not exactly. I couldn't stop missing my Maryellie and then when you mentioned Trissy not doing so well."

Her face fell. He must have seen it with his intense, teal blue eyes.

"But mostly I just had to come see how your foot was feeling now." A grin the size of Texas nearly erupted across his face but she was fascinated by his tongue curling and playing with his upper molars.

"You're a horrible liar but the foot is feeling better than my head."

They burst out laughing together for a nano-second before covering their mouths to quiet back down.

"I know it's late, but can you take me to see Maryellie?"

"Of course. But she's probably sleeping. I read her a book a few hours ago. She was pretty pooped." It would be her pleasure to escort him. She had no reason to covet the attentions this man saved for his daughter. The joy sprouting tiny little lines at the corners of his smile and eyes washed away whatever silliness she'd wanted for herself.

Gosh, she felt so bad for head butting him. His bottom lip was swollen as he rubbed at it and stood, waiting for her to lead. In this fatherly light, he was kind of beautiful. She was kind of, in awe. Lordy put a piggy in her blanket, she was staring.

They walked down the hallway and stopped at the baby-to-be's nursery. Lily ushered Jaxon inside. He walked over to his daughter, pulled up her covers and gave her hand a soft kiss before tucking it under the blanket. Lily watched Jaxon's eyes become shiny while he smiled and walked back toward her. They returned side by side to the kitchen table.

"Is your head okay? I got you pretty good," she asked him.

Why did she feel like kissing that lower lip of his?

"Lily?"

"Yes?"

"Are you okay?"

She was now, strangely.

She nodded at him.

"And that, what did you call it? Crappy fantastic day you were having the last time we talked? Everything okay there?"

Oh my gosh, how did he know about that?

"Stefan," he answered her thought. "He likes you. Thinks you're a cutie." But Jaxon frowned at that.

"He had no idea who I was on the phone." But really the sting of that was long gone. For some reason, being unremarkable to Stefan Calderon didn't matter so much right now.

Jaxon smirked and shook his head. "He's, well, Stefan. He's the boy who pulls the piggy tails of the girls he likes. So hey, you didn't answer me."

Suddenly her throat felt dry. If she *could* answer him, she'd say that Stephanie's words about her being cold-hearted had really hurt and the thought of being followed to Bugscuffle was unsettling to say the least. But she buckled her lips and held it in.

"You're not gonna tell me, are you?" he asked, leaning back in his chair. His biceps bulged when they met up against the wooden slats supporting him and she longed to jump into them.

"It's been a long night. And I'm surprised you're here. Tris's never gonna believe it."

"I needed to come. Stefan's the one who helped me realize it. And you."

A sleepy little girl ambled into the dining room just then, rubbing her eyes and yawning. Jaxon's attention to her was immediate and tender which flooded Lily's heart. He stood and scooped her up into his arms. "Hey sweetums, did Daddy wake you up?" His voice was so soft and attentive with her.

"Yes. I'm so happy you came here, Daddy." Maryella yawned and hugged Jaxon's neck.

"Me too, sweetums. Let's get you back to sleepies, okay? We'll have breakfast in the morning."

"Okay. Auntie Lily makes me French toast."

"Oh yeah, and is it yummy?"

Maryella nodded her head, falling asleep on the third nod.

"I'll be right back," he told Lily before disappearing down the hall.

Lily's worries that her past had seeped into town via that damn letter gushed out in a hearty breath. He might not have come here because of her, but against all odds, Jaxon was here. And somehow that comforted her. Lily stood near the hallway hugging herself. Man, this view from behind—the one of him, a real man carrying his daughter—was out of this world.

* * * *

Was she watching him? Oh hells no, this was not a goody. The week away from her apparently hadn't worked to cool him off. She was the last person in the world he was allowed to be attracted to. Trissy would castrate him for his thoughts alone. And he didn't blame her. He'd be better off running down this sleepy little town's streets, butt-naked, chanting to the devil, rather than lay one more covetous eye on Lily. God, Stefan had been right, her name was even sexy.

Forbidden Lily came closer to his baby girl's door with something small in her hands. "I forgot, um, I picked this up to put in the room with her. Here, I'll give it to you."

"Thanks. Oh, a night light. That's very sweet of you. Why don't you hold onto it and we can find a place for it in the morning. I don't want to wake her up again."

"That's a good idea. We've been keeping her pretty busy; she needs her, how do you say it? Sleepies?" Her giggle was adorable. He wanted to clamp his lips over hers and feel it tumble into his mouth and down his throat.

"Yeah. All righty." He hated turning all short on her. But it was for her own good. He was already imagining Lily wearing nothing but his hands.

"Okay."

She blinked, slowly. He backed away from her, thankful for the few steps he was able to take.

"Well, there are more blankets in your chest. I mean, th-the chest." She pointed to a heavy wooden box on the side of a baby crib next to the air mattress. "Will you sleep in here with Maryella?"

"No, I'll take the couch."

It was done. Something she'd said or did, maybe knowing she'd been here for his daughter when he hadn't been, tweaked at his heart.

Or maybe just how wrong it was for him to want her had done it.

Something damn scary and real popped wide open inside him. He wanted Lily. It wasn't in his nature not to go after that. He scratched at both sides of his head where his hair was shortest and then pulled the longer top pieces through his fingers. "Night, Lily."

* * * *

Shoot, she realized she didn't want that to be it for the night so she followed him back down the hall to the living room.

Jaxon turned to see her following him. "Oh, I just need a drink of water," she said sounding fabulously pathetic.

Where was Benny? Lily noticed he wasn't sprawled out on the couch near the one Jaxon had decided to sleep on.

"I was just gonna say Benny'd already claimed the longer section of couch, but he's gone. Weird."

"Oh shit. He's probably frozen." Jaxon took off out the front door. Lily scooped up a few extra blankets from the chest Lucky had made for her as a "welcome to our family" gift and waited at the front doorway.

Minutes later, Jaxon came back in with his tall, lanky and asleep webmaster in tow. Benny had been out in the car? She guessed he'd been the good sport he always seemed to be and had gone and fetched Jaxon.

"I hope you guys will be okay on the couches for tonight and we'll figure something better out in the morning."

"That's fine," said Jaxon.

"Hi." The sleepy word fell from Benny's mouth.

She couldn't help it; she had to give him a hug. Her arms reached almost all the way around him and then some. He nodded and collapsed onto the longest sofa. Man, he was sleep deprived or something. What had Jaxon put this kid through?

"Good night, Jaxon. It's really nice that you came." She extended her hand to him.

He only nodded in acknowledgment. "Thank you, Lily."

Was he focusing on that spot below her ear he'd tormented and tricked with his mouth? She shivered at the memory, feeling his tongue sweetening her up like a fool.

She stalled like a prisoner of his gaze, a few seconds too long, trying to read his thoughts.

Just as she was about to head back to her room, that disturbed Aussie voice stopped her. "You don't have anywhere to sleep, do you?" He didn't let her answer. "Come here."

For some reason she didn't know, she obeyed him like a little puppy, even though she had a room and a bed. His bare arms, things you just didn't see in Tennessee in the winter, sprinkled with a mix of black and colorful tattoos, invited and promised so much. Maybe he would want to hold her.

"Here, you take the couch. I'll take that window bench."

"You'll freeze," she said. He would, too, if he slept that close to the picturesque pane instead of on the couch.

"I'll be fine," he said so closely she felt his breath tickle her nose.

"No, really, you're our guest, I can't have you..."

"Lily, you gave up your room for my Maryellie. Please, take the couch. I'll be fine." And then he took her into his arms and rubbed his fingers around in the loose hairs at the back of her neck.

"Okay," she mumbled. But no, she had to be honest. Crud. "Jaxon, I have my own room." She hated having to admit that and leave him.

"Oh. Well I guess you better get to it then."

Tris would kick her butt if she knew how badly Lily wished Jaxon would have asked her to cuddle together on the couch. This was going to be an interesting visit. But there wouldn't be much time for confusion. Before she pulled back from him, she spied the pile of work she'd brought home from the dress shop sitting on top of the wooden chest. This was their busiest time of the year. There'd be plenty to keep her occupied and not dreaming about being a wanted woman.

* * * *

Entirely too early the next morning, Jaxon woke up stiff. Hell, if the sun wasn't fully up yet, he shouldn't be either.

He rubbed his neck but it didn't help. Stress filtered through every pore and tissue of his body. He actually felt goose bumps running up and down his arms. He could never live here.

"Jaxon?"

He'd know that voice anywhere. *Trissy.* Fuck, wasn't she supposed to be tucked away in bed? Like until her bitty baby came out?

"Hey you, how are you?" He tried to whisper so as not to wake up Benny who was nose and toes entirely too long for even the large couch. "So where's your long-haired hubby?" He gave her a wink, hoping she was happy to see him as he'd been told. A strange protective notion goaded him into wondering how Lily had slept.

"Wait with the questions. Let me get a good look at you."

She took a few more steps but for a second, he wasn't sure if that was as close as she'd come. He should have known better. A moment later he had his hug. And then a poke in the belly to go with it for his remark. "My gorgeous long haired hubby left a couple hours ago to the main house." She looked magnificent and shiny sharing that with him but then her face changed and she brought her hands to her belly for a rub. "Your...father, and uncle needed help with the truck. So they called Lucky."

Her beaming smile returned, telling him his cousin was good at those things. The last time Jaxon had popped the hood on one of his cars, the thing hadn't started again until a tow trip to the Porsche dealership.

"Give me another hug, I've missed you so much," she said.

He carefully circled his arms around her belly. It was beautiful. "Are you guys having twins?" he teased.

Man, it was just then he realized the last pregnant woman he'd hugged had been Vangie. Those nine months watching her belly fill with his baby girl had been the happiest of their relationship. Had he failed Vangie too? Had she been a better person before he'd gotten his hands on her? Not according to Trissy. Well, he hadn't helped matters, that much was clear.

"I don't think so. Don't scare me," she said smiling crookedly.

"Sorry. You look…so beautiful." So much better than the last times he'd seen her. The time spent here had brought her back to life since the night he'd nearly gotten her killed.

"Thanks, hey let's sneak into the kitchen. I'll make us coffee. Did I tell you how happy I am you decided to come?"

She missed him. It felt too good. But it did nothing to calm his bellyache about being here for the first time. He was a forty-four-year-old man but he felt like that seventeen-year-old kid who had left home with a starved soul all those years ago. Overwhelmed would be an understatement as he tried to figure out each role he needed to play for the people who would soon be waking up. And how the fuc…fudge did he mask his attraction for Lily? Just thinking about her toes tickling the hairs of his shins stroked his arousal.

The smell of Trissy's strong coffee brought him back to their reunion and they sat at the breakfast bar whispering.

"So how did you sleep? I know the big couch was full of Benny." Her head shook and her eyelids fluttered like she was thinking of something absurd. "I should have listened when Lucky suggested adding on an extra room. But no, I shot that down." Jaxon smiled at seeing her unchanged mannerisms and spunky attitude. "Oh oh oh, and did you see Maryella yet?"

Her eagerness to chat about friends and family made him grin. Maybe this was his sign to test the waters. "Yeah, last night. Your sister was awake when I got in and she showed me where my baby girl was sleeping."

It took less than a second for her face to change. Whether she meant to hide it from him or not wouldn't have mattered. He knew this look. This one was a combination of "Oh no you didn't and Keep your hands off her, Jaxon."

"What?" he asked, cupping his mug with both hands and taking a burning hot sip. He'd be feeling that the rest of the day.

"So you were up late with Lily last night?"

Was this a test?

"Well yeah, sort of." Shit, he wasn't gonna say anything to help his cause. "She's uh, she's great. Really sweet, nice girl." That was a pretty PG description, suitable for big sisters. But boy, she was glaring.

"And how would you know all that, exactly, Jaxon?"

"Whoa, was that my belly that just growled? I'm so hungry. Maryellie said the French toast here is pretty good." He just smiled and acted like he had no idea what she was talking about. And where in the hell was Lily? He didn't dare chance a look in the direction of the bedrooms.

* * * *

"Squeeze it. Squeeze it. Squeeze it." Her footsteps broke against the uphill trail in time to the beat as Lily remembered to breathe out on every fourth step. She exhaled and a puff of frozen breath tickled the tip of her numbed nose. "Feel the burn, chica," she chanted aloud and then slapped a hand to each cheek. Damn that jiggle that vibrated beneath her palms.

Oh, she was feeling it all right; may as well have been wearing concrete shoes. Her buns would be on fire when she finally made it back home.

Home. Buns. Jaxon's buh-huns, good gawd.

Lily stepped up the pace to get back to her sister's and the intimidatingly sexy man whose late-night arrival had motivated her to get outdoors on the coldest morning of the year. She could think of at least a half dozen dirty deeds and exactly how dirt cheap she'd do 'em for if Trista didn't have a houseful of guests right now.

Oh wow, what was she saying? Had she sprouted her red hair again? Lily Elstone didn't have those kinds of thoughts. Especially not over completely out of her league men. She knew a little about Jaxon's type, having seen a picture of Maryella's mom the little girl had tucked into one of her books as a bookmark. The woman was unbelievably gorgeous. Skimpy underwear model gorgeous. Plus, she was brunette, chocolate-eyed and could have been a granddaughter of Sophia Lauren. If Lily had a secret celebrity ancestor, it'd be more like Donna Douglas of Elly May Clampett fame. Yeah, you know, come to think of it, she could fantasize about Mr. Sex-comes-before-breathing all she wanted because there wasn't a chance in hell he'd ever be serious about a girl like her. Sure, Jaxon had been nice enough at his house. That thought jacked up her pulse and forced her to step carefully to keep from losing balance. But then he'd thrown her out and the true trust she'd thought they somehow magically shared seemed foolworthy.

The song in her ear buds changed. That voice that lost its Aussie accent when he sang chorus behind Stefan nearly melted her iPod. Tris would blow the house down if she ever found out Lily had already seen those buns in the flesh. "Feel the burn," she chanted. She might not have a real chance with Jaxon, but the thought of being around him and his lethally hot bod at least had gotten her off her duff and away from all the Christmas cookies at home. She made sure to take the long way home, imagining with each squeeze of her glutes that she was feeding Jaxon bites of her scrumptious French toast. A reminder he wasn't there to see her snapped to mind but only vaguely. Who in their right mind wouldn't get carried away with the harmless little feeding food to a rock star fantasy? Especially when they knew it was the only way they could have him.

Chapter Fourteen

Jaxon, what are you doing here, mate? Do you really have to do this to her?

Unfortunately, yes he did.

The small bench in Grace's granny flat where he'd been told to meet Lily could use some new padding. Ha, something Lucky hadn't taken care of. That wasn't fair and he knew it. But fuck if his simpleton cousin hadn't turned out to be golden, all the things Jaxon just wasn't.

Thoughts of goodness and light stirred up his desire for Lily which had grown so strong he could taste the sunshine in the air when she was near.

Across the room in the corner was a headless mannequin, dressed in yellow fabric.

Lily was to surprise Maryellie by teaching her to sew, here at Grace's flat. And he was to have brought his daughter with him now. But, he'd sent her off to the mall to see Santa with Benny. Testing his resolve against that of the soft fabric, Jaxon rubbed it between his finger and thumb, and he lost. Soft like he remembered Lily's skin. He was so stupid.

This flat was too small. Only two rooms, and too far back from the main house. Lily would be here in a few minutes, hurt when he told her what he'd done. Her anger would be welcome but he knew himself too well. Even if Lily was furious with him, it wouldn't matter. He'd just wait it out and then make his move.

The side door opened and she popped in, strawberry blonde and buxom under all her layers. Expressive and fragrant as a real lily.

"Hi Jaxon, where's Maryella? I spent all day looking but finally found a pattern just for kids. It's so cool. You want in on the lesson?"

"She's not coming, Lily."

"Oh, okay. Well shoot. I guess my surprise will have to wait. We were gonna make a Christmas sack dress for the baby."

He had to think up something else to say. Something to push her back across the safe line. "Lily, I don't know if it's a good idea for the two of you to be getting so close."

She took an unnatural step back and shifted her jaw. "Whoa, where did that come from?"

"Can you put yourself in her shoes for a second? She's just a little girl and she's never been around this much family. It's been night and day attention showered on her and it's not like that at our house. I don't want her to get too used to it. You know, then we get home and there's nothing. Just us." *Lame,* he knew it. But he had to have some kind of legitimate reason for backing away from Lily. And some parts of what he'd said were true. It was gonna suck a giant's balls to have to tear Maryellie away from all the love she was getting here. And yeah, he was gonna miss it a bit too, he supposed, but only for his daughter's sake he told himself.

Surprisingly, Lily looked remarkably calm and rational. The frown lines he'd initially caused had already smoothed out. Not good.

"I get it. I do. But Jaxon, you can't protect her from relationships. She's lucky she doesn't need it. Not here. These folks, her folks…they're good people."

He couldn't find anything to say.

"You know, that goes for you too." She let out a sexy, soft chuckle that worked to melt some of his weakening resolve. "Haven't you felt welcome here?"

Yes, he had. Against his will.

Jaxon reached out for her hand, which loosened his rigid stance and allowed his hips to call out to hers. She smiled but chewed at her bottom lip. Honesty with Lily had been rewarding. She hadn't flipped out like he'd expected. He'd try to remember that. Not thinking about much else besides wanting to feel her skin on his, he placed her hand at the side of his neck.

"You're warm," she whispered and shifted her weight from one foot to the other.

He just nodded. In his mind, he already knew her intimately. He was gonna have to talk to Trissy again. This whole keeping his hands to himself was not working out and they were only on day two.

"Well, you're here. I'm here. I've got all this fabric. What do you say? You up for a sewing lesson?"

It was the least he could do to make up for sabotaging her time with Maryellie. But her invitation had him sweating on the inside so he shot off what he'd meant to be a joke. "Are you asking me on a date?"

Her face flamed to cherry red in an instant, reminding him of her weekend at his house. God, that was such a turn on and such a dangerous reaction for her to have this close to him. Alone with him.

"No. I...I just figured since we're both here—" She snaked her hand away from his neck and was rubbing it against her sweatshirt. "Oh, you were just joking, weren't you?"

"Lily, call it a lesson, or a date. I'm looking forward to spending this time with you. What we make is up to you."

Oh shit, she looked like she was about to pass out on a pile of needles.

* * * *

"Okay," she said shakily, feeling like she might just pass out.

Jaxon left her but came back quickly from Grace's kitchenette. "Here, drink some water."

"Oh, thanks." Sure, she would happily blame this episode on dehydration. After emptying the glass, she thanked him again. "Much better."

"No problem. Staying hydrated is just as important in the winter as it is when it's hot out. Plus you've been working out."

He'd noticed that? "Got it. Well, we should get started."

A half hour later and Jaxon still couldn't thread the needle. She'd figured he was good with his hands but hadn't factored in how much larger they were than hers. How would they ever move on to the actual pattern? The pieces they needed to trim for the facings for little baby arms and a chubby neck hole?

"Lily, maybe I should just watch you work. I promise you'll have my full attention."

"I have an even better idea. I'll sew, you watch and learn, *and* we can talk."

"Mmm, okay," he let out. So, where was he going? He moved to sit behind her so that she was sandwiched between his legs. Her shoulder blades felt hugged by his warm chest. Um, she was supposed to teach him to sew like this? Her breathing sky rocketed. "I like talking to you," he said, nearly finishing her off.

Well, she guessed she wouldn't be bringing up last night's dinner with his folks and how much she'd felt for him. Even though she was sure Luke and Bear hadn't meant anything by it, Jaxon had sat there in silence while the men had shared every significant occasion he'd missed over the past two decades. They'd only meant to fill him in, make him feel like he'd been there for everything. Jaxon had exited visibly overwhelmed in a sweat-ringed shirt and had left a mostly uneaten plate to be cleared at clean up time.

She dabbed the end of a long piece of red thread on her tongue to moisten it and then poked it through the eye of the needle. He watched her as he'd promised. He also cloaked her from behind with his massive expanse of shoulders and arms like her own personal heater. Clearly he was very interested in learning. She tried to remember to talk him through each step.

"So then we line up the fabric pieces I've already cut and measured."

"Lily, do you remember the last time we talked?"

"This morning? I think you managed a hello at breakfast before Tris's door opened and she made her way out to the couch."

"That's not talking. Remember that night on the beach? Hmm?"

How could she forget? But they'd barely talked because he'd been under the spell of her foxy temptress hair, finding that spot on her neck so fascinating. "I remember. We determined we liked each other's accents."

"And what else?'

His voice was too deep. Too much.

"We, we, we…"

"I think I did this."

A zillion goose bumps raised their hands, prompting him to their exact location. It was her special spot he'd discovered that night.

"Jaxon, what are we doing?"

"You asked me that before and I still don't have a good answer. Probably getting into lots of trouble. But I don't want to stay away. Can you handle that?"

Nothing would make her happier, she realized, than to explore things with Jaxon further, or as he called it, get into trouble. But one thing was glaringly obvious. She'd have to woman-up quickly. No more of this I can't believe Jaxon James is speaking to me. "I think I just sewed the baby dress to your pant leg." She didn't say it was going to be easy. Just that she had to try.

Because if she didn't, it meant Tom had won.

He took the needle from her hand and gave it a good yank until the red fabric she'd indeed stitched to his pant leg ripped free. "You're like nothing I've ever seen before Lily."

"You're nothing like him."

"Hmm? Like who baby?"

Oh shoot. Oh shoot her dead right now with a double barrel. Why had she let that slip?

* * * *

That was a pretty big slip and he was surprised. Lily might have been a grown woman, but there was something so untouched by man about her. The way she'd said it, whoever *the him* was, she'd been hurt.

He pulled away from her neck and looked at her pretty face. "Hey, you want to talk? I mean really talk?"

His brave little flower crinkled up her brow and nodded her head from side to side. No, she didn't want to talk about it.

"Okay. No talking."

He'd never felt the urge to just hug someone before. No lust, no foreplay or teasing, waiting for the seduction to start. He just wanted to hold her.

If his heart was really pounding as hard as he thought it was, she could hear it right now. Her face was nuzzled over his chest securely. She let him wrap his arms around her and rock her back and forth. Like a ghost hiding in the moonlight, his singing voice came out of hiding. He couldn't hold back the hum because it was for her.

Of course no matter how noble he felt right now, his lecherous body would betray that. He pulled her closer into the hug and realized how hard his dick had gotten. Chest to chest, he could have easily lifted her and set her down on top of him. As it was, if she wasn't feeling him poking into her belly, she had kept extremely quiet about it.

"Sorry about that. My dick, it just has a mind of its own most days."

He'd meant nothing by it, but Lily's head flew up and popped his lower jaw closed.

"Ow, I can't believe I did that again," she said.

"You okay?" He rubbed the top of her strawberry blond head and planted a kiss in her messy part. His jaw knew the excruciating feeling of being smashed in so he ignored the tiny sting now.

"I just, I've never said that word and it's kind of embarrassing to hear you say it so willy nilly."

"What word? Sorry?"

"No, the other one. Your male parts."

"My dick?"

"Yes, that." She brought her hand up to hide her face.

"I'm sorry Lily, I didn't mean to offend you." It was just a word but something about the gaze of the unsure mouse sitting in his lap reminded him she wasn't blatant like her sister and he didn't want her to be. Talk about extremes. If he ever did manage to embarrass Trissy, she'd have told him to shove his dick up his ass. But this one here, she was still sporting her cute flushed cheeks. The question was, did she want to change that?

"I'm such a nerd. Jaxon, please feel free to say whatever floats your boat. I didn't mean to censor you. It's just me."

It felt so good rubbing her back and having this quiet, intimate conversation. "Apology accepted." He grinned, an ornery one he knew she couldn't see. It was his way of easing her embarrassment. "Hey, so I guess this is a good time to warn you that I'm never trying to sound like a perv but sometimes shit just comes out of my mouth…See, like right there, I just said shit when I could have probably used…"

"Shush crazy. Talk like you. Be you. I'm really sorry and I shouldn't have opened my mouth about it. If anything, I wish I could say whatever's on my mind."

"Is there something you'd like to get off your chest now? Anything, free range, go for it." How desperate could he be to get this young woman talking? Maybe he just needed something from her. A bit to hold onto and figure out whether there could be some happy middle ground they could reach between his craziness and her inhibitions.

She's not gonna say anything, dick. You freaked her out.

"I miss the girl I was before. It would be nice to find her again. I think you would have liked her." She gave him a sad wink.

There was no question, he was sure he would have and also that had sounded like a plea. Taking a giant leap here and with her hand setting so close to his crotch, he had the perfect reason to go for it. "Baby, you taught me how to sew today, would you like some lessons in return?"

They were now staring each other in the eyes and she was lit up like a string of twinkly lights. "So now you know how to sew, huh? I must be one heck of a teacher."

"Maybe I'm just a visual learner."

"Oh." She blushed again and nearly knocked foreheads with him when her chin started to dip down. He caught and lifted it.

"So are you interested in what I have to teach?"

He watched her head bob up and down, thrilling him out of the uneasy parts of his visit so far. In his mind, he'd just voted her his table partner for any further family meals.

"Okay, well for starters, are you good sitting here in my lap?"

She swiveled her head around, then tested the ground beneath them with her hands but didn't move. "Actually, yes. I am."

He winked. "Good. So am I. But I'm also highly aroused."

She looked like she didn't believe him. Which was absurd. She let one "Yeah, right," escape and then cleared her throat when he didn't so much as blink. "Okay, you're serious."

"Go on, take a look."

Slowly, like she was tethered to an imaginary string keeping her head from bowing, she glanced at his bulging crotch. "Um, okay, I believe you."

"Good. Can I have your hand please?"

Her eyes popped, "I thought this was a vocabulary lesson, Jaxon."

"It is. I just want to hold your hands while we talk."

"Oh God. See how I do that? Turn everything into a big ole bowl of awkward. Sorry. Here." She offered him her hands which he took and rubbed with his thumbs and then held in the intimate space between their bodies.

"You're sure?"

"Yes, I'm a grown woman and I want to be able to say grown up words without..."

She was butting up against something and he guessed getting over it was the real reason she was daring herself to have this conversation. "Without what, baby?"

A soul-searching stare lingered between them as he continued to rub her hands and wait.

"Without," she pulled her hands back then settled them against her mouth. "Being reminded of how dirty he made me feel when he twisted them and used them."

Fuck. "Who are we talking about Lily?"

"My ex-husband."

Jaxon hated the relief at her answer when she was so obviously torn up over it but thank God she hadn't said her father. An asshole ex-husband was something he could handle. A sexually abusive father, fuck, he had no idea what to do with that shit. Just ask Trissy.

So this was Lily wanting to take something back that some asshole had stolen. That—he could and would help her with. Not that it would make up for past failures but it was a step in the right direction.

"Let's take it slow and start with just one of those words. All you need is a sense of humor about it. Loosen up."

She rolled her neck and shoulders, loosening up like he'd instructed. She was a damned cute student. His groin ached. "Ready," she said in the sexiest voice he'd ever heard.

"Well, since he's awake and wants to be part of the conversation...what word would you use to refer to him?"

"Uh, if by *him* we're talking about your…," she pointed her finger and swirled it in a large circle directly in front of his hugely excited dick, "Oh my God, this is so embarrassing. I guess I'd say your manlihood." Her face pleaded with him not to laugh and he wouldn't. He could tell how hard that had been for her and wondered what kind of sick mental abuse the ex had doled out.

"Okay, that's okay. Well, it is that. But it's also just a dick." He paused to gauge her breathing which she was doing, just a lot slower than was probably normal for most humans. "It is. Think about it, what is it about that word that makes you uncomfortable?"

She gave it some thought. "I guess I just wouldn't want to be offensive to anyone."

"And that makes perfect sense. Even I'd never dare to say dick to Grace. I'm not crazy. I can tell you're not sold yet."

"It's just, it sounds vulgar when I try to hear myself saying it."

"That's because you're a lady. Which, for the record, should never change. But if you're gonna have a guy like me around, you're gonna hear stuff like this. Hey, here's a thought. What about when it's a guy's name? Or that English bread pudding dessert."

"There's an English dessert named after it?'

"Yeah, it's called Spotted Dick."

"No way!"

Her lips curled into delectable, tight vees at the corners, showing him her each and every tooth. He'd lick her from smile line to smile line if he wasn't so enthralled in their laughter.

"Can you say it now?" he asked.

"Jaxon, I could have said it a long time ago. It would just come out sounding really weird and lame. I'm not one of those sexy girls who can pull off that kind of talk."

"Why don't you let me be the judge of that? I promise you won't sound weird. And would it help you to know that your golden boy brother-in-law has said it plenty of times?"

"Lucky?" Her voice hightailed it from beginning to end of his cousin's name.

"Yep." He pulled his lips together and held them like that, trying to keep from tackling her and rubbing himself into her voluptuous body she kept maddeningly hidden.

"What about Stefan?" she asked, setting his jealousy hackles on edge.

"Stefan?"

"Yeah, what does he call it?"

"Okay, but you asked. Stef, he's more of a cock kind of guy. Which we can work up to if you really want to go there."

"Oh no, I don't want to go there."

Her sweetness endeared him so fully he thought his heart might explode under her touch. She was fingering his pointer finger like it was a shiny new toy.

She blew out a breath, making him wish he was the air she breathed. "I'm ready. I'm gonna say it."

"Okay, you can do it," he encouraged.

"Wait, should I just blurt it out, just that one word or can you give me a sentence?"

"For the record, you're killing me, baby. So fucking cute. Sorry, that's one I'm working on not using so much anymore." He thought about it and then leaned into her ear to whisper the one thing he'd die to hear her say. "You could whisper that into my ear for a warm up."

She nodded yes. The second her balmy, cherry scented lips made contact with his ear, he was a lost cause.

He had to pay attention because her words were so very quiet. Letting the immediate tickling sensation smooth its way out, he put his hand to the other side of her head and edged her lips closer to his ear then listened for her to repeat the prompt he'd given her.

The quietest, most erotic voice flowed from her mouth, "I've never met anyone quite so honest and open. Thanks for being yourself with me. And for giving me the courage to be able to say this." Shit, he was dangling by a thread on her every word. "You're not a dick, Jaxon. You're much more, to me anyway."

That wasn't anywhere close to the line he'd fed her to say. To steal her words, it was much more.

A feminine sniff rattled him from the tender galaxy he'd floated off to.

"Lame, huh?" she asked.

"Lily, that's one of the sexiest things anyone has ever said to me. Thank you for being you, baby." He had her hands back in his so he rubbed them again. "Lily, can I ask?" He paused to ensure the sensitivity he intended came out right. "What's the difference between me saying these words to you and how your ex did? Because so help me God, I do not want to upset you."

If she regarded him one more time like that, so needful, he'd have no other choice. She'd be his, in every imaginable way.

"Oh Jaxon, who knows? He was a deceiving, twisted jerk who I let hurt me and wasted entirely too much time with. Whereas you," she smiled, "You are who you are, out in the open, for everyone to see. Good or bad, that's not so scary."

SIN'S FLOWER

Chapter Fifteen

Jaxon stood outside, admiring Grace's converted flat and the nostalgic familiarity of her flower garden. He leaned down and picked up some stray brown leaves that didn't belong. Good for them. They all deserved this. Good men and women, the decent, hardworking people of the world deserved a humble place like this to call home. Maryellie, his baby. She belonged here, way more than where they'd come from.

His next thought nauseated him.

Maryellie was his world. And this was the type of life she needed. This was what he'd been scavenging for in California and coming up empty. No more tricks like he'd pulled earlier that day with Lily and the lesson. He had to at least try to fit in with these people. His father and uncle, men who could live off this land. Maybe Jaxon could learn.

And then there was Lily. Sweet, forbidden Lily. Although he was getting over that and thinking more and more about helping her find the woman she'd lost to the ex. She was sexy as hell and had no idea.

He sat back and closed his eyes. Her innocence made his nerves show up on his skin which became tight with the cold air and his pumping blood. He shivered. It was going to be a long night as Lily had offered to cook another huge meal, enough to feed the four Mason men and the women too. But if he wasn't ready to play the part of whatever they expected of him, he had no business being here.

He drug his hands through his hair, slicking it back on top and then feeling the prickly stubble that had gone too long since its last visit from a razor. Maybe he should try looking less like a crazed maniac. No, he knew better. He couldn't blame it on the razor short sides of his head or the thorn marks he'd had tattooed up the side of his neck. It was his actions, the way he made people feel all jumpy on the inside. Like they didn't know if they wanted to cry with him or because of him. The frustration came from his inability to prove to everyone he didn't want that anymore.

He wanted someone to see him as a daddy. A loving, doting father. Funny enough, and foreign as hell, he wanted Lily to laugh for him. What a beautiful sound that would be if they could be out in the open together. Her laughter would be everyone's proof that he wasn't a bad guy. Not anymore.

"You know, you'd be really handsome if you smiled more."

Her voice pulled his eyes closed. A command to take notice of the butterfly who'd just flown by.

"It's so cold out tonight. Why don't you come back inside, Jaxon?" asked Lily.

"I just needed a little space, to think. I'm fine."

"You're tough, I know." She walked over and stole his arm, making it warm with her soft hands. "Maybe I just needed an excuse to come say hi."

She stepped even closer, tiptoeing like she was creeping up to a tiger exhibit with no protective glass. She had great instincts.

"Mind if I stand here with you for a bit?" she asked.

"I don't. But, uh, you'll be missed inside." He lifted his chin in the direction of Trissy's house. Their breath blew out in puffs together.

"Nah, they're too busy doting on your beautiful little girl." He caught wind of a smile that spread across her face subtly. He didn't normally see beauty in light, airy things. But she cast this adorable glow right now, like a sweet young backstage virgin at her first concert where the neon lights picked her out from the crowd. He'd been with too many like that—young women who'd pretended to be those sweet girls but who were really just dying to show him they would see their teasing through. At least Vangie hadn't tried to hide what she was. Again, an image of that last fight he'd had with her did its best to ruin the moment.

"You know, I have a hard time figuring you out, Miss Lily," he finally said, wanting to get her back inside but needing her presence just as much.

"Why's that?" she asked. Again, her arms rubbed up against his. Thank God for those thick, long sleeves protecting her from him and the cold.

"I think I'm a pretty straightforward girl. Here, I'll prove it. Ask me anything."

"Unh-unh. That's a dangerous game." One they'd tiptoed around earlier at their so called lessons. She'd barely made it out undevoured. "You don't want to play that with me, baby." He pulled her elbow and walked them to a spot behind the raised porch where the chilly wind was at least blocked. There was a corner. He continued to press forward until she was completely protected, by the wood against her back and sides, and his body at her front.

"So you'd rather figure me out all on your own?"

Oh shit, how did she do that? She was all sweetness but played all the wrong way. Like God had made her this innocent demon just to torment him. Shit, how he wanted to figure her out, every molecule. Her mouth made his tongue feel like jelly.

"Lily, I think you should go back inside." He appreciated the visit but telling her would have kept her there longer, in his gratitude, which was dangerous.

"Tell me why you want me to leave so badly and I'll go."

Fine. This girl didn't know when to quit. She had asked and offered up honesty all night. She was going to get it, full blown. "If you don't leave right now, I'm going to do things to you that will make everyone in that house hate me forever. You really want that?"

Ah hell. It took one second for her head to dip nearly to her shoulder, her hand to come up to her mouth and rest at her bottom lip, as she poured out her heart to him in one look. She didn't believe him. But there was no question, she wanted it.

* * * *

Lily couldn't help running her hands over her hips, wondering if he could see that her underwear were too tight against her skin again. Like the universe had heard her and was in a teasing mood, Jaxon's eyes strayed to those parts of her body. *Get a grip silly. He's looked at thousands of women this way. And probably slept with nearly as many.* She couldn't decide if that fact hurt her self-confidence or her feelings more.

"You're right, Jaxon. I would be heartbroken if all those people in their—your—family hated you. Especially if it was because of me."

"Good, I'm glad you understand. Now you'd better get back."

"Don't I get a chance?"

"A chance for what?"

"Well." She cleared her throat and looked down at her rather beat up sneakers. "I appreciate your honesty, again." A smile grabbed her even though she tried to keep it at bay. Its heat warmed her cheeks. "But I wasn't playing when I said I would tell you anything you wanted to know. I don't know why that makes you so nervous. I'd like to get to know you better, too."

"It doesn't make me nervous," he said back casually.

"Then why was your first instinct to blow me off with that silly scare-tactic?"

"That wasn't a threat, Lily. You don't know anything about me."

She knew he was arrogant, that was for sure. Had he already forgotten she'd been married and divorced? She knew about men, both the jerks and the ones worth their weight in gold. There was just something she couldn't shake about his words. The look on his face as he'd tried to scare her off. It was a warning, not a threat. At least that's what she thought for the few seconds he'd stood there looking serious and withdrawn.

A knowing grin barely made its way onto his handsome face. Her first thought was of her father. The next, Tom. The last, Jaxon.

No. She wouldn't condemn Jaxon to that group, no matter how badly he seemed to want her to do it. She'd figure him out, whether he participated in a conversation with her or not. She wasn't going to let him use sex as a threat. That was so wrong. And it hurt her that it had been his gut reaction. She wondered if the rock star had ever loved a woman. She wondered about Maryella's mom.

He leaned in and after a brief pause, whispered into her face, "I don't want to hurt you."

"You can't hurt me. Not like that. I promise."

He pulled back from her and tucked his chin to his chest. She'd said the wrong thing, or exactly the right thing to get him to open up.

"Jaxon?"

"I'm sorry, I was just thinking about something."

"Me too," she said.

They stood huddled in the tight corner together in silence for a few minutes. Finally Jaxon relented. "You wanna talk about it?" His words sounded restricted and uncomfortable but when she felt his hand cup hers, she could only reason he'd meant it to be soothing.

"I don't know if I want to talk about what I think is on your mind right now, but I do want you to know I didn't go through the same hell Tris did. I hate what happened to her, but it wasn't the same for me. It doesn't mean I don't hate my father any less."

He nearly stumbled a step back from her and caught the porch's overhang above her head to steady himself. "Sorry, I just wasn't expecting you to be able to put that out there like that."

"Well, I feel safe around you, Jaxon."

He shook his head as it bowed and he grasped her arms again. "Please, don't say that. You really don't know me well enough."

"Hey, look at me, please?" When he did, she continued. "My father never touched me, but I lived with him and it turns out he was a devil. I know that now. And then there was my ex. You're not bad like that, Jaxon. I'd know it if you were."

"Lily, maybe I'm just a great actor and maybe you scare the hell out of me."

"Why?" she asked. How could she be scary to him?

"I don't know what to do with you."

"I scare you? And you don't know what to do with me? You've been hurt, haven't you?"

"I've been the one who hurts the ones I'm supposed to care about," he said, staring through her.

He wasn't going to let her convince him tonight with her truths and her honesty. She wouldn't push him any further. They'd opened a gaping hole of communication just now, whether he realized it or not, something had clicked even more so than it had the weekend at his place.

It was a real, bonafide start.

She watched as he pulled down with both hands on the stretchy vee-neck collar of his t-shirt. The night should be over for them. She should go back inside and finish prepping supper. Luke and Bear would be there any minute. But the solemn look on Jaxon's face contrasting with the exposed patch of his chest left her unable to move.

She didn't know what possessed her to do it, but she reached her hand out to touch the exposed triangle of skin, the light sprinkling of hairs on his chest. Like a bear trap clamping down on a foot, promising to do permanent damage, Jaxon's hand caught her at the wrist, tight and sharp. She wanted to tell him he was hurting her, like Tom had done, but she didn't. He didn't mean to hurt her, she knew that in her bones. He was merely stopping her before it got to that point.

* * * *

He had to stop her before she ended up another victim. "Lily, go back inside where you belong." He let go of her wrist. It was the nicest thing he could say to her. In two seconds, he would be at her throat, treating himself to the taste of her neck. The smell of her hair. "Go on." The feel of his hand dropping to her waist and then back out again to her amazing hips.

"You know what? You acting like a jerk, it's annoying. But it doesn't hurt." She looked straight through him; tears showed up like a magic trick and filled the corners of her eyes. "Lying to me, saying you want me to leave when I know you don't, that hurts."

"Why?" he asked her, frowning.

"Because that means you don't respect me enough to be honest. And that means we can't be friends."

He didn't know if it was what she'd said or the way her constant look bore down into his aching heart.

"You're right. That's exactly what that means."

And that was not what he'd come here to do. Hurt and lie.

"Come here, Lily."

Too scared now to trust him, she didn't budge from the corner. She didn't even blink.

"Please," he said.

She extended her arm, covered in long sleeve flannel, the wrist he'd undoubtedly hurt earlier poking from the opening. It would be the first thing he kissed. Trying to be tender, trying to be the good man he'd set out to become on this trip, he beat back the insane, intense desire to squeeze her until he felt her pulse beneath his grip. He laced his fingers with hers as she offered them to him.

"I can't stop thinking about your lips," he whispered.

She didn't say anything. As he came closer to her face, she closed her eyes.

"No, Lily. Don't close your eyes."

Two shots of blue, stronger than any tequila he'd ever chased, opened back up, blue fire. His lips were dry but he wouldn't lick them. She would do that for him. God, he felt himself becoming that guy again. That man who didn't know how in the world he was ever going to change. That man, who wanted to have this beautiful flower riding all the way back to California, where he would keep her and never let her go.

Chapter Sixteen

"Okay." She blinked, once for balance, once for a reality check and once more for time. Even a few short seconds would help her adjust to what was happening here. Her breath came out in a cool fog, unbelieving that she was about to make out with Jaxon. So she stood there, eyes wide open, waiting for him to make the next move because she had no idea, apparently, how one leaned in for a romantic kiss with their eyes glued to the other person. "I'm sorry, I don't know how to do this...like this."

"Shh, I've almost found it," he scolded her lightly.

"Found it? Found what?"

"This."

Oh my God. It was wrong to take the Lord's name in vain so often, but she was about to die, she just knew it.

"Keep your eyes open," he said just as she'd begun to slip away into bliss.

"Okay," she said with no more than a wisp of the chilly air her breath made.

Her senses were aware of nothing and everything, like never before. Yes, it was cold but she felt each of his ten fingertips pressing against her scalp, holding her head in place, heating her all the way to her toes.

She wasn't going anywhere, ever.

How long would it be until he did that thing in that place again? She extended her jaw and neck, watching him looking at the spot just behind her ear, the inch of skin between it and her hairline. She'd already memorized how the tip of his nose felt, nudging around the area and then the ridge of his upper lip teasing behind it. Then the way his bottom lip chased all those flowery sensations away. And replaced them with hot, warm, sucking pressure.

Oh my God, again. She didn't know how much longer she could watch the driveway, the cloudy gray sky, Grace's dress form in the granny flat's window that was creeping Lily out right now.

This was crazy.

But as she lowered her chin to accommodate his nuzzling and sucking, what she saw made her never want to close her eyes. It was a beautiful view of his neck and the permanently inked rose thorns, what she'd thought before were tiny sharks' teeth, forever pricking their way up his slightly weathered, tanned skin. The trail of the thorns looked painful, like tracks, while the one his suckling tongue had just blessed her with felt so good.

"Jaxon."

"Hmm?"

"Can I close my eyes, please? As beautiful as your neck is, I feel weird with my eyes open."

"I'd rather you didn't."

"Why?" she asked.

His lips left the lucky spot behind her ear. That wasn't a look of pleasure on his face.

"You said without trust, we could never be friends."

She nodded at his words as he finally touched her again. His fingers glided as far as they could into her hair, pulled back, tangled and messy. "As hard as it is for you to believe this, I do trust you, Jaxon."

His head sunk, causing the tuft of dirty blond bang, half spikes and half pompadour, to fall and break from its perfect form. He let it dip for a few more seconds and then up came a more sincere, less arrogant looking man.

"Lily." She watched as he bit at his lower lip while saying her name. "Did you enjoy what we were doing just now?" He smiled soft and soberly, his voice deep and naughty, his warm breath a godsend.

She blushed. "Yes."

"Then this is your next lesson. Please, just do as I ask."

What was there to think about really? He hadn't even kissed her lips yet and she wanted desperately to find out how that would feel, whether she had turned into a Popsicle or not. She didn't understand what his thing was about this open eyes policy but he'd asked nicely. For him.

"Okay," she gave in.

"Thank you."

"You're welcome, Jaxon."

"Shh," he said, and then stopped himself just as their lips would have touched for the first time.

Surely she looked like a crazy person this close up. Damn it if her eyes weren't about to cross in such close proximity while staring into his. She had to blink. Refocus. When she did, it was like she was staring at a lost soul. But he was brave and tough too. Like he'd fight you if that's what you really wanted, only to admit later that all he really wanted was to go home and sleep it off.

Jaxon's lips were beautiful this close up. She imagined the soft creases in his full pink flesh holding tiny little bursts of his taste.

"What are you waiting for? Kiss me." She couldn't believe she'd just made that request. As soon as the words left her mouth, she wanted to slink back into the corner because she knew he was about to say no.

* * * *

There was no saying no to his Lily. He wasn't letting her get away from him now. Not after that brave little invitation she'd just broken him with. Dammit that he couldn't take her inside.

She inched away but he cupped his hand to the back of her head and gently pulled her face back to his. "Lily, this is going to get me into so much trouble." The worry flashing in her eyes was impossible to miss. He'd sensed her lack of confidence about her body from the very start. The girl lived in too many layers and too many of them made of thick, sweats material. It was a shame. Maybe he could help her learn to own her sexiness. Maybe some more lessons wouldn't hurt but rather help. As much as he wanted to find his way inside her lush body right now, he knew the most she was expecting was a kiss. He'd enjoy that for now but that would be it. Then they would talk. And maybe, if he was lucky, he'd get her to come out of her shell. But first, that request she'd made of him. His way.

"Lily, remember, eyes open please."

"Right. Sorry, I forgot."

He picked up her right hand, took a second to suck at the tip of the fingers resting on his lips and then placed them at the back of his neck. "It's okay." And then he slowly did the same with her other hand and slightly trembling fingers. "Don't be nervous."

"Okay," she said, swallowing.

He scanned the area to be sure the Masons hadn't arrived yet and then reached behind his head to hold her waiting hands, pressing her fingers deeper into the flesh of his neck. He could feel how hot his skin had become. Good. Giving her a little something to do would take her mind off being out here alone with him and clue him into whether or not she'd be able to handle his perversions, should they make it further than just a kiss.

Once he felt her take over the massaging motion of his neck, he left her hands alone to do their magic and for a second, simply enjoyed the touch. But only for a couple seconds because with each of her feminine squeezes of his tense muscles, his dick got harder. He could have controlled it but wanted her to realize and believe in the effect she had on him, or any man for that matter.

With her huddled safely against the sturdy wooden, corner walls, he held tightly to her hips and pushed forward until his chest touched hers. Her arms reached to meet his height and her fingers pressed more deeply to the back of his head, making their way up into his hair.

Fuck. He couldn't just kiss her.

Not with her eyes holding him accountable. Not with her protected by God knew how many layers of clothes. Not even the fear he'd counted on of pissing off Trissy for life would be able to stop him from getting himself inside her should they kiss right now. But he knew that if he did nothing, it would knock her budding confidence. So he went again to her neck, just below her ear lobe and suckled her there until he'd mentally regained enough control.

After a nice long session of memorizing the taste of her neck, he whispered into her ear, "You're so sexy, Lily. I want you too badly." He hoped it had been enough for her. Because it had nearly killed him to have to pull away.

* * * *

Holy cow. That was amazing. She could die right now and go to heaven, that was if they'd let a flaming hot woman with the sweats and the shakes inside the pearly gates. When she got her voice back, she would thank Jaxon for his special kiss. At least her vision seemed to be working. She focused on Jaxon who had stepped back and now stood there so captivating and sexy, a couple feet from her. "Thank you," she said to him.

His eyebrows shot up and then he wiped a thumb over his bottom lip. "You liked?"

She nodded. "I did."

His face quirked for a minute like he was surprised and then it turned down into a sexy frown.

"What's wrong?" she asked him, afraid he would say they were done and she should leave.

"I just realized how hard it's going to be to sleep under the same roof as you tonight and be a good boy."

She loved it when he was silly. But whoa, first off, staying the night with Jaxon was more than fine with her. They were adults and who would care if she invited him to her room? It shouldn't be a big deal to anyone but Lily. So secondly, what the heck was up with his pouting about it? But before she could respond, he shifted his body and reached out for her hand.

"No more kissing for the night. It's for your own good, trust me. And you might want to lock your bedroom door," he said under a sexy but serious raised brow. "Seriously, Lily."

"Okay." If it had been anyone else, she might have felt a hit to her ego but there was just no mistaking the way Jaxon made her feel. She didn't think he could lie about the sexy things he'd said to her and if she wasn't mistaken, neither could his body. "You haven't found the secret stash inside yet, have you?" She would try and make his night on the couch as comfy as possible. Before she ran out of this unexpected gulp of confidence, she smiled and brought his hand to her lips for a kiss. "I'm going inside now. I hope you're coming too."

* * * *

He was in so much trouble for this. *You will not fuck her tonight. And kill the visual lock on her ass. Shit. You could make this easier on yourself. Look away, dickhead.* But Lily's sweatpants covered flared hips and perfectly squeezable cheeks provoked his natural naughty curiosity. She wouldn't lock her door. He would come to her. They would lie together. But that was it. He was a forty-four year old grown man. He could snuggle without sex.

"Lily, you said you were going in. But…you're still here." He grinned, coughed and nodded in order to keep from laughing. "Get inside. I'll be there in a bit," he said to her, holding out his hand but letting it fall back to his side.

Good thing too. Trissy was up against doctor's orders again, poking her head out the door over the front porch as Lily slid past her into the house. That look on her face tunneling right for him might be priceless but Jaxon knew he'd pay dearly, very soon.

"Well, the food nearly burned. And, your father is on his way."

Trissy's knowing eyes couldn't have been clearer. He'd just been warned.

SIN'S FLOWER

Chapter Seventeen

Lily's food smelled delicious and tasted even better. Jaxon pulled his teeth over his fork, enjoying the last bite of spicy smothered pork chops. A drizzle of buttery garlic sauce trickled down the fork to his finger. He wiped it with his napkin rather than risk being shot over a quick lick with the tongue. If it had been a meal for two, he'd have done it just to tease Lily. But there was an audience present and one he didn't want to incite.

"That was so good. Thank you," he offered as everyone leaned back into their chairs looking like a round table of fat, sated house cats. Jaxon's thumbs rapped up against the underside of the table.

Lucky, of all people, echoed him when Trissy remained oddly silent. "Lily is a great cook." His cousin then rubbed at his belly but gave Luke a look. "Dad, if you keep coming over here and mooching supper, your shop pants are gonna need bigger suspenders."

Luke chuckled. Jaxon admired the easy relationship between his cousin and uncle and then couldn't help but glance toward his own father. Bear Mason sat with Maryellie on his lap, lost in grandpa heaven.

Jaxon turned his attention back to Trissy who was frowning. "Yes, Lily is a great cook," she said in her husband's direction. But then she turned to Lily. "I don't know what I'd do without you, little sis. You've kept the family fed while I've been useless. I don't think I realized how much I needed you until this week."

Yeah, Jaxon heard it loud and clear. Translation, *Don't you be getting any ideas of stealing my baby sis.* Problem was, he feared he'd already surpassed that.

"Daddy, did you know who made the green beans?" Maryellie asked.

Jaxon turned back to his daughter and father. "What? There were green beans? Did you sneak some of those yucky things on my plate?"

"Daddy! I made them."

Everyone at the table chuckled.

"Oh wow, I really hope I didn't eat any gross green beans," he said it with a huge grin and a tickle to her belly.

"Oh, I'm sure you did. I made sure to serve plenty on your plate." Lily's voice kissed his ears and she just smiled in his and Maryellie's direction. He was so grateful for her participation in silly talk to cover up his nerves.

He turned from listening to Lily back to his daughter. "Well I must not have realized what they were because they were so delicious. What a wonderful chef you are, sweetums."

Now that Jaxon was smiling, his father must have felt at ease enough to ask him a direct question.

"So Jaxon, any chance you and Maryella might stick around past the holidays?"

"Um, you know, Bear, I hadn't really thought that far out." Jaxon didn't know what else to say.

But apparently Trissy did. "Well, it's time for me to get back to my back, ugh."

Lucky stood to help her but she rested her hand over his arm. "Actually, I was hoping Jaxon could help me this time. We haven't really had a chance to catch up yet."

"Sure, no problem," said Lucky and then kissed her forehead.

"Jaxon?" Trissy asked, "Walk me back to my room?"

Was anyone going to protest? Nope.

Why did that not look like a girl who was over the moon that her best friend was back?

Jaxon excused himself from dinner and followed along, hoping he was reading her all wrong.

Once they were in her room and he had helped her lean back onto the bed, he blurted something out just to kill the silence. "So hey, what's up with all the cheating on doctor's orders to stay in bed? Hmm?"

She was holding it in. She didn't want to have this talk any more than he did. Oh shit, what if this had nothing to do with the eyes he'd had for Lily in front of Trissy but was everything about that night in the field?

"Jaxon, I know how hard it was for you to make this trip, and it means so much to me that you did."

He let out a giant pent up breath.

"I'm glad you feel that way—"

"I wasn't finished, hun. It took all of two seconds for me to see the way you look at my sister. As grateful as I am that you came, we are not going there, Jaxon. I mean it. I'd love to have you stay through the New Year, as long as you promise not to get involved with Lily."

What could he do? At ten years his junior, Trissy hadn't changed and still didn't mince her words when it came to pointing out the obvious to him.

"I hear you and you're right."

"Good," she said, eyeballing him still.

"What? Am I supposed to ignore her completely?" he asked, hiding the hurt Trissy had caused him.

"No, that would be strange and rude. Maryella loves Lily already. Just keep your hands to yourself. Jaxon, please."

"Like I said, you're right."

He leaned over and kissed her forehead then pulled a blanket up and over her lower half.

"I'm just looking out for her best interest," Trissy said as he went to pass through her door.

"I know."

He didn't bother adding that he too, genuinely felt protective of Lily and wanted only to do good things for her. Trissy wouldn't hear that crap. But he cared, beyond belief; he cared about Lily.

The question was, was it inevitable she'd get hurt because of it? As a friend, Lily could end up collateral damage just like Trissy had been in that field. Worse, as a lover, Lily might become twisted into the epitome of jealousy and rage, like Vangie.

Was she screwed either way? He could always refuse to let either of those things happen.

Chapter Eighteen

"Well, I guess we should try and get some sleepies."

"Yeah, I guess that's a good idea."

"Okay."

"Okay."

"Good night."

"Good night."

"See you in the morning."

"Yep, you too."

"Jaxon?"

"Yeah?"

"I can't sleep."

"Me neither. Maybe this wasn't such a great idea."

But the small talk had worked to relax her since he'd knocked at her door a half hour ago. Of course she'd let him in. Locked door her derriere. Like that was happening. She felt less like she was standing tip toes on top of an icy mountaintop after just having drunk a pot of coffee and more like a thirty-one-year old grown woman simply lying beside a man who she could call friend. Tris's cat, who had snuck in behind Jaxon, stepped his way over her face, letting her get a mouthful of fluffy gray tail. Lily giggled and sputtered but averted round two as she picked him up and set him on her empty bed.

"Did you know I rescued that little pain in the ass?"

Well how adorable was that? Jaxon James, one man kitty rescue squad by day, sinful, musical sexy man by night.

"Figjam?" she asked, just to keep the soothing talk going.

"Yep, named him too. It suits him and Jaxon was already taken."

"Odd name, I have to admit."

"Fuck I'm Good, Just Ask Me," he said and then reached out to pet the kitty who had refused her bed offering.

She smiled softly at that.

"You have a beautiful smile, Lily. Did you know that?"

"Um, thanks," she said around what felt like a giant squirt from a tube full of blush.

"I like talking to you. I hope you feel the same." He tapped the tip of her nose and then tucked his hand back to his side.

"I do. You seem so regular."

"Ouch. I bet you wouldn't say that to your real crush, Stefan."

"That's not what I meant. I just feel like I can talk to you about, stuff. Crazy stuff, funny stuff. Messed up stuff. I get the feeling nothing's off limits. It's nice."

The way his eyes settled on her and his shoulders and chest relaxed made her feel even more comfortable.

"Good, because I'm curious to know what you, Lily, like about your body? Lesson three? Are you up for it? Told you...should have locked your door." He winked.

"Oh." She could do this. She wanted to do this more importantly. He was interested or he would never have asked. There was no reason not to be honest with him. And she didn't feel any pressure, not like she had at Tom's requests. Yuck, her ex's name goosed her. She shook it off with an airy flick of her fingers before rubbing them hard into the floor.

"Well?" he said while touching the ends of her hair.

"Well, I like when a woman's body is smaller than a man's."

The sexiest, most devilish grin blazed across his handsome face and she wondered if he was going to bust her out for not really answering his question. "You may have noticed. I'm much bigger than you," he said.

She couldn't have responded even if he'd stopped long enough to let her. Were they still trying to be good and get to sleep because his new line of questions had her pulse playing air hockey under her skin.

* * * *

He hated keeping her up with his admittedly teasing questions, but the thought of sleeping with her scared the shit out of him. If he let her close her eyes, would he be strong enough to keep his hands, arms, legs, and tongue to himself? Doubtful. He coughed.

"So, is there anything particular you like about my body, Lily?"

God, he'd never thought "shy" could equal sexy but here it was, in the flesh. He was dying to hear her answer. Maybe she'd use the new word he'd taught her at lesson one.

"Um, yes...I like your arms and chest," she said a little more quietly. He didn't want to lose her to her shell again. He put his hand over hers and squeezed then petted her fingers with his.

He ached to lose his shirt, only for her but he had to keep the conversation going. "May I ask why you like those particular parts?"

She shook her head, obviously not wanting to share.

"Would you like to know what I like about you?"

He rubbed his hand softly up and down her arm, wishing she wasn't still covered from head to toe.

"I'm not sure," she let out shakily.

183

He couldn't help but chuckle at her honesty. He was telling her anyway and if he wasn't such a pussy all of a sudden, he'd have done it with a kiss.

"Your curves." Then he leaned his lips to her ear and closed his eyes, breaking his own rule, as he committed to telling her the absolute truth of his desire. "I've thought about holding onto your hips, and pushing myself inside you. The fantasy is so much better when I picture entering you from back here…" He stopped, taking a moment to place a kiss in her hair and pet the rounded top of her hip softly then move to her ass. "Your body is so fucking hot, Lily." But she'd become still after hearing that. Maybe it was good that had come out sounding more like a warning. He decided to go with that in hopes of bringing her back to their little talk. "Lily, that's the absolute truth and exactly why I'm so hot and cold. Always talking about kissing you and then never following through."

But all she did was flinch against his cheek. He pulled back because something felt wrong. "Hey, are you okay? I'm sorry, I'll ease up."

Smartly, she pulled back so he could see her face. "It's okay. I uh, I just had a bad experience with my ex."

"What do you mean?" Fuck. Bad ex stories were never good; he had plenty. And he'd gone and said something to remind Lily of hers. "Tell me, please."

She blew out a big breath and fanned her hair at the left temple all the way to the strands' ends just below her collar bone. "He insisted on filming us."

Shit, he'd done that before a time or two. That didn't sound so bad. Which told him there must be more. But he didn't want her to feel dirty that she'd shared that with him. "It's okay. I'd be lying if I said there weren't tapes of me doing God knows what out there."

"Well, he made me watch it." A couple shakes of

her shoulders and her head dunked to her hands.

"Hey, hey, hey, shush, don't cry, Lily. I'm sorry, baby."

"No, it's just…all I could see was the way my fat jiggled and I hated doing it and seeing it. But he didn't care. He never listened to me. I thought he'd stopped after the one time but one day I found a bunch of movie files on his laptop. Basically I'm an idiot."

"Don't say that. No you're not."

"Well, I left him at his family's Easter dinner and he still has the files. I guess I should have been more clever."

"I'll tell you what; I haven't busted anyone's ass in a long time. Just say the word."

"Thanks," she said. His air motions of elbowing someone in the face made her let out a small grin.

"Lily, I never want to make you feel that way. But as you can see, I'm pretty loose talking about sexual stuff. It's just my nature. So if I ever say something crazy, just kick my ass okay?" Even an ankle biter would have known she in no way could see herself kicking his ass from the way her eyebrows hiked up, wrinkling her forehead and making her an absolute cutie. "Or uh, you could just have a poke at my belly. That'd work too."

He loved getting those smiles. It made him wonder what else he could get out of her. A quick look to the clock and he nearly groaned. It was barely past eleven thirty. Unaccustomed to having anyone else awake with him, he decided to take advantage of both the company and his secret task. To get Lily to shed some layers and enjoy herself again like she'd mentioned.

Exhausted, he still couldn't sleep. He eyed the ugly gap keeping her safe on the other side of the blanket pallet she'd made them. "Sure this is okay with you?" he asked.

"Yes."

Coming from anyone else, he'd take that short quickie as eagerness but coming from her…he wouldn't kid himself. Most likely she was on the fringe about having let him in.

"Shit, it's still too early for me to be attempting sleep," he complained and blew out a hot breath while fighting his clothes and the covers. "What's so interesting in your maggy there?"

"My magazine? Oh, um nothing."

Yeah, she wasn't getting away with that so easily. He tried peeping at what had grown her eyes to the size of blue golf balls. "Lemme see."

First she tried turning the page very quickly but he grabbed it.

"Jaxon!"

Well, now he understood what she was trying to hide. There in bold, all caps was his answer. "Don't got sheep? Masturbate your way to sleep. Wow. Now that's a goody."

He'd expected her to have a chuckle along with him at the ridiculously funny title of the article she'd been busting through silently but her eyes were now fixed on the dainty palm covering them. "Aw, I'm sorry. It's a funny title, that's all." What could he do to make up for being an ass? "Hey," he tried for her chin. "Let's give it a read together. I'm very curious now. Please?" He pouted when she finally looked up at him. Most of her cherry red blush had calmed back down.

"Well, I um, I actually already read this last week." Uh-oh, her cheeks were pinking again.

"And, what did it say?"

She took a deep breath but the look on her face told him he may as well be asking her to torture and eat kitties. He tried a new tactic. "Come on baby, you're making me feel like a huge perv here. Do you have any idea how often I've masturbated in the past year? Probably triple the amount of all you Glazmo readers combined."

That got a brief smile to tug at the corner of her kissable mouth. "Oh all right. Well it basically just states that the endorphins released from masturbating help relax the mind and body. Their aim in this issue is getting people to try natural sleep aids with all the recent celebrity overdoses."

He nodded his head in what she would see as agreement but it was really more from personal experience. "So...do you think I ought to give it a go?"

Something was coming out of her mouth that was going to drive him crazy, he could tell by the sudden intensity in her eyes and the tilted downward angle of her forehead. "I tried it the other night and I fell right to sleep." Short, sweet and to the intoxicating point of the sinfully rapturous ledge he was teetering on where she was concerned.

Next came his what the fuck moment. Had he heard her right? Holy shit. He nearly passed out from her admission once it caught up to him what she'd admitted. "Lily? Are, are you okay? Really? That...that's...hot. Are you by chance having a hard time getting to sleep tonight or um, have you been body snatched by a sex-talking alien?"

She chuckled. "Nope. You didn't give me much choice and maybe that lesson of yours is paying off. I can't believe I just said that either." She finally blew out that breath she'd taken a minute ago.

A sudden fear of this conversation making its way through the house's air vents and to her big sister's ears silenced him. But only for a second. Fuck that. This was their time alone and he was going to enjoy it. "I would have liked to have been there for that." A long pause. "Could I interest you in giving it a try now? Please?" he asked soft and serious, confident for the most part she wouldn't haul off and slap him but would most likely say no. It was worth a try. "Safe and under the covers, unless you prefer otherwise," he added.

"Okay. Um, covers sound good, and necessary."

Whoa, she was actually gonna do it, with him there. "Understood." He smiled like a curious devil on his best behavior.

Without much ado, she dipped her hands down into her pajama pants.

* * * *

Cold air licked her stomach like a giant shiver bug as the bottom of her t-shirt inched up. "Hey, what are you doing?" The blanket covering them lay on top of his head, flattening his hair.

"Can't I at least see a little belly? Just up to your button? Please?"

"Okay." He was being very well-behaved which explained why she only felt halfway sick to her stomach doing this with him. Of course that could all change when he saw her flab.

He relaxed back down into the center of the pallet, crossing their imaginary dividing line, watching on the fringe.

Whatever kind of sex voodoo powers this man had, she needed to extract them and start taking daily doses. No wonder he was the leader of the band. He couldn't turn that raw, magnetism off. Closing her eyes and remembering the sensation of his powerful yet tender lips beneath her earlobe, she climaxed, tensing and then relaxing her hips back onto the ground. Sheepishly, she looked over to him.

It was a look she would cherish for all time. His

jaw had gone slack. He swallowed.

"My turn?" he asked.

Her body on fire, she nodded.

"You wanna watch?" he asked.

"Yes."

"You wanna help?"

Trembling, she reached out her hand which he took and showered with kisses. He then placed it on his perfectly beautiful muscled abs.

"You stay put right there," he said directly to her lucky hand. One corner of his mouth quirked up into a decidedly ornery grin and then his eyes caught hers with a spark of warning. "I can't let you go down there, not tonight, but I'll be imagining it's your hand."

* * * *

Lily looked so peaceful, and sexy, sleeping there on her bedroom floor. He heard a knock at the door and wondered who it would be so late. At least he knew Trissy was stuck in her bed.

The door opened and in stepped Trissy. *Fuck. I should have known.* He tried to erase all images of his and Lily's play earlier so his best friend of all these years wouldn't decode the lust on his face.

She started to speak but he put his fingers to his lips to shush her. The peaks of her eyebrows pulled together like a testy vulture as she poked her head in further and snuck a look around the door.

He held his hands up when she glared at him. And then mouthed, "I haven't touched her, much." He'd had to hold Lily's head still in order to get at that spot behind her ear. But technically they'd each kept their hands, albeit intimately, to themselves tonight before Lily had zonked out.

Trissy mouthed back, "Why are you in here when there's a perfectly fine spot on the couch?"

Well, it was a good fucking question anyway. She'd never believe his answer.

"It's hard to explain." No it wasn't. And why should he have to? He hadn't had a drink in two years. Hadn't fucked around with casual sex in half that time. Which was a long ass time. And fuck-him-good, he was ten years older than Trissy, thirteen older than Lily. He understood Trissy's concerns, but hadn't he proved anything by swallowing his pride and showing his face here at her home? Was this new and improved version of himself ever gonna start convincing people? "I'm sorry, Trissy. But I can't sleep out there," he gestured dramatically toward her living room.

She mimicked his flapping hands. "What's wrong with my living room?"

"Nothing. It's perfect." He dry-washed his face with his hot hands. "Hey, shouldn't you be off your feet, in your bed?" He got up to walk Trissy down the hall, back to her room. Carefully he held the door so it didn't slam shut and wake Lily. Trissy refused to budge any further.

"Jaxon, I'm not gonna lie and say I'm thrilled about you two…hooking up. Okay, you know that pisses me off, but whatever—"

"But Trissy, can I just ask why?"

"Do you really have to?"

"Look, you think I don't question myself every fucking day? I do."

"I'm not saying you aren't trying."

"For the record, so far I've done pretty freaking amazingly good. Don't you think I would have stayed in Cali if I didn't trust myself?"

"Jaxon, oh never mind."

"No, say it."

"What if it's not you? What if…"

"Spit it out, Trissy."

"What if it doesn't matter how much you try? How much you change? You weren't a bad guy when our shit happened." She hissed the word shit and shifted, grinding her heels up and down and rubbing her arms in torrents. "What if it's not you, Jax? What if it's your world? Huh? Your fruity karma you're always complaining about?"

His head bobbed under the truth of the very question he'd had to ignore because it always pulled him down into depression. He didn't have an answer to that yet but had been trying to convince himself if he changed, his karma would have no choice but to play nice.

She was right to a degree, but also dead wrong.

"Trissy, two years ago I was a selfish prick, not some good guy suffering because of his seedy world. Okay? That's what led us to all that crap we went through. I'm not that guy now. That's the difference and the one thing I cling to every time I go anywhere near your sister."

Trissy's belly jerked, marking her face with pain and she nearly fell against her door. "I should get back in bed, Jax. I don't know how to feel about all this. I love her. I just got her back. After all this time," she said, rubbing her side and then finally opening the door a crack.

"I understand. And for the record, I haven't *hooked up* with your little sis." He wanted to make note that her baby sister was grown and in her thirties. But he noticed deep flinching gouging the outline of her mouth so he let it be.

Trissy's head rolled back in a deep stretch, extending her throat muscles. God she'd had a hard life.

He wondered what Lily's had been like, hoping for better and safer.

"She was sleeping good when I poked in just now?"

"Yeah, for about an hour already."

She blew out. "Jaxon, be careful." Her eyes weren't shiny with moon glow. That was pure fear. "You might not want to break her heart. Look, I love you like a brother. But we both know what your world is like. It's why I ended up all the way out here. So promise me, now."

"I promise, Trissy."

With that, she let him walk her the rest of the way to her room. And then he made his way back to the girl he'd either end up leaving behind or stealing away. It was too late to avoid those outcomes. One of them was bound to happen by the time this visit was up.

Jaxon crawled under the covers because it was so cold. He hesitated and then whispered to Lily's sleeping face, "I'm so afraid I'm going to hurt you."

It wouldn't be physically. He could control his naughtier desires, even if banging his flesh into Lily's dominated his thoughts.

No, he thought and shook his head. That's the only way I know.

Again he whispered to sleeping Lily, "I'll break your heart."

"What, why?"

Shit. He hadn't expected her soft, sleepy reply.

"Nothing, go back to sleep." He started to sneak out from her covers.

Her hand found his arm and held him there. "You're worried you're gonna hurt me?"

Since they were sleep talking, and she would never stop talking until he was honest with her, he said, "Yeah, something like that."

"So you're concerned about my heart being broken; you don't want that to happen to me," she said without having opened her eyes yet.

He fumbled for her hand and gave it a squeeze.

Lily intertwined her fingers with his. "Only a good man would care about me like that."

She kissed his fingers laced tightly with hers.

She thinks I'm a good man. I fucking want to be.

"We shouldn't be doing this. You and Trissy just barely made it back to each other. I owe her more than I'll ever be able to pay back in this life."

"You love her, don't you?"

"She was my best friend. Ran my life better than I ever could. And I shit on all that, Lily. She should still hate me."

"But she doesn't."

"I know."

"And neither do I."

He wanted to tell her how much that made his frustrated heart swell with pride that he'd gotten better and she'd seen it and appreciated it. But he didn't. "You're a good girl, Lily."

He said it as he held her fingertips, leaned down, and kissed them, then placed them alone back at her side. He rose up and left their makeshift quilted bed on the floor to take up in the chair.

* * * *

Wow, if she didn't know any better, she'd have sworn she'd just seen him try to cover something up. It was looks like that which made her heart take tiny little plunges off the deep end where he was concerned.

She stretched and sat up no matter how much he protested she get back to sleep.

"I get it that she's my big protective sister. But it's really kind of odd that she's so insistent we don't hang out." It wasn't like anyone had planned for her and Jaxon to be the two odd people out. Tris had Lucky and Benny was so good with kids, he pretty much had grown an extra limb named Maryella. "What gives? I mean, she's so happy to have you here, just nowhere near me."

He just shrugged. Guy talk for *he didn't want to talk about it*. Fine. If no one was going to put on their big people panties and give her a good reason for staying away, she wasn't going to worry about it. The boldness of her thoughts made a touch of pride swell in her chest.

    * * * *

"So tell me more about how you and my sister are so close."

Oh man. He really wished she'd roll over and get some more sleepies.

"Well that didn't take long," he said.

"She talks about you, you know. You and the band. And Benny. And Maryella. All. The. Time."

He nodded, liking what he heard but still not sure exactly what Lily was asking as far as his and Trissy's closeness. "You remind me of her. And she was too good for me."

"Jaxon, stop saying that. You've got to stop selling yourself short."

"No, Lily, it's true. I fucked her up and the only reason she's still living and breathing is because she left. Those reasons of hers that you're not so sure about? They're goodies. You should stay away from me." In theory. Not like he planned on letting that happen.

"Well, I don't get it. And I'm not Tris. I'm me."

"You're you. Lovely little Lily. I could destroy you too," he whispered.

"Or maybe you could give me a chance to show you just how strong I am. I've made it through a lot, you know."

Yeah, he was afraid he did know.

SIN'S FLOWER

Chapter Nineteen

"Daddy, can we please go to the drive-thru movies? Please?" Maryellie pleaded on her tippy toes.

Fu...dge. He was going to have to say no to his baby girl. No way in hell were they going to a drive-in mother fudging movie. Especially not out there in the middle of nowhere. Been there, done that. Hells no.

"Sweetums, not tonight." He looked to the couch, where Trissy was laid out on her back, for some help.

"Oh yeah, you know...you know what kiddo?" she started, sounding all out of whack and full of baby.

"What Auntie Trissy?"

"Well, Uncle Lucky and I are going to finish fixing up the baby's room tonight and we could really use your help decorating."

Thank you, Trissy. For a second he was worried she wouldn't have understood his aversion to driving his daughter to the middle of nowhere and then hanging out like a sitting duck.

"Auntie Trissy, you're not sposed to be standing up doing so much stuff." She folded her arms across her chest and made a very serious face.

"Exactly, that's why I need you to stay here and help Uncle Lucky. That way I can be in the room with you guys but sitting down."

"But I'm short. What about Uncle Benny?"

"Yes, Uncle Benny can stay and help too if he'd like."

Jaxon didn't have to press Benny with a stare. He simply pivoted toward him and saw that his webmaster had waved, already agreeing to stay in.

Good, looks like I avoided that mess.

197

Just then, Lily came walking in from the nearby kitchen. "So did I hear the word drive-in? I love the drive-in movies. What's playing? Are we going?"

"No," Jaxon said along with Lucky, Benny and Trissy in unison.

"Ohhhh-kay. Well I'd still like to go. And I think I remember reading something about a special Christmas time showing of the Wizard of Oz. Is it going to be crazy cold, Tris? Are we talking long johns and flannels and sweats and blankets?" Lily asked, obvious excitement making her eyes pop like pretty blue saucers.

If he'd felt anything like himself at that moment, and hadn't been standing in a living room full of people he was trying not to offend, he would have offered to keep her warm. But this drive-in movie thing was the last thing he wanted to do.

"We're not going, Lily."

Jaxon hated driving to most places. But the thought of Lily in his bucket seats, adding her smells to his, and the popcorn's, and the heated air—those were some good fricking, mouth-watering thoughts. But the other thought of being out in the field with her made him nearly puke on Trissy's faux bear skin rug. Too close to his horror show night with her.

"Sorry. No drive-in movies for you, sweetums, or you, Auntie Lily." He gave his little baby girl a stern daddy look, but no matter how much he wanted to deny it, being near Lily in a confined space was something he craved. In the end, Maryellie was just as happy to stay home and help make up the nursery. But Lily on the other hand, she looked about like he felt. Like they needed to get out…somewhere, anywhere.

"Well, I'm going," she said then turned to snatch some keys from the wall-hanger. She left through the side door in the direction of the driveway.

What the hell was that?

Lucky walked up to him and angled his shoulders to keep the conversation between just the two of them. "I'll take good care of the girls here. I suggest you go catch up to the one who just left."

* * * *

"Jaxon, you've spent most of the night tense and preoccupied." How could she have been so deluded about this? Obviously he'd needed to get away from the house but wished to have done it alone. So why had he followed her out to her car?

"I told you I didn't want to go," he half hissed.

"What's the big deal? If you don't want to go with me, just say it."

"I have, Lily. Several times. But here I am."

As soon as he said it, he looked away. But Jaxon refused to give her any more details which left her with all the more doubts.

"You know what? You're right. You did. You don't have to explain anything else. I guess I don't really want to hear it anyway." *I'm such an idiot. To think Jaxon James would actually want to be stuck in a car at a stupid drive in movie theater with me.*

He grabbed her arm. "Lily, we can watch any movie you want, but let's do it here."

Wow. He really didn't want to do this with her. And here she'd imagined it was going to be the perfect escape.

"It's a special once a year showing that I really want to go to." With that, she became determined to make it to her car before she started crying.

She'd nearly made it when she felt a pair of tight arms squeezing around her. She wiggled free and without thinking, made her way past Jaxon and into the driver seat. She fumbled for her keys, not sure of what was going on but feeling incredibly foolish. She had to get out of there.

Her door came open with a gust of cold December air. "Lily, get out of the car."

"No thanks."

"Lily, please, get out of the car."

As crappy as she felt right now, she longed even more for the escape of this special Christmas showing of her momma's favorite movie. She tried to take her door back but he was even stronger than he looked. "Jaxon, you're not making any sense. Just let me go. You're scaring me."

That seemed to stop him cold. He shook his head and when he finally stopped doing that, she could see how tight his jaw was clenched. "Scoot over."

Was he crazy?

"Scoot. Over. Please. It's cold out here. Let me sit down."

It was getting late and she didn't want to miss this showing but once again, Jaxon's sincerity bled through his arrogance and she found herself crawling over the gear shift to get to the passenger side seat.

He sat down with a thud that bounced her rickety old Jetta and then closed the door. Hopefully Lucky had fixed the oil leak from last week. She had a feeling if they actually got somewhere and then broke down, Jaxon might not know what to do with himself.

"Lily, I get it that you want people to just, you know, be able to spit out what's what, whenever you need to hear it. You deserve that."

"But…"

"Yeah, there's a but there. A big one. Listen, I'd really like to spend tonight with you. You know, just the two of us. But…"

"But not at the drive in."

"Right."

"You know that makes no sense to me." Maybe it just wasn't his thing and she should take her own advice and be honest with why she was so insistent on going. "Jaxon, the same way you not wanting to go makes no sense to me, I understand maybe the reason I want to go so badly makes no sense to you. It's just that going to the drive-in used to be my family's thing. We'd go once a month. Have to drive about an hour to get there but Momma and Daddy would sit in the front seat and me, Tris and Jack would all be smashed in the back." His handsome face was marred with a scowl. It startled her into temporarily stopping until he rested a hand on her knee.

"Keep going, please."

"I probably only saw a handful of scenes from who knows how many shows but those nights are some of my best memories. I know it sounds dumb, but I miss that."

"Not dumb. And I like hearing about happy times you and Trissy had."

That said a lot. Tris must not have shared many of those memories with him. Lily understood why. It still hurt to think of her father as a monster when he'd been plain old daddy to her.

She hated him for what he'd done.

It was a giant jumble of twisted up evil and why she couldn't accept dishonesty.

"Jaxon, this was my momma's favorite movie. It would mean a lot if you went to see it with me. But if you won't go, please don't try to keep me from going."

She would give him a couple minutes to turn the ignition and ask her for directions or kindly get out so she could slide back into the driver seat and be on her way.

* * * *

There were very few people he'd go out of his way to make happy, and because of his bananas karma, the one who had quickly risen to the top of that list was currently sitting so close he could hear the impatience in her drumming breaths. He already regretted this. "I'm horrible with directions. You're gonna have to guide me. You for sure know exactly where we're going? How to get there and get back? In the dark?" It was a hot mess of questions he'd just bombed her with but he did it for good reason.

The soft smile threatening to break across her entire face egged him out of the driveway. "Lily? Right or left?"

"Right," she said showing him with her irresistible hands. "And thank you."

He just nodded and followed her cues all the way to the theater. He didn't pull a smile, not once the whole way. That would have constituted a lie, and Lily was hell bent on finding out the truth.

Thirty minutes later, deep into the country of Tennessee, he pulled up to a red and white box office that looked straight out of the Americana past. They made their way to the spaces separated with waist-high, old metal posts stuck in the ground and hanging car speakers. He wished for a place and time when he could have brought Maryellie.

Lily's eyes hadn't dulled since they'd first pulled out of Trissy's drive and he imagined his daughter's would have done the same.

Jaxon tuned her car radio to the right theater station for the movie. Sam Cooke crooned on the oldies station which Jaxon had to admit, gave him some comfort. It made him feel a little better that this place appeared to have been upgraded from the drive-ins of old. It felt less like some forgotten, antique, hole in the wall joint and more like a modern establishment that might get cell phone service in case of an emergency.

He checked his phone's bars. Two should be good enough but he'd have felt much better with a full five.

Fuck. Me. Out of all the places Lily could have begged him to take her, it had to be to a place like this. *Karma. His. Fucking bananas.*

Well, he guessed the only thing left to do was to make the best of it. And keep her safe. The parts of her poking out from behind that chainmail of a tracky suit she was wearing was a good place to focus on.

Fuck, the tension clawing up his neck was killing him right now.

* * * *

Was Jaxon going to speak to her tonight? She waited about a minute longer which actually felt like forever when sitting in a dead quiet car out in the dark with the rock star best friend of your big sister. Especially one who knew about the darkest parts of your past, maybe even more. But his silence woke her up in that hour-long minute. She chanced a look his way only to find him looking stiff as a bag of bricks. All Lily could think of in that moment was helping him. Making up for bad things that had happened to others while she'd been spared.

The pompadour poof of his hair seemed to grow in size the more he shoved his fingers through it.

* * * *

A burning question sizzled through his fingers. Was Lily safe with him right now? The thought was fucking with his head because he felt like an asshole who couldn't protect the people he cared about. He swallowed as much of the fear burning his throat as he could and tried to look happy to be there with Lily.

He rubbed her fingers, massaging her knuckles.

"I hope the movie starts soon," she said, squeezing his hand.

"Lily, I had a bad experience in a place similar to this. That's what my reaction is about tonight. I just wanted to keep you safe."

"Okay, thank you for letting me know."

A shot of humor was badly needed and happened to be hanging out on his tongue. "Well, it's gonna cost you."

Her eyes bulged. "Do I even want to ask?"

"I think I'd like another private sewing lesson."

* * * *

He could have said all kinds of naughty things and she realized she'd sort of been secretly salivating at the thought of him demanding a roll in the backseat as payment. But yeah, turns out he wasn't quite that shallow. Maybe she should have a little more faith in Jaxon James.

"You're on."

His smile seemed a touch more genuine but his shoulders looked like they could bull doze a steel wall. The movie would start when the sun went all the way down. He'd gotten them there so fast, they had time to kill. She twisted and reached around his back as best she could and got her two hands clamped onto the sides of his neck and started rhythmically squeezing and releasing.

"That feels amazing, Lily. I think this might work better back there though. Better angle."

He gave a tilt of his head to the back seat. Her stomach did a triple salchow, front layout, twist, somersault, back flip.

* * * *

"Just kidding." Actually he wasn't but watching her face turn the colors of Christmas reminded him who he was with. He gathered Lily hadn't hopped into many backseats. "Let's go do a snack bar run. I want candy." Jaxon climbed out of her Jetta, narrowly missing the speaker pole as he went.

"Okay." Her voice was as shaky as his freezing body. Fuck it was cold. His balls weren't too happy at being jerked around by winter weather. He and Lily were snuggling, that was final. He wrapped an arm around her and scanning the car-filled lot, walked her to the snack bar.

Back in the car, Jaxon turned up the volume on "Sleepwalk" by Johnny and Santo. Thank God for the good music. It calmed his nerves. With the last spill of daytime still hanging on, the giant black frame for the movie screen stood out, showing how powdery bluethe sky was just before the sunset. But slowly, it got darker, pushing Jaxon closer to the edge.

Their stash of refreshments sat tucked between them. The load of blankets she'd stretched and piled over the both of them hid her curves and all that poked out was her sweet cupid face. How embarrassing that he was the one shivering. He leaned closer to her, hoping to feel her heat, but got caught up on the steering wheel. Shit, he was pretty sure he'd just squashed her box of chocolate mintys.

"I might have to do another candy run. Sorry."

Who were they kidding? He wouldn't leave her alone.

"It's no big deal. Anyway, look the projector just fired up."

A black and white cartoon that had been colorized lit up the screen as a hot dog danced into an open bun. The neighboring car on his side was gonna be banging by the night's end. And the one parked on Lily's side might be rocking later but that's because mummy and daddy had brought their young brood out. He lost count at five heads. They seemed to be surrounded by families and horny teenagers. Safe.

Jaxon hung his arm against the Jetta's door for a few more seconds, debating chancing a run and letting Lily stay warm in the car. Sweat wetted his pits.

"Jaxon, you look like someone just asked you to decide between life and death. It's okay, I don't mind squashed candy. Still tastes just as good."

What would taste good smashed beneath his weight was her delicious womanly body and the neck he'd already sampled. Just looking at her bright pink lips and taffy colored hair made his mouth water with indecision.

"You'll miss the beginning if you leave now."

Those puppy eyes overruled his ass back down all the way into the seat. "Okay, staying put." He manually pushed down his lock and then reached over and did the same to hers. The back doors' locks were secure.

"You okay?" she asked. Iron from the drive-in speaker pole to their rear clanked loudly as someone backed into it.

He jumped.

"Yeah, never better." But he could feel sweat edging his hairline. He dug out the box of soft mints he'd mashed and shook a couple pieces into his hand.

＊ ＊ ＊ ＊

"Jaxon? Are you feverish?"

"Nah, I'm fine. Here you go."

He handed her candy and then pushed their tray of onion rings onto the dash before nearly mashing those too. They fogged up the window and he cursed under his breath. Damn it was probably pretty tame for him. "Thanks." She tried to sound cheery.

He just nodded and with a hand clamped down on his lap, sat staring out the window. First his, then the back, then her side. What was up with him? Was he high? Drunk? Fighting the funk? Oh no, it was whatever bad experience he'd said he had in a place like this.

The sky darkened minutes later. She glanced his way, wanting to at least mouth another thank you, but with him so focused on looking out his window, all she could see was the back of his head. The razored, dark blond hair called to her hand. Except for the longer pieces on top, it was cut short like the boys she saw coming and going from the marine recruiting office near the diner. Proud handsome young men. If Jaxon's hands weren't wrapped around the steering wheel so tight he looked like he could pop the thing off with the tiniest flick of his wrist, she would have considered rubbing her hand up the back of his head, feeling the prickle of the skin-tight buzz cut and then up to the sandy blond top where it was long enough to twirl. A move like that would have let him know she was dying for his kiss on her lips and his hands on her body. But then his head snapped to her as he searched her side of the outdoor theater.

She didn't want to call attention to what was bothering him anymore. Plus, she was quickly becoming entranced by the giant Technicolor visions of The Wizard of Oz. No, she wouldn't pester Jaxon. Even though he looked like a man on his third consecutive shift of guard duty and it worried her. Instead, she settled back into her half of the front seat and tucked a quilt she'd stowed in the trunk under her arms.

The unclaimed bag of Reese's Pieces smelled like a scrumptious sugar-high sandwiched between her cherry Twizzlers and Jaxon's untouched onion rings. Should she offer Jaxon a piece of licorice? Just as she pulled one of the long red candy straws out to hand to him, he jerked his head away from her, back to the darkness outside his half of the truck, and then back to her.

"Open up, baby," he said, offering her another mint.

She did. He bit a small piece from the morsel first and placed the rest on her tongue. Lily watched the movie. Jaxon watched her.

Chapter Twenty

"Hey Tris, I'm home," she called over lightly to the lump on the couch that was her preggers sister. She rolled over knocking the TV remote to the ground. Lily fetched it.

"Hey," she yawned. "How was the movie?"

"Good. Perfect. Thought about Momma the whole time. I wish you could have been there." They both eyeballed her stomach and shrugged. "But this little one is already too eager to come out into the world," Lily cooed to Tris's swollen belly.

"So did Jaxon get any better once you were there?"

"Yeah, about that. He really has something against drive-in theaters. But we had an okay time." She stopped right there, at the safe point, keeping the rest of her feelings for Jaxon secret for now.

"Well I'm glad you got to go. It's a great little place. I was hesitant at first, just like Jaxon, but Lucky's been going there his whole life with Luke and Bear. We go almost every weekend when it's in season. We love it. Plus it's kind of an inside joke."

"What? Really? Oh come on, you have to tell me now." She crossed her heart and sat down on the floor right next to the couch. "Promise I won't tell Lucky."

"Okay, well when I first met Lucky, it was because Jaxon had asked me to let him tag along on my way back to California from Tennessee. So we were at this gas station and you know, he was kissing me while the gas was pumping."

"Wait a second, so you were giving him quite the ride home, it sounds like. Geez, Tris. You hussy!"

"You know it, now shush. So an elderly couple pulled in behind us and I got all shy."

"Yeah right."

"No, I really did. Then Lucky took over the pumping…" Lily tried not to bust out laughing at the unintended pumping pun to her sister's sinful tale.

"Shut up, oh forget it," Tris said, irritation grating her words.

"No please, please tell me the rest." Lily zipped her lips with her finger.

"Well, he finished pumping our gas and gave me some money to go inside and get snacks. But as I was walking away he mumbled something about my jeep being a sin wagon."

"Aww, just like Danny and Sandy in Grease."

"Exactly. And then I kind of told him I'd show him a sin wagon. The R rated version of Danny and Sandy of course."

"Oh God, I love it, Tris. That is so cool. You guys make me smile."

"Hey, it'll happen for you someday too. Don't be in a hurry. You're only thirty-one years old, Lily. Okay? And Tom was just a bump in the road. Any word on those final papers yet?"

Lily shook her head no and then jumped when Benny wandered past and on into the kitchen.

He nodded at them, tilting his head back up but his eyes and nose were masked by his long shaggy bangs. "Hey Benny, need help?" Lily asked.

"Uh. No. Water."

Aww, he was out for a little sleepwalking drink. They waited for him to pass back by to his couch. "Night night Benny," Tris said as he scooted his long lanky legs past them and then collapsed.

"He's a real sweetie." Tris winked at her.

"Is there something in your eye, Tris?"

"No, nice try. You know, Benny is a great guy. Sweet, tall, dark hair, cool funky style. Good manners. Hard working. Great with kids. Music trivia genius. There's not an 80's song he doesn't know every word to and that includes all the glam rock."

"Whoa, whoa, whoa. Whoa," Lily sputtered out.

"Those are all true statements. Thanks for pointing all that out." She gave her sister a meaningful stare.

"I think he likes you."

"No you don't and no he doesn't. Not like that. You and I both know he's lovesick over that Kirby singer girl."

"Erby."

"Right. And I've only known him for a month. What's her deal?"

"She's a rock star." They had a good laugh at that term. "They suck!" Tris snorted out.

"You said it, not me."

"Shh, you're cackling and you're gonna make me pee and give birth."

Lily stilled and stopped to make sure Tris was just joking. "You okay?"

She nodded. "So about that. I've been meaning to tell you there's a women's clinic not too far from us where you can get your annual exam, pap, birth control..."

"Thanks. I know I've been lazy about getting set up with a new doctor. I think I'm gonna be here for a while so it's probably a good idea." Lily smiled because Tris's face was smothered by a goofy grin.

"You're *really* staying? For good? I mean I was definitely hoping for that with the shop and I swear I'll be back on my feet and helping with that at some point..." Now she was doing that frowny but happy weird smile.

"Well, I really like Bugscuffle. And seriously, being around you and Lucky is healing. And yes, I love that we run a shop together. Even though I'm pulling all the weight right now, you slacker," Lily said teasingly.

"Come here." They hugged. "That makes me so happy."

"Me too."

"Remind me in the morning and we'll get out the clinic phone number, since you're staying."

"Okay. You've got great timing. My Pill prescription is only good for three more months. Hopefully I can get in before it expires."

"Oh, okay. So you are actively taking it?"

"Yes," Lily said, drawing out the short word. "Why do you sound so shocked?"

"I'm not, I mean....you haven't said much about boyfriends. That's all."

What did she say here? The only thing she was ever comfortable with was the truth but Lily had never been in this situation before. Rather than add to whatever Tris's issue was over her and Jaxon becoming close, Lily divulged the ultimate reason for why she'd decided not to come off the Pill when her marriage had ended. "That jerk ex-husband of mine in Oklahoma taught me to always be prepared."

She wouldn't lie about it but wasn't ready to share that a disgusting picture had shown up in their dress shop mail box the other day. She didn't want her sister thinking she was a trouble magnet. There hadn't been any more contact so hopefully the still photo from the video was a one time, last ditched, parting shot at how she'd broken things off with Tom.

"Okay. So, are there any other boys you'd like to talk about? Lucky's got a really good friend who doesn't live too far away. I could totally set you and Paul up."

Tris twisted her mouth, looking like she would enjoy some sisterly guy chat and for Lily to start drooling over the prospects of this Paul guy.

Too bad there was only one man controlling her salivary glands at the moment. Maybe she could dish just a little with Tris. After everything else they'd shared…and this was even happy stuff. Not sad and depressing.

"So I've been spending some time with Jaxon the past week..."

"Oh geez, Lily. Really hun?"

"See, I knew I wasn't imagining you getting all grumpy whenever we were all in the same room. I don't understand what that's all about. You do realize that right?"

Tris did not want to respond. Not with those twisted lips and disappointed eyes. But why?

"Tris, you know I went to California because it was obvious you needed your best friend back. Right? I mean you seemed so happy when he first got here."

"Yes, Lily. By the way, thanks for not believing in that bush everyone else in the world likes to beat around. Not my little sis. Crap. Of all the things we've talked about, I don't know if I'm prepared to have this one conversation with you. Or anyone for that matter."

Well what a way to scare the crap out of a girl. What in the world was Tris so afraid of and what did it have to do with Jaxon?

What should she do? Did her sister need to get this off her chest? If it was something bad about Jaxon, Lily should probably hear it, considering how blinded she'd been over Tom. But being that blatantly honest just now had affected Tris differently than any of their other honest talks. Lily decided not to press.

"Tris, maybe we can save this one for another time."

Tris nodded but added, "I'm sorry, Lily. I just feel so protective of you. I want you to find someone who is going to light up your life and make everything good."

Funny how she knew her sister was making a case against Jaxon but those were the exact ways he'd made Lily feel that week.

"I understand." She'd wanted to ask for some mutual trust but stopped short and instead tucked Tris's warnings about getting involved with Jaxon into her heart's back pocket.

Hey, there was one safe guy who Lily knew she could honestly gush over. "How freaking hot is Stefan Calderon?" she asked Tris with a poke.

Streamers may have well shot from cannons. "Oh lordy. You have serious issues, child. Stefan Calderon is a handful of hot-mess."

"I know! That's why I have his face on my pillow. Tell me more about him, please?" she pleaded.

Tris went on to lavish many details about the sexy lead singer of Sin Pointe onto her and she soaked up every bit. But in the back of her head all she could think about was Jaxon and him never seeing the still photos Tom had sent of them in bed. Oh yeah, and what in the world Jaxon had with Tris that was more unspeakable than her sister's childhood abuse.

Chapter Twenty-One

It was two days before Christmas and she'd vowed to spend as much time as was needed knocking out candy cane doggy sweaters and the remaining mommy and me holiday muumuu dresses due to customers that afternoon. She'd be doing some home delivery when all was said and done at the shop. Good thing she had a helper.

Jaxon greeted a customer who wandered in. They spoke a few pleasantries and Jaxon brought the elderly lady up front with a dashing stride that made her proud. "Ma'am, this is Lily, she'll be able to point us in the right direction."

"Oh, thank you, young man. Yes, Lily, I have a great granddaughter who was born a preemie and still doesn't fit any of the stuff at the department stores. Might you have something tucked away here dear?"

"Oh wow, well first off, congratulations. Um, about how much does she weigh?"

The elderly lady dressed in a burgundy wool coat and swathed in what looked to be several neck scarves held up her hands to show Lily how long the baby was. "I think she's just barely seven pounds as of yesterday. Which doesn't sound like much but when you consider she was only three pounds at birth."

"She sounds like a downright miracle to me," Jaxon chimed in which brought an undeniable rosy pride to their customer's wrinkly cheeks.

That was tiny. Lily didn't think she had any preemie sized items left. She shared a quick look with Jaxon who stood holding the lady's umbrella. Something about seeing him like that washed away the worries that had been bugging her ever since Tris's warnings the night before. While Lily went to the back to search for something small and special, she overheard a sweet comment made by Jaxon's customer.

"Young man, thank you for being such a good helper. But I do have to say you should probably ask for some time off to go home and rest. Poor dear, those circles under your eyes."

All Lily heard in return was, "Yes, ma'am, I will do that. Thank you for supporting this shop. It means a lot to the girls who run it."

Lily returned as warmed as a pie sitting under a heating lamp but unfortunately without anything small enough. "Ma'am?" she prompted.

"Oh dear, please call me Elaine."

"Mrs. Elaine, I don't seem to have anything but if you don't need it right now, I'd love to make something up for your little grandbaby today and then deliver it tonight. Would that be okay? I feel so honored that you came looking here."

Elaine's crinkled, hunched fingers clasped over her heart. "If that's possible, I would love it."

Lily wrote up an order with Elaine's color and pattern choices and then accepted a sweet kiss on the cheek. Jaxon walked Elaine all the way to her car. When he returned, if she hadn't already believed he was an actual knight in shining armor, his words tipped the scale.

"You know, I can handle doing more than just greeting customers. Make me up a list of what all needs to be done so that you can concentrate on creating. I'm serious, mopping, dusting, folding—I'll take care of everything. That was very sweet what you did for Elaine." He leaned down and pushed her hair out of the way so he could give her a quick kiss. Yes, most chivalrous gentlemen would have gone for the hand or cheek, but this was her Jaxon. And he was allowed to go for the neck whenever he wanted. "And consider me your delivery driver too."

He was like the rebel without a cause of Bugscuffle, with his ripped jeans and torso hugging black shirt that only covered him down to the middle of his forearms. She'd stolen him just as he'd stepped out of the shower and knew his blond hair was still dark and wet under the wool hat he wore to hide it. She'd never seen a more dashing man.

"Yes, sir," she smiled, giggling at how his stubble tickled her neck again. "I'd better get to work."

"Yep, you'd better do that," said her sexy helper. "Don't forget my list."

"Two down, two to go." She held up a medium-sized pooch outfit.

Jaxon walked his sexy strut, trying to distract her, she was sure, and sat on a stool nearby her work station, sorting fabric scraps by color.
"This is a lot of hard work you've put in here."

"Not just me, Tris too. In fact, that whole wall of shelving over there," she pointed, "that's all made by her hand."

"Hmm. So what do you prefer? Hand stitching or sewing machine?"

"Oh, ask me how many times I've sewn my thumb into a seam."

"Really?"

"Yeah, I really dig the simple, monotonous in and out of a good old fashioned hand stich."

He watched her hands as she continued the needle work with the red and white yarn. She repaid the notion and caught herself staring at how strong his fingers looked just sitting there holding a piece of fabric.

"I'm sure you know a thing or two about sore fingers. I've heard it's a special kind of pain playing guitar all the time."

"Nah, you build up callous and get used to it," he shared in a humble tone.

What a moment for them. It felt like any old regular day between two completely normal people. Good and boring, sometimes those were perfectly fine days to have.

"Hey helper, can you do me a favor and grab the hand lotion out of my bag over there? The green tote. Thank you," she asked nicely.

Although her hands had lost their moisture to the constant handling of the yarn, she really just wanted to watch his tight butt while he walked away from her in those ripped jeans. They'd been at the shop for four hours now and her mouth watered with each step he took. On his way back, she noticed he had more than just her lotion in hand.

"Lily, sorry for prying, but what's this about, baby?"

Oh no.

"Please give me that."

She got up from her station and held out her hand. It wasn't shaking yet but she could feel her blood turning jumpy and it was just a matter of time. She'd forgotten about hiding that stupid picture from Tom in her bag so that no one at home would find it. And now Jaxon had seen it and she felt humiliated.

"Sure, here." He made no games about handing it over to which she was thankful. "But can we talk about it? Why you're carrying it around?"

There went her perfectly boring day.

"This is going to be short and to the point, Jaxon. And then I have to get back to work."

"Sure, no problem. I understand."

"My ex-husband is very unhappy that our divorce has finally gone through and this is just part of his campaign to let me know. If you've wondered why I'm like a hawk at the mailbox first thing every day, that's why. Now I'm not just waiting for the final judgment papers to show up but also anymore of his special packages. This one came yesterday."

"Shit Lily. That came to your house?"

"No, just here."

"So he knows where you work?"

She nodded.

"You seem pretty calm about that. Why haven't you said anything, baby? This is harassment."

"Ouch," she squawked after stabbing herself with the thick needle. "It's Christmas, Jaxon. My first Christmas here with my family."

"And you don't want to ruin it."

"I guess we both know a little something about that," she said. "I should rip that up right now."

He walked back over to meet her at her station. "As much as I hate to say it, you might want to hold onto it as proof."

All she could do in answer to that suggestion was shake her head side to side.

"Hey, how about this—if any more of these show up, will you promise to give them to me? I'll take care of it."

Oh, thank God for that offer. She had no idea what she was going to do if it was more than just this one. But did she really want Jaxon seeing her like that? Naked and posed so obscenely over her ex-husband?

"Promise me you won't look at it anymore. Please swear it, Jaxon."

"I promise." He touched her hair gently. "But did the picture show up alone?"

"You're wondering if he sent a note."

"Yes, that's what I'm concerned about," Jaxon said chewing the inside of his cheek.

"Nope, just the disgusting picture."

"Okay. If you receive anymore, I'll just hold onto them for you. They'll stay hidden in my luggage. And if it becomes anything more than a guy milking his wounded pride, I'll help you figure out what to do next. Okay, baby?"

"I didn't know how much I needed you to take this from me, Jaxon."

"Well, I'm just glad you were so desperate to see me swish my ass that you sent me over to fetch your lotion."

"How do you do that? Make everything melt away just with a smile and a sexy strut?"

"I'm a fucking rock star, baby." He winked. "It's just my nature."

She hadn't thought of him as the leader of Sin Pointe in quite some time. Not since he'd become very real to her and very close. If she could keep him, Maryella and Benny, she would. Her network of yarn had become tangled so she worked out the kinks and started in again on doggy sweater number three.

* * * *

"Not very many of you rock stars walking around Bugscuffle. Maryella seems to like it here."

"Maryellie loves it here. But don't do that. That's not fair. I have to go back." *Lily. Lovely little Lily. I wish I could stay for you baby. Fuck this hurt more than he'd guessed it would.*

"That's not what I meant, I mean, I was just being stupid and talking you know. I guess just the whole picture thing had me out of my head a little. I'd never ask you to do anything like that. Um...yeah, sorry for the ridiculous suggestion."

He shook his head, knowing he was in deep with her, and had sent her into a non-sensical rant. "Lily, why do you do that?"

"Do what?"

"You told me I sell myself short, but you're the woman who took a bus out to find me and bring me here. You have every right to ask me what my plans are. Don't sell yourself short." What exactly was he saying though? That he'd leave California if she asked him to? The fantasy where he stole her away to his seaside villa had crumbled when he'd seen first-hand the connection she so desperately was rebuilding with Trissy.

"That whole crazy trip was for Tris. That was important. She and Maryella needed you here for Christmas."

He didn't want to interrupt her knitting rhythm but her tender cheek called out to his hand. Stroking her gently, he couldn't stop wondering what it was that she wanted and needed. She'd proven to be the type who never asked anything for herself but moved mountains for others.

But how did he just up and leave Cali and everyone he owed in it?

"Jaxon, how...how did you love, Tris?" she asked him out of left field.

"Too much, not nearly enough." Pause. "But not like that, Lily. Never like that."

"As a sister, then."

"Yes, very much like that."

He waited to see if she'd ask what his feelings were for her, but she didn't.

"You're a brave young woman, Lily. I admire that about you, more than you'll ever
        know."

        "How am I brave? Remember, you're not the scary guy in this situation."

        "You're right. I used to be though."

        "I don't think you've told me exactly how old you are, Jaxon."

        "Okay. Forty-four."

        "Forty-four," she repeated. Maybe she found him too old for her now.

        "I've been wondering if you have a problem with our age difference."

        "Mmm, no. Not at all." She blushed, her fingers working furiously but with a gorgeous rhythm he coveted. "You're…a grown man."

        "Yes, I am." He came closer, sensing her nerves, wanting to ease them as well as explore them. Where were they coming from? "Thank you for noticing. I appreciate that." He took another step toward her. "Lily, am I making it so you can't get your work done? Should I go back to my post over there?"

        She shook her head no, impressing him with her ability to keep on knitting and not have to watch her fingers. It was the first time he'd missed his guitars since he'd been here.

        "You know how sweet you look doing that?" he asked.

        She bit her lip and then edged back away from him, taking her doggy sweater with her. "I know you think I'm too sweet. Sometimes I wish I was grittier, like Tris." She shrugged her shoulders like she'd just come in second and he saw her confidence fade. It would have been one of those instances he should have taken advantage of. To step away. Leave her be. But he couldn't. More than anything, he wanted to be good for her. And somehow, he knew he could be, eventually. *Now, be good for her now.* But what was good and what was bad? He was clean, sober. Hadn't touched liquor in twenty-five months. That was the good part.

The bad?

Maybe the way he'd completely given up on finding Vangie. Shouldn't he be trying to help the mother of his child? Or was it better for Maryellie that he'd given up? Vangie had never listened to him. Not once. Lily would though, like no other he'd been with ever had. She would be so good for him.

"You're a beautiful, sweet woman, Lily. One who *I* want and don't care to share with anyone else." It was a huge admittance to make out loud but it was the truth.

Her mouth swirled into an "oh" and her lips looked like they wanted to ask how he could possibly want that. She paused her handiwork because she'd made a mistake with one of her loops. Fussing over it was only appearing to make it worse.

He'd have to show her. Later when she finished her work. For now he'd be good, walk back to his corner, let her enjoy the view of his retreat.

* * * *

Lily couldn't help it. Not with the private show Jaxon was treating her to with that strut. Crazy that she came to this decision as he walked away.

She trusted him.

She wanted him.

If he turned around, stalked back to her and told her he was going to make love to her there in the dress shop, her simple answer would have been, "Yes."

SIN'S FLOWER

Chapter Twenty-Two

They were finally home from the last delivery and Jaxon wanted Lily. Badly.

He held the front door open and let her step inside first. Ready to relegate himself to the spare couch, his pulse exploded when she reached for his hand and tugged him down the hall toward her room. Man, it had been a long night. Maybe she was so exhausted, she didn't care what anyone in the house would think. But Benny was snoring, so was Maryellie through her open door, and the light was off in the master bedroom.

Oh shit, Lily was in trouble. He would devastate her body if she pulled him any further.

At least as much as she could handle. Which he honestly couldn't guess. The damn image of the picture he'd stashed for her in his luggage pounded at his brain. She looked so sad in it, so dejected. That asshole ex-husband of hers who'd taken it had obviously left her broken. And that didn't even come close to the fears he still had of the things her father may have done to her.

She'd denied it, but he'd heard of repressed memories. Thank God he could at least say he'd been there to work through some of those with Trissy.

His worries over her reaction to that embarrassing photo he now had were lost to the lust he felt as he trailed her to her room. She opened the door. The blanket pallet was still there on the floor. He stepped inside but let her close the door behind them.

When he heard the click of the lock, he knew it meant she was willing to give herself to him. But what if something he asked of Lily triggered blanked out memories in some horrible way? Vangie had told him on numerous occasions that his requests were perverted. He'd thought of them as direct.

Lesson four lingered hesitantly on his tongue as he followed her to the edge of her bed. She sat down and pulled him with her. They would have tumbled onto the small mattress but he held himself up. There was something he had to know first.

"Lily, have you experimented with sex much?" He hated having to ask her so boldly but it was the only way he knew to be sure. Scaring her with something unexpected was not an option.

She paused before answering. "I'm not sure what you're asking, Jaxon." Her face fired up into a cherry red blush. "God, am I that pathetic? I was married, remember?"

"Not pathetic." Scrambling for something to make up for his butchered question, he said, "You're way too beautiful not to have had boyfriends. And there's no way in hell those boys didn't do their best to be with you." He wouldn't bring up her marriage. That bastard wasn't getting any credit, ever. The seduction soaked his mouth and tongue, making him need hers. He could hear it in his words. "So I'd be bananas to think you hadn't had men before. I just wondered what you were open to."

He decided it was time to let her answer and rubbed a small circle around her chin, just so he could be in the zone with her.

"Well, you've seen enough to know I'm no saint. But there was only my ex."

"I really hate that asshole."

She smiled. "Me too."

"Good." His voice sounded incredibly thick. Much like Stefan's when he sang. She had to hear that desperation blasting its way through their quiet space.

"You're nothing like him, Jaxon. You talk to me. You listen. And you seem interested."

Good girl. She had noticed that, then. "I'm very interested in you, baby. Tell me, are you interested in…"

"Yes."

"How do you know what I was going to say?" he asked.

"Well, I'm not as innocent as you think."

At that, he tugged on the bottom of his t-shirt. "It's hot." *It's the dead of winter.* What a horrible lie she would see through in a second. He smiled and hoped she would enjoy his attempt to seduce her. But it was still a surprise when she tried yanking her sweater over her head before he could do much with his own. His heart warmed to see that she wore a flannel top underneath that. It didn't matter if she'd slept with one man or one hundred. She was exactly that inexperienced. "Hey Lily, let me be in charge of that, okay?"

"Oh, okay. Jaxon?"

"Hmm?"

"Your shoulders are…nice."

"Would you like to feel them?"

She nodded and puckered up her lips like she was about to blow him a kiss.

Yes, she had just given him the okay he needed. He couldn't swear on it, but in her own sweet way, he was sure she was trying to say she wanted him too. For the first time ever, he worried about being too forward but still took her hand in his and placed it on his lap and then pulled his shirt up and over his head. He then moved her fingers to his shoulder. His muscles were too big and dwarfed her hand but it didn't tremble as he'd expected. Instead, her palm did its best to hold on.

"Hey, Lily. Look at me." He waited for her eyes to make their way inch by inch up his chest. Her gaze appeared to be stuck on his tattoos. Sensing her curiosity, he moved her one hand to touch his ink. "We can do this. I want to do this. But the same way you need complete honesty, I need complete openness from you. You have to trust me."

"I do." Pause. "I just don't want to disappoint you," she let out.

He took her hand, wrapped it around to his back, and guided her fingers to his waistband. "You would never disappoint me." He kissed her knuckles. "Touch me, Lily."

"I don't know if I can."

"Have you changed your mind?"

"No. But you make my stomach flip around. A lot."

That made him smile. "But you want to be here, doing this with me, now?"

"Yes."

"Okay. Tell me what you want to see next."

"Really?"

"Mm-hmm."

"Okay, um, there is one thing I've been checking out."

"Yeah?"

"Yeah."

He slowly undid his pants and let them fall to the ground. Standing there barefoot and bare-assed naked had never felt better. Aside from the fact he was cold as fuck, Jaxon realized he could fall in love with the adoring look in her eyes. Until she closed them and turned away with a big breath.

"Hey, it's okay." Maybe his thickness wasn't what she wanted to see. "Will you rub my back if I lay down?"

"Yes. Your backside is very nice."

"Thank you, baby. Maybe when you're ready, you'll let me see yours."

"Oh. Oh. Okay."

"Sorry. You think I'm perverted right?"

"No, not at all. It's just that you said you wanted to take care of undressing me, that's why I stopped earlier."

Fuck. She was right. She had him off his game. God, she was beautiful. If he took her clothes off, he was going to plunder her hard and fast. He pulled one of her quilts over his lap.

"Jaxon, what's wrong? What did I say?"

He wanted her more than he'd wanted any other female, ever. But he couldn't be sweet with her. If he was going to take pleasure from her, it had to be on familiar terms. Lily was nowhere near being ready for that. His plan to get her there started in earnest now. No more vocabulary lessons. This was very real preparation he would uphold for her sake. Their hourglass had been tipped and the sand was draining fast.

"Sit like that, just like that. Now, let your head relax and fall back."

* * * *

Lily tried to follow the specifics Jaxon had just given her on how he wanted her to sit. Unexpectedly, she flashed back to a night when Tom had insisted she do things his way, holding awkward positions which made her feel dirty, so he could film them. Then he'd played the video back, taunting her to watch, as he made faces without even trying to conceal them. There was just a certain way a person looked when they were disappointed. And a very obvious way when they were disgusted. Yeah, that one was impossible to mask. What if she turned out not to be as sexy as Jaxon believed? She had a choice to make now. Either trust Jaxon or admit she didn't have it in her to do this with him.

The look in his eyes now as he waited patiently for her to comply to his request made her dig for that confidence. She closed her eyes and pictured herself with flaming red hair.

"I can help you. Here, like this, baby," he said, pulling her over to the chair in her room.

Jaxon touched his hand to her back, making her sit up straight. The correction to her posture helped. She sat taller, with her knees bent, her head hanging back so that her shoulder –blade skimming hair appeared to hang that much longer. Her arms and hands braced her weight as her chest heaved slightly forward in anticipation of what he might ask next. Her sitting like that brought a sparkle to his turquoise eyes. If she held so much power in her hands to make him happy, how could she ever be weak enough to let him hurt her?

"Lily, I want to sleep with you, but I want to do it in a way you're going to enjoy too."

"And I don't want you to feel like you have to be anyone but yourself around me," she answered back.

Jaxon looked at her as if he wanted to tell her the ways in which he'd like to peel off her skin and suck her dry of every cell in her body. She'd never seen anyone so hungry and so hesitant to go after that dangling bone. And he still hadn't undressed her yet.

She undid the first button of her flannel shirt. But he stopped her.

"Let me. I like that part."

Oh dear lord, that meant he'd be paying extra close attention. It was a dangerous and scary thought. To be that bare. She held tight to her breath, hoping the extra inch of side flab wasn't bulging from the tight-waisted yoga pants she'd chosen to wear tonight, her motivation to drop a size sooner than later. He began removing her flannel top. How many thousands of women had Jaxon James undressed throughout the years? Lily prayed she didn't disappoint him.

Her flannel fell to the ground which left her last layer. The snug but thin cotton undershirt she'd borrowed from Tris really was a size too small when worn alone. Boy did she ever feel that now. When she caught back up to his gaze, she found he was fixated on her chest. Thank the heavens men loved boobs.

"Stand up, Lily."

She would have agreed to but her legs had gone numb from practicing such strict and straight posture. She'd been holding her thighs together so tightly she must have cut off circulation to her lady parts. A springy-like cramp popped between her legs and then spasmed its way all around the tense area. Unable to get up and not knowing what to do with her hands, she fumbled around the elastic waistband cutting deep into her skin as she hoped he couldn't make out her hips in the semi-darkened room. A curse riddled through her mind that she'd left on the one small lamp up on her dresser. "I think I'll just stay sitting," she mumbled.

"Okay." He lowered himself and sat comfortably in front of her on the backs of his heels. In that squat position, the thick muscles of his thighs expanded and doubled the size of his legs, making him look all the more strong and hunky. She knew if the room were brighter, she wouldn't find a single dimple of cellulite marring his physique. She, on the other hand, felt like she could give Swiss cheese a run for its money. "Hey," he said rubbing her clothed thighs. "You know what my secret favorite part of your body is? Hmm?"

She carefully shook her head no because it may very well fall off her neck at this point.

"Here." He rubbed a calloused, large hand over hers at first and then nudged it out of his way so he was the only one holding onto her hips. "Your curves remind me of Wineglass Bay."

"What's that?"

"The most beautiful, rounded beach in the world." He emphasized by caressing his hands over her hips until she was sure she felt the tingles all the way to her scalp.

"Lily? Lily, take a breath."

She almost prayed out loud to Jesus. Boy, the room was starting to spin.

* * * *

She'd been holding her breath, probably sucking her stomach in the way girls did for some insane reason. When her eyelids started to flutter closed, he grabbed for his pants with one hand and held onto her by the shoulder with the other. Her head did a severe rubbernecking once which seemed to snap her back to life.

"Oh my god, what just happened? That felt so strange."

"Yeah um, you almost passed out."

"Jaxon? You're dressed?"

"About that baby, we need to slow down. It's my fault for pushing too hard." He tried to put the blame on himself, always sensing how fragile her confidence was and not wanting to shatter it. "I really like what we started but...hey, there is something special I'd like you to do for me tonight. Think you might be up for it?"

"Yes."

He had his pants pulled up but hadn't zipped the fly yet. Not against his straining dick. Her gaze had dipped down twice now. He gave the zipper a quick yank. Knowing Lily wanted him was torture but he wanted her ready and prepared for their first time. And she clearly wasn't yet. But he pulled that earlier plan he'd thought up out, with a new exercise that might just help her with her insecurities over her body.

"I want you to sleep naked tonight."

"Like as in without clothes, naked?"

He had to remind himself that this was going to help her because her lack of comfort with her body really was a foreign concept to him. If he could run around without clothes and not get thrown in jail or lose Maryellie, he would. "That's the kind of naked I'm referring to."

"Oh, I don't know. I've never done that."

"I gathered that much. You do like your PJs. Which is fine. They're keeping you warm." *Until it's my turn to do that.*

"You always sleep in the nude?" she asked him setting her eyes upon his face now and not letting them wander even a tiny bit.

"Every day for as long as I can remember."

"But I like feeling snug when I sleep."

In the future, when she was ready, he'd revel inbeing her snuggly something. But he had fast work to do to get her there. He'd been so clueless about that weekend she'd shown up at his house. If he'd had any idea then about her ex, he would've been so much more careful. Exposing her to that weekend, and with Stefan showing up. God, he'd been such a fool. Women did that to him though, didn't they? It was still his best explanation for his Vangie episode. Thoughts of his ex still fucked with his head again. He hoped she'd gotten her shit together, wherever she was. God help Maryellie since he was apparently her sole parent and role model. Even if he could be as good as he was trying for, there were just things he lacked that a little girl needed. He focused again on Lily who was indeed holding herself in a tight hug. If she did this for him tonight, he'd take her tomorrow. She'd be ready.

"That's what your blankets are for," he reminded her. *And me.* He wished on all his stars for that day to come soon. "You don't have to give those up. I sleep under the covers too. Just do this for one night. And if you really don't like it, then no harm done. But I think you're gonna dig the freeing feeling of your skin breathing the nighttime air and the sheets warming to your body, not trapped by all the extra layers. Just give me one night like this, please?"

"I wish I was as comfortable as you with this stuff, Jaxon."

Me too. "Is that something you want?"

"Yes. But it's hard for me. I mean, body wise, there's you and Tris and Lucky. Even Benny. You're all tall and in this crazy good shape. Even pregnant, Tris isn't fat. I fit in more with Bear and Luke." She rubbed her lips and then bit down and chewed on a tiny piece of chipped pink finger nail.

God, he had to picture really terrible things to keep him from chuckling at how cute and funny she was. But he knew that was just her defense mechy. She really believed that about herself. Tonight while she was safely sleeping away from him in her room, he was getting on a laptop and googling all the gorgeous examples of curvy women he could find to show her. The iconic curvy beauty Marilyn Monroe leaped to mind. He'd be awake all night without question. Just the thought of Lily sleeping naked would keep him up. All the way up.

"You are not built in any way, shape or form like mine and Lucky's fathers. That's just bananas. Now lay your beautiful, about to be naked butt down and get some sleep." He kissed her shoulder. The best part was seeing how much she felt it whenever he did something so small.

"I'll try."

"Good. So I'm looking forward to breakfast with you in the morning. Want help with the French toast?" He twirled a lock of her hair between his fingers and then kissed that too, not ready to leave her and make his way to the living room and the empty couch.

She twisted up her mouth. "I'll make you some if you like. But I'm probably gonna try yogurt. You know, just for a change of pace."

"All right. Yogurt then."

He didn't like the sound of her ditching her favorite meal. His gut was urging him to snatch her up, lay her where he wanted her right there on their bed of blankets, and make her his, inside and out. That'd be the quickest way to say "Lily, you're fucking hot and you're fucking mine." But the cavemen had gone extinct for a reason. Lily deserved better. Jaxon would not be that ass anymore.

"Okay, it's a date," she said.

They were both standing now and he leaned in and gave her arms a quick couple of rubs. "I can't wait."

To his fervent delight, she went up on her tiptoes and singed his lips like a dripping hot wax seal on a yellowed piece of paper. She'd closed her eyes for the two seconds it had taken. Good for her. He guessed he was okay with her breaking the rules every now and then.

"That was our first real kiss, Lily."

"I know. Guess I was tired of waiting." Her chin lowered and she peered up at him, contentment binding happiness to her features. She blew out. "Wow, it's so cold. Maybe I'll just run out to the hall closet and grab us some more blankets."

Oh yeah. There was that one tiny detail he'd left out. "Baby, you're gonna have to do this in here on your own."

* * * *

Visions of waking up in her birthday suit with the blanket having fallen off in the night and everyone in the house standing there staring gave her the twitches.

"I wish I could stay in here with you and help more but trust me, at this point, I've got to go."

Gosh, what was he going to do if he was near her and she was naked? Gobble her up? Could be, she guessed and then wished on every star she'd ever seen shoot across the southern sky it would be true.

"Well, all right, I promise I'll give it a try."

"Good girl."

"Hey Jaxon, I know this is your way of trying to help me. I hope you can see what that says about you." She turned and went to her bed to sit down. Lily hoped Jaxon didn't plan on changing himself too much. He'd grown on her a whole lot. She had vowed never to get naked for another man, yet here she was.

Lily moved a set of small, square lavender pillows to the head of her bed. They were her favorite because Tris had somehow scented them with lilac. She hugged one to her chest and inhaled the invisible bouquet that wafted up.

"Why am I doing this? What am I trying to prove?" she whispered into the cotton stuffing. Jaxon wasn't even here and he wouldn't know whether she'd gone through with it or not. The thrilling feeling she'd had near Jaxon when he'd made this request had faded. The feminine tingles he inspired in her body and the seductive hug his stare gave her curves only seemed real when she was standing in front of him. Without him here, simply put, she wasn't feeling it.

Afraid of disturbing those who had found sleep in the house, she quashed the urge to tiptoe her way back out to the couch and snag Jaxon. Yep, that desire meant in the morning, she was going to have to spill this secret to Tris. It was time Lily started acting like the grown woman Jaxon had awakened within her. Still dressed, she closed her eyes and thought hard about the most delicate way to tell her sister she'd fallen for Jaxon and there was no turning back.

SIN'S FLOWER

Chapter Twenty-Three

Christmas Eve...

It was plainly obvious Jaxon could learn a few things from his younger male counterpart. When it came to treating a woman right and being a man about it, Lucky turned out to be a stud. Packing up a defiant, pregnant woman's bags and carrying her out to the truck under protest took a brave man but he'd watched Lucky handle it with a cool calm just a few hours ago. Trissy's early contractions had persisted so it was for her own good they'd taken off to find a hotel room near her birthing center.

It was Christmas Eve, complete with a heavy smell of pine and sweet, spicy pies hanging in the air and colorful twinkly lights sparkling up against the shadows of the darkened living room. He sat on the couch alone, taking a quiet moment to look around at the photos framed on the walls and the way this family room made him feel a part of something but still stranded on the outside.

The smell of buttery, hot popcorn beat Lily into the living room as she showed up balancing two large bowls for the movie they had on cue. She set one down on the coffee table for when Benny came back and then moved to Jaxon's side and offered to share.

"Thanks baby," he said, guiding her closer to his lap. "I saved you a spot."

"Welcome. Um, on your lap?" she whispered. "What about Benny?"

"He's too big, won't fit."

Her nervous smile lit up his innate dark hole and he may have pinned her with too needy of a stare because she turned and sat down exactly where he wanted her. "Okay." She let her back melt into his chest and folded her legs up criss-cross style, settling in easily while he widened his straddle to take in her lush curves. He wanted all of her tucked into his lap. Her hair tickled his cheek and smelled divine. God, he wanted to fuck her like crazy.

"So hey, while we're waiting for Benny," she said quietly, "I made his Christmas present this morning. It's a wool hat. I hope he'll like the colors. Forest green and charcoal grey."

"He'll love it," he nearly moaned into her ear. "He apparently lost his at the mall with Maryellie the other day."

"Perfect. He's so good with her and it's really sweet that he took her Christmas shopping for everyone's gifts. Think he'd consider letting me adopt him?"

Jaxon was so attuned to her every move and apparently this talk made her giddy; she wiggled her ass over his groin, bringing him along to her happy place. "If I didn't need him so much back in Cali, we'd work something out. Shared custody maybe." He tried desperately hard not to nip at the soft flesh of her jaw or round his hands to the sweet valley between her criss-crossed legs. Talking like this brought him into the realm he'd felt locked out of before. Lily's devotion to Maryellie was precious. They could be a couple. That would fulfill his every desire as of late.

"Hey, you haven't asked what I want for Christmas," he teased playfully at first, using a suggestive voice. But, as he committed to his proposal in his heart, his voice had no choice but to lull just as deeply.

"So sorry. What would you like? A sweater?" she asked.

Her head twisted past her shoulder so she could see his face. The sparkle in her eyes launched his ego to the stars as he whispered into her ear. "Time is doing its best to fly by, baby. New Year's will be here soon and vacation time will be up. I'm gonna miss you."

"Me too," she hushed out with shiny eyes.

"I don't want you to leave here, to leave your sister. This is a good place." He took in a deep breath, being sure to smell every strand of her cherry scented hair, and then wrapped his arms around and squeezed her to his chest. He was about to do it. The thing he'd thought about all day as he recognized the better person he'd already become this past week. He'd genuinely wanted to help out around the shop, to drive her places she needed to be and to accept he had to be honest with Trissy. There was no reason not to say this to her now. "What I do want is for you to be mine. I'll figure out a way to make it work. You can visit me as often as you like; I'll come here as much as I can. We could make it work, if you'd be mine."

Her head slowly dipped, and kept dipping lower and lower. "Breathe Lily."

She took in a lungful but it was shaky.

"What do you say, baby? Will you be my woman?"

Shit, please say something.

Even better, she turned until her entire body brought her chest to chest, face to face, still in his lap. He saw that she was having trouble with where to put her legs and while he was dying to feel them hugging his waist, his help wasn't helping much. She sat with them bunched up; her toes prodded into his bulge. This time he took the deep breath.

None of that mattered when her shy smile turned up. "Are you sure?" She leaned in closer and whispered, tickling his ear. "I chickened out last night, you know. Do you really want a woman who's never slept necked?"

Maybe she was being playful, maybe dead serious. He hoped for a little of both because it was what endeared him to her.

Their faces were close enough to kiss. "Okay, I want two things for Christmas. Will you be my woman and will you please sleep naked?"

Because like Jaxon's karma, Benny's timing was bananas, he came back from the bathroom in that same second. The refrigerator motor sounded from the kitchen while Benny filled a glass with water.

"Benny, mate, I officially have a woman."

Lily poked him in the chest. "Yes."

He kissed the tip of her nose for her answer he'd accidentally skipped over.

"Great. You should officially get a room. Seriously, if you two are gonna be out here on the couch tonight, tell me now so I can go enjoy Lucky's king size bed. Unless you guys want it. I'm chill either way but I'm bouts to conk out."

Jaxon steered his complete attention to Lily and quirked his eyebrows up in a question. She shook her head no with a "that's gross" look.

"I'm chill with the couch for now," she offered, mimicking Benny. And then only for Jaxon, "I can't imagine being in their bed but mine on the other hand...maybe after the movie." She scrunched up her nose and to his ultimate pleasure, bit down on her bottom lip. "You can definitely have the giant bed, Benny. Stretch out and don't forget your popcorn."

"Merry Christmas Eve, mate."

Benny disappeared down the hall with a goofy peace out wave.

"It's just you and me, kid. Let's start the movie."

With Maryellie safe, snug and deep into sleepies in the nursery, Jaxon couldn't strip his eyes off Lily, sitting so intimately in his lap. The things he could do with her, knowing what a womanly body she had been blessed with, even if he'd yet to see it live. Tonight he wasn't sleeping until he'd finally proven to her how desirable she was.

That pent up desire was currently driving him insane.

He'd fought his urges all day and night. Something about tonight and things happening beyond his control that put them in this house, together, made him feel like maybe she didn't need protecting from him anymore. He was enough of a dreamer to believe maybe someone wanted them together.

* * * *

In her wildest dreams, she'd never have put herself with Jaxon James, here in the cozy living room of her long lost sister's house, on Christmas Eve of all the magical nights.

"I love this movie," she said to her man, trying not to hyperventilate at the brand spanking new term. "Maybe I should turn around so we can actually see it."

Under a near pout, he agreed and laid down on his back with his legs stretched out down the couch's length. "Plenty of room." He patted his chest like a gentle caveman calling his woman to bed and gave her a tug.

Her body melded over his while they lay there staring at each other stomach to stomach, Jaxon on his back, Lily with her eyes at his chin. "But the movie, don't you think we should do the sideways spooning thing so you can see it without straining your neck?"

"I'll be fine," he said.

"Okee dokee." She stretched her right arm to the coffee table and grabbed the remote then hit play.

It wasn't long before her apprehensions died down about laying there with Jaxon so intimately; she became lost in the sweetness the young man in the movie showed to his girlfriend. A half hour into it and they'd come to her favorite part. The young man, a wounded veteran who should be closed off to the world had seen the woman through an emotional breakdown. He held her so close which always did it for Lily. But when he looked at her, somehow it was just one of those perfect Hollywood looks where you could see just how badly he wanted to make love to her but how much more important her feelings were to him. He'd wait until she was ready. And then in return, his lady feels so safe that she makes the first moves and they end up in a passionate embrace which of course leads to their first time. All beautiful and lovey dovey and sexy and everything Lily loved about this movie. Her squirming and toe curling led to a loud sigh and then a few tears.

* * * *

Well, they wouldn't be watching many of these romantic movies together. Her wiggling was just too damn distracting. With her so wrapped up in the dude on screen, Jaxon had decided to stay wrapped up in twirling Lily's hair in his fingers until he felt a few tears drop from her eyes land on his forearm.

"Don't cry."

"I can't help it."

He thumbed the ridge of her cheek bone, taking away the tears. "I thought this was one of your favorite movies."

"It is. That's why it makes me cry. He's so sweet with her when he could easily be a raging jerk. He's been through so much but he keeps her away from that. And in the end she heals him."

"That's a nice story, Lily."

"I know, it's corny right?"

"I didn't say that." He had no choice then. He hooked his hands under her armpits and brought her up until their faces were close enough to kiss. "It's my favorite movie," he said after surprising her with his tongue on hers. She tasted so good.

"No it's not. You're so strange sometimes," she said with a loose smile, her mouth still open from his kiss.

"You like it, I like it."

"Jaxon? If there was something hurting you so deep like that on the inside, I hope you'd let me help you like she does for him."

He blinked a few slow times and felt his pulse slow the lower his heart sank with fear that she saw the darkness inside of him. It wasn't a question of "if". The problem was that he couldn't see a "when" in the near future. He was trying to forget. Telling Lily what he'd almost done to her sister would only serve to destroy the two girls' fledgling relationship. As much as he wanted to be free and healed like Lily described, he wouldn't cause her that pain of knowing what had gone down with her sister. He wouldn't steal what she'd regained with Trissy, and couldn't imagine losing what they had miraculously built since meeting not so long ago. He was selfish in many ways, but he wouldn't put his grief on Lily. He doubted she would cry heart stinging tears at a movie where the guy tells his girl about the time he was almost forced to rape her sister. That wasn't romantic shit. It was fucked up and evil. And something he would take to his grave before burdening his Lily.

She was staring at him. He gave her what he could. "If I'm ever hurting and you can help me, I promise to ask. Right now, I just want to finish watching you watch your movie."

She smiled and kissed him back then turned her head as the scene changed for the couple. He'd thought his chances of making love to Lily out on the couch were all but nil, with the sweetness she seemed to crave and his lack of it. The way he wanted to have sex with her was not nice. It was raw and wild. There were things he longed to ask her to do while he watched.

As the movie played now, he pictured her in the privacy of his bedroom this way and that, every way and everywhere. When Lily cooed, Jaxon looked up and then over at the flat screen. The guy was standing on a ladder fixing something in the woman's worn down house. Jaxon's images became like stop signs warning him she might not like what he had to offer. Then the scene changed to the man and woman standing outside her fixer upper house later that night. He was expecting there would be a nice, long and tame kiss under the stars but the rain started falling and apparently all their inhibitions were washed away. Within seconds, they were up against the wall of her house and although the camera angles kept things PG-13, it was obvious the guy was inside her, making her pant.

Lily's nails dug into his forearm. Her one knee slid up his thigh. Her breath came out in short, hot hitches. Shit, she liked it. Maybe he could have his Lily how he wanted after all. Not here on the couch; he'd keep it tender and quiet since they'd be at the mercy of the open room. But once they went back to her room...mmm, he exhaled at the thought. Jaxon waited patiently for the movie to finish. It was difficult and he was hard.

Chapter Twenty-Four

"I won't hurt you. I promise," he vowed, still aware of the care he had to take with her and how exposed she must feel being with him out on her sister's couch. "Thank you for being out here with me. You're brave, baby." He nipped at her ear lobe. She shuddered.
"Okay."

"Can we take some of these off?" He gestured toward her layers of clothes. "Can we? And then wrap up in the blankets?" It was a stretch but he had to feel her like he had to breathe. "I promise I won't let anyone see you. Just me."

She nodded for him. "Yes."

His hands made fast work of the hoodie sweatshirt. A sense that she wasn't going anywhere dawned on him and he slowed his stripping of her flannel shirt next which also calmed her heaving chest. He had to remember her tendency for getting light headed around him.

Before he stole anymore of her clothes, a jolting need to be naked in front of her spun his head. With fever controlling his movements, he tugged his one and only top layer over his head and tossed it to the floor.

"Hi," she said when he moved so that he could lay down lengthwise and stretch his legs down the couch.

"Hi," he said back and tugged her to sit straddling him this time. It didn't matter that they were both still in their pants, he could feel her woman's heat coming off her core. It scorched his belly underneath her. "Doing okay?" he asked.

Searching the living room, she hadn't looked down at him yet. "Hey," he gave her shoulders a tug downward until she had no choice but to rest herself on his bare chest. "Benny's in the back bedroom for the night. Trust me; he knows not to come out here. Maryellie is zonked out in her room until morning, dreaming of Santa and Rudy. It's just us. Just you and me, baby. I want you here, now. But we can go to your room if you're not okay with this." Not having had the chance to practice many doting gestures with past partners, he delighted to cup her cheek with his hand until she let the weight of her full breasts fall onto his chest.

"Let's try this, here," she let out quietly.

He nudged her up after stroking her back for a few turns. "Baby, pull off your shirt for me please."

She began nodding that she was going to do so when she stopped with her hands stuck at the bottom hem. "Jaxon, what if you don't like it?"

"Not it, silly. You." He padded her nose with his fingertip. "And that's not possible. I promise you that." The picture from her asshole ex he'd seen disgusted him but not for her lack of beauty. Before she went any further, he assured her with a slow, hot kiss. As he worked her mouth with his tongue, she lifted her top inch by inch until they had to part heads to slip it off.

"See, you're perfect." Her breasts weren't huge like he'd thought, picturing and growing them day by day in his imagination. But they were full enough to overflow the cups of her bra and his hands once he held her. With one glance up and down her hot body, he knew her size and what he'd be next day shipping to this address tomorrow. Sexy, properly fitting lingerie she would feel comfortable in and he would relish taking off. It would be her secret New Year's Eve present from him. He'd be sure to include a few feminine styled tracky suits for her too since sweats seemed to be what she liked.

She shook her head but smiled softly. "You're the silly one."

In only minutes, he had her stripped down to just
her bra and panties. All of his clothes were gone. He'd
tossed them here and there but she'd piled them neatly by
the couch in case he needed to dress quickly.

"I want to taste you, baby." The elastic clung to
her skin so tightly it left marks in her wonderful hips. He
leaned down and peeled the offending waistband back
from her skin and kissed the marks.

Before he could go any further, she reached down,
grabbed her t-shirt and pulled it back on over her head.
She then mugged him with a very sad and disappointed
looking face. "I'm sorry but I just can't be out here
completely naked."

Carefully he raised himself up to look her in the
eyes again. "If you're not sure about this tonight, tell me
now. I'll let you go." Not what he wanted to say but
still, he should offer her one last escape.

"Where would I go, half…mostly naked? What's
wrong? Now that you've seen me you don't want me."

"No, no, no, no, no. That's not what I meant. Of
course I want you. But baby, I take a lot, and I don't
know if you're ready for that." If she stayed with him
now, he prayed to be that slower, gentler man she
obviously needed, just for this one night.

"Jaxon, I want you to want me the same way
you've wanted every other girl you've ever been with."
Her eyes shone true blue for him and he felt like he'd
found home right there in her gaze. He bit his tongue to
keep from licking her so hard he stole all taste from her
neck.

He couldn't tell her that was impossible since
he'd never cared about any other woman the way he
cared for her. And also that his hesitation was due in part
to the fact that the last time he'd had sex was nearly a

year and a half ago. And never since he'd been forced to lie on top of Trissy.

"I want you." He paused for a kiss on the chin. "You deserve soft and slow." He nipped at her lips after soft and after slow.

"Will it bother you if I keep my shirt on?"

He'd prefer she didn't but knew that with it, she'd feel more comfortable with him. "As long as you don't mind my hands sneaking up under it."

God, the beauty of a woman he could make blush with mere words.

"Should I touch you? Will that help make up for it?"

He didn't know what it was going to do other than drive him crazy. "Mmm, can I make you a deal? Aside from your tee shirt, get the rest of the way naked for me baby. Then we'll touch."

She stood, anxiousness wicking like a lit candle in her blue yes, and wiggled out of her lavender cotton panties. He counted one half of a breath before she hurriedly lay back down on top of him. He knew she'd moved like lightning to hide his view but her light brown curly hairs poking out from the shirt's hem had driven him to ecstasy.

"So where would you like my hands?" Her voice came out in a sexy whisper as she lay there wiggling her toes.

Shit, here went his stab at honesty. *Baby, please don't think I'm a disgusting perverted fuck.* Vangie's detested voice chanted those words in his mind before he spit it out. "My dick, Lily."

Another "oh" nearly made it around her lips and then she bit it back. He was about to explode and her mouth making that round little cheerio shape was not helping. He fought to maintain control because as badly

as he wanted to let go and be himself for her, he refused
to hurt her.

Her hand touched his thigh and then slid to where
his balls hung, strained and heavy. Butterflies were
things girls felt in their tummies, they shouldn't be
flitting around in his sack. Fuck, she felt so good
touching him there.

"Lily, where can I touch you, baby? Tell me."

She shook her head no. Shit, he thought he'd
gotten her past that. He tried again. "Show me?" he
asked.

She nodded yes, saving him from his doubts. She
left his balls and quickly found his hand but held onto it
for a long minute. And then she placed his fingers to her
mouth, kissed his palm, and scooted herself as close to
him as was possible on the borrowed couch, making his
arms have no choice but to wrap around her. She wanted
a hug. God, how could he have used those vulgar words
with her just now? *Jaxon, you really are a dick, you
asshole.*

"I'm sorry, Lily," he said, crossing his arms over
her bare back since he'd edged her shirt up to uncover her
shoulder blades. She curled her shoulders inward and he
tightened his embrace even more. "I should never have
said that to you."

"Why are you sorry?"

"Because I told you to touch my dick."

"But I liked touching you there and I don't mind
you saying what's on your mind. You're not being dirty
with me. I know that."

"Um, baby, did you really just want a hug or…"

"I wanted a hug to start out with, but now I want
you to take over. If you don't mind."

He did not mind. He just had to decide where to
start.

Her body was his home. It was time to own it.

"Lay underneath me baby." He lifted himself and she did.

He knew how this had to go. Blanket up and over them, the heat from their breathing instantly created summertime moist warm air in the dead of a freezing Tennessee winter. His hands started out rounding back and forth, up and over from her hips to her fine ass and back. When he easily found the womanly bone of her hip jutting out, he wanted to scold her for thinking she had anything but the heaven sent body of a goddess. He squeezed in, applying pressure with his thumb into the skin and flesh right below that bone. He'd found a sensitive spot. She rolled her body from the shoulders down to where he was pressing in at her hip toward him like he'd found and brought her home from a night of stripping. Her short soft hairs brushed against his thigh so he brought it up and nuzzled it against her opening. She gifted him by rubbing herself further up his thigh and nearly up onto his hip. Fucking hot ass woman and her gifted pussy. He knew exactly where he had to go next. His mouth watered at the thought.

* * * *

Half of her felt like a cornered rabbit just waiting for the trigger to release and end her days. The rest of her felt like she was already there, frolicking around and populating the bunny heavens. She hadn't done much except for gawk and lay still so far. Back to the gawking part, that was her man? Really? Holy cannoli, his body could fire up the space shuttle's engines.

Of course she'd already known about his buns of desire but that had been a squelch of a fraction of how tantalizing Jaxon's body was built from the front. He was currently squeezing her hip which sort of sent her to her horrified place worrying about the squishiness he was discovering. Except he glanced up at her for a second long enough that she could see something like pure admiration mixed in with an "I want to eat you" look.

He squeezed harder, applying this crazy pressure just below where her hipbone jutted out and it felt so amazing she immediately downgraded her hip from gross to okay. She couldn't help but rub herself over his thigh. She'd never felt a man's leg hairs making contact with her sensitive lady parts and spent a little longer in that rhythm than she maybe should have. He wasn't helping by flexing his thick leg muscle each time she rubbed. She was ready to go back to just gawking and laying still when he dipped his head to travel down south. And then he said something to her but she couldn't hear it so she flapped some air into the blanket, holding it open by her end at the top.

"Jaxon?"

He wasn't smiling but he was happy, that was for sure.

"I was just reminding you to breathe, baby." He gave her a wink and then a kissy face too. And he licked the air with his tongue. Was he trying to send her to her bunny grave? "Don't pass out on me."

"What makes you think I would do that?" she asked in his direction.

His answer was lips finding this spot on her thigh, his tongue probing it with more strength than she thought a tongue could have, and then nibbling teeth. Her answer was squirming and an accidental assault by her two knees coming together in a fiercely fast clap.

"Ow, baby."

Sometimes a girl having her brand spanking new boyfriend go down on her for the first time will say the darndest things. "Jaxon, I haven't showered yet today."

She thought that would bring him back up to the surface and save her from the pending heart attack.

"I don't care."

Shoot. "Well, I do."

"Are you sure? Because I'm really doing just fine."

Yeah, sure he was. Aside from the concussion he was probably suffering from. The thought locked her knees together again.

"Ow. Okay, you win."

She stood and found her undies, slipping them back on while Jaxon just sat completely at home with his surroundings and his naked body.

She took a seat on the floor then and hung her hand over his knee. "I wish that had gone better."

"Me too, Lily."

"I know, I'm sorry. I'm gonna go take a bath."

Please hear how badly I want you to join me without making me say it. Please take just one more chance on me.

* * * *

"I'm coming with you. I hope you don't mind," Jaxon said, unwilling to let Lily's unfounded self-consciousness ruin this for her.

He knew an invitation when he heard one. Even though it felt like she was asking him to run laps around the track until they both ran out of gas, he didn't care. She was finding her way and he wasn't the dumbass who was gonna say no thanks due to silly pride.

"I'd like that," she said.

She sat on the toilet while he filled the tub.

"Here, toss this in there," she said with her eyes locked on his.

"What's that?"

The pink ball she held out to him smelled like circus cotton candy but he took it and held the salty hardness in his hands.

"It's a fizzy bath bomb. Tris keeps them stocked and they're always different. Sometimes when they melt away, there's little trinkets inside."

"This one looks glittery. You sure about this? It could get in your eye," he said, wanting to be able to see her clearly without too much fluff in the way.

That was it, another cleverly worded warning to her that every moment he spent with her, he was closer and closer to pouncing. He'd always stop when she asked him to. But she'd have to be clear.

The tub was a third full and he let the bath ball fall. It dunked and plummeted, fizzing pink curdles quickly. And glitter.

"So, my lovely Lily. Are you ready to get sparkly with me?"

"Yes, but hold on." She rubbed her hands together and then ducked to rummage through the cabinet under the bathroom sink. "There we go."

He watched her body's intricate movements as she plugged in a small radio and then set a small white plastic globe on the counter. She then locked the bathroom door, testing it twice and pushed a button on the globe before finally turning off the main light switch. The bathroom had become warm from the water filling the tub and on the ceiling he saw stars. Not because his head was swimming with lust for her shapely thighs, hips, calves and the way her breasts bobbed beneath her loose tee. The globe was a star shooting night lamp. And it projected a midnight purple sky scene on the ceiling. Other than that glow, the bathroom was dark. He sat there on the cold edge of the tub, in a trance.

"Do you like it?" she asked.

"I love it. Come here."

"Wait, one more thing."

She hit play on the portable mp3 player and uttered the word shuffle as she pushed one more button to make that selection.

Jaxon just sat there watching her try to douse the nerves he knew were biting her in the ass right now. He'd learned her anxious cues in their short time together.

"Better?" He reached a hand out to her.

She nodded. "You're so beautiful Jaxon," she said to him while finally letting her gaze lower over his body, down to his toes and back up, slowly.

Until the day he died, he'd never forget her hand reaching out to his and putting it on the hem of her shirt. "I really need that bath," she spoke so breathily.

"I like your shirt by the way. Purple makes your eyes intense," he told her as he lifted it up and then set it on the toilet seat where it would be in hands reach if she felt the urge. He reached back to turn off the water before it became too full for two adult bodies to sink in. "Oops. That's pretty full. Guess I was distracted by the sexy, hot woman standing right here in front of me."

She stood there hugging him. With her skin melded to his, he knew her problem wasn't being close to him, but him seeing her body. "I'm just going to slide these off." He kept his eyes with hers and felt his way to her waist band to slide her panties down. He put those on top of her tee and felt back around until his hands rested over her full cheeks. "You have a great ass baby."

As he squeezed and rubbed it softly, he swayed with her to the solemn song playing on her player. He knew this one. Not one of his but similar to Sin Pointe's style. When they did a ballad, they did it dark and raw. And this one by Phosphorescent reminded him of home—guitars, late Los Angeles nights, and disappointment. He craved a new memory and so he strummed his fingers up her soft, warm back, fingering pressure points along her spine and bent down so he could cover her mouth with his. Eventually she would see that he only wanted to worship her, spend time with her, talk to her, make love with her. Eventually she would know how beautiful she was. He kept up his whispered words, helping her to get there. "I like your bath time set up. You should always pamper yourself like this." He had the feeling she probably only indulged once in a while.

"Special occasions," she said so softly it was like her voice had been claimed by the shadows of the mostly dark bathroom they swayed in. "I don't want to use up all my sister's bath stuff."

"Have you thought about getting your own place?" The song changed to another slow one, this time one of his favorites by Sheryl Crow. "I mean, here in town, so you stay close but have something of your own." He kept his kisses attuned to her mouth, cheeks, nose, and eyelids.

"I hadn't thought that far yet. Everything I make, I put back into the dress shop," she said distractedly.

He held her with one hand at the shoulders now and as they talked and swayed, he stepped them closer to the tub. Only one slow step at a time. "Mmm. Maybe you should. For my visits," his voice tickled her ear. "But close because I wouldn't want you out in the middle of nowhere on your own."

Maybe he could talk Lucky into contracting with him to build Lily her own flat, something like what he'd done for Grace. The lot here was plenty big enough to accommodate another two-bedroom sized home.

He lifted his leg and hers obediently followed, their two feet landing in the hot tub water together. And then the other. They remained standing and swaying up to their mid shins. Lily hugged herself to his chest and while Jaxon would love to have a moment to simply gaze at her silhouette, he loved the warmth their bodies created when pressed together. Even the overly sweet smell of the sugar bomb appealed to him, standing there holding her to him so intimately.

"Oh, this is one of my favorite songs," she said, stirring the fluffy water with her foot. He took it as a cue to sit down. He then scooted all the way back until his skin touched against cool porcelain. He spread his thighs so she could sit between his legs and lean back into his chest.

"I haven't heard this one," he said burying his face in her hair.

"He's new."

"Reminds me of Dave Mathews."

"That's what I said too but Trissy said I was crazy and deaf."

They shared a laugh at that. "Your sister has a way with words."

"Jaxon?"

"Yes?" he asked and skimmed his foremost wet fingertips in a trail of water and desire up the center of her belly, through the division of her rib cage and then up to her collarbone.

"Kiss me."

He steadied himself and helped her turn to face him. It was so dark with just the lavender glow of the star show beaming up onto the ceiling that everything his hands asked her body to do, she obeyed without hesitating. With her now laying on top of him and the water cuddling them in its warmth, he plunged his tongue so deeply into her mouth; her taste would stay with him for days. In the dark, her hands knew where to touch him. His pecs burned as she massaged them. "I trust you, baby," Jaxon said. He didn't realize that had ever been a question for him.

* * * *

"I trust you too."

The other thing she trusted in? That her perfectly capable boyfriend knew what he was doing and this would be a night she'd never forget.

SIN'S FLOWER

Chapter Twenty-Five

It was obvious where things were going and that she no longer had the will or felt the need to stop him. And being the man he was, probably didn't want to worry about getting her pregnant.

"Jaxon," she pulled back from his lips and he nipped her right at first but she didn't mind and it only stung a little. "I just wanted you to know I'm on the pill so we'll be okay there."

"Okay." The way he said it made it sound like the furthest thing from his mind but she felt better. As wishy washy as she'd been, it couldn't hurt to let him know how sure she w—oh, time for mind numbing silence.

A thick head nudged at her water-sealed entrance and erased her brain.

Hair not long enough to grip. She stopped her petting of it and went lower where she met up with his wide, herculean shoulders and squeezed.

"Sitting on you."

"Yes, you are baby. And it feels amazing," he said as he pulled her body, sliding her up his abs and torso in a slick ride so that he could delve his tongue back into her mouth and suck at her lips.

"You're so beautiful."

"Thank you, baby," he said.

She'd meant hard, that he was so hot and hard and perfect. It felt like she'd waited her whole life to have him making love to her like this. The way her legs fit perfectly over his narrow hips, the only narrow part on his gorgeous lover's body. No sex she'd ever had felt like this. The four years she'd wasted her womanhood with that creep threatened to poke its awful head into this perfect moment but she refused and squeezed Jaxon's

waist with her thighs. For the first time, they felt
muscular and not just big.

"Do that again, baby," he said, his accent coming
back stronger.

"What? This?" She knew what he wanted. The
last two times her thighs had hugged him he'd gulped for
a breath inside her mouth. She flexed and felt the inner
muscles become tight around his hips because she'd
slinked a little lower this time, her aching need searching
for Jaxon to fill it.

"Mmm," he groaned. "Do you want me inside
you, Lily?"

She nodded.

He spun her around in one of his strong arms so
that she lay on the bottom of the tub, that arm of his
cushioning her spine and neck. His fingers slid into the
fullness of her hair and he held her there tightly. His
other hand was tenderly at her cheek and just because it
was dark didn't mean she couldn't see the immense need
in his eyes. "Tell me, baby," he said.

"I want you inside me."

"Jaxon."

"Huh? Oh, I want you inside me, Jaxon."

"Mmm. Thank you, baby."

"Welcome."

While she lay there remarkably still, his hips
shifted over hers, finding their natural place and
suggesting she spread her knees further apart so he would
fit. As far as was possible within the slick, cool confines
of the tub, she opened herself to him. Making herself
proud, she found the dip where his back, waist and buns
all met up and pressed down hard enough that he knew
she was ready for this. Ready for him. Candy scented
foam ebbed in the water kissing their skin and his perfect,
tight buns.

After one last kiss on her lips, he let his mouth slip to her neck just below her ear; she had a feeling he might like to keep talking to her now and then. She was right.

"Has it been a while, baby?"

His thick fingers petted her opening and then slipped inside, one by one. She hadn't meant to but the muscles lining her neglected female walls squeezed in response. She nodded, knowing he could feel it against his cheek.

"Me too."

She knew that meant he needed more of her. She waited a few heartbeats and breaths, secretly working up the courage while enjoying the way his fingers explored her insides.

"Jaxon," she made sure to begin with because he seemed to like her saying his name, "I want—" but the words stuck in her throat. Even a quick cough didn't loosen her up.

He nuzzled her jawline with his smooth cheek, still suckling the skin under her ear lobe. "You want my dick in you?" he asked with a tiny hint of struggle which she appreciated.

Well yes, that is what she wanted. She smiled to herself. "Yes, Jaxon."

His fingers slowly came out, and took hold of her hip, squeezing that thumb of his into her flesh with an immaculate pressure.

If she didn't help him now, he would have to remove his arm that was acting as her spine's cushion so she swam her fingers through their warm bath water and found him. She'd seen him hard, both through pants and naked. But feeling him was another matter. He lifted his hips, giving more space for her hand and then slid himself between her fingers. "Ohhh," she let out.

"That's it baby. Fuck. I'm so hard."

"I know, you really are," she said sounding amazed because she truly was. His erection was hard like something that could do damage to other hard things. And most certainly to certain soft things. But she didn't fear him hurting her. Just filling her up and making her feel things she'd never felt.

"Like this?" Her hand slid down the length of him and then back up.

"Yeah." He nipped at her skin, holding a slice of it in his teeth before he let go. "No, I mean no. I'll come in your hand." He stilled his hips until his tip found its way back to her entrance. "Just relax, okay baby?"

"Okay."

"And breathe."

She inhaled and exhaled for him while he watched her with his eyes, pinning her in place. He blinked a couple times and then breathed with her, not looking away for a second. If eyes had a voice, his were saying he loved doing this with her right now. When she let out her breath, his grip tightened both in her hair at the back of her head and over her hip, and then he was inside. Full, hard, perfect and beautiful. Thrusting until the tender skin under their short hairs touched, making contact because he was inside her all the way.

She hadn't really wanted to cry. He was making love to her like a sex god, a practiced one who had made General in his time amongst the other sex gods. What was about to bring her to tears was the adorable smile on his face that grew each time he pushed into her. "You're smiling."

He nodded. Maybe he couldn't talk. Maybe she'd left him speechless.

A girl could dream.

* * * *

Jaxon knew he was grinning like an idiot but he couldn't stop smiling. Only four songs had played but fucking Lily's tight, hugging lips were about to make his dick sing. If he did come before her this time, she was first next. They had all night.

"Baby, is it good? Do you like it?" He pumped into her again, sloshing water up to the rim of the tub.

"Very good, Jaxon. Very good."

So she was close too. He bit his lips together, holding them with his teeth from the inside. Maybe what she needed was a rolling thrust. Yes, she moaned while he grinded himself against the soaking wet mass of hairs and arched his back. He felt her begin to squeeze not because she was playing with and taunting him but because her body was about to rip into a very well earned orgasm.

Her mouth opened for him. Only her soft pants came out.

He'd rather not take his eyes off her but he wanted to suck on her sweet pink tongue. Which was different. He'd never had that particular urge right before shooting his seed. Fuck, why was he thinking so much? But the genuine look of womanly lust for what his body was doing to her brought back his smile. He plunged himself in deep, all the way, splashing water this time onto the floor, again and then again until her eyes widened, her pussy gave him one last squeeze and then he let himself go. When he sank down onto her, their chests suctioned closed over each other. *Mine* whispered through his conscience. *Mine.*

* * * *

Whether Jaxon realized it or not, she was his. Even if he left here and his promise to make things work faded with time, or even if he showed up every weekend

like she secretly hoped for. She was his pure and simple.
All his and nothing could change that. She hoped.

Nothing could take away the pure joy she felt
right now with him laying on top of her in their candy
sweet bath. Oh boy, her eyes had adjusted enough to the
darkness to see that the surprise in this bath bomb had
been a center burst of glitter. Jaxon's back was bathed in
it. She tried not to laugh while rinsing his skin with
handfuls of glittery bath water that only made it worse.

"What are you doing, baby?" he asked while
nibbling at her ear lobe as they semi-floated together.

"Um, just trying to wash off your sparkles.
Glitter filled bath ball. Sorry."

"Okay."

He didn't mind. God, who could have ever
counted him as a jerk? She was baffled. And curious
about Maryella's mom.

"I can't believe it'll be Christmas in a few hours.
I'm so glad Maryella is here. Kids always make it more
special."

"Yep, and it's my job to make sure she believes in
Santa for a very long time. Otherwise, you're right, not
as special."

"You're a good dad, you know that?" She cupped
another handful of water and sprinkled it over his back.
He shivered while she stayed protected and warm in the
water beneath him. For some reason, making love and
talking about a baby he had made seemed natural.

"Oh, I don't know about that. I love my baby girl
like no other though."

"Jaxon?"

"Hmm?" he asked and nuzzled his cheek over her
collarbone.

"Can I ask you about Maryella's mom?"

The water rippled with small waves when he shifted onto his elbows and then laid his head back down where it had been. "You could."

SIN'S FLOWER

Chapter Twenty-Six

Lily could guess there was a *but* lingering around his short response. But, if she didn't, she'd always be bothered by the pestering questions surrounding the mother of his child.

"So I get that you two aren't together but with it being Christmas, I was wondering if Maryella sees her much."

He did his best to prop himself back up and washed his hands over his face. The pompadour of his hair was so sexy slicked back. With it flat like that, he looked like just your average totally hot guy with a rockin' bod. Not at all like the creative genius behind one of the best-selling rock bands of her time.

"So here it goes. I'd never try to be rude to you, Lily, but talking about her just flat out pisses me off. She and I never married but when Maryellie was born we tried to make a bad relationship work. After five years it was obvious that was a huge mistake. Things finally blew up at Maryellie's fifth birthday party. That was the last time I saw the woman. She chooses not to be in our lives and I'm fine with that."

Maryella was seven now so Lily could do the math and figure out that Vangie hadn't been around for two years now. Wow. She guessed she had her answers to that question. The way he had half of his fist curled around his mouth and his thumb digging into his cheek said it all.

"Okay, well thank you for sharing that with me. There's nothing else I need to know. I won't bring it up again, unless you ever just feel the need to unload. Unfortunately, I've been there, done that, so I get it."

Oh, why did she end with that? Was she trying to ruin this perfect moment for them with talk of exes? How could he not…yep, there was the question in his eyes.

"If I ever cross paths with your fucker ex-husband, I'm kicking his ass, baby. Whatever shit he did to you, I'm gonna do whatever I have to, to make sure you forget that crap. Just so you know."

How could she not smile and when was she gonna learn never to assume she knew what was going on in that genius head of his?

"Deal. I guess it's time we got out and dried off. I'm all pruny," she said examining her hand in the shadows.

Jaxon laid his lips into hers just as the knock sounded at the bathroom door.

She felt her eyes become wide. But she also flashed an easy smile. After all, Benny had to have known this was coming. Somehow, his being on the other side of the door wasn't terrifying in the least. She kissed Jaxon's cheek to let him know she was totally comfortable officially being his woman.

* * * *

He was sated and ready to go again but that knock at the bathroom door had probably quashed all Lily's sexy inhibitions of the last half hour.

"Boss?" came Benny's call, a loud, forced whisper followed by a few knocks.

"What's up, Benny?" he called back, sure it was nothing and hopeful he'd be able to dismiss him quickly and make Lily forget about her wrinkly fingers. He wanted more.

"Uh, there's uh, some visitors. You might want to—"

"Hold on, mate." Jaxon climbed out of the tub dripping wet, trying not to step on Lily, and toweled off his legs, ass and chest quickly before wrapping it around his waist then opened the door a crack. He looked back over his shoulder to see Lily still dunked below the water. He protected the small opening he'd made with his body so Benny wouldn't see his goods. "What's up?"

"Dude, your dad is here. And your uncle. And Trista's grandma Grace. Just thought I'd let you know."

"Shit." That was a lot of visitors. "Okay, just give us a few minutes and we'll be out."

He turned around after closing the door. "Did you hear that?"

"Yep." She sank below the water's surface.

"Hey, hey, come back up here," he said, reaching into the tub and bringing her back by the shoulder. "It's no big deal."

"Jaxon, it's kind of a big deal."

"No it's not. So what? We were in the bath together. News flash, I'm fucking old and you're old enough. I don't give a shit what anyone thinks and the good news is that they aren't gonna think anything anyways. It's none of their business."

"Well I don't know about Bear and Luke, but I guarantee you Grace is going to think something. Oh my God, she's gonna know we had sex in the bathtub and then she's gonna tell Tris. And then Tris will kill you and kick me out of the house. I'll be homeless; you'll be banned from ever visiting again. I'm gonna pass out."

He just shook his head realizing thirty-one wasn't so far from being in her twenties. "Whoa, whoa. Slow down. None of that is going to happen. I thought you were okay with us, Lily. Have you changed your mind?"

He didn't believe that was the case. Even though he was sure her worries were non-issues, and that not

Grace nor his uncle nor dad would go flapping about something as mundane as Jaxon's sex life. The skin on the back of his neck did prickle at Trissy's reaction if she learned about what he'd done, however. So she'd left him alone with her baby sister for less than twenty-four hours and in that time Jaxon had asked her to be his and consummated their relationship, in Trissy's bathtub. He nearly chuckled but Lily was now out of the tub and rubbing profusely at skin she'd already dried to the bone.

"Hey, are we okay? I get it this isn't how we pictured things. I for one was not quite done with you yet, but at least we get to walk out of here together. Right?"

"Uh, do you think that's a good idea?"

"Hmm. Ouch."

"That's not what I meant," she said.

"No big deal. I'm dry. I'll go on out. You take your time."

"Jaxon. That's not what I meant."

"Lily, I don't know if it's me or you or the asshole who made you feel like dirt, but it's feeling like one of those battles."

"Don't say that."

"Okay, I won't. But don't make it feel like I'm losing every time I try to help."

Her chin nearly clapped against her breastbone and she wrapped herself in her towel then got dressed over it. As much as he wanted what was underneath, and not just her body—had he gone after too good a prize? He was all about aiming high but was Lily even attainable? Moments like this made him wonder. If her instincts were constantly to pull back and protect herself, what did that say about him? It said he needed to keep working on his patience. "I'm sorry, baby. Come here."

He wrapped his arms around her still moist skin now poking out from a lumpy layer of stretched shirt over thick towel. She relaxed into his embrace a few seconds later.

"Okay, well I'll be out there waiting. Don't take too long." He made to open the door when she sniffled.

"Your clothes are out on the couch."

"Yep, if we're lucky, Benny saw them and scooped them up for me." But Jaxon knew better. If Benny had done that, he'd have handed them over through the crack in the door. Most likely they were still in the neat pile where Lily had left them for him. Easily accessible, she'd said. "All right. Just breathe. It'll be fine."

* * * *

A half hour later and Lily sat still and sinking like an old rotting tree stump there on the couch, listening to Luke and Bear wind down their excitement over the call they'd gotten not an hour ago from Lucky.

"They're just giving the baby another hour to turn on his own and if he doesn't, then they're going through with the C-section," said Luke.

Grace folded her hands as if in prayer and smiled warmly. "That's wonderful, Luke. You're about to join the grandparents club. I couldn't be happier for you."

Lily couldn't help but glance in Bear's direction, wondering if anyone else was as worried as Lily that the baby was three months early.

The tall, still blond but turning white haired, and as Luke had described him, cocked diesel, giant of a man had technically been a member of that club for seven years now, only this was his first true visit with his one and only grandchild. It was hard to imagine Jaxon having kept Maryella away from his dad like that. Lily knew better than to ask any more questions about Vangie,

273

but something told her the girl's mother had nothing to do with that. It would have been a father's decision.

Lily had never met a kinder man than Bear Mason. Other than his brother, Luke, and of course Lucky. So what in the world had kept Jaxon and Maryella away for so long from this place overabounding with loving family? If it had nothing to do with Vangie like Lily believed, the topic shouldn't be off limits. If she ever made it off this couch and Jaxon ever rejoined her from his stoop in the kitchen, maybe she'd ask him. Then again, with the strained look on his face, maybe not.

Bear just dipped his humble head and feathered his large hooked fingers through his healthy head of hair while his younger brother Luke donned a set of sparkling eyes. "Hey, we've kept the kids up way past their bedtime. Let's turn off some lights and hit the sacks. Don't wanna be scaring off Santa for little Maryella." His cheeks were rosy, just like Saint Nick. "Everyone know where they're bedding down?" asked Luke.

Jaxon spoke up with clear respect for his elders which impressed Lily. He'd seemed so aloof and swaggerly around them the few times they'd been together this visit. "Lucky and Trissy's room is available if you'd like a bed to sleep in. Maryella's in the nursery. Benny's on the long couch and I…"

"And Jaxon and I are in my room," Lily chimed in. He blinked while his face relaxed and a grin quirked one corner of his mouth. Lily went and stood by his side.

"Luke and I'll do just fine out here on the couches. Let Benny make use of the open room." Bear said, stretching his shoulders and rotating them when Lily smiled inside. She'd seen Jaxon roll his shoulders just like that a couple times now.

Well it was settled and with relative ease. The brothers Mason would hunker down on the couches,

Grace would presumably retire to her flat, Benny could go back to Tris's room, and she and Jaxon would slink off to her room.

She didn't know why, but Lily immediately spun her head to see Grace's reaction.

What she got was herself in a hard place. "Well, I'll see you gentlemen in the morning for coffee and biscuits and Lily, you're welcome to stay out back with me in the grandma quarters if you'd prefer to let Jaxon have your room to himself."

Oh boy. Was there a polite way to say no thanks, I'd rather sleep on the floor with the one man on earth I'm supposed to stay away from according to the sister I'd do anything to make happy? She didn't think so either.

It seemed like all six of them looked around the living room together. Then Benny backed his way down the hall and disappeared into Tris's room. Luke plopped down on his couch, sending shock waves through every tassled throw pillow in his wake. Bear stretched once more then chimed in, "Grace, I think I recall hearing Maryella say she wanted to wake up and make special Christmas morning French toast with Lily. Probably easier if Auntie Lily's already here. You know my granddaughter likes to get up bright and early."

Thank you, Bear. You are a life saver.

Grace didn't seem affected either way but Lily believed somewhere inside, she'd hoped that Lily would have gone with her. Oh well. Grace came over and gave her a light squeeze. "Okay dear, whatever you feel most comfortable with. I'll bring over a carafe of coffee to go with that French toast in the morning. Sleep well kids."

"Good night, Grace."

That left just Jaxon, Luke, Bear and Lily in the living room and she was sure Luke was already snoring.

"Well, see you in the morning, Bear," Jaxon let out.

"Yep. See ya in the mornin'. Merry Christmas Eve, son."

Lily watched Jaxon give a slow but short nod and then she followed him down the hall to her room. Her heart was about to explode from having just seen the father reach out to his son only to be shunned. But her heart also went out to Jaxon who had to have his reasons. Before she racked herself emotionally any further, she took a deep breath because it was about to be the two of them alone in her room with Maryella sleeping soundly next door. On Christmas Eve. Almost like a little family of their own. Her shoulders rose and the step she took through the opened door was on her tippy toes.

"After you," said her man.

Once inside, they used the glow of her small lamp to find their blanket pallet on the floor. "Come here."

"You say that a lot to me. It's a good thing I like it," she whispered.

He stretched out on his back and patted the fluffy carpet they would call bed that night.

"I really wish I had an adult size bed."

"Your bed's adult size, it's just made for one. I've grown pretty fond of this floor thing. It's kind of like camping. Do you like camping?" he asked her, pulling his shirt off and leaving it on the chair. It took her a minute to remember drooling wasn't cool.

"I don't know. Never been. And you don't seem like the woodsy type," she said, swallowing.

He pulled her into his bare, hunky chest for a hug and a rub. "First of all, the Aussie in me is insulted. I haven't been in a while though. But the guys and I used to make a special trip once a year out east for band bonding. We haven't done it in a couple years. Maybe

I'll have to start that back up. Come on, you know you want to go camping with Stefan Calderon," he teased her mercilessly and she actually loved it.

With the pending disaster of surprise visitors averted, Lily found herself wanting to be with Jaxon again. When she joined him, he scooted and pulled so that her head rested comfortably on his bounteous bicep. It didn't matter that her face was buried in his armpit. Only she would know what a man who'd been dipped in cotton candy bath water smelled like. In one word, delicious. He then tucked a quilt around her and sealed it shut with his thigh hanging over her hip. She wondered if he was also thinking about how wonderful they'd felt joined together.

"For a second there, I thought you were gonna send me on my way out with Grace."

"Maybe I should have."

"Why do you say that?" she asked.

"Let me ask you this, what are you thinking about right this very second?"

"Honestly? Maryella and what she's gonna think of seeing her daddy and aunty coming out of the same room in the morning. I hope she's okay with it." They were nice, family like things to be thinking about. Why did his stare make her feel like she'd failed some test? "Why?"

"And all I want is to be inside you again." He kissed her forehead. "That's why."

　　　* * * *

Lying on the floor in Lily's room—he wanted his woman. After that one taste, he craved another.

"You, well, I mean that's on my mind too, obviously," she whispered into his underarm hairs, tickling him. "That wasn't a fair question, Jaxon."

"Shush," he said, sorry he'd unintentionally tried to one up her.

"No, I thought about us. I just have other things I worry about too. I'm sorry, but that's me. Then there's Tris and Lucky and the baby too."

He edged back an inch.

"Okay, I believe you." Great, he'd insulted her devotion and she'd cracked his ego. On the whole, not so bad actually. "Can we forget I said that?" But Lily wasn't biting. She'd even pulled her nose back from where it had been nuzzling. "Never mind," he said to the top of her head which then shot back so she could look up at him.

It was a good thing she was dressed. Her anger was sexy.

"Are you ignoring me now, Jaxon?" Really, either we have sex or you turn off?"

"I'm not doing that. I promise. Now shush and lay back."

She huffed and it sounded so cute. "Did we just have our first fight?" she asked.

"Are you refusing to let me inside you again?" he whispered into her ear.

"Jaxon, are you teasing me?"

"Yes. Get some sleepies. We'll be up and making breakfast far too early for my likes. I'm sorry if I got a little cranky with you. I just enjoyed our first time so much. I want more. I'm always gonna want more, Lily. Sleep on that and make sure you're okay with it."

The truth was that the old him would have taken what he wanted. An unwilling girl wasn't kept around when it was him and the guys. Not when there were so many eager to take her place. But Lily was different. Her honesty was the best thing he'd felt in ages.

"Jaxon, I'm sorry about leaving you like that."

"Yeah, you better watch out or I'm gonna start calling you V."

The peachy complexion he'd grown quickly to love blanked and she looked like she'd just watched a marathon of horror movies.

"V?" she said, her face crumpled.

Shit, not that V. Not Vangie. "For Viagra, baby. Viagra." He took her face into his hands and held her there until she saw that it had been a mistake what he'd just said.

Her hand hovered near the club that had once been his neglected but relatively stress free dick. Now his shit was fuc...fudging in distress. "It's all right. Just close your eyes and let's get some sleepies." He was thankful for the crazy hours Trissy's absence at their dress shop had tolled on Lily. *Fall asleep baby, please.* He needed to roll over and jack his shit.

But no. That wasn't happening. Lily rolled over so that she was now facing him. "Can't sleep?" he asked her.

"No, not really." She loosened a hand and it effectively sent shudders up and down his entire body. She'd accidentally swiped between them and touched his groin. "Oh man. That's my fault. Maybe I could offer you some assistance." She sounded so technical and stiff. Not to mention nervous, unsure, adorable.

Before he could say what a bad idea her assistance probably was, before he could worry about the people who thought the two of them together was treachery, her hot thigh escaped the burrito he'd tried to make of her and was up and over his hip and her head tilted down looking between the darkened space between their two bodies. Her fingers started at his belly button and zigzagged around in his hairs. "God, that's sexy." He knew it the exact moment when those beautiful fingers met the base of his dick. They circled around it slowly and then he felt her fingertips join around him with the pad of her thumb. "Fuck, Lily." He was so sorry he'd cursed in front of her again but he couldn't help this. "Sorry baby."

"Shhh. Don't be sorry. Stop worrying and just be you."

"Hey, that's my line to you."

But he couldn't joke around with her right now. He moaned and swore to himself and the saints that he wasn't sorry. That he never wanted to feel another woman's touch on his body again. "Unnnhhh," he moaned again trying to muffle the noise in her hair.

* * * *

Jaxon's body felt wonderful under her hands. Not just the one wrapped around his manhood. His hip bone was so sexy as she focused on the differences and similarities of the two areas she stroked now. One area was hot, soft and hard all at the same time, a little bumpy from hairs sprouting out and the small veins rising under the tightly stretched skin. His hip had her entranced. She hoped she wasn't neglecting the hand job she'd offered him but his hip was...perfect. No extra padding from unwanted fat. Just taut muscle over bone. Bone covered by tanned soft skin. Had he been born that way, so sinful but heartbreakingly gorgeous? She wondered if she could convince him to walk around freezing Tennessee in his lowest rising pants and a short shirt to show it off. That would be so mean.

The thoughts of being with him in sunny and warm California suddenly became ecstasy. Could she imagine it? Oh yes she could. Him walking around naked whenever he wanted. Jaxon had to take Maryella and Benny home in one week. And somewhere in her heart, she knew she couldn't leave Tris. There was going to be a flipping farewell taking place soon. One where she'd try to be confident, and dammit, work her sexy for him.

Chapter Twenty-Seven

"You don't like this part of your body, do you?" he asked her after some time had passed and some space had been created and then erased between them.

"No, not really."

"Did you know that I wish I could lay my head down, right here, and just pet you without ever stopping? Your body is gorgeous, Lily. See this?" He let his hand slide up and down in the valley of her waist and the hill of her hip. "I love this. A woman is supposed to have this here. It's where I need to hold onto you. Where I did hold onto you. Remember? So fucking sexy."

She gasped. "I do feel kind of sexy when you put it that way. And yes, I remember."

"Good girl."

"Jaxon, where does it come from? The way you feel so sensual about your body?"

"Mmm. I feel an immense desire at the thought of having sex, and sharing myself, I always have. Maybe it comes from Australia. We're special down there like that." Every time he winked, her cheeks warmed against his bicep.

She chuckled lightly at his joke. "But is there a part on you that you like? Kind of how I hate my hips a little less now that we've had this talk."

Who could help themselves from smiling? Neither of them.

"My hands."

"They are beautiful. They really are. You know what part I like?"

He loved that they were having this conversation, so open and natural and raw and sexy and real. Especially after the near fight they'd gotten into only minutes ago. He'd rather think of it as a misunderstanding. Once Lily understood that he would always want to stop time to make love to her, they would be much better off. They continued their whispered conversation.

"What part, baby? I'll make sure I take very good care of it for you."

Her mouth had to stop smiling like that. "Right here." And then she touched his neck where the rose thorns tattoo traveled up from his shoulder muscle, along his pulsing artery. "I think if I kissed you there now, I'd never want to stop."

She had no idea he'd had the tattoo put there back in his younger years as a statement of what he thought about the women professing their undying love to him. All thorns, no roses. And then so many hadn't paid attention and thought they were teeth marks. The assumptions grew that he liked to be bitten there because of one damned song he'd done during a blood sucker fascination phase. And he'd been wasted at the time.

"You look like you'd rather be castrated, Jaxon."

"No, no." He didn't want to explain because then she'd know more about that man he wanted to forget and never ever introduce her to. "Your sweet perfect lips would feel incredible in that spot."

"Yeah?"

"Yeah, go ahead. Have a taste."

But before he had the chance to enjoy that, his phone buzzed in his pocket. He ripped it out, set to heave it across the room. But the contact name flashing at him was Vangie's mother. No matter how dead against he was talking about his ex right now, Mrs. Acosta had generally been decent to him and to that he owed her a few minnies of his time. He caught Lily's face in his palms just as she was about to send him to heaven.

"Lily, I'm gonna step out to take this," he said and flashed her his phone. "Be right back," he mouthed to her. See, if he'd been without his pants, he would have avoided this interruption. Pants could kiss his ass.

She nodded and he hopped up then quietly left the room. "Just a second," he said, deciding the only place where he wouldn't wake anyone was outside. Shoeless and freezing, he stood on the side porch steps marching softly to keep his toes from turning to ice cubes.

"Hello? Elva? Is that you? I can't hear too well. Can you speak up?" The connection wasn't great, making her voice small and distant.

"Jaxon? Jaxon? Are you with Maryella?" Elva Acosta had always surprised him with her soft-spoken voice, so glaringly opposite of Vangie's, and he'd had plenty occasions to hear her cry over her daughter's behavior. Shit, he'd shared a few of his own tears with her.

"Yes, Elva. It's me and I'm here at my family's home in Tennessee with Maryellie. But I can't hear you too good. Are you all right?" He continued to prance on the porch.

"Oh Jaxon, it's Vangie."

So help him, not a word for two years. If she had gone and booked herself a room for the night with the Vegas PD, at motherfucking Christmas, he was gonna be so pissed. As much as being a single dad was kicking his ass, he wasn't ever fucking up again. This was the best gig of his life and he'd never forget that. If he could get his shit together, then Vangie should do the same. But her problems had never been about addiction. There probably wasn't a cure for bitchiness and a passion for fighting. Those were just unfortunate personality traits that Vangie had in spades.

"Have you heard from her? Does she want something?" He sighed, not letting down his guard. In the two years since she'd disappeared, he'd finally gotten her poison out of his system.

Then he remembered the ad and the looming deadline for her to respond about amending Maryellie's birth certificate. Shit! That's what this was about. God dammit with the games.

He cracked his knuckles. For as much as he'd wished in the past that they could have worked things out, the thought of Vangie being near Maryellie set his hackles on edge. Elva hadn't said anything in response yet.

"She was at a boyfriend's house, I think." The calm had left Elva's voice and it quivered.

"The one in Vegas?" Why did he care?

"Yes, probably," she choked out.

"Elva, what are you not telling me? Did she ask you to call? Because I'm sorry. She left us, without a word. Two years ago. I'm done. I have to protect Maryellie from that right now. She's too little to understand."

His daughter hadn't seen her mummy since she was five. That had been the last time Vangie had stolen Maryellie from him. Later, thanks to a call from Elva, he'd found out Vangie'd taken off to Vegas. And a few days after that, had called Elva to come get Maryellie while she *figured things out*. Darkness clawed at his eyes, his throat felt rough when he swallowed. The worst part? He hadn't done anything to help Vangie once she'd left like that.

"Vangie died, Jaxon. An officer called me about a couple hours ago."

Vangie was dead? Jaxon fell back against the house, stunned. "Elva, are you okay?"

"I'll be okay. I'm sorry I had to call you with this news tonight. I really am, so so sorry."

"Oh Elva, please don't worry about that. Do you know what happened?"

"Jaxon, my daughter, she just never figured things out. The officer said there was a fight with a boyfriend. Vangie left the apartment in his car and pulled out in front of someone. They hit her on the driver side. It was fast." Elva began to cry a desolate mother's tears. She was able to catch her breath for a moment. "I didn't call to say this, but thank you for not shutting me out of Maryella's life. I know it must be hard. But I'm so grateful right now."

Jaxon's emotions had deserted him. He couldn't even address the subject of his baby's mum being dead. "Elva, you're a great grandma. Maryellie loves you, very much. I wish you got to see her more." Elva had always come to them in California. He'd yet to make a trip to see her in Texas. That would change now. "I don't know what to say, Elva. But, I'm sorry. For a lot of things."

Elva sniffled. "You've done all you can. You're a good man, Jaxon. And a great dad. And for what it's worth, I'm sorry too."

"Elva, I'm not sure what final plans there will be, but please let me take care of those. Please let me do that on behalf of Maryellie."

She made a wet, snorting sound like she'd just crossed the line into delirium for having to think of those. "You just take care of my grandbaby and yourself. How are you doing, Jaxon?"

He wanted to promise her so many things but knew that would be wrong. He couldn't imagine the crap she'd gone through having Vangie as her only child. Shit, how much of that crap had been his fault too?

"I'm in a good place, Elva. Because of Maryellie. God, I'm so sorry. If you change your mind or need anything, please call me. Please take care of yourself."

"Hug Maryella for me, Jaxon. Hug her and tell her I love her."

"I will. I promise."

The phone disconnected from Elva's end.

For a few minutes, he stood there in shadows of the porch's overhang. The intersecting wooden beams of the frame reflected a slanting cross onto his chest. He tried but failed to rub the shadow away. Raindrops falling just to his right sprayed him and began to drip from his face and shirt until he moved to sit down on the porch bench. Outdoor smells of old, wooden beams and even more ancient trees being washed clean bled through the home's sidewalls. What more was there to think about?

The woman he'd fathered his baby girl with was gone. That twisted his heart. The tumultuous years he and Vangie had plowed through together and the countless times they should have called it quits for good rumbled around his soul. All the people they'd hurt. He knew better than to lay the blame solely at Vangie's feet. At least she'd had the guts to be the one to leave in the end. Thank God she'd had the wits to return their daughter before she went and fucked herself up even worse. He'd let Vangie treat people he cared about like crap for so long but had done his best not to let Maryellie feel any of that. Now he had no idea what to say or do.

His mind lost, a deep cough choked its way out his throat. The back of his head lobbed backward, hitting the house as he sat there on the bench. Never had he wished she'd die. Why couldn't she just have gotten better? Why hadn't she made it easier on one single person who would have cared to help her?

"Damn you, Vangie," he whispered to the lonely country. Grabbing at his hair, he slouched down onto the cold bench further, pissed she'd never come back and make it up to their daughter. "I'm sorry, baby girl."

He needed something to hold. Against the cold, hard wall, he banged his head until the numbness went away and pain showed up in its place. He understood the years of crap he was owed to make up for the past but his daughter? What had she done to deserve this? Nothing. Nothing but be tied to him. Nobody should bear that fucked up fate. "I hate this shit," he yelled out in a thundering roar. Let them all hear him. The real him.

* * * *

Lily could have sworn she'd heard something on the other side of the door. She'd already slipped into her coat to go look for Jaxon. He'd been gone a while now. Before heading out, she made sure Maryella was sleeping like a rock. All was well.

There wasn't much she could do about the ice cold rain pelting against the outside of the door. She was going out in it to find her man and apologize for not being more focused on them and their beautiful first night together. No doubt about it, she wanted him, and in her heart, wished everyone knew. Well, wished everyone was okay with the knowledge. But Jaxon was right, she shouldn't worry about what anyone else thought. It wasn't their business.

She had it in mind to make a lightning quick beeline to the covered RV pull through on the far side of the driveway but found she didn't need to go so far. Jaxon was sitting on the porch bench just off to the side from the door. Heat sizzled up her neck to her cheeks at the thought of him not having to stay out on the couch anymore.

Until she looked more closely. He looked so cold with his bluish lips she just wanted to get him back in the house. Oh no, he was barefoot. He would freeze. After a few unanswered smiles, she reached her hand out to his cheek but he looked down. Weird because before he'd left, they'd been in the middle of something mind-blowing. At least it had felt that way for her.

"Jaxon. Hey you."

He moved over on the bench, signaling he didn't mind if she sat with him but he wasn't going in yet. She huddled close to his side, hoping to avoid the rain's splatter.

"Hey. Where've you been? Fall asleep out here? You know the anti-Jaxon/Lily squad is all the way in Nashville. It sank in for me about five minutes ago; we don't have to sneak around anymore," she teased, excited to give him a…well what did she give the guy who just an hour ago had offered her a taste? And before that the best sex she'd ever experienced in her thirty-one years. A hug? A high-five? A lick? As she moved closer, she saw that there was no place for her humor. Something had come up and changed his red hot lust into ice cold blues.

His proud and playful shoulders slumped which she'd never seen from him and he was gonna rub his forehead raw if he kept up with working the heel of his palm against it so roughly. It became obvious they weren't picking up where they'd left off. "Hey, what's going on?" she asked lightly and then dipped her head down low so she could try and see his face.

"Don't wanna talk about it."

"Okay. We don't have to talk. I just was worried because you lef—"

He silenced her with a single wounded look. The purplish circles she'd gotten used to under his eyes from the times she'd seen him perform with his guyliner were darker now from the shadows. He hadn't worn any rocker stage make up since she'd personally gotten to know him but his hypnotizing teal blue eyes usually appeared rimmed with darkness. Suddenly, his face was right in hers. If he didn't look so gone, she'd have smoothed her fingertips under his eyes and along his cheekbones in some kind of gesture. Something had definitely happened. He wasn't talking so how could she know what was wrong?

"Jaxon, you're scaring me." They were supposed to be working on this trust thing together.

"You know I'd never hurt you," he cut out a reply and then went back to squeezing his head between his palms. Somehow she sensed he meant more than physically. Like he was vowing something to her, the house, even the town.

"Of course I know that." As soon as she said it, his tension level seemed to draw down but not completely.

"How's my Maryellie?" he asked, sounding so far out of touch.

"Still zonked outright next door to our room. She's okay, I promise." Yes, she'd emphasized *our* on purpose, surprising herself.

The black shirt he wore looked like it was bothering him, or it could be that everything was bothering him right now. He stood up and tugged at the sleeves and kept his eyes just about everywhere except focused on her. Harder than a steel boxing glove, reality punched her in the gut and it tugged her heart down with it to drown.

"Jaxon, you changed your mind about us, right? This, whatever all this is, it's not necessary." She made to leave but he caught her arm tight. She was about to shrug free from his hold and obvious guilt at having led her on when she saw him choking for air. "Jaxon, just breathe. Tell me what's wrong. "

"Maryellie's mum called." He licked the moisture running from his nose down to his lips and then wiped the rest away with the back of his hand.

"Oh. Oh, I'm sorry. You talked to her?"

"No. Mrs. Acosta," he said, seeming to have a difficult time acknowledging that name. It must be Vangie's mother. He looked to the sky like life was a complete mystery to him. "I've been so out of my mind that she'd show back up someday. That I'd finally get my shit straightened out and be doing good for baby girl and then she'd show up and turn it to hell. Well, she died today."

Lily's hand flew first to cover her mouth and next to soothe the splitting headache he looked to be dying under. "I'm so sorry." She felt like a first-rate, stuttering idiot but one who wanted to get him inside the warm house. She knew all about having to live on antacids because of the fear your ugly past would mutilate your pretty new fresh start. Not like this though. It was obvious he'd been rocked by the call.

"Hey, why don't we go check on Maryella?" Lily put her hand on the doorknob and waited. It took a few seconds, but he turned to her with his hand over hers. Unfortunately, she *could* imagine what he was going through, barely keeping ahead of his past.

His eyes darted to the side, reminding her of a tough guy who didn't want to ask or answer for anything. He took a few moments but finally responded. It was both a surprising yet expected response from her boyfriend who was hurting. "Lily, fuck—"

"It's okay. Hey, whatever it is, just tell me," she said, aware she was nearly numb to the curse word he dropped like insignificant crumbs off the counter. She went ahead and smoothed the hair hanging in his face back without worrying whether he'd protest. His pain was too present not to feel some of it herself.

He snorted up a full sounding sinus cavity of mucus and coughed. And then he nearly laughed at himself before slipping away from her back into his grief. "I really need you tonight," he said plainly. She knew his seductive side intimately, and this wasn't it. This was different, although she wouldn't deny he still looked at her with immense longing.

"All right...but," she stuttered out. If some space was better for him, she had to offer it. "Don't feel like I'm expecting anything. If you need to be alone I completely understand."

"Lily, I'm an alcoholic. I need someone to remind me why it would be a very stupid thing for me to go looking for a drink. You're the only one I trust telling that."

She was proud of him and heartbroken for his struggle all at once.

She flashed back to the night at his house when she'd wanted to make a wine sauce for a meal and astonishingly hadn't found anything remotely close to containing alcohol. Crap, what if Lucky and Tris had liquor lying around or tucked into a cupboard somewhere? Should she run in and scour the place first? But then she risked waking the men and causing a scene. Gosh, how did he deal with being on the road and in a band known for its bad behavior and badly behaving crowds? An itch bugged her scalp and the muscles lining her brow bone tensed. It wasn't much, but she offered what she could. "Hey, after we check on Maryella, I have something I think will make you feel better. Okay?"

Jaxon nodded and followed her inside, still uncharacteristically slumped.

The toast burnt her fingers but she knew the butter would melt best that way. A thin layer of strawberry jam came next. Lily had never served anyone else this go to stress reducer and never in a bathroom, but it went best with her tears, maybe it would go with the ones Jaxon looked to be holding in. She set the toast on a small plate and handed it over to him on the toilet seat. Relief poured through her that she hadn't crashed and banged around with her arms full of bread, butter, jam and a few utensils, and the toaster, from the kitchen to the bathroom.

He bit down. "Thanks."

"Welcome. Always makes me feel better. So I just figured…"

He sniffed and she tried to look away because watching him avoid his feelings the past couple hours was turning her to emotional mush. Her magical toast might do wonders to boost her sad times, but it was just strawberry toast to him. He'd been very accommodating to sit there and eat it while she watched.

"So, Maryella was sleeping soundly. You know, she's a great little kid. I've really enjoyed my time with her."

Sometimes hiding your feelings just took too much work. When Jaxon's head hit his forearms, she knew he was dead tired from it. She grabbed his plate just as it teetered on his lap and threatened to smash to the ground.

"Lily, we have to be sure of what we're doing by the time your sister comes home with the baby. I'll stay as long as I can but I can't promise how long that will be."

A thought she'd been tossing back and forth all evening solidified at his words. "I agree. You go be with Maryella. I'm going to go spend some time with Grace."

She cleaned up the crumbs into the sink, bundled her arms with her supplies and let him open the door for her. "Really?" he asked dumbfounded.

After laying a kiss on his cheek, she assured him. "I have questions and I've come to realize you don't have the answers, Jaxon. That's okay." She kissed his cheek again. "Maybe Grace does. You think you're not a good friend, but you are. And I know how hard it will be for you to hurt Tris by being with me out in the open when she comes home. If I can figure out why Tris is so against us being together, I can at least try and fix it so we don't feel like we have to hide."

She didn't miss the way he worried his fingers along the silver zippers of his pants as she got up to leave.

* * * *

Here he'd found Lily, the perfect woman for both him and his daughter, only he'd have to steal her away from someone he'd already wounded in order to have her in their life. Life wasn't just unfair, it was cruel.

Grace. It all boiled down to whether or not Trissy had ever confided in her grandmum about their vile night.

In a matter of seconds, the memories shot through his mind, clawing to be seen and acknowledged. He flipped up the toilet lid just in time and heaved. All he could see when he opened his bulging eyes were the pink chunks of Lily's strawberry toast.

He should have told her the truth then and there in the bathroom.

She was on a mission to get answers and if she got them from anyone but him, he knew this little thing

he'd started with her would be done. His excruciating
headache plummeted to his heart.

Chapter Twenty-Eight

Grace's flat took on an entirely different feel now that she was back. The potted plants lining her windowsill perked up, like the cold winter was of no consequence now that their mama was back. Grace took up her spot, petite and solid, at the kitchenette's sink, petting the ivy's leaves as Lily sat on the loveseat.

Lily admired Grace as she tended to the smaller details that the younger generations let slide and slide and slide until they became too small to see. The doilies setting here and there, ready to host dishes or knick-knacks or just look pretty were her favorite. The white lace reminded her of being a little girl and learning to sew. She wondered if Grace and her momma had been close. With the way Tris's father had died so suddenly, and then how quickly Momma had married Daddy, she wasn't sure if Grace had any ill feelings that her daughter-in-law had moved on too fast. Lily wished her relationship with Grace felt as easy as it looked. Maybe someday they'd be closer. For now, Lily at least trusted she'd get the no-nonsense truth in this modest dwelling.

"I hope you don't mind, but I've been doing some sewing in here while you've been gone. I even tried teaching Jaxon. I hope we didn't disturb it very much."

"Oh, it's no problem. I'm glad the place was of use."

Interesting. Grace didn't seem too concerned over the lessons. "You know, I'm surprised Jaxon didn't try to hideout in your flat this whole time. There were a couple heated dinners over in the main house."

Grace offered Lily a quilt and a throw pillow. "Here you go dear. One thing's for sure is no one made much use of the space heaters." She took her own set of quilts with her to the bed and turned up a small portable heating unit before sitting and tucking her slippered feet beneath her. "Lily, you used the words 'hide out'. I suspect that means you have an understanding of Jaxon's situation, maybe more so than you think. And with that understanding, no, dear, I'm not surprised."

The woman didn't mince words and tiptoeing around what she wanted to know would tire them both sooner than later. "Grace, you're right. I do know enough to get why Jaxon feels uncomfortable in the main house. With all those years he stayed away from his dad and uncle and then especially after Maryella was born. I sense he's got a ton of guilt over that."

Grace nodded and rubbed cream from a rosy colored, palm-sized pot into her crinkled skin. She offered some to Lily. "Thank you, that smells wonderful. Like roses." They both smelled their fingers at the same time and smiled.

"So it sounds like you've had a chance to get to know Jaxon. That's good. I've always felt bad for that young man. He could use a friend now that Trista Jeane has found Lucky."

"You speak surprisingly well of him."

"Why does that surprise you, dear?"

"Um, I guess because he looks like…"

"Like he's here to cause trouble?" Grace chuckled. "The first time Trista Jeane brought Jaxon to my old trailer park, I had to spend three weeks vouching that he hadn't robbed me blind or snuck out with any of the neighbors' precious lawn decorations. So silly. That was about fifteen years ago. Do you know that every year he'd visit, I'd have to go over the same complaints and questions with the same old ninnies? Of course it would have helped if he'd let me brag about all the nice things he did for them at night when he couldn't sleep.

You haven't lived until you've seen a young man in his ripped up pants kneeling by a plastic Easter bunny pulling weeds after midnight, in a seniors' trailer park." She stopped to take a breath and have a chuckle. "But he asked me nicely to zip my lips about it so I did."

"That's very sort of sad and funny all at the same time. He has gotten a few odd looks the days we've gone to the dress shop together. Hmm, I guess I never really thought of it because I don't think of him as a..."

"As a bad guy?" Grace asked with her soft, thinning eyebrows raised just so.

"Right. He's not a bad guy at all. He's wonderful."

"Lily dear, you are welcome to stay out here and chit-chat with me; it's why I offered earlier tonight. But I am surprised that you've taken me up on it. Especially now."

"What do you mean, Grace?"

"One of these days you're going to realize that you have a good knack for answering your own questions." Grace smiled. "A young man who values his privacy has helped you out at the shop. I bet you if I walked the perimeter of my garden, there'd be less weeds and debris in my flower pots. You said yourself you don't see him as a bad guy and obviously his less than traditional looks haven't caused you to judge him unfairly. Yet you're here with me instead of with him."

Lily was genuinely shocked to hear that coming from such a moral and sound woman. There, she answered her own question again. If sound and moral Grace thought she was fine staying with Jaxon, why in the world wasn't she? Because. Her confusion didn't lie with Jaxon or Grace, it was tangled around her sister.

"You're absolutely right. I do want to be with Jaxon. But there is a reason I came to talk to you, Grace. And I honestly don't believe I have this answer."

"Well what is it, dear?"

"Do you have any idea why Tris is so against Jaxon and I being together? She all but transforms into Medusa with her stony looks whenever we're in the same room. Those glares are never for me though. They're always for Jaxon. It makes me feel so bad for him. But I owe Tris so much. And Lucky, and you too. You all are the last people I want to upset, especially Tris. I just don't understand. And, now that I've gotten to know Jaxon, it's really mind-baffling. I was hoping you might be able to shed some light on what Tris's beef is with him. It's like she's so happy he came out but can't wait to see him leave sometimes."

Grace rubbed the pads of her thumbs into the pads of her pointer fingers and then folded her hands, letting them rest gently over her quilted lap. "If I knew for sure, I would do my best to help you figure this out, Lily. But all I have are my own guesses. And you know what happens when you plant a rumor weed."

"What happens?"

"It grows. If I knew anything behind Trista Jeane's behavior for sure, I'd tell you. And I don't. Which means it could be too hard for her to have shared with me."

"Right." Lily let out a loud sigh.

"You really care about him, don't you, dear?"

"Grace, I respect you so I will be completely honest. Jaxon and I are in a relationship, of some sort. It's very new and so far I feel like I'm stumbling through it. But, yes, I already care deeply about him. That's why I'm out here. I have to figure out how to make this all work. I don't wanna upset the family I just barely got back but I also don't like having to hide how happy I am with Jaxon. Maybe it really is just Tris being the over protective, big sister."

"Lily, listen to me, very closely. You and I both know about the dark places your sister has come through. God bless her soul." Grace seemed to eyeball her at that.

Lily nodded, wondering at the sudden stare, and then leaned in and listened intently to Grace. In such close proximity, Lily picked up on the earthy notes of soil and wood mixed with the creamy rose and she took as much of it in as she could.

"I believe Jaxon was able to be that kind of rare friend to Trista Jeane all those years because his soul was suffering too. How else could he have stood by? Hmm? But Trista Jeane has Lucky now. Lucky, who has brought a special light to her life. You remind me a lot of Lucky. Maybe your sister is afraid Jaxon's darkness could block out your light, dear."

"Well, I never thought of it that way. But Grace, maybe what Lucky has been for Tris, I could be for Jaxon. Why can't she see it that way?"

Grace stood and huddled herself in her thickest housecoat. "I don't know. But you're exactly right. Which is why I am walking you back over to Jaxon now. People have to be together to figure these things out. I have faith that you will." Her thin, cold lips left a tender, warm kiss on Lily's cheek.

"Thank you, Grace," she said, slightly stunned.

"Lily, I'm always here for you. I don't suppose Jaxon is the only one dealing with guilt."

Lily didn't have to ask to know that Grace referred to taking Tris away from her and Jack when they were too little to understand why. "For the record, you have nothing to feel guilty about where I'm concerned, Grace. I am eternally grateful for what you did for my sister," she said into Grace's short, dark pageboy hair while hugging her close.

Grace nodded and then kindly told her to get her tush in gear; it was cold outside.

A spring took up in her step that would rival any rosy-cheeked, jolly old elfas she and Grace shuffled quickly back to the house. The odds were definitely in her favor now. She was two for two in the "It's just Tris being your over protective big sister" column. That, she decided, she could live with. It didn't hurt that she seemed to have Grace on her side.

Chapter Twenty-Nine

One o'clock in the morning. Well, Jaxon had bugged Benny at worse hours for much more trivial things.

He kissed Maryellie on the cheek, propped her koala back under her tiny fingers and got up to leave the nursery. He made a stop in Lily's room. His toe caught on the bottom of the quilt he'd burrito wrapped her in, making him miss her even more. How amazing was she that he was sleeping on floors without pillows and blankets to be with her? Pretty damn amazing. Knowing she was there for him helped the pain dull.

As he was passing the dresser by the door, he noticed a few small photos lying scattered on top. He didn't know what he thought he might find. Honestly, it was his desire to feel closer to her, to discover what kinds of things she liked to surround herself with so that maybe he could provide her those same types of things. Her closet door opened without a screech. The sight warmed his heart. He'd never seen so much space between the hangers in a woman's closet. She might have had ten items hanging, max.

One pair of jeans was pushed furthest back. Four pair of sweat pants, not the sexy ones with words scribbled across the butts in flirty colors, but thick, heavy and dark instead, weighed down their hangers. The other few bits were the matching tops to the dreary pants. Folded on the top shelf looked to be tee shirts. Oh, look at that, three whole pair of shoes and not a stiletto among them.

It made him wonder if this simple, bare bones style was really her or if it was the woman she'd had to be when she'd fled her ex in Oklahoma. That tiny bit

saddened him but soon, he realized the minimalistic sense
of the closet, the nearly bare room except for the bed and
the dresser, might mean she hadn't really laid down roots
here. At least not in this home. It still wasn't his intent
to take her from her sister, but it sure as hell convinced
him he was finding them a place nearby of their own. It
would take too long for Lucky to build something and
Jaxon's heart raced with impatience at the thought of
complete privacy, with Lily.

Now he had a valid reason to go wake Benny.
Jaxon needed to borrow his laptop.

"Hey Benny, you awake?"

"No," he grumbled out.

"I need to borrow your laptop. Just tell me where
it is and I'll get it. You don't have to get up. Where is it,
mate?" He gave the big foot hanging off the end of the
bed a flick.

"Ow. I have to sign on. Password."

"Just tell me what it is. I can do it."

"Unh. I'm up. I'll get it." Benny flopped over
then crawled to his gargantuan sized backpack.

"Your choice."

Jaxon watched and waited patiently as his
webmaster finagled the familiar rectangular black hunk
of folded machinery out from his backpack. When it was
opened, Jaxon stepped closer so he could take over as
soon as Benny signed in. He hadn't meant to be spying
but the poor guy's predictability was both charming and
sad. "Your password is Erby? Mate, you are devoted to
that girl like nothing I've ever seen."

"Whatever. Here."

Benny started to lie back down but Jaxon wasn't
sure which web browser to use. Geez, there were too
many choices. All he needed was to crash Benny's

system. Even his non-techy ass knew that would be catastrophic.

"I guess I'm not that tired. What are we looking for boss?"

He decided to let the name calling slide this time. "Homes in this area for sale."

"Uh, okay, is there something you need to tell me? Like as in, I need to find another job because Sin Pointe is about to be minus their leader? You would give me the heads up right?"

"Benny, your job is safe, mate. Nothing's happening with Sin Pointe. That's the problem actually. That's why we're finding a place to live out here."

"I know I'm sleep deprived most days and have been for the last decade, but I'm not following, boss."

"Well, the leader of the band might be ready for a change of scenery. A new playground. I'm hoping Nashville is a big enough enticement to convince the rest of the guys to move our sandbox out here. What do you think? Had enough of Rock Star, California?"

While Benny sat there readying his settings and browsers and windows and such, Jaxon realized he'd just put something major out there. The thought had teased him a few times now. He loved his villa by the beach but what good was paradise if you felt trapped in your own personal hell every minute of every day? While Jaxon wasn't the most comfy guy stuck under this roof with those he'd let down, he felt a strange kinship with the town. Maybe it was calling him home. Hopefully Stefan, Will and Marion could handle this apparent change of heart.

"What's that smirk all about there, mate?" He and Benny sat side by side on the extra-large bed but the only lap the computer was topping was Benny's. "You don't trust me with that, do you?"

"Uh, no and I'm not telling you, uh in the other order."

"Okay. Well pull up some sites and I'll tell you specifics of what we're looking for." He would let Benny off the hook for a few minutes while they searched but then they were getting back to the smirk his pal didn't care to explain.

"So give me some criteria. Are we talking house, condo, apartment, cabin in the woods?"

He shot Benny a dirty look for the last suggestion because he'd used his creepy voice to say it. "Let's shoot for a house, minimum three bedrooms, no make that four." The mental tally he'd done at first was wrong. He realized he'd need a room for himself and Lily, Maryellie, an office, and Benny. "Okay, so preferably five if we can find it." The experience here had taught him that an extra room was priceless. And, who knew? As much amazing sex as he planned on having with Lily, one could never be too sure. Not that he planned on making a baby with her, but it could happen. And if it didn't, fine. They'd have an extra play room he was sure they could find something to do with.

"Now you're the one grinning, boss."

He smacked Benny in the arm and then tugged him back upright. "Also put in there a pool or at least a lot with enough land to have one built."

Benny got hot working his input magic; his fingers flew fast and sure. By the last pause, Benny had found two matches with immediate availability. "Sweet. Let me get the numbers; I'll give them calls tomorrow. Wait, tomorrow's Christmas."

"Uh okay, boss, but it's not the stone age. We can just shoot them emails right now if you want. And technically, I believe it's the wee hours of Christmas day already. Merry Christmas, boss."

These were the things that made him feel old—the ability to conduct business at any hour, from any place on earth. "Right, okay let's do that. Make sure you put in there that I can buy it outright in one lump sum. That ought to persuade them to sell quickly."

"Or to think you're a drug dealer."

"Which is a good point. Leave out the part about the lump sum. Just say something clever that lets them know I'm a serious buyer and I'm looking to own ASAP."

Benny began composing a very professional looking email to each seller. As he typed, he blew up at his bangs, parting them with his breath. Jaxon watched in admiration.

"Hey Jaxon?"

"Yeah mate?"

"I know it's none of my business, but is this place just for you and Maryella?"

"Yes. And for Lily if she'll have me. And you too, mate. You'll always have a place with us. You're like family, you tall ass gangly bugger." Hopefully Benny picked up on the love that lay under those words. Benny hit send once and then again. "Goody. Now you owe me an explanation for that smirk earlier."

"Oh that."

Jaxon eyeballed him until he caved.

"I kind of figured you were looking for a love nest or something and it made me remember that a few weeks ago, Lily had been with us for like two days before you even said hi. It sounded funnier in my head now that I've gone and pointed that out though. Sorry."

"Hey, it is what it is. Did I uh, did I put on a full-blown asshole show those days I was avoiding her?"

"Do you really want to know? Aside from the fun of house shopping just now, you seem a little bent tonight, boss."

Yeah, talk of Vangie did that to him. "You know me so well. This is why I can never let you go. And yeah, I really want to know."

"She cooked three meals a day for us both days. And snacks in between. There was also some laundry she sort of did and you know, minor things like dusting, sweeping, polishing…Oh, and the time I walked outside and found her pulling the stray weeds and putting the pretty rocks that had scattered out back into the landscaping."

"Shit."

"Yeah, she's super short and it was a real stretch to reach those outside windows. Um and that's not all."

"What else could there possibly be? I already feel like I should cut her a check and go groveling on my knees to deliver it with a giant basket of girly stuff."

"That whole red head job she pulled that weekend? Not her idea. I sort of mentioned how you weren't real receptive to blondes and brunettes one night when I was messing around with my hair. I had an extra box of color. We used it on her because we thought maybe you'd give her a chance if she didn't look so familiar."

"Are you fucking kidding me, mate? That whole Leeloo thing was because of me?"

"Yep. I personally thought she looked real cute, though. Leeloo is super-hot. She's the perfect woman, you know."

"Well hell yeah, Lily looked hot. But we both know that's beside the point. Shit."

"She's a really great girl, Jaxon. For the record, I hope things work out between you two. And…oh you're probably gonna have a minute where you feel like strangling me, but I think she'd make a great assistant at the studio. You know, the new one we'd find out here if we move and all. I like her a lot. She's nice to me. And I really need help, boss." After that, Benny's gaze dropped to the midnight blue and dark brown stitching of the comforter they sat on.

Yes, Jaxon needed a minute to control his breathing.

It wasn't that Benny had said anything that wasn't true or equally appealing to his ears. But the one thing Jaxon could not do was insert Lily into the spot Trissy had left vacant. She could be his woman, his lover, his muse, because Trissy had never been those things to him. But Lily could not be his assistant. No way, no how. No matter how perfect it would be to have her with him on the road and off, always so close by and keeping him company. Not in a million years on this earth, in this lifetime or the next. He could feel his scalp heating which would soon bead up into worried droplets of sweat.

"Hey, let's leave the grand planning to me. I have a viable idea going here, mate. It can work for all of us. Me, Lily, the band, you. Your firecracker Erby. Have you forgotten that Loner by is based out of Nashville?"

"That is true. But it seems like there's a lotta *if* involved. If you find a place, if Lily says yes, if the guys agree to relocate."

"Benny, my friend, everything we do, everything we've always done, has been because of that tiny little word. I haven't had a good feeling about something working out in a real long time. But this is different. To be honest with you, *if* I went back for good to California, that would probably be the thing to tear Sin Pointe apart. I can't get right out there. The music coming out of me, if you can even call it that, is all wrong when I'm there."

Benny's face turned sheepish; he squinted before asking, "Have you written new stuff since we've been here?" The skin stretched over his face then spread so wide Jaxon saw Benny's hairline move back a centimeter or so.

"Not on paper, but it's in here." Jaxon rubbed a circle around the center of his chest. "I can feel it. I think this is home." Which was the craziest part. He remembered exactly how much he'd dreaded making this visit. He knew it was Lily's doing.

"Whatever you need, I'm on it, boss. Where is Lily, by the way?"

Presumably, she was still at Grace's and hopefully not hearing things that would spell out The End to the dream life he'd just gone on and on about with Benny. Jaxon knew then and there he'd have to come clean with Lily about that night. As much as he'd like for it to just fade away, he was realistic enough to know his karma would never go that easy on him.

If Grace was aware of what had happened with Trissy, and had told Lily, then Jaxon would man up and take whatever heat he deserved. But if his dark secrets hadn't been revealed yet, he vowed that before he left here this week, before he offered his woman a life and a home, Lily would hear the truth directly from his lips.

He felt content enough to actually get some sleepies so he crawled off the king-size bed, thanked Benny, and pulled the door open. Standing on the other side was Lily. Her face glowed in the dark hall; her adorable crooked smile shaved at least a few layers of his earlier funk off for good. She didn't appear ready to slap him, so that made him breathe easier. God help him if he fucked this up.

"Hey baby, whatcha doing here?" He gently pulled the door closed behind him and wrapped his arms loosely around her waist. Her nose tasted good like nature on his lips. He should and would plant more kisses there. Life was short; he'd learned that a long time ago but had been brutally reminded of it tonight. He'd think of what to tell Maryellie, if anything, after he'd gotten some rest.

From a dark shadow behind Lily, Grace stepped to his side and patted him on the arm. Her sudden appearance startled him but he knew he was one of her favorites. Grace never judged a book by its cover, no matter how dinged up, chain-laden or tattooed it was.

"Hello Son." He leaned down so she could kiss his cheek. "I missed you. Just wanted to walk Lily back over and see your handsome face."

He leaned down further and gave Grace a sincere hug about the shoulders. "Thank you, Grace," he said full of heart. "Did you want to stay here tonight? You're welcome to snuggle up on the air bed with Maryellie."

"That's sweet but I think I'll make my time up with sweetie poo tomorrow. Who knows, you may even want a babysitter in the next day or two." Grace winked at him and then she turned to face Lily. "Remember what I said dear." He thought they were done but she held onto his elbow a moment longer. "Oh my, I almost forgot. Must be getting old. Lucky called a few minutes ago. Mom and baby boy are doing okay. The baby is little and will have to stay in the NICU until he can pass all the newborn tests, but Lucky and Trista Jeane will be home as soon as they can. And they've asked if we can hold off celebrating Christmas until they're here."

Thank God they would be okay. Maybe the night had taken a good turn. He wouldn't lie. Familiar angst was flocking back to his conscience over what it was Grace wanted Lily to remember. But when he checked Lily's face, she appeared spirited and happy. "Wow, that's great news," he said. "Another Mason man joins the clan, even if he's just a little booger."

"That makes five of you now, son. Good night kids," Grace said then turned and made her way to return to her flat.

Jaxon walked Grace back to her place and then returned once again to Lily's room. He'd used the short trip to breathe and remember his earlier decision. Tonight was his and Lily's last night before she knew his darkest truth. And then tomorrow, for better or worse, he'd tell her everything.

* * * *

If this was the part where someone pinched her and told her she wasn't really seeing one of the most sought after men in the country who was totally into her for some God only knows reason, she'd return that pinch with a southern goody she'd learned growing up in Oklahoma. They'd get a consolation kiss on the cheek while Lily whispered into their ear that she knew it was crazy, but honey, he was hers and she wasn't doing any sharing.

The thought made her smile which caught Jaxon's attention. He didn't lick his lips or bite down on them to let her know he wanted her like she'd read in so many of her steamy books. Nope, her guy just opened his mouth and started talking. She was never quite prepared for the things he'd say and she bet this would be no different. One side of his mouth darted up giving him the naughtiest one-sided grin she'd ever seen.

"Hey baby, about that taste I offered you earlier," he let out in a warm, low baritone. Of course she couldn't speak for the awe she felt over being the girl he was talking to. He generally seemed to pick up on this and continued slowly. "I hope you won't be mad, but you won't be getting that tonight."

What? Again he had her perplexed. "I won't?"

As if a loose melody held his head in its musical hands, he bobbed it back and forth to a smooth silent beat, this time taking that delicious pouty lip between his teeth just like in her books. "I decided I get to be the one to taste. I need it more."

There was no place else for it to hit her but right at sex's home base, where his body was made to be inside hers. "You do." Her entire body quivered.

"Mmm-hmm. And I promise to be quiet. Although I don't think I'm the one we have to worry about."

"What do you mean?" she asked while he covered them up in the blanket with one hand and slid the other underneath, massaging up and down her rib cage. To her surprise, he left her t-shirt in place.

He grinned. "My mouth is going to be too busy to be making any noise. You, on the other hand, might want to find your Stefan pillow I know you have in here somewhere and bite down."

"Why in the world would I want to bite down on that pillow?"

"To keep from screaming out how good my tongue feels inside your—"

"Stop, stop, stop. Okay, you're going to kill me."

He waited a second, probably to gauge her face to see if she really meant stop. She'd help him out there. "I don't mean stop what you were planning on doing," she said, feeling the rouge staining her permanently.

"You said you wanted me to be me."

"I do want you to be you, but remember those vocabulary lessons you gave me?" She waited for him to nod. "Well, you're like a black belt in sexy talk and I'm the girl who just barely walked into the dojo for the first time who's looking at flyers and admiring trophies. I need a little time to catch up there, sensei."

"Sensei. Sounds nice." His fingers teased her skin, applying pressure and making her squirm. "Lily, I like talking to you."

"Me too," she said, knowing that had come out slightly wrong but unable to correct herself with his lips pressing against hers. With his slow kiss, he released the pent up bunch of nerves he'd created with his scandalous talk and all the pain he'd somehow hidden. "That's nice," she let out with an exhale.

"Shhh, see I told you…"

He was right; he had told her that she'd be the one to get them in trouble. Her knees squeezed together because she knew where he was going for his taste.

* * * *

Usually when a girl's knees were clamped this tight, it meant it was time to thank her for hanging out and hope for better luck next time. Jaxon didn't want Stefan's words stuck in his head right now, especially not with the damn little pillow with his goofy ass face on it in the room. This wasn't all for one, one for all. He worked her sweat pants down but left them bunched at those locked knees.

The airspace he breathed was hot, not that he minded. The steamier it got, the more her womanly scent fragranced his body. But he'd been down here under the blanket for a bit now, kissing Lily's soft, supple skin, admittedly driving her mad with his exploring. He dipped his tongue into her belly button and felt her tummy muscles contract. He smiled to himself. Pulling back and resting his cheek ever so gently against her belly, he waited to feel the rise and fall of her breathing. When he didn't feel that, he ran a finger up the middle of her ribs and breasts, and gave her a tap. "Lily, breathe."

A second later, he felt her body inhale and exhale. "Thank you baby," he whispered against her skin, taking a mouthful of flesh from her side and suckling it. If he wanted between those sexy legs, he was gonna have to pull her knees apart himself. In the three decades he'd been having sex, he could honestly say this was a first. A thrill spun around in his belly as if to celebrate the momentous occasion.

Moving his lips to her belly button again, he used only the tip of his tongue to circle it while he slid his hand over her womanly thighs. How he adored this woman. *Open up for me baby.* He thought it again as he spanned her body with his touch. One hand reached under her shirt to hold her by the breast and the other traced the crevice of her clenched thighs slowly up and down. As long as he felt her breathing, he didn't worry about the time she needed.

They would get to their destination. She would open up for him.

With his cheek resting on her belly, he could hear her heart beat, soothing him. He traced his finger down once more but this time drug it all the way down to her nest of soft hairs. Even with her knees closed, he had plenty of access to this very special spot. Maybe she hadn't realized that because she wiggled her hips when he slid his fingers through her silkiness. The small, extra sensitive nub of flesh peeking out from her cleft was so swollen. He knew what he was doing to her was ecstasy and torture mixed together. His fingering was okay but he knew his true talent lay in what he could do to her with his tongue. If she would only open up for him.

He waited, savoring her scent and smiling. Without thinking, he began humming the melodies to her songs.

* * * *

Lily could swear her lady parts were humming. God how she wanted to open up and accept the gift he was primed and ready to give her. Boy, he'd been down there a long time. He was so expert with his caressing and kissing, she'd nearly drifted to sleep a few times. How long could he stand to be down there? She should check on him to make sure he hadn't passed out.

Lily lifted the blanket and held it up a couple feet to allow fresh air to flow downward. "Jaxon, are you still awake?" she whispered. But of course he was because his lips peeled away from her rib cage and he looked up at her with his usual poof of bangs so sexy falling into his eyes.

"Yes. Are you?" As soon as he asked her that, she felt his fingers slide deeper into her body which made her gasp. "Yes, you are." He licked her up the center of her rib cage, staring at her the whole way. "You taste so good. I'm ready for more, baby."

Trying to speak would be a severe mistake because she'd say something crazy like stop or slow down, she just knew it. Instead she opened her trembling big girl legs and swiped his hair out of his eyes so she could see him as he inched his way down.

God, please let him like this.

"Hey, I'm gonna love this. I promise."

Lily relaxed at their uncanny connection and the way he got her. When his warm tongue touched her opening, she made herself take a big breath, in and out. It was so intimate with him watching her while licking and suckling her at the same time. She tried to smile for him but was too far gone in awe of the splash of pleasure she saw in his eyes. Her hips rose at the tickling sensation that grew each time he dipped his tongue deeper inside her. A pleasure burst was building so fast, she searched for his hands, at least one of them to hold onto. She was afraid if she left her fingers in his hair, she might tug on it and didn't want to hurt him. His warm palms were harnessed to each of her hips but he let one go to grasp her hand in his. "You taste so good baby," he whispered up to her. "Do you like it? Does it feel good?"

"Uh-huh," she managed to get out.

He smiled and dipped his mouth back down and reopened her lips using only his tongue. Whatever kind of rolling wave thingy he was doing was amazing. She'd been enjoying that tickling sensation for a couple minutes now and wasn't prepared for the intense pressure that built a second before her hips popped up and her buns tightened underneath her. All her tender parts began to spasm. As soon as that happened, it felt like Jaxon sucked as much of her flesh into his mouth as he could and held her tightly within his lips, his tongue milking her senseless. Her body jerked tiny ups and downs in response but he held on. It was so erotic; she'd never experienced anything like this. Tom had only ever gone down on her once and told her she really should have showered first. She refused to let that errant thought ruin her moment with Jaxon. The good news was that it hadn't ruined it. What Jaxon had done for her just now couldn't be crumbled. It was an untouchable feeling where past hurt and pain was concerned and he owned it.

Once her hips stopped shooting up and down, he kissed her folds and then slowly made his way to her mouth.

So that's what satisfaction looked like on him.

No grinning, no winking, just a soft, sleepy kind of expression. He kissed her several times, as if letting her taste herself on his lips and tongue, and petted her hair. He lifted himself onto his fully stretched muscled arms for a second before sliding back down to her.

She would have gladly taken her turn pleasing and tasting him but he didn't ask and seemed so peaceful and ready for sleep. And it had been one heck of a day and night.

So many possibilities flashed through her mind as she took the outstretched bicep he offered her to rest her head. While he pulled her body into his and draped her with his heavy thigh, she knew they were meant to be together, through thick and thin, for better or worse. She knew those terms scared him, especially the "for worse" part. It terrified him to his core that he might hurt her somehow, just by being himself. She'd decided it was why he had taken so long to greet her at his home. And probably why he hadn't just gotten them a hotel room somewhere for the privacy they desperately wanted. If he kept her here, he must feel she'd be protected by the family members who didn't think the two of them were a good idea.

Well, they were all crazy.

He was good. She was good. Together they would be great and together they could give their funky pasts the boot.

Jaxon nuzzled her hair with his lips and planted a kiss on her head before she heard his breathing become heavy. Later when they were awake again and had a moment of privacy, she was going to have him dig out that picture Tom had sent her and together, she and Jaxon would have a good laugh at it and then it was getting wadded up and chucked into the fireplace.

"Enjoy your sleepies, Jaxon," she said into the protection of his arm. *I love you.*

Chapter Thirty

Letting December twenty-fifth pass by quietly with a seven-year-old girl bouncing around the house was difficult on him as a daddy, but Jaxon was glad for the extra day to ease into his role as a member of this family. The amazing night he'd spent with Lily had done wonders for his attitude as the excruciating pinch of guilt he felt around his father and uncle had faded. He still hadn't dealt with the news of Vangie's death. That would have to come, he knew it. But not now.

They'd prepared a few nice meals, with Lily, Grace and Maryellie at the head of kitchen ops while Jaxon had joined Bear and Luke in the surrounding woods gathering firewood, a first for him. He'd tried to snag Benny from the kitchen on the way out but laid off because his mate was setting up an unimaginable Christmas day viewing of one of the two available homes in town. Apparently the owner was eager to sell. But before he and Benny secretly headed over for a look, he'd had Mason man business to tend to. It was a good thing he was built like his father and could keep up. He'd expected questions and uneasy small talk from them but had found to his pleasure and surprise that they were men of few words. They hadn't lured him to the woods for an intervention or to yack his head off. They really just wanted an extra hand with the wood.

The best part? Coming inside to an angel's smile and adoration.

He'd showered and then used Lily and Grace's request to take Maryellie to the dress shop as his and Benny's chance to go see the home. He couldn't help but kiss Lily out in the open at her offer to bring home enough kid-friendly sewing projects to keep his baby girl's mind off the fact that Christmas was coming a day or so late. The thought made him wonder if Lily wanted children of her own. She'd make a great mom. And at this point, he'd give her just about anything she asked for.

Jaxon was sure Trissy hadn't noticed much of his growing public displays of affection all day because she'd been napping for most of it but now, her stare was definitely tuned in and zeroed on him. A modest pile of prezzies was spread under the tree, most of them made out to Maryellie and the baby, little Lucas Alan Eddie Mason whose picture had melted everyone's hearts. Big guy had another month at least, more likely two in the NICU. Trissy and Lucky would be on their way back to the hospital soon. The proud parents had done a great job of naming the kiddo after every male family member present for his birth and perhaps the one man they all wished could have been there, Grace's only child, Eddie Hart, Trissy's father.

Jaxon just felt happy to be included, sharing his and his father's middle name with the bundle of joy. Trissy couldn't hate him that much, right?

"All righty, we only have a few hours until we need to get back to Lucas so let's see what Santa brought," Trissy said with a warm but worried smile.

First she opened the baby gift that Lily made and complimented her handy work, saying how much she needed Lily at the shop with her and how valuable she was to their work. Much of that had been aimed at him, he was sure. Then as she opened her own present from Lily, Trissy noticed him holding Lily's hand. He watched Trissy's eyes circling to the same rhythm which he rubbed circles around Lily's back. The moment they made eye contact, Jaxon knew she wanted to speak with him privately. But, neither of them said anything.

Trissy opened her present while Maryellie cheered her on. It was the two frames he'd encouraged Lily to wrap the day before when he'd come home from sealing the deal on their home. Trissy held the picture of Maryellie and him posing in front of the tree from a couple days earlier.

"I love it!" She gave Maryellie a soft squeeze as she was still tender. "This will remind me of you guys coming all the way from California to visit me. Thank you so much."

She hugged her baby sis next. Jaxon breathed easier seeing Trissy wasn't taking her irritation at him out on Lily.

"You're welcome, Tris. There's one more under it," Lily said with a bit of hesitation. He renewed his rubbing of her back when he saw Lily's posture straighten and tense.

Trissy padded the discarded wrapping paper and found the second frame. For a few seconds she just blinked but then her hand flew to her mouth. "Oh," was all she got out before raising up, wincing, and grabbing her lower tummy. Lucky was at her side in a heartbeat.

"You okay, darlin'?" Lucky asked his treasured wife.

With her head tilted downward, she said, "Feeling woozy, must be pain meds."

But it was obvious to Jaxon something else was wrong. Lucky wasted no time helping her up and escorting her to the back of the house.

"Is Auntie Trissy okay?" asked Maryellie.

Jaxon wasn't at all quick enough with what to say when Lily spoke up. "She's fine, sweetie. When mommies have babies, they need a lot of rest to get their energy back. Here, I think Santa must have dropped these off when we weren't looking yesterday." They were two small boxes, one for Maryellie and one for little Lucas. Lily handed them to his baby girl and Jaxon noticed her hand was trembling. "Do you think you can open your baby cousin's for him?" Lily asked.

Jaxon inched even closer to Lily where they sat on the floor near the festive tree and whispered into her ear. "Hey, your hand's shaking. Are you okay?"

She gave the smallest of nods but he saw the worry welling up in her shiny eyes. Shit. She felt at fault for giving Trissy that picture from their childhood.

He was about to ask if she'd like to go for a walk to the back yard patio where the fireplace was warming up but just then Lucky came out from the back bedroom.

Discreetly, Lucky approached him. "Jaxon, can you go back there and talk to Trista? She's not doing so hot and she asked to speak with you."

Jaxon blew out a breath, hating to leave Lily when she was being so brave but looking so fragile. "I'll be right back, baby."

* * * *

The twinkly blue, red and green lights on the tree blurred as her eyes kept on with the embarrassing show of tears. She held those suckers in though. She would not spoil Christmas for the rest of the family, as she'd obviously already done for Tris.

Lucky, bless his heart, came up behind her and watched from over her shoulder as Luke looked again at the pictures of his grandson. Lucky's hands weren't the same as Jaxon's, but he did his best to give her shoulders friendly, soothing squeezes.

"Hey Lily, why don't you come with me for a second," Lucky said, urging her with a soft tug toward the back porch.

She nodded okay.

"Dad, we're just gonna step out for some air. We'll be right back," he said to Luke.

As soon as they were out of sight and hopefully hearing range of the family, Lily let out a sob. Lucky pulled her into a light hug and patted her back.

"Oh Lily, hun, I'm so sorry for Trista's reaction to your gift. She didn't mean to hurt your feelings. She cares so much about you. Shh...," he tried to calm her but while she appreciated Lucky's sweetness, all she wanted was Jaxon's strong shoulder to lean on and arms wrapped around her. To hear him say something wild that would crack her up.

"What did I do? What didn't she like?"

"Hun, this has nothing to do with you, okay? Promise me you believe that?"

"I don't see how."

"She didn't say much, just that seeing your..." Lucky pinched his lips together like he wasn't sure how to proceed. "Seeing a shoe in the corner of the photo freaked her out. That's all. It was nothing you did and has nothing to do with you."

Wrong. It had everything to do with her.

All she'd seen in that picture was three happy little kids with lopsided socks, messy hair and milk mustaches.

What a great and equally crappy example of her awkward situation since she'd arrived here. How did the ashamed daughter of the man who'd abused someone function as that person's supportive sister? Was it even possible?

"Lucky, be honest with me, I'm begging you. Would it be best if I moved out? Am I a constant reminder of what Tris went through when we were little?"

He rubbed at his soul patch. "Trista loves you. Yeah, it's bound to take some time to get over what happened, but she knows it's not your fault. It would devastate her to lose you again, Lily."

Her sister wanted her to stay but to remain in such close proximity, under the same roof, Lily would have to constantly keep herself in check. The times she wanted to let go and share the happier stories of their childhood, she'd have to worry about hurting her sister. She could do it, but for how long? Lily's biggest dream was having and keeping her big sister again. But maybe it was time to consider finding a small place of her own. Should she confide to Lucky her feelings for Jaxon?

"Lucky, maybe this has nothing to do with anything, but I guess you should know that Jaxon and I are together. I don't plan on moving away from here, but it's a very likely possibility that I'll go visit him in California. At first I was worried about being gone, but maybe it'll be for the best from time to time. Tris won't have to be constantly reminded that way."

"Oh hun. I am happy for you, if you're happy, I really am. But I wouldn't feel like I'm being much of a big brother if I didn't share this with you. When I went chasing after Trista in California, to make a long story short, it wasn't a good idea. I had no idea what I was getting into."

"But you wouldn't change any of it, right? Because going after her brought you two together?"

He nodded slowly. "Yes, but we also ended up hurting each other out there and I don't think that was necessary. If at all possible, I'd like to keep my little sister from going through that."

Lily warmed at his endearment. It made her miss Jack so much but she would always have a special place in her heart for Lucky and the way he included her.

"But…I love him. I can't say no to that. It's been so long and I need that, Lucky."

"Trust me hun, I understand." He paused for a long few seconds. "You want me to go with you and we'll talk to Trista together about this?"

"You would do that?"

She figured most guys would take off running the other way rather than get involved in something as deep and feeling-based as this pending conversation.

"Again, I'm looking out for my little sister. Plus, I've never seen Jaxon this happy. You two are worth it."

She hugged Lucky and they made their way to his room where they'd left Tris and Jaxon. This was it. She was excited and nervous all in one crumpled up, crazy heap.

* * * *

"Look Trissy, I hear, I understand, I get it all." And he really did understand her every concern. "But do you know what she does for me? She lets me hold her. I go everyday places with her. And I'm the one who drives! I know it sounds crazy, but I'm just a man with her and I can't tell you what that means to me."

Jaxon knew Trissy would remember all the times he'd been so desperate for genuine, human touch that he'd gone like a sad little puppy to his best friend. How many nights after shows had he cuddled with Trissy whether it had been on the bus, the plane or in the hotel? How many times had Trissy seen Vangie chewing his ass about hanging on her in public? And then Trissy wouldn't know that Vangie had had the same complaints in private. Maybe it went with his sensual nature, but Lily letting him hold her was not only miraculous, it was right.

"Jaxon, hun, I can hear it in your voice and your face says it all. You care about Lily. A lot. But I don't think she's ready for, well, for you. Tell me you can see that too."

"No Trissy, I don't want to hear that. She's doing just fine with me." No doubt, that had been the wrong thing to say.

"Jaxon, you're sleeping with her. I knew it. Why would you do that, given everything you know about our childhood and everything you and I have been through?"

Did he have a good enough answer for Trissy? He'd wanted Lily and he'd taken her. What was wrong with him that he didn't regret it? He was about to stammer through an explanation when Trissy crucified him.

"You are too much for her, Jaxon. You're talking about a girl who was abused by her ex-husband for four years. Did you even know that? And I can't even think about the possibilities of what her father may have done to her when I left. I know you Jaxon. I love you like a brother. But Lily needs time in a stable, wholesome environment and I'm not going to let her get hurt by you."

"Trissy…"

"No Jaxon, don't Trissy me. You of all people should know better." Then her voice dipped low. "Tell me you haven't forgotten that night…"

"You know I haven't."

"Right, and neither have I. And I'll be damned sure that my baby sister is never dragged into that. Your world, Jaxon, it's shit. You can't take Lily into that. You can't."

"I would never hurt her," was all he could say in the face of Trissy's sobs.

"You never meant to hurt me but we ended up on the hood of a car with you being forced to rape me."

He couldn't speak. There were no words.
Everything she said was the absolute truth.

Hearing Lily's voice join in was the ultimate pain.
"Oh my God. What?"

"Lily," Trissy said, reaching out to her sister but
Lily kept her distance.

"I can't believe…, what are you two saying?
How could you not have told me any of this?"

* * * *

This wasn't happening, her head banged with too
much pressure.

Jaxon's lips opened and she hoped he'd tell her
she'd heard it all wrong. "Lily, I was going to tell you
tonight. I just wanted to wait until…" he said low and
reserved, until she cut him off.

The man she'd given her heart and body to
because she trusted him wasn't taking it back. He wasn't
waking her up from some nauseating nightmare.
Everything she'd overheard had actually been spoken
from his lips to her sister's and back.

"Until what? I was good and hooked? Until
you'd made me believe I could trust you?" Then she
turned her shocked heartbreak to Trissy. "If you hadn't
left, you would have known that I was fine. My father
remarried within three months of your leaving and I
swear to you, he never hurt me the way he did you. I
would have remembered that." Lily's bottom lip was
pulling downward with the weight of the sob she couldn't
allow for. "I would have told you, Tris. You think I'd let
you pour your heart out to me about what he did to you
and not share that it had happened to me too? I would
not have kept that from you."

The doubting looks on their faces said they didn't
believe her. In her peripheral she saw Jaxon's hand

reaching out to her. She backed away and her eyes darted between him and her sister.

Tris's jaw clenched. "I didn't want to leave, Lily. I wanted to die. And if I hadn't left, he probably wouldn't have remarried. And who knows what would have happened then. To me, to you," Tris choked out between her sobs.

Snot slalomed down Lily's nose to her mouth and chin. "As if that's even the worst I just overheard."

"Lily—no," Jaxon nearly cried.

"Is this why you've been trying to keep Jaxon out of my life?" Absolute loneliness cut through her as she stood there in that room.

"Baby, it's my fault. I should have told you about that night before." Jaxon's voice echoed against the throbbing in her head but she'd lost her grip on who to trust, who to believe. She felt his hand on her shoulder. It was heavy.

Lily held up a weak hand to her sister, unable to deal with her heart that grieved for yet feared Jaxon. "How would you feel if I took Lucky away from you, Tris? Just like that, with a few words. That's what you've done; you've taken Jaxon away from me. I guess you got what you wanted," Lily said, her grief about to drop her to the floor. "Why? I loved him."

"You." She pointed at Jaxon. "You were never mine, were you? LEAVE, LEAVE, LEAVE, LEAVE, leave," she screamed and then collapsed against the door.

The memory was as clear and sharp as newly cut glass. Earlier that night, before Tris had run off to the creek, Lily had fallen asleep, balled up in her father's closet where she'd been playing with her momma's old shoes he kept. She woke to watch Tris getting up off his bed and then leave the room quietly. After she'd spied her father making his way to the bathroom, she'd snuck out, back to her room. She'd lost everything that night and had fallen into a trance whispering to herself, *leave, leave, leave, leave…*

Her eyes darted between Jaxon and Tris.

Jaxon didn't budge. He wasn't letting her pass.

So she gathered herself as best she could and shoved past him. How was she to deal with the fact she'd witnessed her father molesting Tris?

"Lily, come back here!" Jaxon's voice tunneled after her.

Within a matter of seconds, she was outside the house. A package lay on the steps which she nearly tripped over in her escape. After kicking it down the stairs in her fury, she realized it might be a gift for Maryella or the baby so she carefully deposited it back down on the bottom step. She got to her Jetta, plunked down, slammed her door and turned the ignition. It chortled to life, needing a minute to warm up.

Jaxon was the first one she saw make his way out of the house and onto the porch. With her only thoughts being getting away from this confusing house, she forced the gear into reverse and backed as quickly as she could out the driveway. With the uncanny speed of a cheetah, Jaxon ran down the driveway and caught up to her. She could hear him, even through her closed and dirty window. She slammed her hand down on the door lock.

"Lily I'm sorry; I was going to tell you. I wasn't ready before." His pleading lips held her still; moving with what looked like truth. His palms flattened against the glass that shook from his force. She just watched, held in a trance, wishing she didn't know. Wishing she hadn't been so insistent. Now she had her explanations and they wretched her heart that begged her to roll down her window and give him a chance.

But, the one thing she'd learned was she couldn't trust that heart.

Look where it had gotten her all these years. She'd loved a father who was a living, breathing monster. She'd married a winner who'd turned out to be the worst kind of loser. And now she'd fallen in love with a man who could never be hers because too much of him lay buried in the past with her sister. Part of her didn't blame him for keeping the secret. But what she couldn't get over was the way he'd looked at her when she'd walked in on the revelation. And the way he was looking at her now. Unbelievably horrible and evil things had happened to her sister. He worried he'd bring the same kind of pain to Lily. Well, he had.

"Please, Lily. I'll leave. You stay."

She shook her head and concentrated on getting out of there. The view out her windows and mirrors was a huge blur as she passed his silver Range Rover she and Benny had driven out here on the side. She shouldn't be driving and had no idea of where she was heading. But she needed out and away. Someplace Jaxon wouldn't step foot.

A couple places came to mind. As she drove, she absentmindedly flipped on the radio. It scanned until it came to a clear enough station. The song would make her cry if she didn't change it. Johnny and Santo's "Sleepwalk" always did that to her. She let it play.

Chapter Thirty-One

This was not happening. Not again. Karma and the universe could kiss his ass if they thought he was going to let Lily be their next innocent victim. Hell no.

"Shouldn't you be asking Lucky or your dad or I don't know, the police, for help?" Benny was upset and cold. It was obvious as his long toes curled under where he stood, shivering. Jaxon understood. "They obviously know the town better than us."

"The police, Benny? Really? Lily left because she was pissed. I can't just send the sheriff after her for that. You stay and take care of Maryellie. I'll be back as soon as I find Lily. But uh, have your bags ready to go when I get back. Maryellie's too."

"Really? You think she's that pissed?"

"Yep," he said, frustrated and saying as little as possible to avoid lashing out.

Benny nodded at his instructions but not before pointing out the obvious. "She could have gone anywhere. Have you tried calling her?"

Of course he had.

"She won't answer my calls. But that gives me an idea. Give me your phone."

Benny quickly snatched it from his loose pocket and handed it over.

Jaxon dialed Lily's number. When she answered, he knew she wasn't screening Benny's calls at least. "Lily, it's me, please tell me where you are." The song playing in the background had never inspired him to feel hopeful in the past but it did just then. His memory of hearing it at the drive-in the other night gave him a clue as to where she'd fled. "I'm on my way. Please just stay in the car—"

Click.

That had been his one chance. She wouldn't pick up any more calls coming from Benny's phone.

"What did she say?"

"Nothing. Benny, I've got to go." He tossed him back the now useless phone. "Thanks. I'll check in."

"Where are you going?"

"To the movies."

Silence.

He pushed his shoulders back into the leather driver seat and pressed with even more weight on the gas pedal. He'd let Trissy down so many times the past twenty years…all the awful things his best friend had survived in her childhood, which is why it had been so hard to believe Lily hadn't been hurt too. But Lily was adamant it hadn't been that way. Like that mattered. Her ex-husband had made up for it apparently. Jaxon may have made a career of not being there, but he had a chance to help them both right now. He'd be damned if he didn't set things right, the way they'd been before Lily had shown up at his house, and stumbled upon the most selfish beast—Jaxon James.

* * * *

"What'll it be, sweetheart?" The twenty-something bartender in his skinny jeans and western shirt was cute and obviously confident, but not enough to cheer her up. She knew the only sinfully beautiful naughty smile that could do that belonged to the deceitful man she'd foolishly given her heart to. It was with his face in mind that she'd ended up at Slangers. "Not the cream of Nashville's crop," she echoed her sister's words about the place she'd met Lucky to no one in particular.

Jaxon might have broken her heart tonight, but he would never step foot in a bar. He loved his daughter too much to risk it, which made it Lily's perfect hiding spot.

The bartender eyed her.

Well, she was here to drown out her sorrows. If she thought they'd serve her an extra thick Oreo shake, she'd have ordered one with a can of whipped cream on the side and a jar of cherries. "Can I just get a cherry coke please?" Oh, what the hell. Her heart begged her for more. "Do you happen to have anything sugary back there? Maybe a secret stash of brownies?" The scruffy-bearded bartender flipped his bangs to the side with a toss of his head and gave her a pity smile. He ducked down and a second later tossed a bag of M&M's her way. "Oh bless you child." Lily let a twenty dollar bill lay under her fingertips a moment before she slid it his way. It was all the cash she had but the guy had earned it. She spun her bar stool seat around at the sound of a guitar being tuned.

Great. She prayed they sounded nothing like Sin Pointe.

After a few minutes, all four of the band members had taken the stage. Something about them was familiar to her but she couldn't place it. Their name was rather generic, The Brothers and That Guy. Or TBTG as was written across the chests of an ample group of women lining the very edge of the stage. That was quite a fervent following.

Relaxing back into her tall seat, she couldn't help but notice the way the lead guitarist bent over to check something on his amp and stayed low as two tight T-shirted admirers fawned all over him. Yeah, he was soaking it up like a true sponge. Why not? He looked young, although she wouldn't describe him as happy. Something in the way he was already sporting enough sweat around his hairline to slick it back each time he ran his hands through it. Maybe he had the flu. Whatever it was, he put a smile on his pale face, looking like he'd already had a long night. The girls didn't seem to notice and he made no move to extract himself.

How many hands had copped feels of Jaxon's hair, shoulders, and zippers? How much bigger had his hordes of adoring women been and how much more aggressive? How much did he enjoy that? Enough to keep at it all these years, she supposed with a bitter, lemon-sized lump in her throat. Not like she blamed him for any of it. Not like it would matter if she did. Not after tonight. Well, she sighed, at least she wouldn't have to worry herself over sharing him. He was theirs, not hers. Lily sucked down her cherry coke and without thinking, tore off the corner of her bag of candy and funneled the whole thing into her mouth.

* * * *

Retracing his route seriously sucked right now. Not only was his mind a wreck for what had just blown up back at the house but he had no idea what he was gonna do when he got to the drive-in and found Lily. He'd watched the budding trust she'd had for him die out when she'd shouted over and over for him to leave.

So of course she'd gone there to escape him. She probably didn't believe he'd chase her there knowing how much he'd detested it the first time. Dammit, again he'd hurt someone without trying. In fact, he'd managed to do it even though he'd gone out of his way not to hurt Lily.

"What are you doing, mate?" he asked himself. Surrounded by complete country darkness, he flashed his headlights to his brights and prayed he didn't strike any wild animals crossing the road. That would be pretty fitting. So what was his plan? What did he want? What did he expect would come of tracking Lily down out in the middle of nowhere?

The answers to his questions were solid, even though they didn't fit together quite right when he was the one forcing them into place. He wanted Lily but more than that, he wanted her to be safe and happy. His plan consisted of finding her and taking her back to her sister's. That was the only way he knew to fulfill the part about keeping her safe.

If she would hear him out, he'd apologize and then tell her everything. And then when she refused to have anything more to do with him, he'd do what was right and leave her be. As much as he dared to imagine the sweetness of her forgiveness, and her granting his sorry ass one more chance, Jaxon wasn't a fool. That wouldn't be happening. Trust and honesty were deal breakers with Lily. And he'd obliterated them with his hands tied behind his back.

Twenty miles flashed by in a heartbeat as he saw the drive-in theater's marquee reflect against his high beams in the distance. Great, the place was dark and she'd come here anyway. He pulled in to the entrance, tasting blood under the pinch of lip skin between his teeth, for a better view since it wasn't roped off. Even doing that made his skin freeze to ice.

Whether the assumptions he had made about her past were wrong or right didn't matter. She didn't belong out here. Whether she'd known and didn't remember the monster her father had been, didn't matter. Out here in a place like this, she'd find her monsters like he'd found his that night in Virginia with Trissy. And if she didn't find them, they'd find her.

That was the way it worked.

So no matter how much he wanted to scream at her right now for foolishly and stubbornly coming out here, he wouldn't. Because she'd seen enough bad guys in her life. If this was the last thing he got to do for her, it would be as a calm, reasonable grown man. A bead of sweat fell onto his hand. He clenched the steering wheel and lurched his Range Rover into the lot.

He tasted the vomit a second before it gurgled out onto his lap. He doubled over. The car engine sputtered dead.

Crying, he smashed his hands over his ears to mute the echoing of Lily's pain, "*Leave, leave, leave...*"

"No, you weak bastard. She needs you right now," he screamed at himself inside his car.

He wiped his eyes, making them sting from the sweat and bile coating his hands. Closer to the snack bar, he focused on the two cars. Neither one of them was Lily's Jetta.

"Where are you, baby?"

* * * *

Where in the world had she seen these guys before? And where was her M&M supplier? The guy sitting on the stool next to her was seriously macking on her personal space. For a second, she considered going and joining the TBTG groupies just to get away from him but was that really who she wanted to be tonight?

No. She wanted to be the girl who hadn't just overheard her boyfriend talking about being plastered over her sister on the hood of a car. In fact, while she was busy being other people, why couldn't she be the girl who was actually believed when she said she hadn't been abused as a kid or the girl who wasn't thirty-one and already divorced? Huh, how about those girls? Where did they live? Maybe Lily could drive her pathetic butt over to one of their doorsteps.

The loud slurping sound that always came when the straw sucked up the last juicy remnants got her a wink from old Mack who was now almost elbow to elbow with her. "Can I get you another one of those or maybe something a little stronger, baby?"

Did she have to acknowledge that? He had picked the wrong pet name. She wasn't anybody's baby, not anymore.

Well, she hadn't developed amnesia in the past hour like she'd hoped and that jerk calling her baby had only served to bring Jaxon's sinfully handsome face back from the mind fog she'd stuck him in. Looked like it was time to go be somebody else. Someone without her ghosts.

Looked like it was time to join the girls.

But before she did that, she had something to do as Lily first.

She dialed and it only took a half of a ring for him to answer.

"Lily, is that you?" Benny asked her. "Are you okay? Did Jaxon find you?"

Okay, she was going to have to do this quickly because breaking up with Benny was way too hard to fathom. "It's me, Benny."

"Where are you?" he interrupted. "It's loud."

"Benny, I'm not telling you that because I don't want Jaxon to know."

"You're at a club, aren't you?"

Geez, this kid was good. She couldn't stay on the line and let him keep answering the questions she refused to address but there was the whole point of her making this call to get to. "Benny, I'm at a bar and Jaxon can't come here."

"Because he's an alcoholic," Benny finished for her.

"Right. I just wanted you to know I'm okay. Please tell my sister."

She didn't want them worrying. That was about it for her conscience concern.

"You know that's not how it works, right? He'd go to a distillery if he knew where to find you—"

Even though it broke her heart, she clicked the end call button. Jaxon could not step foot in this place. The smell of alcohol from Mack's belch knocked her the rest of the way off her seat and motivated her towards the swarm of TBTG devotees.

Weird, she knew this song. Huh, could be because the chorus kept repeating while the lead singer pounded his fist into his chest. "We reap what we sow." By the fifth time he'd said it, her sugar high was buzzing through her veins. Her own little song played in her head, "*I will not think about you, I will not think about you.*" Maybe she should call it, "Love sucks and you're a liar."

With her arm raised above her head, and her fingertips popping the air to the beat, she became the heartbroken girl lost in the crowd.

* * * *

Fuck, he was lost.

And he stunk like puke.

He'd thought he'd just follow the same state highway back to Trissy's house but there'd been a fork in the road and he'd made his best guess in the pitch dark. His mind was swamped. It hurt to think. He'd guessed wrong. A gas station came into view on his right. He'd have remembered The Lucky Pump.

Jaxon just shook his head.

It was time to call Benny.

"Hey boss, I was just about to call you."

Jaxon's ears alerted. "Did Lily call?"

"Actually, yeah she did."

"Where is she? Is she okay?"

"Yeah, so I think she's fine."

"You think?" Jaxon hated being stuck out here.

"She was calling from a bar to say she was okay but wouldn't say where because—"

"Because I hurt her tonight and she's holing up somewhere I won't go." Little did Lily know how dead wrong she was. She must have forgotten what he did for a living. He had to battle his addiction every night on the road. Being with her, not having that thrown in his face whether on purpose or by accident, had been a Godsend. He knew he deserved this.

"Pretty much. But I think I know the name of the place she's at."

His foot nearly stomped its way through the floorboard in anxiety. "How do you know that?"

"This is crazy, but I swore I heard "The Reaper" being sung in the background, except for it was a dude singing, so that threw me off. But anyway, I Googled where Loner by was playing tonight and turns out they aren't playing anywhere. But then I saw that there was a thread some fans had started on the Lonberby website about a pop-up show by some band Liam, Oscar and Noah put together and one of their old session musician buddies called The Brothers and That Guy. Dude, I'm pretty sure Lily's at this place called Slangers in Nashville."

Holy shit, did he want to kiss Benny right now. Even though Jaxon was sure Lily would hate seeing him again tonight, he didn't care. She was at Slangers, which was an okay establishment until some drunk asshole forgot his manners. Typical local bar shit he'd seen enough of. Now he knew where to find her. Only one problem, he didn't know where he was or how to get to Slangers.

"Hey Benny, that's great news but fuck, I'm lost."

"No you're not."

"What?"

"Your phone has GPS. I'll give you the address and you just type it in and then follow whatever the nice lady's voice says."

Benny gave him all the specifics which was work trying to remember but he would have memorized the phone book if it meant finding Lily. He then called Benny back.

"I owe you, mate. Big time."

"So you're going, right?"

"Already on the road. I'll check in later."

He had sixty miles to go and no time to waste. Lily was a smart girl; she could take care of herself. But Trissy had been that ten-fold and look where it had gotten her. He rammed his boot onto the gas. "I'm on my way, baby. Please be careful."

Chapter Thirty-Two

Dancing had never felt this freeing. If she wasn't the sexiest thing in the room, then the room wasn't full of the feeling wrapping itself around her waist and pushing her tush around the floor. Her jeans were tight but sexy tight. Yeah, her friend, the inch of flab, was still there making the waistband snugger than a thumb in a pinky ring but guess what? She didn't care. Lily went for a spin, arms in the air like she was a disco queen. She spun again. The lights twirled by in a pretty blur. Okay, she was going for another one. Yeah, that giddy, wonderful sensation tickled her again. Her emotions swirled in her chest; she could cry at how light she felt.

"Excuse me, hips. Watch out. You just stepped on my girlfriend's toes."

A hard elbow jabbed into her back and then it and the voice disappeared into the crowd. "Oh, oh I'm sorry," she mumbled to whoever she'd offended, turning to try and see if she'd hurt anyone, until she realized she was the one who'd been hurt. She tugged down on her top, one of Tris's prettier maternity peasant blouses she'd put on for their Christmas celebration. She didn't know if everyone was staring at her, but they might as well be.

"I was happy, pretty," she mumbled, making little sense but feeling the raw truth of her words. She didn't want to say why because she knew whose face would rock her façade of escaping from the night. A second after his teal eyes flashed her one of those devastatingly deep looks, she got knocked into again.

And that's when her shoulders started shaking uncontrollably. She brought her hand up flat as if to salute but kept the unsteady, no good thing balanced on the bridge of her nose. How much of her face could she hide? For a second she thought everyone was cheering her pending melt down until she heard the band announce they were going to do a cover of a band they had opened up for in the past.

"Here's 'Play' by one of our favorite bands, Sin Pointe."

It wasn't Stefan's voice barreling over the crowd, but it was close. And in her head, it didn't matter. The only man she heard was Jaxon.

For a second, the sound held her up. In the next second, it dropped her flat on the floor. Her knees buckled and there she was, crying big girl tears.

Distant calls to help the lady who'd just passed out sounded all around her. God, she hadn't passed out but her head felt like it had just rolled between the cowboy boots and heels of the couple trying not to step on her. Oh holy heavens, what was she doing?

She scrambled to her knees so she could get up on her feet when she felt unwelcome sets of hands fitting under her arms and at her sides. She was still so wobbly, and her tears hadn't stopped embarrassing her either. Under a bowed fringe of bangs, she thanked her helpers but let them know she was okay. They backed away while she kneeled there, frozen and mortified. Lily watched the floor, now feeling extra self-conscious about every choice she'd made. She was caught up in all her recent pretending and fretting over the spectacle she'd just made of herself when the most expressive and tormenting hand she'd ever known extended to offer her help.

She wasn't taking that hand. He'd already done enough. She was out of trust.

* * * *

He tugged down on Benny's wool hat, keeping his head mostly bowed and uttered quick, low-key thanks to the couples who had tried to help. Shit, he hadn't planned on finding her so quickly after making his way inside. What was she doing in a heap on the dance floor? He'd expected angry, pissed, and belligerent even, but not this. "I've got her, thanks again."

Good, they hadn't recognized him. The chances of keeping up that streak were dicey. The male contingency of Lonerby was playing and when he'd been standing at the bar's front door, he'd heard a cover of one of his songs. He'd like to get Lily out of here as quickly as possible. They needed to talk. And then if she still hated him, so be it. It'd be what he deserved.

Just then a loud voice rumbled over to him from the side. "Hey, your hippy chick stepped all over my lady. You need to get her off the floor."

Oh, hells no.

"Fuck you."

He knelt down, focusing on his baby. No, she wouldn't want him thinking of her that way anymore. "Lily, let's get out of here. We need to talk."

She swiveled her head from right to left, never looking up at him. He heard a faint whimper coming from her.

"Please," he begged.

"Don't touch me," she said icily.

"Get her off the floor, douche bag."

Shit. This guy was asking for it. It would feel so good to crack a fist into the dipshit's jaw but fuck, he knew he couldn't do that. "Say one more God damned word about her and I'll fuck you up."

"Lily," he pleaded again.

"Go away," she hissed.

Onlookers who had given them space began crowding back in and he didn't know how much longer he could stand the stench of booze bleeding through their pores and the shit for brains who clearly wanted to get his ass whooped.

"Lily, we don't want to make a scene here. Come outside with me, I'll take you anywhere you want. Look, you don't have to talk to me, just come with me. Please."

Good girl, she was reconsidering and pushing herself up. She still refused to take his hand but at least she'd seen his reason.

* * * *

What? Had he lied about being an alcoholic too? What was he doing here? She thought she'd known this man, as much as a girl could in such a short time, with all the things they'd shared.

Exquisite fun and soul-baring pain.

Why did he carry on with her the way he had? Maybe it was just to be close to her sister. Maybe he just couldn't let go of her and Lily had provided him the means to show up. She hated thinking in those terms, but she'd heard it from Jaxon's own lips tonight. Tris was the woman he'd confided in; Lily was the one he'd slept with. Rage at her unending stupidity bolted her upright.

She was full of words for him and he was gonna get an earful. "Why? So you can fuck with me some more? No thanks." With that, she fisted her hand over her keychain and tugged it loose from her belt loop and then made like a speed walker to the front door. She should have included his name nice and loud at the end of her dismissal but deep down inside, she couldn't hurt him that way. Slamming the club doors open, she punched it to her car.

"Lily, wait."

"No."

She'd never gotten a true jump on him, so as she went through the fumbling task of getting her old doors unlocked and open, he was standing right beside her, waiting. Guess he thought she was going to have a seat and they were going to talk. He was sorely mistaken.

Lily landed in her seat like a watermelon being chucked over a balcony. She chanced one look at him and it was a horrible mistake. For a split second, she considered hearing him out. That's why she had to slam the door as hard as she did, and hit the locks.

Ready to put the key in the ignition and drive herself away, although not to Tris's house, she now felt safe glancing his way one last time.

Big. Mistake.

He had all the space in the world standing there in the parking lot but he looked like he'd been locked up in a clear plastic box only big enough to fit him. His fists pounded at his temples and he clearly was pissed, strained.

Those clenched fists opened up and clapped against her window, making her jump in her seat. Because she was a fool, her heart started reaching its desperate little fingers out to him. No, she replayed what she'd heard coming directly from his mouth earlier. How could he not have at least mentioned something to Lily about the night with her sister? She wasn't even interested in the gruesome details. The only answer was he didn't trust her.

"I'm leaving. Don't follow me."

"Lily! You're not safe," he screamed at her and even the glass separating them didn't mute his ire. "Lily, open the door. Open the goddamned door! Now!"

Geez, he was going scary berserk out there pounding on her window.

Someone was going to hear him and call the cops if he didn't calm down. More than that, he was really scaring her. Why was he screaming that she wasn't safe? God, had Tom come to town to hand deliver another smutty shot? But that was only about humiliating her. He didn't have the cojones to show up and make threats in person. Aside from drunk old Mack invading her personal space inside or the random jerks who'd pointed out her hippyness, she couldn't think of any threats Jaxon should be so amped up about where she was concerned. But his bewildered eyes and clenched expression told her something very real had him terrified out of his mind.

Good grief. I can't let him keep on like this.

She left his shattered gaze and rolled her window down a couple inches. Only loud enough so she would hear, she rehearsed a few reminders. "You can hear him out, but that is all. Giving your heart to him again won't do you any good. He's had it and enjoyed it but now he's done with it and has given it back. You should be thankful." She blew out and then faced the opening, readying herself for the onslaught of pain she'd just invited in through those two measly inches.

"Keep your doors locked and drive yourself back to your sister's house," he ordered.

There was something very wrong about him. She couldn't decide if the pallid complexion and jittery hands meant he was racked with guilt or strangely bludgeoned by fear.

"Jaxon." She had no idea what else to say. Somehow what's wrong didn't feel right. Her heart moved her hand from the steering wheel to her knee.

His breath came out in force, fogging her window with each gasp. Had he been driven to drink? This completely foreign man sitting shotgun must be Jaxon James the addict, the man she'd never met but had heard about. That's right, he'd trusted her enough to tell her that much. Completely baffled, she hoped that by the time this night was over, she at least understood what the hell had happened today. Because right now, nothing made sense. And she wasn't going anywhere with or being ordered around by someone who had made her believe in trust only to yank it back once she'd fallen for him.

"Lily, have you ever been so sure you were going to die, that you prayed God would just end it?"

Things had certainly been tough, humiliating, and frightening but no, she hadn't feared for her life. But there was no mistaking, he had.

Why was this all happening like this? Why was he here when he obviously didn't care that much about her? Lily could never hurt another human being, but her heart was lost right now. She decided she'd let him think she was driving back to Tris's just to calm him down and get him back to a safe place, away from this bar. But once he thought she had done as told, that was it. She was done. No more trusting people who were incapable of being honest with her.

"I'm going home now," she said before rolling her window back up.

Good, he'd taken that and gone back to his Range Rover parked a few spots away.

Lily had the sixty miles from Nashville to Bugscuffle to figure out where home would be now that she realized she'd made a mess of her sister's.

SIN'S FLOWER

Chapter Thirty-Three

Losing his mind in front of Lily had actually served to whip him back to his senses. Tall dark pines blacked out most of the midnight sky except for when the road climbed to the top of a hill and the view was then one of stars and more midnight sky. He had little hope she was happy with the way he'd just ordered her to go home but at least she'd agreed and would be safe again at Trissy's.

He trusted her enough not to ditch him on this long ass drive so he muted the voice of the GPS and followed Lily closely through hills, over train tracks, the creek, and the neighboring dairy farms.

Jaxon had gone over what he knew he had to say a hundred times as Lily drove on. If only he had any idea of her thoughts right now. God, she probably had 9-1-1 set to dial after that performance he'd just put in. But she could never do that to him again. It wasn't safe to be outside in a car in the middle of nowhere in the dead of night. And he was about to tell her why. Finally, they reached their destination.

She pulled up alongside the curb of Trissy's home, letting him pull in first. It was so dark out here. He knew he'd done the right thing going after her and insisting she come back. It was gonna suck and be very uncomfortable, but hadn't Lily and Trissy dealt with the most awkward parts of becoming reunited already? He'd admired Lily so much when she'd shared with him that some of the first conversations she and Trissy'd had were the ones about why Trissy had left. Why Grace had shown up and rescued her from the abuse. If they could get past those blocks, couldn't they do the same now?

They had to or else he'd live with knowing he'd been the cause of yet another series of heartaches for women he'd give his life for.

Ducking down to pick up his fallen phone from the floorboard, he quickly worked out what would happen when he and Lily went inside. He'd ask to explain himself. If Lily refused, he wouldn't push her. He'd just make his way out to Grace's and wait it out until morning.

He exited his driver side and saw that a few yards behind him, Lily's car was already dark too. She must have gone inside quickly, which wasn't a surprise since it was freezing cold out. No doubt her mind was still spinning and she wasn't ready to speak with him yet. He'd leave her alone for tonight. In the morning then. But something inside his gut nagged at him. There was an urgency to go inside and force her to hear the truth she'd deserved right here, right now, and then let the pieces fall where they may. It wasn't like he could fuck this night up any worse.

With determined strides, he made his way up the porch steps and into Trissy's home.

* * * *

As soon as Lily saw Jaxon go inside, she sat back up and turned on her car, leaving the headlights dark for now. She glanced over to the front porch while backing down the drive, hoping it would take Jaxon at least a few minutes to realize she hadn't gone inside. When she pulled out onto the road and the porch remained dark with the house door closed, she knew she'd have enough time to get far enough away that once he realized, she'd be too far to follow.

Within minutes, Tris's home was out of sight. Lily made the turns that took her to the low, narrow bridge crossing the rushing Duck River and then out to the two lane highway. Normally she'd have gone left to head toward Nashville and the dress shop, so instead she made a right. She knew she shouldn't stop, not until she'd put more than five miles between her and the ones she just couldn't be around right now. She drove a few more miles through the darkness, sure she was passing homes now and then, and probably a farm or two. But her heart ached so heavily that she was having a hard time catching her breath.

She pulled over onto the side of the road to clutch at her chest and let the engine die. God, how did people who cared about each other lie so coldly to each other? The anguish of what she'd done to Jaxon just now, deceiving him into thinking she was home safe, was crushing her ability to breath. She couldn't even cry over the huge lump blocking her airway. Her head spun with the question of how he'd been able to be so intimate with her while keeping such crucial secrets.

Hoping the fresh air would help, she climbed out of her car and looked around at her surroundings. The frozen cloud of her breath followed her every step. A creek sounded just a few feet away so she followed the trickling noise to its bank and sat down to splash her face. Never in her life had she felt something as painfully cold as that icy water just then. The burning sensation served to steal her breath for one full hitch before the lump caught in her throat felt like it exploded and she was finally able to get a full inhale and exhale. Then came the tears. Teeth chattering and in pain from the intense freezing temperature, Lily realized this hadn't been her best idea and made her way back to her car. Except for when she pulled on her door handle, she found it was locked. And there on the seat, were her keys. Next to them was her phone. Which was now lighting up and flashing with an incoming call.

If she'd have been able to see, or feel her fingers, she'd have searched for a rock to bust her window, desperate for warmth. But the only rocks she'd find out here were probably in that frozen creek which she wasn't too keen on dipping into again.

What choice did she have though? Was she gonna hoof it back to the highway? Not out here in the frozen pitch black of night with the critters. Without a single house light on this stretch of road, her only choice was back to the creek to find a rock. She had to get herself inside something if she wanted her jaw to stop trembling and her blood flow to return to her hands.

You can do this, girl. Come on now, Lily.

Shaking, she forced herself back to the trickling ice and began fumbling around. She didn't know where the thought came from, but in her mind, all she could hear was the rationale that the stabbing sensation gouging her frozen skin was painful but it wouldn't kill her. How many times had she walked to school on wintery mornings, hand in hand with Tris saying that very thing in her ear?

"It ain't that bad, Lily. Folks live with pain all the time. Just think of something warm."

As Lily continued dragging her hands through the creek in search of her rock, she couldn't help but feel that somehow, someway, her big sis was there with her, trying to help her out. She also couldn't help but think of something warm. An image of standing on the beach, wrapped up in Jaxon's hug, did cruel yet warm things to her heart. A second later, her fingers scraped over a solid, rough chunk wedged into the sandy creek's bottom. She'd found her rock.

Now she had to muster up the will to go and smash it through her window. Guess it was a blessing she couldn't feel her hands.

* * * *

The more minutes ticked off the clock, the closer Jaxon got to alerting the sheriff. He'd wasted precious minutes assuming Lily had gone inside to quietly slink into her room to bed down for the night. But when he'd entered, he didn't find Lily. Then he'd peeked in to the nursery and she wasn't in there either. The only one on the couch was Benny. Lucky had come out to ask if Jaxon had found Lily and assuming he had, Jaxon told him yes. It was after he'd gone to see if she was with Grace that he saw her car was not pulled in behind his.

And that's when he realized what a fool he'd been not leaving his car at the bar and driving with her.

Before, he realized he'd hurt her. Now, he realized just how badly he'd done it.

He called her phone from his number, Benny's, and then Trissy's land line. Nothing.

Benny, Grace, Lucky and Trissy now stood around the kitchen with him, saturating it with their combined worry. Everyone had a suggestion, a possible place she could have gone to. The inaction was starting to piss him off. This was his doing. But he was going to need help. A clear plan finally ripped through his mind.

"Benny, you go back to Slangers. Lucky, you're more familiar with the drive-in theater, you check there. Trissy and Grace, please stay by your phones in case she calls. I've been to the dress shop enough times I can get myself there. Everyone check in once you get to your places."

Lucky caressed Trissy's face, planting kisses on her forehead before letting her go to grab the keys to his truck and toss Benny the set to Trissy's car.

Jaxon was almost out the door when Trissy made her way to him. "When you find her, tell her I was wrong. And I'm sorry."

Jaxon nodded, understanding her every word and then squeezed her in a short hug.

"Let's go."

The three of them headed out. God help them find his woman who didn't want to be found. Fuck everything else, the moment he had her in his sights, he was telling her how much he loved and needed her. There would never be another woman for him.

Jaxon pulled out after Lucky and Benny and made his way following the caravan until they came to that damn fork in the road where'd he'd gotten hung up before. The guys had each made that turn in front of him, on their way north to their particular destinations. Jaxon was supposed to make that turn as well to head to the dress shop. Listening to his gut in the past had nearly always led him into deeper and darker realms of hell. But the house he'd gone to look at earlier that day had been to the south. At the last second, Jaxon went with his gut and made a right turn. In the daytime, he'd noticed how remote but peaceful a drive it had been. He'd been thinking the whole way how much Lily would love making the trip from their new country home to the dress shop, with the cows and the creek so close to the road.

He hadn't gone more than five miles when his high beams showed her car parked off to the side. The window driver side window was busted out.

"Oh shit, no," he said in a panic as he pulled up alongside her car and scrambled out. "Lily," he called. But there was no answer. He scanned the car inside and out but all he found was her dead cell phone. He pulled the car door open and sat in her seat, trying to think and see what she might have seen sitting there. He picked up her phone even though it was useless. That was when he felt the moisture. When he dropped it to look at what had smeared into the palm of his hand, he saw the blood.

And then it started showing up everywhere. On the steering wheel, all over the remaining pieces of window glass, on the keys that were stuck in the ignition.

His head hit his forearms which hit the steering wheel. Jaxon cried out. "No, not her. Not her God dammit! Lily, where are you, baby?"

* * * *

"I'm over here," she called out but knew it hadn't been loud enough for him to hear. Funny how his voice motivated her up from the creek's edge when freezing to death hadn't. Even though it hurt like hell, she lurched up onto her knees and coddled the bloodied club that was her probably broken hand to her chest. "Here," she said faintly, crawling as best she could. If she could just make it back up to the road's shoulder, he'd see her.

"Lily? Oh God, oh baby…" That was all she heard before she realized he'd picked her up and was carrying her back to the car. Her entire body had become numb instead of just the broken bloody hand she'd held in the creek water. "You're so cold baby. Fuck, I'm so sorry. This is all my fault. I'm gonna take care of you. I'm gonna make it up to you."

He just kept repeating those things over and over. There had been no chance for her to tell him she loved him too.

SIN'S FLOWER

Chapter Thirty-Four

The mailbox that was made to look like a mini-red barn made her smile.

God that was a beautiful thing to see after the night they'd had. He had spent his last reserves of sanity insisting her nurse take another look because there was no way Lily could have bled that much from a simple gash. He was convinced she'd severed an artery. But no, it had been a very bad cut that was cleaned, stitched and bandaged and a broken hand that was set in a cast. In fact, the biggest concern had been how low her body temperature had measured upon their arrival. But once that had risen to normal, they'd gotten the okay to leave the nearly deserted ER.

That was when Jaxon had asked Lily if he could take her somewhere quiet to talk, just the two of them and the rising sun.

Quietly, she agreed.

This would have been the perfect place for them. The least he hoped to get out of Lily after his explanation and apology was her acceptance of his gift. He still wanted her to have it. Her own place to do with whatever she wanted.

"Jaxon, I don't understand. Why did you bring me here?"

He adjusted in his seat so he could see her. The last complete sentence he'd punished her with had been his order at the hospital that she promise never to pull another stunt like that again.

"I owe you an explanation. And I feel better about telling it to you here."

"Here? Parked outside some empty house at the crack of dawn? You know this is the back hills country

357

of Tennessee. The neighbors could shoot us for trespassing and it wouldn't even make the news."

The neighbors wouldn't do any such thing. He'd met them the day before when Benny and he had driven out to take a look at the place. He'd wanted to see it before making an offer. In a matter of days, the for sale sign would be gone and either Lily would be calling it home or it would be his empty country home, in name only, if she refused.

"Jaxon, last night, why did you think I was in danger? Do you know something I don't?"

Yes, he did. That there had been a package left on the steps last night from her ex. It was a copy the jerk had apparently made of the final divorce judgment papers and a cryptic note that said he hoped everything worked out for her in Bugscuffle. Jaxon didn't believe for one second that the ass had written that as a peace offering. No one who humiliated a girl the many ways Tom had did anything out of the kindness of his heart.

After the things life had shown Jaxon, he wasn't putting a single ounce of good faith in Lily's ex.

Not to mention that any ole drunk, rowdy, no good guy out with his buddies last night at the bar could have hurt her in that parking lot. "Lily, whatever you heard me saying to your sister last night, you couldn't have heard it all. You have to have missed some very crucial parts. I, I want you to promise to hear me out now and then my promise to you is that whatever you decide, I will respect it. But yes, I had my reasons for being out of my mind about your safety last night."

Her tongue was working the side of her cheek like she couldn't believe the shit flying out of his mouth. He could tell his use of the word respect was grating on her. Which meant she felt he didn't have any for her. Sad, considering she'd earned his admiration within hours of their first meeting.

"Well, you might feel cozy parked out here but I don't. Please just say what you need to say."

"Fair enough." He huffed out a breath, remembering how much physical pain she had to still be in. This was it. "A little less than three years ago, your sister was still working for me but she'd met Lucky and realized it was time for her to part ways with me and the band. She didn't know how to do that because I had her so wrapped up in what I needed. We ended up driving out to this venue we'd played at earlier that night for some privacy; it was very late. She needed to talk and I thought I was doing the right thing by listening. Well, because of my stupidity, we ended up getting attacked by this group of sadistic pricks who wanted me to do things to Trissy while they watched."

"What things?" Her expression shifted from pained to concerned.

"They wanted me to have sex with her on the hood of the car, Lily."

"Oh, my God. You guys couldn't fight them off or get away? Or just stay locked in the car?"

"That's where my ego screwed us. I got out of the car because I only saw two of them at first and I could have handled that. But it turned out much differently. They, uh, they…" He fingered the scar bisecting his brow. "They messed me up pretty good with their metal poles. And then it turned out there were five of them. Your sister was a tough girl but at that time, she was in such a bad place. She'd recently met Lucky on a trip to visit your mum's grave but going back to Oklahoma really hurt her. When we got stuck out there in that field, her mind slipped away and I couldn't fight all five of them on my own. I had to go along with their sick game because I was afraid they'd gang rape her if I got myself knocked out."

"So, you had to do it?" Lily's voice crept out of her mouth, surely afraid to hear his answer.

"I had to try. But I couldn't go through with it. I just couldn't. She was like my baby sis."

"Did, did they rape her, Jaxon?"

He licked his lips with his no good, dry tongue and tried to swallow. "No, luckily Stefan and Lucky figured out where we were and showed up and the coward bastards ran off, back into the woods, but not before leaving Trissy and me beaten and bloodied. Your sister finally saw that life with me and the guys was no good for her. She left and that was that."

"That was the last time you two saw each other since that night?"

"Not exactly. Trissy and Lucky came to that show we did this summer in Nashville."

"The one where I ran into her."

"Yeah, that one. I saw her briefly afterwards but it wasn't the time to talk."

"So you two have never talked about that night, have you?"

"Not until you walked in and heard what you heard last night." He turned more to face her even more dead on. His hands were dying to caress her cheek but he couldn't interfere in any decision she made regarding him. "I'm so sorry that happened like that. Lily, you have no idea how badly I wish I could have had that conversation with you first like I'd planned."

"You planned to tell me yourself?"

"I did. But then everything got out of whack during our gift exchange and Lucky said your sis needed to talk to me pretty badly. And, um, I don't mean to disrespect you, but I think I'm having a hard time accepting Maryellie's mother is gone."

Lily slunk back into the seat, breaking their face to face connection.

"That's why you hated being at the drive-in movies. Why you refused to take Maryella," she said while looking out the front window.

"Yes."

"And when you looked so scared last night in the parking lot."

How did he tell her that was what he looked like broken hearted *and* terrified?

How did he explain that as they sat here having this talk, with her seeming to accept what he was saying, and desperately needing her forgiveness, it was also the thing that scared him most?

"I understand that I overreact, but I can't help it. I just want you and Maryellie and Trissy to be safe. I guess that's all." He sat on his hands to keep from wiping that tear that had escaped and rolled down her cheek.

* * * *

That was a start, but that didn't explain why he'd brought her to this vacant house or the other things she'd heard him and her sister talking about.

"Jaxon." She finally looked up at him. "I'm truly, with every fiber of my being, sorry you went through that. And even worse, you've been living with this horrible thing hanging over your head. I clearly misunderstood that part of your conversation with Tris. And I'm very sorry for that too."

"You're not the one who's supposed to be apologizing out here, Lily."

"Well, I'm not perfect. I get it wrong just like everybody else from time to time. But there are some things I'm very sure about. And I think that's the part of what I overheard that hurts me most." She bit her lips together, sealing them shut from the inside so she wouldn't cry out loud to go with that tear that had fallen. Her lips quivered, her nostrils quivered, everything did. She pulled in a shaky breath through her nose. "What do I have to do to prove I wasn't abused by my father?"

"Lily, I want to do my best by you. With the accident you had at my house that weekend and the way you've been uncomfortable with your body...Baby, I didn't know what to think."

She shot him a sharp warning. "Please...don't call me that." It hurt her worse than her throbbing hand because up until last night, she'd hung on that one word every minute of every day.

It stung him. She may have well have slapped his cheek. "Okay."

"Did you know that I've had bladder infections my whole life and there's a medical reason for it? Okay, it's just something that I and thousands of other women deal with as adults. It doesn't mean I was abused by my father but in an unfamiliar place, apparently it means I may occasionally wet the bed. Which is completely embarrassing and something I could have explained if you'd have talked to me and not my sister."

Her breath hitched and frustration routed through her sore, recovering muscles, twisting them into tight knots while shame latched itself over that. It was exactly the way Jaxon had probably felt and she'd paid no mind to that. All she'd cared about was her need to hear him say it out loud.

"Okay, well I didn't know that and with Trissy's childhood history and then all the shit I did to fuck her up even worse, I was scared, Lily. Scared I was going to hurt you, too. Is it so hard to believe that I honestly just didn't know how to approach you with all this?"

She put herself in his shoes and yes, she could see his glaring point. She just wished he'd found a way to her first, even if it had taken him more time.

"I don't know what else to say," he told her, keeping his hands in his lap.

"Me neither."

Her mouth might have reached its limit, but her heart sure hadn't. She laid her hand out palm side up on her knee. He noticed but only stared down in that direction.

Now she knew what it meant when people said not to wish for things because they might actually come true. Where did they go from here? The angry firestorm, that had burned so intense she honestly hadn't wanted anything to do with him, had fizzled to a scalding burn. He hadn't reached for her hand yet. All night she'd been pissed that he hadn't trusted her enough to come to her first.

"Jaxon, for what it's worth, I do have one more thing to say."

His teal blue eyes locked on her, waiting. "What is it?"

"Thank you."

A laugh escaped his throat. "What for?"

"Even though I looked like a complete idiot on that dance floor, for a few songs, I actually felt pretty. And pissed, but pretty too. That was only possible because of you."

Now he was the one sealing his lips with his teeth from the inside. What was he not telling her?

* * * *

How did he tell her this should be goodbye?

363

SIN'S FLOWER

Chapter Thirty-Five

The longer they sat in front of this house, the less she felt like a burglar. It had grown on her in the thirty minutes they'd been holed up in the Rover, figuring some things out and not yet brave enough to venture in other directions. For example, he hadn't tried to call her baby again and she didn't bring up the fact she wasn't planning on sleeping at Tris's for a few days. It would feel entirely too awkward. Bingo. That must be what Jaxon had felt like this whole time.

When was the last time he'd said anything, anyway?

He just sat there keeping his mouth shut and listening to her talk. God knows what she was babbling on about now.

"Jaxon, I'm sorry I rushed you to tell me the truth when you weren't ready for it. But I can't handle having someone hide their dark side from me. Those things are scarier when they slip out. You had me terrified last night."

That was when his body, big and muscled and covered mostly in black turned to her. He finally took her hand.

"Lily, I know what I want. But I've taken everything I've ever wanted in the past. And I won't do that to you."

He won't do that to me. So that's what this was about. Dragging me out here to a place of his choosing. He is giving me the boot, again.

"Are you trying to say goodbye to me?"
* * * *

He was supposed to be. Letting her go to be happy, keep up her work with Trissy, find someone golden like his cuzzy. That was where the thought kept screeching to a bloody stop. He couldn't picture her loving anyone else. Or anyone else loving her.

* * * *

God, could she do this?

She knew what she wanted too. And as much as that included hearing him make the invitation, he was right. He wasn't playing stubborn, selfish games. This felt like the last lesson in that crazy little plan he'd apparently cooked up after that first night she'd shown up on his villa's door step. What started out as a grin turned down into a frown at that thought.

She realized showing up was the easy part. It was sticking around that proved who you were.

How nice it would be to make her next arrival as someone who'd been invited, though. But the one she desperately wanted to do the asking was sitting right there with a smug and maybe worried look on his gorgeous, zipped lips and face. One look into his eyes molded her decision. By not saying anything out loud, he was in effect asking her something very important. To make her own decision.

She wiggled a few wonky side-to-sides in an effort to face him again, blew out a breath she tried not to let out in a whoosh, and then let her un-casted arm hang freely at her side as she turned all the way to face him. She looked straight into his eyes. Something told her he was dying to reach out and hold her hand but just as certainly as she knew that, she also knew he wouldn't do anything to interfere.

"Jaxon, a year ago, it became obvious I needed to make some changes. Get rid of the bad stuff I'd acquired and find the good things that had gone missing. I thought running into my big sis that day at your concert was it. The thing I thought was going to be the reward at the end of this journey I'd imagined ended up landing in my lap like a big ole present dropped straight from heaven.

"It happened so fast. There I was with my sister back practically on day one of the journey. And then she asked me to stay with her and Lucky and run the dress shop in Momma's honor. It made me feel so needed. Even Bugscuffle made me feel safe. That raging Duck River was like my own personal troubles washer-away-er."

She caught him smile at her description and then he bit down on his lips from the inside to get back to serious. Maybe he didn't realize it, but his hand had stretched and crept closer to hers. She knew he hadn't done it on purpose so she decided not to go for it with hers. He wanted her to do this on her own. And so did she, come to think of it. She licked her dry lips.

"It all happened so fast, I just figured it was fate's way of telling me I was right where I was meant to be and we were square. But, I fell out of balance. That's why I came to find you. For Tris. I needed to do something for her. And I'd learned quickly that she was hurting pretty bad over something to do with you."

She could see him listening intently to her, that manly hand of his inched toward hers bit by bit. He probably regretted insisting she be the one to do the talking. But he had to hear this if he was really going to believe her, trust her.

"The first time I heard your voice. The most beautiful but sad words came drifting down the studio hall. I've thought of them practically every night I've laid down to go to sleep."

Lily reached out and touched the very edges of his rough fingertips with hers and sang those words to Jaxon. "*I love her because she's gone. I have no idea where she is and I couldn't care less. You were always my chosen mess. I'm not the only one who needs you; wish I could say the same for myself. I'll never get another chance if I won't ask for help. Just change me, then someone can save me. I'm the mess. I'm the mess.*

"Jaxon, I thought that song was about my sister. But now I realize it was about Vangie too." She paused to see how he felt about her mentioning the hurtful pieces from his past but he kept an even face. How did she tell him this without sounding selfish? The thing was, she knew this was crucial and that she owed him the truth if that's what she expected in return. "It's taken me awhile to feel like I have any business even saying this. But I want to be the girl someone writes a song about."

His brow crinkled in a manly sort of tender way. "Someone?"

"You," she admitted.

One time when she was fourteen, she'd been hit smack in the mouth with a softball. Her lips, gums, and teeth had all felt like they'd been hit clear from her face. Jaxon's sudden kiss knocked her back just as hard as that softball had. Her lips, gums and teeth all felt like they'd disappeared from her face just now. It was heaven.

"I have a little secret to tell you. I've kind of written you twenty-two songs. But only thirteen of them are making it onto the new cd. I hope that's okay."

"You wrote me a CDs worth of songs?"

"I did. And Stefan thinks they're pretty good. Well, the lyrics anyway. He's even willing to talk the guys in to coming out here and recording in Nashville. Switch things up a bitty."

"Oh. Well, that's cool. Um…"

"Lily, I'm prepared to stay here with you. If that's what you want. That's sort of what this spot is all about."

"What do you mean?"

"Well, yesterday morning I made an offer on this house. I was planning on bringing you here last night after our gift exchange and telling you the truth. Depending on how you took it, I was going to ask if you'd let me and Maryellie...and Benny, live here with you."

"Wait, I don't understand. That wouldn't be my offer to make." Now she felt her brow crinkle.

"Yes it would be because it was...it is my Christmas present to you. Your own place. Of course I hoped you'd want some company. Lily, after the way you found things out last night, I don't expect you to make that offer."

"Of course that is what I want," she said.

Did he need more convincing? No. No, he'd written her songs for goodness sake.

"Can I hear a little piece of one? Of the songs I mean?" she asked.

He cleared his throat. "It will sound much better coming out of Stefan's mouth but..."

"I disagree. Things sound much better to me coming out of your beautiful mouth." She winked.

"Yes ma'am."

"Ma'am? What happened to baby?" She smiled for him.

He swallowed and picked at a few pieces of string at the rip in his jeans. Then he looked up at her and rubbed his throat.

"What's a matter?"

"I think I've got stage fright. For the first time in my life."

She drew her fingers over the razored-short hair of his sideburn and up and over his ear. Then she kissed him. When he pulled back he had the taste of a song on his lips.

"I can't help from drowning in your eyes. You make me wanna come and clean up all these lies. Let me up before I die. Mine."

"Mine?"

"Mm-hmm. You like it?"

"It's beautiful. I don't know how I feel about hearing those words coming out of Stefan's mouth someday though."

"Well, that's another new idea I'm kicking around. I'm gonna sing the lead on this one."

She was a big enough fan to know he'd never done that before. Oh my God. He loved her.

"Jaxon, I would like you to stay. Here in Tennessee with me. And Maryella. In my new house."

"And Benny?"

"Yes, Benny too."

"I thought you'd never ask," he said playfully.

"Is that a yes?"

"No, not yet."

"Wha—?" But he tugged her up before she could finish. In true caveman fashion, Jaxon hiked her over his lap, except he did it with care. It seemed like he might have his own point to make. She couldn't focus and breathing had come so much easier in the minutes leading up to this.

"I need to get you somewhere private."

"Do you have the keys to this place yet?"

"Not yet. Hopefully later today."

"Hmm, well, I feel pretty comfy right here, where we're at."

As soon as she said it, she knew what she'd done to him. But if they were going to live here together, they had to feel safe. Whatever he decided, whatever he was comfortable with, she would go along for the ride. Then she had another stroke of brilliance.

"Hey, you know what? I'm a little light on cash…so….do you think you might spring for a hotel room?"

"Baby, I'm already so sprung."

She found directions on her phone to several motels within twenty miles. Jaxon insisted on splurging on the only one that offered a king size bed. And yes, he paid extra for early check in.

SIN'S FLOWER

Chapter Thirty-Six

Around suppertime, Jaxon set Lily down on Trissy's porch. Her face told him she was confused but the cute way her forehead creased in the middle with a little "w" melted his fear that she'd changed her mind about facing the music, now rather than later. Maybe too abruptly, he found her hand, took it in his and gave it a good squeeze. Hopefully she'd know there was nothing to fear or worry about because they were doing this together. He certainly felt the strength having her by his side inspired. "This is my yes, baby."

God he wanted to kiss her first, but that wasn't the deal he'd made himself that morning. He opened the door, blanking out all the things he could let slow him down. The family inside he'd spent way too long alienating. The best friend he'd initially saved only to destroy later on. The little piece of him walking around in sparkle boots and pig tails who he owed his life to. And the brand new baby who, thank God, would only know a happy and healthy Uncle Jaxon.

"Jaxon? What are we doing?" He heard Lily ask, trying to be patient and sweet with him as he stumbled in the entryway.

"My yes to you doesn't count unless I can face this house full of people I've hurt."

"Hey, you stop right there."

"No Lily, come on. Let's go in."

"No, not yet." She pulled the door closed. "I get it. Okay. I could actually be a big baby right now and cry at what you're doing. But I need you to promise me something first."

He sniffed in a breath because she wasn't the only one who could turn baby out here on the front steps. The fact she felt the confidence to stop him and demand a promise blasted through him like sun heating an icy ocean. "What baby? I'm ready to give you everything I am. Just ask."

"I'm gonna have so much fun loving you when you're at your best. But on those days when you're not up for being perfect, for the world or anyone else," she smiled and poked a finger into his chest, "Promise you won't hide that guy from me. I intend to love your entire package."

"Kind of like how you did all morning and afternoon at the hotel? My package could handle that."

They both cut into a loud roar of laughter. Which brought Lucky to the door. "Hey, what are y'all cracking up so loud about out here? And it's freezing cold. Get inside."

"Yes sir," they said in unison to Lucky and stepped through the doorway. Jaxon made sure to keep Lily's hand tightly in his.

Watching Lily coo over the baby picture Lucky carried around everywhere made him almost forget his mission. "Hey Lucky, where is everyone?"

"In the sun room. Got the chiminea going so our, uh, dads can show Maryella the fine art of roasting snowmen marshmallows. You coming? Trista and I have to head back to the hospital soon. She'd like to see you two."

He looked to Lily and then brought their laced hands up to his lips and kissed her knuckles nice and slow. "Yes," he said. "We're coming."

Lucky chuckled to himself and grinned. "This way, then." A second later his cuzzy seemingly was lost in thoughts over his brand new bundle of joy. But he managed to come back for a moment to wrap one arm around Lily's shoulders. "Glad to see you're okay, sis. I missed ya," Lucky said to her.

On their way through the home heading toward the sun room, Jaxon chanced a quick look over at Lily. She couldn't have looked more like he felt if she'd tried. She was his soul's mirror. All the butterflies popping around in his belly were busy kissing her cheeks. "I love you."

It didn't surprise him that she thanked him first. Silly Lily. "I love you too, Jaxon. Wow, here we are."

They followed Lucky into the home's glassed-in back porch. Lucky made his way to Trissy, leaving Jaxon and Lily to head up the group of concentrated stares focused entirely on them. Feminine hands that had been icy and dry a few minutes ago warmed and wetted inside of his. He gave them another squeeze. His baby girl sat bouncing on his father's knee, watching the glow of the fireplace melting her marshmallow snowmen against a darkening sky. She looked up and blew him a kiss which he caught and tucked into his fist then rubbed it into his chest near his heart. Like always.

"So hey there." *God I suck balls at this.* After scanning the intimidating small crowd, being sure to make a connection to each person giving him their full attention, Jaxon loosened his vice grip on Lily's hand. "I uh, don't wanna take up a whole lotta time. But I'd like to say thanks for letting me be here. It's turned out to mean a lot. You all played a biggy in that, but mostly I owe the thanks to this beauty standing here with me." He turned to Lily and re-took her hand in his. "I love you, baby. That's all that matters."

"I love you guys too." A voice that sounded so sincere, the fact it had shuttled out from a grown man's mouth had them all laughing together now.

"Aww, Benny, mate. I love you too, brother."

"So…does this mean you're staying?" Trissy asked, lacking her usual moxie.

What could he tell Trissy except for the absolute truth?

"Well, I put an offer on a place not too far from here. Pretty sure it'll be ours by the end of business today." He'd found the perfect love nest and Lily had said yes.

"Yours?" came Trissy's shaky voice. "Not far from here?"

She looked and sounded so hopeful. He hoped Lily heard it loud and clear too.

"About ten miles from your front porch."

Trissy nodded and cried and then Lily nodded, spilling a new tear each time her chin tilted downward. He couldn't wait to be the new owner of the place, with Lily. But for right now, time couldn't pass quickly enough. The rest of his surprise awaited them at Grace's borrowed flat.

Unexpectedly, Trissy came over and gave them both a big hug. "I'm an idiot. And I'm sorry. You guys make a beautiful couple and I know you'll take good care of each other." Trissy winked for him and gave him another hug. Then she whispered into his ear. "Thank you, Jaxon."

Once the last log had been burnt for the night and Maryellie's face had been wiped clean of melted sugar, Jaxon and Lily tucked her into bed and sang her to sleep. Then they made their way hand in hand over to Grace's. Lily stopped him at the door.

"So the house—"

"Our house."

Lily smiled. "So our house…ten miles is pretty close. Are you sure you're okay with that?"

"Twenty minnys drive from our front door to the dress shop and just a bit further back here to Trissy's." He nipped at her bottom lip and warmed her with his breath. "Yes, I'm okay with that. It was never my plan to take you from your family, baby. I just had to figure out how to insert myself into your life. I think I finally worked it out."

"You did, perfectly. The house is perfect, by the way. And private."

One more grin like that and he'd caveman her inside Grace's. On second thought, that was a great idea. Up she went in one swing over his shoulder.

"Mine," he said and made his way out the door. Her hot laughter tickled along the bared skin of his back where his shirt hiked up. "All mine."

Inside, he laid her on top of the lush set of blankets he'd scavenged from the main house, covered in lily petals. And lots and lots of pillows, probably six or seven. Her hand flew to her mouth and she nearly bust out laughing when she saw that Stefan's face peeked out from one on the bottom.

But then her laughter sucked back in when she must have realized what he had planned next. On his knees, he slowly began stripping his clothes off. He tried to take it nice and slow, seductive like he'd done in the hotel room, but a mere minute later, he was naked.

"This is the rest of my yes," he said. "I love you, Lily."

"Mine?" she asked as she touched her hand to his heart.

"Yours." He covered her hand with his. "All yours."

SIN'S FLOWER

Epilogue

Rock Star, California...

"Yup, knew you'd be back. Good to see you brother. Lez go."

Jaxon trailed his trusted tattoo artist back to the private room. He missed Lily already but looked forward to the meal she was probably concocting back at the villa. They'd decided to keep their oceanfront home for the times when their little family needed warm beachy breaks from the cold Tennessee winters. And honestly, there was no one else Jaxon trusted to ink him. Coming to see Ryan this one last time was on Jaxon's bucket list. He had an unfinished work of art to fill in.

"So what am I doing you for today?"

Jaxon stripped off his shirt and extended his neck to the side. As soon as he exposed the trail of thorns, Ryan started nodding like he was grooving on some insanely deep but silent tune. "Yay-uh. All right. Whatcha need? We finally gonna give those pretty thorns a flower?"

Jaxon went into full detail of how he wanted Ryan to weave the phrase *My love, my life, my Lily* inside the trail of thorns with Lily's name at the tail end of the stem, closest to his heart. "I want this part up here to have the lily flower." He pointed at his neck.

"Cool. Okay, so, the lily was the symbol of innocence for some cultures but sexuality for others. Which is yours bro? We gonna go passion red or sweet peach for the color?"

"My girls the perfect mix, mate."

"So like a pretty raspberry mixed with some cream. I think that gives us your girl, man."

"That's why I come to you."

"I can translate it into Latin if you want. Just give me a few minutes to go jump on the translator."

Jaxon stopped him before he left his stool. "That's not necessary. No more hiding for me."

Ryan chuckled. "Yeah man, I wasn't gonna say anything but you got that puppy love glow. Looks pretty good on a dude your age."

"When we're done, I might kick your ass, mate."

"You come back next month when you're all healed up and we'll *arreglar cuentas.*"

Jaxon flipped Ryan off with a star-studded smile and then relaxed his head against the back of the tall chair, translating the phrase in his best rusty Spanish. "Well, there won't be much to settle; I trust you man," Jaxon said.

Ryan came at him with the ink gun. "You know, all the times I've done you, you've never said that to me. Must be the girl."

"Oh, there's no question about that. It's definitely the girl. Put her on me," Jaxon said with a wink. He couldn't wait to get home and show her his half of their one year anniversary present.

The End

www.carlenelove.com

Evernight Publishing
www.evernightpublishing.com

www.ingramcontent.com/pod-product-compliance
Lightning Source LLC
Chambersburg PA
CBHW051523250626

47156CB00001B/205